I0760780

CRESCENT CITY WOLF PACK COLLECTION TWO

Carrie Pulkinen

This is a work of fiction. Names, characters, places, and incidents are either the product of the author's imagination or are used fictitiously, and any resemblance to actual persons living or dead, business establishments, events, or locales is entirely coincidental.

Crescent City Wolf Pack Collection Two

ISBN: 978-1-957253-07-7

Contact Information: www.CarriePulkinen.com

A DEAL WITH DEATH

CARRIE PULKINEN

CHAPTER ONE

16 Years Ago

Pissing off the Voodoo Spirit of death wasn't in anyone's best interest, but that's exactly what Odette had done. When Baron Samedi visited her dreams last night, he'd made it clear what she had to do: free the soul fragments she'd helped her uncle trap and command the spirits to cross over.

Sending the spirits to the other side would be easy; she'd been able to see and communicate with ghosts since she was little. Freeing them from their *ouangas*, the magical jars that contained them, would require the Baron's assistance. She'd done the proper Voodoo rituals to allow the loa, the Ancestral Spirit, to cross to this realm. Now, all she could do was wait for her dad to take her to her weekly lesson with her uncle.

She rolled onto her back and stared at the ceiling fan, following the path of a single blade as it revolved round and round until her stomach soured and she squeezed her eyes shut.

How was she supposed to know her uncle had been lying to her about the souls? She was only twelve years old for Spirit's sake, and the man was supposed to be her mentor. A bitter taste crept up the back of her throat, and she swallowed it down.

With his looming presence, dark powers, and heavy hand, Odette had been terrified to cross the man, much less question his morals. Now she had to right the wrong she'd helped him commit.

With a heavy sigh, she glanced at the clock and rolled out of bed. Jerking the earbuds from her ears, she shoved the iPod into her back pocket and closed her bedroom door before padding toward the living room. With any luck, Baron Samedi could make her uncle see the error of his ways, and he'd let his prisoners go willingly. Not that luck had ever been on her side.

The irritation in her father's voice as he shouted into the telephone slowed her pace, and she leaned against the wall in the hallway, peering around the corner, hesitating to enter the living room.

"For the last time, Agnes, she's fine with her uncle. She'd tell me if there was a problem." Her dad let out an irritated grunt. "I don't go to mass, but that doesn't make me any less Catholic..."

He pinched the bridge of his nose and shook his head, the gray strands of his curly salt-and-pepper hair glinting in the sunlight streaming in through the window. "I realize I'm no vodouisant, but I was married to one for ten years. Adelaide was your *Mambo* for Christ's sake. If there's one thing she taught me, it's that Voodoo is a *family* legacy. Mathias is the only family Odette has on her mother's side, and until she objects, he'll be the one to train her."

Odette's heart flopped in her chest like a fish in a flat-bottom boat. No one ever told her she had the option to object. Well, after today, she'd be done with her menacing uncle and his questionable magic. If she had the choice, she'd learn from a Mambo, a Voodoo priestess like her mom had been.

She straightened her spine and strode into the living room as her dad ended the call. He started as he turned to her, a flash of guilt crossing his features before he pulled her into a hug. "How much of that did you hear?"

Odette shrugged from his embrace. "Enough. Agnes wants me learning at the House."

"She was your mom's best friend. She worries about you...and the trouble you've been getting into at school. She says children of Baron

Samedi need extra guidance or the loa's carefree ways can keep you from succeeding."

"Please, Dad. I'm fine." Odette rolled her eyes. There was nothing wrong with having a little fun every now and then. "Can we go? I've got an important lesson with Uncle Mathias today."

"Oh yeah?" He grabbed his keys from a hook and ushered her out the door. "What's he teaching you?"

Odette waited until she climbed into the seat and buckled her seatbelt before she answered. "It's a…role reversal today. I'm supposed to be the teacher, with Baron Samedi's help, of course."

"Sounds like fun, sweet pea." He mussed her hair, and she swatted his hand away.

She stuffed her earbuds into her ears and cranked up her favorite Beyoncé album, tapping her thumb on her knee to the rhythm. Fifteen minutes into the drive to the swamp, her dad put a hand on her shoulder. She freed one ear and turned the volume down.

"You're okay with getting lessons from your uncle, right? I mean… your mom never mentioned much about him when she was alive, but he seemed thrilled to take you on as a student when I approached him."

She missed a beat in her reply. "Yeah. He's fine."

Her dad nodded absently as he stared out the windshield. "He doesn't practice any black magic or anything scary, right? Everything is on the up-and-up?"

Odette swallowed and gazed out the window. Spanish moss draped from the cypress branches, giving the swamp a creepy horror movie vibe, and a blue heron swooped from a tree to catch a mouthful of bayou water and crawfish.

She couldn't lie to her father, but if he knew what she'd been tasked to do today, he'd turn the car around and take her straight home. Baron Samedi would never forgive her if she didn't take care of this problem.

Wiping her sweaty palms on her jeans, she turned to him. "I don't know about *everything*, but like Mom always said… 'There's nothing wrong with a little *gris-gris*.'"

Her dad glanced at her, smiling wistfully before focusing on the road. Bringing up her mom and all her words of wisdom was the best way to deflect any unwelcome conversation her dad tried to push on her. Guilt gnawed in her gut for manipulating him, but she couldn't refuse Baron Samedi's demands. She owed the loa her life, after all.

After saying goodbye to her dad, she trudged through the front yard toward the rickety old house. White paint peeled from the wooden slats, and a porch wrapped around the entire structure from front to back. A garden overflowed with herbs, some edible, some poisonous, and she made a wide berth around it before heading up the stairs and around to the back door.

With her hand on the knob, she paused and inhaled deeply, hoping the fresh air would untie the knot her insides had tangled into. The scents of mud and decaying foliage did nothing to calm her nerves. "I'm ready when you are, Baron. Please make it quick."

A heaviness formed in the air behind her, pressing onto her shoulders as the hum of living energy gave way to the void of death. Baron Samedi was ready too.

As she pushed the door open, a chime made of chicken bones rattled from above, and her uncle shuffled into the room, wiping something that looked a lot like blood from his hands. He kept what was left of his curly, black hair sheered short to the sides of his head, and the yellowish tinge of his bloodshot eyes reminded her of rotten eggs burrowing into his dark-brown, leathery skin.

"'Bout time you got here." The deep creases in his forehead turned to canyons as he frowned at her. "I need heron blood, and I had to send Emile out hunting for one instead of you. Come here." He crooked his finger to call her close as he reached for the belt he kept wound on the shelf.

"I'm not late, and even if I were, it's not my fault. It's not like I can drive myself." She crossed her arms, refusing to budge.

He folded the belt in half, gripping both ends and snapping it. "You listen to me, little one. Talking back'll get you nothin' but a bruised butt. You want that?"

She uncrossed her arms and lowered her gaze. "No, sir." She'd faced the wrath of her uncle and his belt enough times to know better now. This would all be over soon anyway. "Can I please see the *ouangas*?"

His smile revealed three missing teeth. "Later, honey. I have a patient coming in who's agreed to let me store a piece of his soul, so you'll get to work your magic soon enough. Now go on out to the garden and fetch me some sage."

Baron Samedi's presence behind her intensified, giving her the courage to let her own power build. She drew on the energy of the spirit realm, concentrating her magic into her words. "I want to see them now."

Her uncle's eyes widened, and he started toward the other room before shaking his head and swinging the belt toward her, the leathery end slapping across her side with a crack. Sharp pain ricocheted through her ribcage, and she squealed.

"Don't you ever try to use your power against me again. You understand?" He shook the belt toward her. "I got plenty more of these lying around."

With a hard exhale, Odette released control, opening herself up to Baron Samedi. Pressure built in her chest, a burning sensation ripping through her veins as the loa took control of her body. Her spine straightened, and her head turned toward her uncle, but she wasn't making herself move. She tried to run, to turn around and get the hell out of that place, but her will had no effect on her movements. She was like a puppet, Baron Samedi her master.

With long strides, the loa carried her past her uncle, and with strength not her own, she jerked from the man's grasp as he tried to stop her.

"You get back here, girl." He followed after her, and she whirled around to face him.

"Baron Samedi wants to see the *ouangas*. Who are you to stop me, *bokor*?" The Baron made her mouth form the words, and though she fought it, she'd lost all control.

Her uncle's mouth hung open, his arms falling slack at his sides before he ducked his head in a bow. "Baron Samedi? I had no idea it was you. Please accept my apology."

"Why are you stealing souls that belong to me?" Her body should have been trembling, but her voice was strong and confident, not her own.

"Stealing?" He chuckled. "Naw, I'm not stealing. Most of those people are still alive. I'm just holding onto them while they're sick. I'll give 'em back once they heal."

The Baron used Odette's body to grab her uncle's shirt and twist it in her fist. "You've lied to the girl enough. You're not dealing with her right now, you're talking to a loa." She released her hold, giving him a light shove, and her uncle smoothed his shirt down his chest.

"I'm sorry."

"I'm taking them back." She turned toward the *ouangas* and lifted her hands as an ancient energy buzzed in her veins, growing in intensity until she felt like she would explode. Sweat beaded on her forehead, and her muscles cramped like a Charlie horse had overtaken her entire body. *Please, Baron,* she begged in her mind, *it hurts.*

If she'd had control she'd have crumpled to the floor, her desperate screams piercing through the swamp. Instead, she stood tall, focusing the searing, vibrating energy into her palms and throwing it at the *ouangas.*

The first jar shattered, the pieces flying across the room as the soul trapped inside it was freed, the Baron's magic joining it with the living being to which it belonged.

"No!" Her uncle begged. "Don't take them."

The second *ouanga* shattered, the soul swirling into the air and hovering on the ceiling, confusion furrowing its ghostly brow. Though it had been stolen from a living person, the victim had since died, so the soul had nowhere to go.

It would be Odette's job to cross the dead over to the spirit realm if she survived this possession. The Baron called on more of his power, and her blood felt like it boiled in her veins. It was too much magic for a human to endure. Her muscles screamed for relief. Her steady pulse begged to race in her chest, but the Baron kept her under tight control.

She lifted her hand to free the next soul when her uncle grabbed her shoulders, attempting to tackle her. Baron Samedi's otherworldly strength held her still, and she threw her uncle against the wall, holding him there with the loa's magic.

Jar after jar shattered, the living souls exiting the moment they were freed, the dead collecting in a mass by the corner. Her uncle screamed, angry, hot tears streaming down his cheeks as he struggled against Baron Samedi's hold.

As the last of the *ouangas* broke, the ghost joining the others, the Baron's voice echoed in Odette's mind. *Cross them over and go home, child. I'm proud of you.*

The loa ripped from her body, and she collapsed in a heap on the floor. Her muscles felt like pulverized meat, her nerves raw and exposed as she heaved in breath after breath, the air slicing through her lungs like razor blades.

She scrambled to her feet, doubling over as dizziness threatened to force her to the ground. The mass of ghosts glared at her, their anger palpable in the air. All seven of them drifted toward her, their energy converging into one impenetrable wall of hate.

She stepped backward into her uncle's chest, and he gripped her shoulders, throwing her to the ground. Her head smacked the wood with a clunk, and her vision swam. Dropping to his knees, Mathias clutched her throat, tightening his grip until she couldn't breathe.

"You little bitch," he growled between clenched teeth. "How dare you bring your loa here to steal everything I've worked for?"

Stars glittered in her darkening vision as she clawed at her uncle's hands, but he was too strong, her own strength zapped from the loa's possession. If she couldn't fulfill her duty and cross over the souls, Baron Samedi probably wouldn't accept hers.

"Dad?"

Her uncle loosened his grip as her cousin, Emile, stormed into the room, and Odette gasped for breath.

"Get off her!" Emile tackled his father, freeing Odette from his clutches, and she scrambled to stand, panting.

Mathias focused his anger on his son, wailing on Emile like he'd been the one to free the souls. He landed punch after punch, bloodying his son's face until his eye swelled shut.

"Stop it!" Odette screamed, but the men ignored her. Mathias continued pounding on his son, Emile lying motionless beneath his father's rage.

The ghosts advanced on her again, and she threw up her arms. "Stop!"

The spirits froze, and a euphoric sensation swept through her body, making her tingle from head to toe. "Turn around."

The spirits did as they were told. As *she* told them to do, and her heart sprinted. "Stop Mathias." She pointed to her uncle. "Get him!"

The ghosts converged on Mathias, but their essence passed right through him. Odette opened herself to the spirit realm, channeling the energy of the dead through her body and into the ghosts, making the specters' ethereal forms solid.

A burly ghost grabbed her uncle and yanked him off Emile, while a female spirit punched him in the stomach.

A hysterical laugh bubbled up from Odette's chest. These ghosts were hers to command. No wonder her uncle had been so willing to tutor her; she had a power unlike anything she'd known possible, and he had planned to exploit it.

The ghosts continued their assault, beating her uncle until she screamed at them to stop. The burly spirit dropped Mathias's lifeless body to the ground, his head lolling at an unnatural angle. His neck had been snapped.

Oh, no. No, no, no. She didn't use the ghosts to kill her uncle. That's not what she meant when she told them to get him. This couldn't be happening.

She could fix this. She could use the ghosts to… No. No, she couldn't. No matter how amazing it felt to use her newfound magic, she made a promise to Baron Samedi to cross the spirits over, and that's what she would do.

Raising her hands toward the ghosts, she used her magic one last time and called on Baron Samedi to take the spirits. One by one, they disintegrated into the spirit realm, leaving Odette alone with the man she'd murdered and his bruised and bloodied son.

Tears brimmed in her eyes as she dropped to her knees between them, and Emile rolled to his side and looked at his father. Odette followed his gaze and found Mathias's eyes wide with fear, the light in them gone, and a knot wedged in her throat, blocking her sob.

The room spun. A million thoughts raced through her mind, but she couldn't grab onto one. She'd lost control. First with the Baron using her body and then with her own powers. She'd killed a man. Her own uncle.

Lost in her attempt to form a coherent thought, she didn't notice that Emile had risen until he spoke. "Help me bury him."

Her cousin didn't say another word. He lifted his father's torso, Odette took his feet, and they carried the body to the swamp, laying it next to the water's edge. His expression blank, Emile trudged to the house and returned with a cinder block.

Odette wiped the tears from her cheeks and followed him back up the slope, gripping another cinder block and hauling it to the water. The concrete dug into her palms as she dragged the heavy block through the dirt, and she focused on the physical pain, using the sharp, agonizing sensation to ground her, to keep her from getting lost in the tornado of thoughts in her mind.

With a long piece of rope, Emile tied the cinder to his father's body and shoved it into the swamp. As the corpse descended, a bubble rose from the depths, releasing a cloud of steam as it popped on the surface, and Odette's stomach lurched.

Silently, his face unreadable, Emile returned to the house. She followed him into the living room, where he stood by the wall, staring at the chicken bones hanging over the entrance.

"Emile..." She tried to speak to him a few times, but he clamped his mouth shut and shook his head, refusing to look at her. She sat on the couch, chewing her bottom lip and clutching her hands in her lap until the rumble of an engine signaled her dad's arrival.

Emile slammed his bedroom door, and her lip trembled as she darted onto the porch and scurried around the house to the driveway.

"Everything okay, sweet pea?" Her dad smiled as she climbed into the car and slammed the door.

"Fine." She stared out the window as the rickety old shack and all the horrors it contained faded from view.

Odette waited until her dad drove her home and they were safely inside the house before she opened the floodgates. She told him everything, vowing never to use her magic again.

"Please, Daddy, can we move away? I never want to see this place again." She was done with Voodoo, done with Baron Samedi, and done with New Orleans.

CHAPTER TWO

Present Day

The sense of foreboding tightening Odette Allemand's throat didn't mean anything. The sinking feeling in her stomach was merely anticipation, and the fact that her heart hadn't beat this fast since the time she'd come face-to-face with an opossum she'd thought was a poltergeist proved this house was worth every penny she'd be paying for the next thirty years. Who wouldn't be excited to own a historic Creole home like this?

Heat clung to her skin, baking her in the summer sun as she peered at her prized purchase. The salmon color of the exterior would be changing soon enough, but the pristine white front porch looked exactly as it would have in its glory days.

Pausing on the second step, she inhaled the sweet scent of the bougainvillea blooming in her new front yard. The familiar perfume stirred nostalgia in her soul, and a feeling of finally being home mixed with the anticipatory emotions swirling through her chest. She had this situation completely under control.

She climbed the next two steps and stood on the front porch. The moving box tucked under her right arm dug into her hip, so she shifted it to her left side and fished the key from her purse.

An oval window of cut glass in the center of the front door provided a distorted view into the darkened foyer. Rays of sunlight spilled across the wooden floor, giving the entrance a warm and welcoming vibe, but she hesitated to step inside.

The nineteenth-century mansion wouldn't have had a door like this in its original condition, and though she intended to restore the home to the grandeur of the 1800s, it wouldn't hurt to make a few modernizations. Maybe the light would help clear out the darkness that followed her around like a storm cloud waiting for the perfect lightning strike to unleash its fury.

"You gonna stand outside all day or are you going inside?" Natasha, a Voodoo priestess and Odette's closest friend, laughed as she ascended the steps, breaking whatever trance Odette had succumbed to.

Pressing her hand to her heart, she spun around. "Sweet Spirits, Mambo, don't do that. You scared me to death."

"You look plenty alive to me." One corner of Natasha's mouth tugged into a teasing grin, and she crossed her arms over her burnt-orange blouse. A matching orange scarf encircled her head, and her dark-brown hair sprouted out from the center of the fabric in tufts, like a potted plant. "You still haven't figured out the meaning, have you?"

Odette let out her breath and forced herself to open the door. "It's a beautiful Creole mansion that I've admired since I was a little girl. There is no other meaning."

"Mm-hmm. You know you can't lie to your Mambo. What's wrong?" Natasha followed her into the foyer.

If you only knew. Gripping the box in both hands, she carried it to the kitchen and set it on the counter. She'd hired a contractor to do the renovations, and she hadn't felt a hint of this ominous dread when she'd opened the house for him last week. But now she was moving in, and that made her more nervous than she cared to admit.

"Nothing's wrong. Once I do a smudging to clear out the old energy and get my altar set up, I'm sure it will feel like home."

Natasha leaned a hip against the counter. "There's something else."

Could the Voodoo priestess sense her emotions in her energy, or was her body language that obvious? Whichever it was, discussing it was pointless. She'd bought this place, and she intended to stay. Straightening her spine, Odette put her hands on her hips. "I'm not thrilled about having to move in before the renovations have even started. Karma should be biting my old landlord in the butt any day now."

"And sending that kind of energy out into the world will bring it right back to you."

Odette crossed her arms. "I'm not the one who promised my tenant an extension on her lease and then changed her mind at the last minute. That's no way to do business, and I'm lucky I have a place to live."

"You can call it luck, or you can admit fate might have plans that required you to move in sooner. That maybe you don't have as much control as you think you do. Everything happens for a reason, and *everything* has meaning. Even this old house. My guess is that it's related to a past life."

She clenched her teeth and took a bundle of sage from her box. Staring at the herbs, Odette whispered, "I would rather not know," before flicking her gaze to her Mambo, pleading with her eyes. Natasha had guided her through several past-life regressions, trying to help her overcome her fears in her present life, and she'd learned more than she needed to know.

Her past couldn't help her with the present, anyway. Her current issues stemmed from this life alone, and she wasn't about to divulge the reasons why. To anyone.

"It will help you understand—"

"I understand enough to know I can't go through that again. Maybe I did live here in a past life, but you know that life ended in tragedy. I don't need to experience it again." She *couldn't* do it again. Reliving the horrific murders of her former selves had left her emotionally drained and physically ill for days afterward. She glanced at her watch. "Would you mind doing the blessing now, so I can smudge and have this place clean when my furniture arrives?"

"Always on a schedule." Natasha gave her a knowing look—one that said Odette would eventually give in and do what the Ancestral Spirits guided her to do, but Odette never gave in. Not anymore.

Closing her eyes, Natasha took a few deep breaths, her body swaying slightly from side to side as she whispered a prayer in Haitian Creole. With a long exhale, she opened her eyes. "I thought you said there weren't no ghosts here."

"I've been here several times since I bought the place. No one has made contact." Not that she'd tried very hard to find any. All old homes held residual spirit energy. Odette could see it if she wanted to, but if she left herself open to the spirit realm twenty-four-seven, she'd never have a moment to herself.

Ghosts were everywhere, all the time—especially in New Orleans—and if they didn't feel the need to contact her, she'd let them be. So long as they weren't malevolent. The bad ones *always* made themselves known. No searching required.

"Did you command the ghosts to reveal themselves? You know some of them can hide."

Her fingers curled into tight fists, her nails biting into her palms. "And you know I will *never* command the dead."

It was the same discussion over and over. Natasha would say she wouldn't have been blessed with the powers if she shouldn't use them. Odette's retort would state the power in question was firmly planted on the black side of magic and she refused to dabble in the dark arts. Her friend would call Odette's ability to command the dead gray and follow up with, "There's nothing wrong with a little *gris-gris*," like her mother used to say.

Natasha opened her mouth as if to continue the argument, but she let out a long sigh and grasped Odette's hand instead. "Open your senses and feel. Someone's here." The priestess closed her eyes again and shook her head. "He's a strong one too; took me some searching to find him, but he's here. Can you sense him now?"

Odette closed her eyes and took a deep, centering breath. Allowing her walls to fall away, she opened her mind and reached out to the energy in the house. The same bumpy, vibrating charge, left behind by the countless families who'd called this place home, hummed around her. The sensation swirled through the house, creating a rough cacophony of energy grating against her senses like sandpaper.

She pushed through the bramble, opening herself even more, but all she felt was the static leftovers of those who lived here before. Natasha squeezed her hand, reminding her to focus, and she gave one more push.

There, in the corner of the kitchen, she felt him. A spirit unlike any she'd encountered before...and she'd encountered plenty. Even when she'd turned away from Voodoo and refused her connection with Baron Samedi, the loa of the dead, Odette could never get away from ghosts. This was the first time in as long as she could remember that a specter had been able to hide itself from her when she'd reached out.

"Will you please show yourself to me?" She opened her eyes, ready to see at least a faint outline of the ghost, but nothing manifested in the spot where she felt him. "Who are you?"

Her chest tightened, and she gasped as a feeling of overwhelming love expanded in her core. The sensation grew, her heart aching at the intensity of the emotion.

"Are you okay?" Natasha released her hand and wrapped her arm around Odette's shoulders.

"He's making me feel his emotions. How is he doing that?" No run-of-the-mill ghost could affect her this way. In her relations with the spirit realm, she always stayed in control.

"What do you feel?"

She sucked in a trembling breath as tears welled in her eyes. "Adoration. He loved someone deeply. And happiness. So much joy."

"I told you he's a strong one. If he has no ill intent, the blessing of the home won't get rid of him. We'll have to cross him over ourselves."

The happiness and love swirling in her heart converged, slamming into her like a knife twisting in her back. Gripping the countertop, she pressed a hand to her chest. "Betrayal. Unrelenting sadness." The tears of joy brimming in her eyes cascaded down her cheeks in trails of sorrow. "Will you please stop," she whispered, and the ghost released his hold. The emotions dissipated as quickly as they had formed.

She straightened and wiped the tears from her cheeks, grabbing her bundle of sage. "I'm okay. The ghost can stay." Forcing a spirit to cross over…one who wasn't ready to leave…required Odette's magic. The mere thought of opening herself up to that much power made her stomach turn. She rummaged through her box, moving aside the items for her altar, and found a lighter. "Can we begin?"

Natasha's brow furrowed. "Are you sure you want him to stay? You're not an empath, so if he can send you his emotions like that, he can cause you a world of trouble." She nodded to the box. "You've got everything to set up your altar right there. Maybe we should call on Baron Samedi for help."

"No." Her *met tet*, the main loa that guided her, hadn't completely forgiven her for turning her back on him—and the entire religion—when she was young. "I don't want to bother the Baron with this. I didn't sense any hostility from the ghost. It'll be fine." She'd save calling on her guardian Voodoo Spirit for the big things.

Anyway, there had to be a reason the ghost lingered. If she could figure it out, talk to him and get him to cross over on his own, maybe she'd get back into Baron Samedi's good graces. Talking to a ghost, she could handle. That ability was built into her soul and didn't require calling on any dark magic from the spirit realm.

Odette toyed with the purple and black braided bracelet adorning her wrist. Wearing the colors was an act of honoring Baron Samedi, something she should have been doing her entire life. "I'll open the windows if you'll continue the blessing."

"Stubborn as ever, just like your momma was." Natasha closed her eyes and resumed her Haitian prayer.

A familiar pang of longing tightened Odette's chest. Natasha couldn't have been older than fifteen when Odette's mom died, but from the way she talked about her, she'd idolized her.

Pushing the thoughts from her mind, she scurried around the house, opening all the windows—upstairs and down. Cleansing a home required positive energy, and dwelling on the fact that her mom had died saving her life was anything but.

Back in the kitchen, Odette struck the lighter, setting the end of the sage bundle ablaze and then blowing out the flames. She walked the perimeter of her house, fanning the smoke to the four corners and waving it around the windows and doors. "Negative energy be gone. Only peace and love may remain in my home."

The ghost followed her as she and Natasha cleansed each room. She could feel its presence as a solid form, almost as if a living person stood behind her, but when she turned to look, nothing was there. She'd coax him out eventually—no commands necessary. Her ability to communicate with the dead had intensified when she'd returned to her Voodoo roots.

Unfortunately, as her magic strengthened, the blackness grew in her soul. She had powers no living person should have, and if she lost control of herself, even for a minute, like before… No, she would never let that happen again.

They closed the windows, and Natasha shut the front door, ending the cleansing. "That should do it." She hugged her. "You sure you can handle that ghost?"

"I think I need to." Whomever the dead man had been in life, Odette couldn't ignore the emotions he'd sent to her. Maybe this house called to her because the ghost called to her.

"Then you must." The Mambo picked up her bag. "Some of us are meeting at Rusty's tonight for dancing and drinks. You should come."

"Thanks, but I'm sure I'll be exhausted from unpacking. The movers will be here soon." She followed Natasha onto the porch, avoiding eye contact.

"How much you gonna unpack when the renovations start tomorrow? Come have a little fun."

"I'll pass." When vodouisants, magical beings who practiced Voodoo, got together for dancing and drinks, the epic party lasted into the early morning. Odette had things to do. Responsible things, like getting to work on time and making sure her company ran in tip-top shape.

Natasha chuckled. "If Baron Samedi hadn't told me he was your *met tet* himself, I wouldn't believe it. What child of the Baron doesn't like to let loose?"

Most vodouisants reflected the personalities of their *met tets*, their deep connections with their guardian loa affecting every aspect of their lives. Known for his antics, his love of sex, rum, and cigars, and his gyrating dance moves, Baron Samedi's personality was the exact opposite of Odette's.

"People go to bars to meet other people, which is exactly what I'm trying to avoid. Falling in love will end with a horrific murder that I'd rather not experience in this life if I don't have to. It's happened enough in my past lives." She shivered at the memories. After her fourth past-life regression revealed the same gruesome ending, she'd resolved to spend her life alone. It was her only chance at making it past forty.

Natasha gave her a sympathetic smile. "Some people go out to spend time with their friends. If anyone hits on you, I'll shoo him away."

She sighed. "There's also the *other* reason."

"Letting loose and having a little fun ain't gonna turn you evil—not that you have an ounce of evil in your soul, whether you believe it or not. Your powers are strong because you can handle them. Your *met tet* has faith you won't use them for nothing but good. You should too."

She forced a smile. "Maybe next time."

"Between my hair salon and running the Voodoo shop, I don't get out much, so I'll hold you to it." Natasha nodded. "Next time it is."

"I said maybe." Odette waved as Natasha descended the steps and sashayed up the path toward the sidewalk.

Stepping inside, she closed the door, and with a deep, cleansing breath, she opened her senses once more. The blessing the Mambo had placed on the home rid the air of the rough, grating energy, replacing it with soft warmth…a clean slate. Well, except for the ghost hovering in the corner.

Odette put her hands on her hips and stared at the area where she sensed him. "I'm willing to listen whenever you're ready to talk."

As she shuffled to the kitchen, that same overwhelming feeling of utter adoration expanded in her chest, making tears brim in her eyes. Whomever this guy loved in life was one lucky lady, but if Odette didn't put up some barriers now, he might figure out a way to take advantage of her.

She picked up the extinguished sage and waved it in his direction. "Will you please stop that. Right now." The sensation dissipated, rolling away from her and into the invisible entity. "Let's get one thing straight. I don't want you to force your feelings on me, understand? I'm not an empath. I don't deal with other people's emotional baggage. If you want to communicate with me, you're going to have to figure out another way. Like with words."

Grabbing her box from the counter, she carried it into the living room and set it on the floor. She smiled at the grand mantle on the enormous wood-burning fireplace. The dark-wood ledge stretched across the entire front of the brick hearth and wrapped around the sides to meet the doorframes on either side. The first time she'd stepped foot inside the house, the mantle had called to her—the perfect place to set up the altar honoring the loa who walked with her.

She glanced at her watch and quickened her pace. The movers would arrive within the hour.

Pulling a deep-purple scarf from the box, she shook it with a flourish and draped it across the front of the mantle. Then she hung the Baron's *vévé*, the spiritual symbol to represent the loa, on the wall behind it. Composed of a cemetery cross, which represented the crossroads, and two coffins, the hand-stitched *vévé* had been a gift from Natasha after Odette's initiation into the Mambo's House of worship.

She continued setting up the items to represent and honor her guardian Spirit: a human skull replica with a top hat and dark glasses, purple and white candles, a small bottle of rum, and a fine Cuban cigar. A string of silver and black Mardi Gras beads completed the altar, and she stepped back to admire her creation. "That's a beautiful testament to my servitude, don't you think, Baron?"

A heaviness in the air formed behind her right shoulder, and a woodsy scent, both familiar and foreign, crept into her senses. She turned, and though she couldn't yet see him, the presence of her resident ghost was unmistakable. "I'm not scared of you. Why don't you show yourself to me?"

The presence drifted closer, until the empty energy of the entity reached her skin. She sensed in her mind an arm reaching toward her, and the sensation of fingers gliding down her cheek raised goose bumps on her arms. For a dead guy, he sure was warm.

Her heart thrummed, and she swallowed the dryness from her mouth. "Who are you?"

A deep, musical voice danced through her head. "Have you forgotten me?"

CHAPTER THREE

James Malveaux scanned the crowd, searching for the woman of his dreams, but the likelihood of finding someone in a dress that looked like it came straight from the set of *Gone with the Wind* in a crowded nightclub was nil…even in New Orleans.

The DJ played a mix of modern music, the heavy bass line masking the melody so that it sounded more like he stood inside a giant heart beating an irregular rhythm. Bodies gyrated on the dance floor, moving in time to the vibrating tempo, and the scents of alcohol, sweat, perfume, and Axe body spray swirled through the air.

His friends Noah and Cade had wandered off to hit on women, and James would have normally been right in the middle of it, but that damn dream had him so confused he didn't know his head from his tail. The mystery woman was all he'd thought about since the dreams started three weeks ago. Every time he managed to get her off his mind, his wolf would throw her back into his thoughts front and center…as if he'd already claimed her…but how could he claim someone he'd never met?

And that dress… He rubbed at the scruff on his chin. He hadn't planned on attending any costume balls in the foreseeable future, but plans could change.

Leaning an elbow on the bar, he tossed back a double-shot of whiskey and focused on the warmth trailing down to his stomach. He needed to get out of his head and into the moment. Or at least dull the thoughts with a little libation. Unfortunately, it took three times as many drinks to get a werewolf buzzed. His body processed the alcohol at lightning speed, so the buzz—if he managed to get one—wouldn't last half an hour.

"You okay?" The bartender, Nikki, a witch from the local coven, leaned toward him, her shoulder-length earrings swishing as she tilted her head. "You've usually found a date by now." She grinned and popped the top on an Abita beer, sliding it to the man next to him.

He chewed the inside of his cheek. He *should* have found a date by now. "Give me a rum and Coke. Make it a triple."

"Who is she?" Ice clinked in the glass as she filled it.

"Who?"

"The woman who broke your heart." She held up a bottle of Captain Morgan. "The usual?"

James huffed. His heart couldn't be broken when he'd never been in love. He'd never allowed himself to even come close to that emotion. He glanced at the rack of liquor behind her and focused on a bottle with a purple label. A skeleton wearing a tuxedo jacket and a top hat stared back at him. "Is the rum with the dead guy on it any good?"

She shrugged. "The Baron? I like it. The distillery is here in New Orleans. Been around since the late eighties, I think. It almost went under a few years ago, until the owner sent his daughter in to whip it into shape." She poured in three shots and topped it with a splash of Coke before sliding it to him.

Gripping the drink, he focused on the chill seeping through the glass. Beads of condensation formed on the surface, and he wiped them away with his thumb. "You know a lot about your liquor."

"I'm a bartender. It's my job."

He took a sip and swished the concoction around in his mouth. Warm, earthy tones greeted his taste buds, with an undercurrent of cinnamon and some other exotic spices he couldn't place. The Coke added a touch of sweetness to the robust aroma of the rum. He closed his eyes to savor the flavor and took another sip.

Nikki chuckled. "Good, huh?"

He opened his eyes. "I've found my new favorite drink. You said it's called The Baron?"

She held up the bottle. If O'Malley's didn't stock it, he'd have to convince the pack's headquarters to start. Where had this delicacy been all his life? "The woman who runs it now…do you know her name?"

"She's a vodouisant, and everyone calls her the Baroness. She comes from money, and she runs a tight ship." She leaned in closer. "I've heard rumors that some kind of black magic was involved. Baron Samedi is the Voodoo god of death, after all. I don't know much about Voodoo, but why would you dedicate your business to death? Sounds dangerous to me."

He took another sip of his drink. "Sounds like my kind of woman."

Nikki arched an eyebrow. "No offense, but a woman like that wouldn't bat an eye at a werewolf construction worker. You wouldn't have much to offer someone who's made a deal with the devil."

He straightened his spine. "I've got plenty to offer. Werewolves are known for our stamina."

She snorted. "Was that supposed to be a reference to your prowess in the bedroom? If so, you'll have to forgive me. The only wiener I'm interested in is the kind that's smothered in creole mustard and comes on a bun." She returned the rum bottle to the rack and nodded at something behind him. "Speaking of vodouisants. There's the Queen herself."

James turned to find Natasha, the Mambo of the biggest New Orleans House of Voodoo, waltzing through the door, followed by six other vodouisants.

"I bet she'd know who the Baroness is," Nikki said.

James downed the rest of his drink and slid off his seat. His head spun as the buzz he'd been so desperate for finally fogged his senses. His interest in the distillery owner dissolved as he strode toward Natasha. He had another question for the Mambo.

He waited until she finished saying hello to a woman near the bar before offering his hand to shake. “Hi, Natasha. I’m James Malveaux. It’s nice to finally meet you.”

She accepted his outstretched hand and paused as his magical signature registered on her skin. “Werewolf?”

He nodded. “I need your help.”

“You’ve visited my readers at the temple a few times. I remember seeing your name on the books. Did they not answer your questions?”

He raked a hand through his hair and tried to collect his muddled thoughts. “They did. Kinda. Not really, but I’ve been having these dreams…”

“Why don’t you stop by the temple tomorrow around seven, and I’ll read your cards?”

His heart sank. “Yeah. Okay, I will.” He blew out a breath and shoved his hands in his pockets, kicking a flattened plastic cup toward a trash can.

Natasha sighed and motioned for him to follow her. She disappeared into the crowd, and he stumbled around the patrons, catching up to her as she went out the back door.

Two wrought-iron tables occupied the small, grassy area of the courtyard, and a cobblestone path led to a separate building that housed a storage area for the club and the restrooms. A thin layer of wispy, white clouds stretched across the crescent moon, and pale stars twinkled in the midnight sky.

The humid, summer air clung to his skin, and the vibrating bass from the club muffled, giving his ears a reprieve from the incessant noise as he strode deeper into the courtyard.

Natasha settled into one of the metal chairs and gestured for James to take the other one. As he lowered into the seat, she chuckled. “Your eyes match your shirt.”

He glanced at his pale-blue button up. “I’ve been told I look good in blue.”

“My Spirit Guides approve.”

“Spirit Guides?”

She nodded. “They’re the reason I’m out here, about to give you a reading, instead of having drinks with my friends.”

Thank goodness for Spirit Guides, then. "What else did they tell you?"

"That I should talk to you. What have you seen my readers about?"

He swallowed and glanced up as two women, walking arm-in-arm, disappeared into the restroom. Talking to a vodouisant in the privacy of a reading room at the temple had been hard enough, but to spill his guts out here in the open? He wiped his sweaty palms on his jeans.

"You don't have to be embarrassed; I won't tell a soul. We take our readings seriously."

He ran a hand down his face. How could he explain this without sounding like a complete wuss? "I'm having these dreams about a woman, and…" Heat crept into his cheeks, but he couldn't tell if it was embarrassment or the alcohol. He blew out a breath and looked into the Mambo's eyes. "I feel like I love her. My wolf does anyway. It feels like he's claimed her."

She arched an eyebrow. "*Claimed* her?"

"It's a werewolf thing. My wolf wants me to take this woman as my mate. He's telling me she's my fate-bound…my soulmate. But I've never met her. I don't even know if she exists." Saying it out loud made it sound more ridiculous than it already was. His wolf *couldn't* claim a woman he'd never met. It wasn't possible.

"Mm-hmm." Though her tone sounded doubtful, with her blank expression, the woman was impossible to read.

"Anyway, all the readings have said the same thing. That I have to *break the cycle*, but I don't know what the cycle is. I just want to know who this woman is. My wolf won't rest until I find her."

Natasha held his gaze for what felt like an eternity. His buddies inside must have been looking for him by now, but he *had* to hear whatever the priestess had to say.

He'd been perfectly happy living his life as a bachelor, seeing a woman a time or two and then ending it before any emotions had time to bloom. He'd been counting on his wolf to let him know when it was time to settle down. Mating with anyone but his fate-bound was out of the question. If fate didn't have a specific mate in mind for him, he'd rather stay single for the rest of his life. He'd seen what could happen to a werewolf who mated with someone fate didn't choose. His dad was a broken man because of it.

Natasha inhaled deeply and swayed slightly, almost as if she were slipping into a trance. Then, she straightened her spine. "Let me see your hands."

Reaching across the table, he placed his hands palm up in hers. Her magical energy pricked at his skin as she gazed at the place where his right pinkie finger should have been.

"I thought werewolves were fast healers."

He fought the instinct to jerk his hand away. He'd been asked that question so many times, he'd lost count. *Most* werewolves were fast healers. "We can't regrow limbs."

"You couldn't reattach it?"

If his body worked like a normal werewolf's, then yeah, he could have. "It got caught in a cement mixer. There wasn't much left to reattach."

She frowned. "This makes sense. My guides told me a piece of you was missing, and here it is."

He ground his teeth, trying to quell his frustration. His buzz was already wearing off, and he needed answers. "What's the cycle people have been talking about, and who is the woman from my dreams?"

With a sigh, Natasha reached into her purse and pulled out a deck of tarot cards. She shuffled them and then offered the stack to him. "Mix them up, and I'll do a quick card reading. Don't expect much though. The alcohol you've drunk is mucking up the waters."

He shuffled the cards and handed them back to her. "I didn't drink that much."

"You've had enough." She turned over three cards and narrowed her eyes at them. "You are stuck in a cycle that needs to be broken. Not just for your sake. There are others involved."

His heart raced. "What's the cycle?"

"It's unclear." She turned over a few more cards. "Your dreams are trying to tell you something."

No kidding. "Who is the woman?"

She turned over another card and frowned. "Also unclear."

"Damn it." He fisted his hands and slammed them on the table.

Natasha arched an eyebrow at him. "If the Spirits say it isn't time for you to know, then it's not time."

"I'm sorry." He opened his fists and folded his hands on the table. Being an ass to a priestess wouldn't get him anywhere.

"I'm sensing an unrest."

He'd never felt more restless in his life.

Placing two more cards face up, she shook her head. "This is bigger than you."

She turned over another card, and his heart sank. The most recognizable card in the tarot deck stared up at him, and he could barely force the word through his tightening throat. "Death."

Sympathy softened her eyes. "In tarot, the death card rarely means literal death. It's the end of one cycle and the start of something new. Whatever cycle you're stuck in, you gotta end it soon."

"But you can't tell me what the cycle is? What I need to do to stop it?"

She stacked the cards and returned them to her purse. "The Spirits ain't sharing that information with me. It could be something you're supposed to discover on your own, or it could involve another person, and you'll have to end it together." She rose to her feet. "Or it could be the alcohol. The waters around you are murky. Come see me when you're sober, and we'll try again."

"Thank you."

She bowed and shuffled into the club. With his elbows on the table, he held his head in his hands. That wasn't what he'd wanted to hear. And the fact that the Mambo, the most powerful vodouisant in New Orleans, couldn't give him any new information didn't make him feel any better about his problem.

Natasha was right when she'd said a piece of him was missing, but it wasn't his finger like she thought. He'd always felt that way, even before he'd lost it in a construction accident. A piece of him was missing from somewhere deep in his soul. He'd never felt whole, and he blamed it on his mother. If she'd been around more, maybe he wouldn't be so opposed to love and his wolf wouldn't have claimed an imaginary mate.

His mom had cheated on his dad more times than he could count.

Probably a lot more than James was aware of, since it started when he was a kid. There was no guarantee that a werewolf would find a fate-bound, so many chose to mate with whomever their human side fell in love with, rather than waiting to see if their wolves would bond with anyone. His dad mated with the first woman he fell for, and look how that worked out for him.

James shook his head. A fate-bound mate would never cheat, and he wouldn't settle for anything less.

Of course, his mom being human didn't help his circumstances either. He was already slow to heal because he only had his father's magic running through his veins. Maybe his human side made him incapable of finding his fate-bound too.

"There you are, man. I was starting to think you jetted on us." Noah, a second-born were with auburn hair and dark-brown eyes, sauntered into the courtyard. "He's out here," he called over his shoulder to Cade. With a flick of his wrist, Noah dragged the chair through the grass and plopped into it.

James glanced through the doorway, but luckily no one had seen his friend's display. "Are you drunk? Don't use your power where people can see."

Noah grinned. "I checked. No one saw." Second-born werewolves lacked the ability to shift, but most of them had some sort of psychic power. Telekinesis was a rare talent for a were, and Noah's cocky attitude about it grated on James's nerves.

"It's not parlor magic; it's a unique werewolf gift. Don't flaunt it like it's cheap."

"When did you become a grumpy old fart?" Noah crossed his arms.

When indeed?

"Cade's holding down the fort in there. We met a group of three, and they're up for leaving the club. We need you."

A quick glance inside revealed Cade standing near the doorway, a mug of beer in one hand, his other arm wrapped around the waist of a tall blonde. Cade's own blond hair had that mussed, just-got-out-of-bed look, but James knew better. He'd seen the amount of hair products his friend used to make himself look thrown together.

James held in a groan. With his buzz gone, he wasn't in the mood to play wingman. "You can handle two, can't you?"

Noah narrowed his eyes. "What's wrong with you? You—"

"Hold on." James inhaled deeply, and the distinct scent of rotting garbage and death assaulted his senses. "You smell that?"

Noah sniffed. "Is that…demon?"

He rose to his feet. "Sure smells like it. Get Cade."

James crept toward the back of the courtyard and glanced at his friends. When Cade didn't respond to Noah's shout, Noah flicked his fingers, making Cade spill his beer down the front of his shirt.

"Goddammit." Cade stormed out of the club, but he stopped short, his nostrils flaring. "Why didn't you tell me we were going hunting tonight?"

They flanked James on either side and slinked out of the courtyard and into the alley between two clubs. A two-foot-tall dark mass darted behind a dumpster, and James ran toward it. The fiend leaped into the trash container, and a rancid wad of rotting meat flew out, slapping James in the face. He wiped the slimy substance from his cheek and stood on his toes to peer inside the dumpster.

An array of garbage and empty beer bottles hurled from the container, and James sidestepped around the spray.

"What the hell?" Noah used his telekinesis to slam the dumpster lid shut and held it closed as the tiny demon knocked against it, trying to escape. "What is it?"

James shook his head. "Some kind of lower-level demon. I'd guess it answers to a bigger master, but this is the only one I can sense." He scanned the alley, finding it empty.

"What's the plan?" Cade asked.

"Check the alley entrance. When we're clear, shout. Then Noah will release the lid, and I'll shift and take it out."

"You sure, man?" Cade made his way to end of the alley. "Shifting in the city is against the rules."

"When have I ever cared about rules?"

"Inside, when I…" Noah laughed. "All right, maybe you're not such an old fart after all."

"Clear," Cade shouted.

James tensed, calling his wolf to the surface. He looked at Noah. "On three."

Noah nodded. The demon thrashed inside the bin, denting the side of the container from the inside.

"Three," James shouted.

Noah released the lid, and the fiend sprang from the dumpster. James leaped toward it, shifting in mid-air as the creature bounced off a wall and clamped its razor-like teeth onto his front leg.

James held in a grunt as the demon's teeth met bone, and he bit into its neck, ripping it from his leg and tossing it across the alley.

"Make it fast," Cade said between clenched teeth. "Group of tourists heading this way."

Advancing on the fiend, James swiped a massive paw across its chest, piercing its heart with a claw, and the demon exploded into a cloud of ash. As James shifted to human form, he shoved his hands in his pockets and coolly strolled toward the sidewalk as the group of women came into view. They glanced at the men in the alley and quickened their pace, linking arms as they hurried past.

"That was fun. I told you I'd be a good demon hunter." Noah's grin slipped into a scowl as he nodded at James's arm. "Oh, man. It got you."

Blood oozed from the puncture wounds, trailing down to his wrist, and one of the fiend's teeth had torn a two-inch gash near his elbow. The bite stung, but the bleeding had slowed. He'd heal. Eventually.

Cade sauntered closer, reaching for James's arm. "Do you need medical attention? We could call Alexis…"

He jerked away. "I don't need medical attention, dammit, and I definitely don't need a healer. I'll be fine."

"Are you sure?" Noah cut his gaze between James and Cade. "If I had a gash like that, I'd need stitches."

"You're second-born; I'm not." His voice came out in a growl, and Noah flinched. James might as well have been second-born too, at the rate this wound was healing, but he'd be damned if he'd let his pack-mates fuss over a little demon bite.

Noah gritted his teeth, crossing his arms over his chest. "Thanks for the reminder, Captain Obvious."

"I..." James let out a slow breath. His old man had warned him not to join the demon hunting team. Hell, his dad wouldn't even let James hunt gators with his friends when he was a kid. *The pack is only as strong as its weakest member,* he'd say. *Never let them know that's you.* But James wasn't a lone wolf. He belonged in the pack, and he refused to be the weakest link.

"Look, it's healing." He held up his arm. The small punctures had already closed, and the gash was beginning to seal. "Let's get out of this alley before someone calls the cops. I'm going to text Luke, and we'll meet him at O'Malley's."

"We don't have to report it to the alpha right now, do we?" Disappointment was evident in Noah's voice. "It's barely past midnight, and if you cleaned up the blood, we could..."

"There could be more out there." James jerked his head toward his Chevy, indicating his friends should follow. "This is what demon hunters do. You want to be on the team, don't you?"

Noah gazed wistfully at the club. "Yeah. Let's go."

They trudged up the sidewalk to James's truck, and he found an old paint rag in the back seat to wipe up the blood. It killed him that his friends saw his weakness like that. If they'd have been in the swamp, he could've stayed in wolf form until the wound closed—and he'd have healed much faster—sparing himself from their sympathy.

He more than made up for his...limitation...with his faster-than-normal shifting speed and his keen demon-hunting abilities. Cade and especially Noah...he outranked them for God's sake; pity was the last thing he needed from the pack. From anyone.

CHAPTER FOUR

ODETTE GROANED IN HER SLEEP AND ROLLED OVER. AS A spectator in her dream, she stood on the side of the road, watching the same event she'd been forced to relive in her mind countless times since it happened in real life.

A little girl with shiny black ringlets and freckles across her nose played with a bright-purple ball in the front yard, while her beautiful momma pulled weeds in the flower bed. Odette remembered the scene as if it happened yesterday. The sun warming her light umber skin. The sweet fragrance of bougainvillea drifting through the summer air.

As the girl tossed the ball into the air, she spotted a little boy with blood running down his face across the road. The ball bounced on the grass and rolled into the street, and a car zipped past, catching it beneath a tire and flattening it. Too young to recognize the difference between the living and the dead, the girl called to the boy, *"Are you okay?"* and he met her gaze with fearful eyes.

"He's a ghost," Odette tried to say to the girl in her dream, but her mouth wouldn't form words. The girl stepped off the curb to help him, and her momma yelled, *"Be careful, child."*

The girl turned to see her momma running to her, her face

contorted with fear. She pushed her, and the girl tumbled, rolling across the street and smacking her head on the pavement.

Odette's heart raced in her dream. A truck rounding the corner slammed into the girl's momma, the tires rolling over her neck, crushing her. The sound of crunching bone and tearing flesh was so real and loud it echoed in her head like razorblades ripping through her skull.

She wanted to scream. To run to the woman and do something… anything to save her. But there was no saving this woman, even if her feet weren't stuck to the ground in the dream. Odette couldn't save her then, and now she'd been buried for twenty years.

She looked at the eight-year-old version of herself, and her heart wrenched. Young Odette scrambled to her feet, screaming, and threw herself onto her momma's lifeless body.

"No, Momma! You can't leave me!" The little girl sobbed and lifted her gaze to her momma's spirit hovering near her body. The ghost drifted higher, and young Odette sobbed, *"You have to stay with me always."*

Her momma's ghost jerked, obeying the command, and drifted toward her daughter. *"You have to let me go, child. It's my time."*

"No!" Odette said in unison with the younger version of herself, and she covered her mouth.

"You're going to stay with me always," the girl repeated. *"Baron Samedi will bring you back."*

Sirens sounded in the distance, and a crowd gathered around the girl and her momma's body. A neighbor rested her hand on young Odette's shoulder. *"Your momma is gone, sweetheart. Why don't you come with me, and we'll call your daddy?"*

"No!" Young Odette shrugged away from her touch and stood, blood—her momma's and her own—dripping down her face and covering her dress, making her look as if she belonged in a Stephen King movie. *"She's going to come back to life. Baron Samedi's going to bring her back."*

The neighbors glanced at each other uncomfortably. *"Her body is ruined,"* one of them said. *"If you brought her back now, she'd be a zombie. Is that what you want?"*

"She won't be a zombie! Baron Samedi can bring her back whole like he did me."

"Nobody brought you back to life," another neighbor said.

The paramedics and the police arrived and ushered the on-lookers to the sidewalk.

Tears rolled down the little girl's cheeks, and her hands trembled. *"I died when I was born, and Momma did a ritual for Baron Samedi to bring me back, and he did."*

"Hush, child," her momma's ghost said.

The neighbors whispered to each other, and a paramedic guided young Odette to the back of an ambulance. Another pair of EMTs loaded her momma's body onto a stretcher and covered her head with a sheet.

"Don't take her!" the girl screamed. *"She's coming back to life, just like I did!"*

Odette woke with a gasp, sitting up in bed and clutching her sweat-drenched sheets. Tears streamed down her cheeks, and she pressed a hand to her chest, trying to slow her frantic heart.

A presence gathered in her bedroom, a solid form taking shape in the atmosphere. Sympathy warmed her chest, and the calming presence moved closer, stopping at the edge of the bed.

"While I appreciate the support, I asked you not to push your feelings on me." She swung her legs over the side of the bed.

The calm dissipated, allowing her to feel the grating, raw emotions her dream left behind. She rolled her neck, stretching the tightness from her muscles. That dream always left her with a headache.

Rising to her feet, she padded across the wood floor and headed for the shower. The entity followed her to the bathroom door, and she paused in the threshold without turning around. "I would appreciate it if you didn't come into the bathroom. Will you please give me some privacy?" She closed the door, and thankfully, the ghost respected her request.

Avoiding the mirror, she stripped and showered quickly. The contractor would be there soon, and she didn't want to keep the alpha werewolf waiting. He seemed like a nice enough guy, but magical beings that strong should never be tested. She emerged from the bathroom thirty minutes later dressed in a black pencil skirt with a matching blazer, and ready for work.

The ghost followed her to the kitchen, hovering in the corner as she brewed her coffee and ate a container of strawberry yogurt. "I wish you would show yourself to me." She looked in the direction where she felt the presence. "It's not fair that you can see me, but I can't see you."

A deep, masculine voice drifted to her ears. "Have you really forgotten me?"

She shivered as goose bumps rose on her neck. "Maybe I would remember if you let me see you. Or at least tell me your name."

The air in the room grew cold, which was typical when a spirit was trying to manifest. The goose bumps on her arms turned to pinpricks, and the air around her seemed to thicken. An image wavered before her, the air shimmering like heat coming off a blacktop in the summer.

"Keep trying. I'm starting to see something." A pang of guilt flashed in her chest as she watched the ghost struggle to appear. She could easily give him the power he needed, her own body acting as a conduit, allowing the energy of the spirit world to pass through her and into the specter. Letting go and supplying the power would be easy. Shutting it off was another issue altogether, and she'd learned the hard way not to start something she couldn't stop. Give a ghost too much power, and the consequences would be dire.

After a few more pained minutes, the form solidified, and a man stood before her wearing a dark-gray suit with a vest and pocket watch. He was handsome, with fair skin, a strong jaw, and bright-blue eyes, but his clothing and the style of his light-brown hair were reminiscent of the early 1800s. Definitely not someone she knew when he was alive.

"That's better. Can you tell me your name?" She waited as the ghost opened his mouth a few times to speak, closing it again when no sound would form. "That's okay; becoming visible zapped your energy, which is normal. You probably haven't shown yourself to anyone in a long time, have you?"

The man shook his head.

"Are you stuck here?"

His brow furrowed, and he looked at his surroundings with a confused expression. Lifting his shoulders, he turned his palms up as if to say he didn't know.

"That's okay. We'll figure it out together. Most people won't be able to hear you speak, but I can. Direct your energy to your voice so you can tell me your name."

The spirit stiffened, his eyes widening as his mouth opened. "My name is Nicolas. How did you do that? You told me to speak, and I felt…compelled to." He drifted toward her, stopping a few inches in front of her.

Taking a step back, she swallowed the bile from the back of her throat. She'd accidentally given him a command. That was worse than giving him energy.

Nicolas smiled. "It's wonderful to speak to you again, *mon cher*."

Cher? Who did this guy think she was? "Listen, Nicolas. I'm glad you're talking now, but I have some men on their way over."

He tilted his head.

"Construction workers. I'm having the home restored to its original state, and I would appreciate it if you left them alone. Will you please make yourself scarce when they're around, so they don't get scared?" Not that she thought werewolves would be scared of ghosts, but there could be humans on the team.

The ghost's smile returned, and he reached a hand toward her. Curling a strand of hair around his finger, he slid the back of his hand down her cheek as he released the lock. "You look different."

Her breath caught at his tender touch, the warmth of his non-existent skin making her shiver. She had so many questions for the ghost, but with the contractor about to arrive, she didn't have time to deal with him now.

Clearing her voice, she took a few more steps away. "Right. Well, we all change. I have to get some work done, so if you don't mind, maybe we can talk some more this evening when I get home?"

The ghost opened his mouth, but he could only emit a tiny squeak, like air releasing from a balloon. His form faded, the energy he'd expended to say those few words taking its toll. Confusion clouded his eyes, and he dissipated.

Odette reached out with her senses, but he'd gone wherever it was that Earth-bound ghosts went, leaving her alone. Settling at the kitchen table, she fired up her laptop and logged into her work e-mail in an effort to make a dent in her inbox while she waited for her contractor to arrive.

As James sauntered through the door into O'Malley's Pub, a curtain of crisp air blasted his skin. Shaded lights hanging from exposed beams cast a smoky glow over the bar, even though no one had been allowed to smoke indoors in the last ten years.

He slid onto a barstool as Amber, the alpha's sister, poured him a cup of black coffee. Clutching the mug in both hands, he inhaled the rich aroma and took a sip. "Are you picking up on anything new? Any more little monsters for me to chase?" After he'd reported the incident to Luke last night, they'd patrolled the city for hours and found nothing.

Her brow furrowed. "The feeling is muddy, but I think you're going to be fighting more evil soon. There's…" She shook her head. "Something is going to happen, but I don't know what."

"I'll be ready." He winked, and she gave him a curious look, tilting her head. He didn't dare ask the next question dancing on his tongue.

As a second-born were, Amber had the ability of empathic premonitions. She felt things about the future, but she rarely picked up on details. She'd already told James she sensed change in his future…of the romantic type…but it seemed that change would be his wolf trying to claim a dream woman he'd never meet. And if the modern-day Voodoo Queen of New Orleans couldn't help him solve his problem, he was up shit creek without a paddle.

Amber opened the coffee maker and put in a fresh filter. "Luke's not in yet. Do you want breakfast while you wait?"

"Nah. I'm good."

A high-pitched giggle emanated from the sidewalk outside and turned into a squeal of delight as the door opened. Emma, a seven-year-old were with dark hair and hazel eyes, darted inside, and her mom, Bekah, sighed as she followed her.

Emma scrambled onto a barstool, but the joy on her face transformed into a scowl as she glared at Amber. "Where's Uncle Chase?"

"That's rude, Emma." Bekah stood behind her daughter. "You should say hello first."

The girl rolled her eyes. "Hi."

Amber laughed. "Hi, Emma. Chase had to help Rain in the bakery this morning. He'll be in later."

"Sorry, kiddo." Bekah took Emma's hand. "Maybe we can see him this afternoon."

Yanking her hand from her mom's grasp, Emma crossed her arms. "We'll wait."

"No, we won't. You have to go to school."

The girl's shoulders slumped. "Please, Mom. I haven't seen Uncle Chase in a week."

"We've all been busy." Bekah tried to tug her off the stool, but Emma gripped the edge of the bar.

"I'm not leaving until I see Uncle Chase."

"Hey now." James sauntered toward her and sank onto a stool. "Don't you know what happens to kids who don't listen to their moms?"

Emma cut him a sideways glance and pouted. "They get in trouble."

"Worse than trouble. The Rougarou knows when kids are misbehaving, and he'll wake up from his deep sleep in the swamp to come and *get you*." He tickled her ribs as he said the last words, and she squealed.

"I'm not afraid of the Rougarou." She grinned.

James crossed his arms. "No? Why not?"

"Because *you're* the Rougarou." She tried to tickle him back, but her fingers caught his arm instead.

He chuckled. "I'm not the werewolf boogeyman. Do I have red eyes and fangs?"

Her smile faded. "No."

"You've seen me shift. Do I have a wolf's head on a man's body, or am I a full wolf?"

Her little brow furrowed. "You're a full wolf."

"I don't sleep in the swamp either. So how could one of your pack-mates be the Rougarou?"

Her eyes widened, and she slid to her feet. "I'm ready to go to school, Mommy."

Bekah held back a laugh as she waved goodbye and led Emma out the door.

Amber shook her head, fighting her smile. "You shouldn't scare her with made-up stories about a werewolf boogeyman."

"Why not? My dad scared me with it when I was a kid. It's a rite of passage." He picked up his mug and drank the rest of his coffee as Luke sauntered through the door.

At six-foot-four, Luke stood two inches taller than James—the biggest wolf in the pack, like an alpha should be. His light-brown hair was tied back in a band, and he carried a tablet computer beneath his arm.

James chuckled. "I can't believe I beat the alpha to work."

Luke fought a grin. "I was…distracted this morning." And by the gleam in his eyes, his mate had something to do with the distraction.

Longing tightened James's chest, adding another layer of unwanted emotion to his inner battle with his wolf over a woman he'd never met, who might not even exist.

Sliding onto a stool, Luke tapped the screen of his tablet. "I wanted you to go to the new site with me on Esplanade today. The owner wants to restore the house to its original state."

"Those are my favorite."

Luke nodded. "Mine too. But we're running behind on the Ursulines project, so I need you there to pick up the slack."

Damn. He'd much rather work on a restoration than the modernization they were doing to the building on Ursulines.

"Mmm…" Amber tapped a finger against her lips. "I feel like James needs to go to Esplanade."

Luke arched an eyebrow. "Details?"

"I feel like both good and bad things will happen if he goes." Her brow scrunched. "But there will be a disaster if he doesn't."

Luke paused, cutting his gaze between his sister and James. Then, he typed on his tablet screen and nodded. "I sent you the details. Read through it before you get there, and have her walk you through the house to confirm everything she wants done."

"Got it, boss." A drip of adrenaline rolled through James's veins… just enough to clear his head and straighten his spine. He'd get to work on his favorite kind of project, and there was the possibility of impending doom. His day kept getting better.

The alpha looked at his sister. "Does this feeling have anything to do with the change you've been predicting for him…female-wise?"

"Possibly." She refilled James's cup. "But I'm feeling good and bad things, so be careful."

Luke squared his gaze on James. "No sleeping with the client unless you plan to take her as your mate."

James choked on his coffee, spewing it across the bar. "I've never slept with a client."

With his hand on the bar, Luke paused, narrowing his eyes before rising to his full height. "Something tells me this time might be different."

CHAPTER FIVE

JAMES PARKED ON THE CURB IN FRONT OF A SALMON-COLORED two-story mansion on Esplanade. Four steps led up to a wrap-around front porch, and a dark-wood door framed an oval cut-glass window. White columns held up the second-story gallery, where two doors on either end of the house were painted white.

The colors were wrong. The doors were wrong. Shaking his head, he pulled up the file Luke had sent him. The corners of his lips tugged into a smile as he scanned the document. Everything the owner had requested accurately portrayed what it would have looked like in its nineteenth-century prime.

He chuckled. This particular house had always been his favorite. Since he was a teen, his dream had been to own the place, but he didn't even know the property had been for sale. Not that he could have afforded the two-million-dollar price tag attached to it. Being in charge of the renovation would have to suffice.

Scrolling to the top of the document, he glimpsed the owner's name. Odette Allemand. *Hmm.* He'd known an Odette once, a long time ago. He hadn't seen her since seventh grade when she'd moved away, and she'd hardly spoken to him…to anyone…in junior high. A strange flush of excitement rolled through his veins. How many Odette Allemands could there be?

He slid out of the truck and tucked his phone into his pocket. Slamming the door, he paced up the walk and climbed the front steps, wiping his palms on his jeans.

He knocked and held his breath. The sound of heels clicking on the wooden floor emanated from inside, and a tall silhouette appeared in the glass oval.

She opened the door halfway and gave him a once-over with her gaze before speaking. "Can I help you?"

His throat thickened, making it hard to force out an answer. This was the same Odette from his childhood, but she'd grown into a stunningly beautiful woman. She wore a black skirt that stopped two inches above her knees and a tailored black blazer with a purple silk shirt beneath. Her black hair hung in ringlets down to her shoulders, framing her delicate face, and the same sprinkling of freckles across her nose that had made his heart race in junior high accented her light umber skin. Her dark eyes narrowed as she waited for him to answer.

He cleared his throat. "Odette?"

"Yes?"

"I'm James. We had a few classes together in school. I…" *Damn it.* His heart raced, and his palms were still sweating. He never got nervous around women, but that was exactly what this unwelcome emotion felt like.

She gripped the door handle, probably ready to slam it in his face if he didn't get his act together. "What can I do for you, James?" Her brows lifted, and she pressed her lips together, her expression indifferent.

She didn't remember him. Or if she did, she didn't care. The sting of rejection brought him out of the past, reminding him why he had come here. "I'm with Mason Remodeling. Luke had to attend to an emergency at another site, so he sent me to finalize the details with you this morning."

She glanced at his truck on the curb, squinting as if trying to read the magnetic sign on the side. Seemingly satisfied, she opened the door fully. "Welcome. Come on in."

He stepped through the threshold, and she closed the door. The size of the floorboards indicated the wood was original to the house. The previous owner had kept it in excellent condition, though it shined more than it would have in the nineteenth century. A modern, chrome light fixture hung in the foyer, but the switch was off, allowing the morning sunlight cascading in through the windows to light the room.

"I was hoping you could show me the place, so we can go over any last-minute changes you might want to make."

She blinked at him, her gaze sweeping down the length of his body before meeting his eyes. "I don't want to make any changes. I want this house as close to the original as possible. All of the paint and wallpaper selections are based on that." She glanced over his shoulder with a curious expression.

He turned to see what she was looking at, but an empty room was all that lay behind him. He raked a hand through his hair. "Do you mind if I have a look around myself, then? So I can make sure everything Luke wrote up is clear?"

She glanced behind him again and gave her head a tiny shake. Confliction sparked in her eyes before she let out a sigh and relaxed her posture. "I suppose I have a few minutes to show you around before I leave for work. Are you starting today?" She turned and headed for the kitchen. "This way."

He followed, allowing his gaze to focus on her swaying hips for a moment. An image of the woman from his dreams flashed behind his eyes, like it had been doing every time he'd seen someone who piqued his interest for the past three weeks. But this time, the picture of whom his wolf wanted didn't kill his libido instantly.

Instead, a confusing mix of attraction and longing drew his wolf to the surface, and if he didn't know any better, he'd say it felt an awful lot like his wolf was considering Odette a possible mate. His chest warmed at the idea, his mouth curving into an involuntary grin.

Whoa. Put the brakes on, man. He wouldn't consider anyone a potential mate until his wolf told him it was ordained by fate, and there was far too much confusion swirling through his mind. Fate didn't get confused, and werewolves only claimed one fate-bound mate.

He hadn't been laid in over a month. That's all it was. Feeling sexual attraction to anyone but his dream woman had taken him off-guard. And sexual attraction was all this was. It was all it would ever be.

James wiped the thoughts from his mind and focused on the architecture. The modern kitchen had an island and stainless-steel appliances. Granite countertops reflected the recessed lighting, and the cabinets had chrome handles and glass fronts.

"I realize some of the amenities of this home didn't exist in the early eighteen hundreds." She reached for the sink and opened the tap. "But I would like to hang on to the modern luxuries of indoor plumbing and air conditioning."

"I can't blame you." He looked at the notes Luke had written. They'd be changing out the cabinetry and lighting, but the appliances and all the plumbing would remain intact.

She led him through a few more empty rooms downstairs, and his breath caught when he spotted the altar she'd set up on the fireplace. A skull with a top hat and lots of black and purple items occupied most of the space. He stepped toward it to have a closer look, but she cleared her throat and motioned toward another room.

James had learned a little about Voodoo over the years, but the religion, and the people who practiced it, remained shrouded in mystery. She obviously wasn't open to questions, so he followed her into the next room. A queen-sized bed sat against the far wall, and half a dozen moving boxes were scattered about the space.

"All this room needs is a coat of paint, so I'm using it as my bedroom until the renovations are done and I can finish moving in." She held his gaze with another curious expression before strutting toward the door.

The back of her hand brushed his on her way out, and her magical signature tingled across his skin, sending a jolt straight to his heart. *Get it together, man.* Just because his wolf didn't revolt at the thought of being with this woman, it didn't mean anything. That strange stirring in his soul was not his beast attempting to claim a second person. It wasn't possible. Anyway, she was a client, so she was off limits.

Unless he planned to make her his mate.

He shook himself, stopping the ridiculous thought before it could wriggle any further into his mind. If he slept with her, the feelings of attraction would dissolve, and he'd turn tail and run like he always did. Until he figured out how to break whatever cycle he was stuck in, and either find the dream woman or convince his wolf she didn't exist, he was screwed.

Odette showed him the upstairs, and he glanced at Luke's notes. Everything was crystal-clear as he'd expected from the alpha. They returned to the room with the altar, and she turned to him. "Any questions? I need to get to work."

"You don't remember me, do you?"

Her expression softened, but as she parted her lips to answer, something slammed into his chest, knocking him off his feet. The air *whooshed* from his lungs as his back smacked into the hardwood floor, and he skidded across the room. The side of his head slammed into the brick fireplace, and the room spun before everything went dark.

"James!" Odette raced toward him. "Nicolas, stop it! Get out of him." Reaching with her mind, she grabbed hold of the ghost invading James's body and ripped him out, throwing the entity across the room. She dropped to her knees next to James. Placing her hand on his chest, she relaxed at the gentle up and down motion of his breaths. The bloody gash on his forehead was already healing, and she rushed to the kitchen, grabbed a clean dish towel, and returned to his side.

She gently wiped the blood from his face and marveled at the way he healed. Anyone else would need stitches and weeks of recovery to mend a wound that deep, but his body took care of itself, the fibers of his skin slowly reconnecting in front of her eyes. Blood oozed from the partially-healed cut, and she dabbed the cloth on his brow to keep it from running into his eye.

Dark lashes fringed his closed lids, and the stubble peppering his jaw gave him a rugged, handsome appearance. His wavy, dark-brown hair was sheared short on the sides and long enough on top to have that messy, care-free look. He was cute in junior high; time had made him downright sexy. His head rolled to the side, and she pulled him into her lap, cradling his shoulders with her hands.

Lifting her gaze to Nicolas, she glared at the ghost. "You will never do that again, do you understand? You will leave him alone."

The spectral figure stiffened as her command took hold of his consciousness.

She cringed as her magic flared in her veins. A magic no living being should hold. Taking a deep breath, she got herself under control. "Why did you do that to him?"

Nicolas began to fade.

"Answer me." Another flush of magic raced through her veins, and she tried to ignore how good it felt.

His figure grew opaque, and his eyes widened. "My home."

The last thing she needed was a territorial ghost attacking the men who came over. Her house would be full of them for the next few weeks until the renovation was done. "This is *my* home now. You can't attack people like that because you're jealous. You are not allowed to do that to anyone again."

Nicolas's brow furrowed, and he disappeared.

James's eyes fluttered open, and she wiped another trail of blood from his forehead. Glancing at her briefly, he lowered his gaze. "Thanks." He reached for the towel, his fingers brushing hers, and his magic seeped into her skin.

Her stomach fluttered at his touch. *Uh-oh.* That was not a good sign. "Are you okay?" She glanced at his hand and bit back her next question. If she recalled correctly, he'd had all ten fingers as a kid, but how he'd lost one was none of her business.

"I'm good." He tried to push to a sitting position, but he clutched his head and lowered back into her lap. "Give me a minute." He gazed up at her. "What happened?"

"That was my resident ghost. He seemed harmless before, so I'm not sure why he did that to you."

He sat up, gripping the towel in his lap, avoiding eye contact as if he were embarrassed. The bleeding on his head stopped, a thin crust of scab sealing the wound. "What did he do?"

"He jumped you." She caught his gaze, and the intense blue of his eyes made her breath hitch. Forcing herself to look away, she shifted to her knees and smoothed her skirt down her thighs. "He was trying to get inside you, but you don't have to worry about him anymore. He won't bother you again."

He gingerly pressed his fingers to his head and winced. Something between a grunt and a chuckle resonated in his chest, and he rose to his feet and offered her a hand up. "How do you know he won't?"

She took his hand and rose to her feet, slipping from his warm grasp as soon as she was steady. "Because I told him not to."

"The dead do what you say?"

She wrapped her arms around herself. "I've always been able to communicate with the dead. To see and hear them." That wasn't a lie. Hopefully, he wouldn't notice she'd avoided the question.

"I see." He looked at the blood on the towel, and a strange expression crossed over his face. Was it disappointment? Disgust? She didn't know him well enough to tell yet.

Yet. As if she planned to get to know him at all. "Here, let me take that for you." She reached for the towel, but he jerked it away.

"That's okay." He shoved it into his pocket. "I'll take it home and wash it and bring it back to you tomorrow."

She started to argue, but he was a werewolf. They had rules about their blood. "I wasn't planning to use it for a spell."

"I didn't think you were, but..." He shrugged.

"I understand." She lowered her gaze, trying to avoid his mesmerizing eyes. She could get lost in them if she looked too long. "I do remember you." She'd recognized him the moment he'd introduced himself, and an undeniable spark had flared in her soul. A fire she'd been trying to extinguish since he stepped foot inside her home. She refused to fall for a man in this life...but James was one hell of a man. Tall, muscular, hotter than hellfire. Sweet Spirits, it was happening.

A tiny voice in the back of her mind whispered, *he's the one*, but she silenced it.

"What do you remember?" He smiled, and her heart melted.

Warning bells went off in her mind. She needed to end this conversation now. Tell him she was late for work and walk out the door before the heat building in her core turned into an inferno.

But her feet felt glued to the floor. "After my mom died, when I came back to school, you were the only kid in class who didn't call me…zombie girl." She held his gaze, refusing to allow the memory to consume her. The ravings of a bloodied little girl in the middle of the street had turned into rumors that spread like a prairie fire with a tailwind. Her dad eventually stomped out the blaze, but not before the kids at school overheard their parents' gossip.

"You looked plenty alive to me. You still do." He stepped toward her, and she instinctively took a step back. "Although, when you disappeared in seventh grade, I did wonder… Where have you been all these years?"

"We moved to Alabama. My dad bought a company there, and he needed to be closer to it." She did not need to get into the real reason they'd moved. That was a memory she'd rather forget.

He angled his body toward her, and though his feet didn't move, the distance between them seemed to shrink. "No one knew what happened to you. One day you were at school, and then you were gone."

She laughed dryly. "And I'm sure people spread all kinds of rumors, right? The devil took me back to hell?"

"I've never been one for rumors." He shrugged. "Is it true, though? What happened to you when you were a baby?"

She chewed the inside of her cheek and glanced at her altar. She really should get to work, and that would be the perfect reason to excuse herself from this conversation. But something about being near this man made her want to be closer. The warning bells sounding in her head turned to full-blown sirens, but she felt compelled to tell him the truth. At least a little of it. "I did die when I was born, yes. But my mom didn't make a deal with the devil to bring me back; she prayed to Baron Samedi." She nodded at her altar. "He's the loa of death, and he's in charge of the crossroads… whom he takes to the spirit realm and who gets another chance at life."

James clutched his hands behind his back and stepped toward the altar. "I've heard of this guy."

She moved next to him, close enough to invade his personal space, but not nearly as close as the fire inside her urged her to be. When he didn't step away, the flames grew hotter. "He's not evil or a demon or anything else people claim. He granted my mom's wish, and he spared my life."

He leaned in closer to the altar, examining the offerings she'd laid on it. "He's the rum god, right? He makes good rum." He grinned and winked.

She laughed. "He's not a god, and he doesn't make rum." Taking a small bottle from the mantle, she ran a finger across the label. "I make the rum to honor him. My parents opened the distillery as an offering to Baron Samedi in exchange for my life. Now that I'm back in New Orleans, I'm running it."

He blinked. "You're the Baroness?"

Returning the bottle to the altar, she ground her teeth. "Only people who don't know any better call me that. Baron Samedi crowned me when he gave me my life back, but I'm not his wife."

"Crowned you?"

"He's my *met tet*. Sort of like a guardian angel. He's the main loa who walks with me, and he gave me my abilities to communicate with the dead."

"Fascinating." He looked at her, an expression of awe softening his handsome features.

Her pulse quickened. The self-preservation instinct caused most people to back away the moment she mentioned her guardian angel was death himself, which was why she rarely mentioned it. "You're not afraid of me now that you know I'm crowned by death?"

He chuckled. "I've never been afraid of death."

She held his gaze a little longer, and the spark she'd been failing miserably at extinguishing grew hot enough to consume her. If the suspicion gnawing her gut was true, he needed to be very afraid.

She'd done everything she could to avoid this. Ever since she figured out her horrific life cycles, she'd steered clear of men to prevent the possibility of falling in love. She needed to squelch the desire burning in her core and get away from this man before her feelings could form into anything more than attraction.

"Right, well, I have to get to work. Is there anything else you need from me?"

He opened his mouth as if to say something, but he closed it again. Sweeping his gaze across the room, he shoved his hands into his pockets. "You're sure your ghost friend won't be an issue?"

She couldn't hide her grin. "So, you are scared of something?"

"I'm not scared, but I'd rather not wake up on the floor again."

"He won't try to jump you." A sense of unease settled in her stomach. Nicolas was strong, and controlling him had been way too easy.

He nodded. "The rest of the crew should be here any minute, and we'll get started. I'll always be the first one here and the last to leave, so I'll lock up if you aren't home. No worries."

"I'm not worried." Not about the renovation, anyway. "Thank you, James."

"My pleasure." His smile could have lit a city block. And the way his eyes crinkled with the curve of his lips had her mouth watering.

Not good, Odette. Walk away now.

She turned on her heel and strode to the kitchen. Shoving her laptop into her bag, she swung it over her shoulder and headed out the door without looking back. So she was attracted to a sexy werewolf. Who wouldn't be? Just because she'd felt a little something for a man for the first time in more than a year, it didn't mean he would be the one to doom her to death. Everything would be fine.

CHAPTER SIX

Rolling his neck to stretch out the soreness, James shuffled into the living room. He'd spent all day in the house prepping it for the retexturing of the walls and painting, and his shoulders ached from hunching over to tape off the baseboards.

As Odette had promised, the ghost didn't mess with him again, but he couldn't shake the feeling that something was watching him, following him through the house as he worked.

The crew had done their best to steer clear of this room. His men had taken one look at Odette's altar to death, and they'd found any excuse they could to work somewhere else. He couldn't blame them. Voodoo was a mysterious religion, and people on the outside…werewolves included…often misunderstood it. Once she'd explained her reasoning for having the altar, though, it made sense.

James wiped his hands on the towel he'd been carrying all day and peered at the smear of blood on the fabric. After staying wadded up in his pocket, the stain was probably set. He owed Odette a new towel. He wouldn't mind taking her to dinner for the trouble too. Getting to know her.

He scratched his head. His wolf had been dead set on claiming a woman he'd never met, but the moment he'd laid eyes on Odette, his beast started having second thoughts.

Normally, any inkling of wanting to know a woman on a deeper level stopped him in his tracks, warning him it was time to move on. If his wolf wasn't on board, he wasn't wasting his time. But as this train of emotion blew its whistle, preparing to depart the station, the beast seemed to have one foot on the train and the rest on the platform. *Make up your mind, buddy.*

Luke would have his ass if he made a move on her without approval from his wolf. Not that she would be receptive to his advances if he tried. Up until that ghost slammed into him, knocking him out, she'd lived up to the rumors he'd heard about the Baroness. Stiff. Proper. All business.

It was a shell though, and he'd witnessed it crack when she'd cradled his head in her lap. She had a soft and tender side, and it intrigued him.

"I have to admit, I was expecting a shit hole." Noah sauntered into the living room, pulling James from his thoughts. "But this place is nice. We'll probably finish ahead of schedule."

"Yeah." James scanned the room, but he couldn't remember why he'd wandered in here.

Odette didn't want anything done to the fireplace, and he could see why. The previous owners had kept it in…or restored it to…its original grandeur. A dark wood mantle lined the exposed brick of the hearth, and with winter lasting all of two or three weeks in the South, the inside was as pristine as if it had never been used.

"That's creepy." Noah reached a hand toward the altar, and the skull and top hat flew into his palm. "It's not real is it?" He turned the skull, and the hat slipped off.

James caught it before it hit the floor. "Put that back, dumbass. It's a religious altar." When Noah didn't move to return the item, James yanked it from his hands and gingerly set it back in place. "Would you go into a Catholic person's house and take their crucifix from the wall?"

"I guess not." Noah leaned in to examine the artifacts. "Is she a devil worshipper?"

"She's a vodouisant, and she has psychic medium abilities. She can talk to the dead, so she honors the Voodoo loa of death."

Noah curled his lip. "Like I said. Creepy."

"She's not creepy. She's…never mind." There was no use in trying to explain it. Odette had close ties with death. Hell, she'd been dead at one time. Most people would find that disturbing, but James had grown up around death. It was part of life.

"At least she has good taste in liquor." Noah reached for the bottle of rum on the altar.

James slapped his hand. "Don't touch that. It's an offering for the loa."

"Not like the dude's ever going to drink it." He rubbed his hand and cut his gaze between the bottle and the skull. "Is that the same guy?"

"Yeah."

"So she's offering The Baron rum to Baron Samedi. Kinda cliché, isn't it?" Noah laughed.

James ground his teeth. His friend's clowning attitude usually didn't bother him, but when Noah's jokes were directed at Odette, they struck a chord. "She owns the distillery. The whole operation is an offering to the Spirit."

Noah lifted his eyebrows. "Wait. We're working for the Baroness?" He let out a disbelieving huff. "No room for mistakes then, I guess."

"You know her?"

"One of my old man's drinking buddies works there. I've heard stories. She's all business. Dresses like she's on her way to a funeral. Never smiles." He crossed his arms. "They don't even have company picnics or Christmas parties or anything. They go in, get the job done, and go home. Have to save the socializing for their own time."

James furrowed his brow. His friends knew more about Odette than he did—he hadn't even known she was back in town, and that bothered him more than it should have.

Noah grinned. "I recognize that look."

James tried for a neutral expression. "What look? I don't have a look."

"You've got the hots for the client."

"No, I don't."

Noah slapped him on the shoulder. "Whatever you say, man. Better not let Luke know. He'll have you reassigned faster than a topless woman gathers beads at Mardi Gras."

James narrowed his eyes. "I don't have the hots for Odette."

"Then why are you still here? The crew left half an hour ago."

If he were honest with himself, he'd admit he was hoping Odette would come home from work before he left. That she'd show up and invite him to stay for dinner. Then one thing might lead to another, and… *Damn it.* She was a client. He couldn't think of her that way. "Why are *you* still here?"

"I came in to see if you needed any help patrolling tonight. You're on the first shift, right?"

Crap. After his run-in with the ghost and his strange feelings for Odette, he'd forgotten about his demon-patrol duties. Those little minions rarely showed up alone. "Yeah. Let me lock up, and I'll meet you outside."

Noah paused. "You don't think she's responsible for summoning them, do you?" He nodded to the altar. "I mean…"

"No." He shook his head. "We were friends in school. I know her; she's not like that." At least, he didn't think she was. Really, he didn't know the woman at all. Being acquaintances in grade school didn't count as much of a relationship, and based on the rumors he'd heard about her, she wasn't the sad, scared little girl he remembered. His judgment was based on a feeling he had about her, but unless his wolf put all four paws on the train, it would be leaving the station empty.

"If she is responsible, we'll find out soon enough." James jerked his head toward the exit. "Let's go patrol, and we can hit the club after." With his wolf finally allowing him to notice another woman, maybe he could satiate his desires with someone other than Odette and forget all about his feelings for his client. That would prove his attraction to her was nothing more than the shallow desire of a man for a beautiful woman.

Shoving her key into the ignition, Odette leaned her head against the headrest and closed her eyes. The cool leather seat pressed into the backs of her legs, and the air freshener stuck to the vent filled the car with the subtle scent of lavender.

Her secretary had fielded her calls, sending through the important ones, while Odette spent most of the workday locked in her office. She'd meditated, but it didn't clear her mind. She'd hyper-focused on the marketing proposal for the upcoming line of white rums, but it didn't distract her from the sinking feeling of dread hollowing out her stomach.

Her prayers to the Baron hadn't been answered yet. Her *met tet* would know if James was the one who'd doom her to a horrific death, but Baron Samedi was either too busy to provide insight, or the question was too big for a simple prayer.

She ran her hand along the soft leather of the console and reached for the key again. Turning it, she started the car, the engine purring to life as she gripped the steering wheel and eased on the gas, exiting the parking garage. Driving along Tchoupitoulas Street, she took in the majestic view of the Mississippi River until she turned onto Poydras and headed into the Central Business District.

Breathing deeply, she tried to keep herself calm as she made a right and headed into the French Quarter to Mambo Voodoo, Natasha's store that doubled as both a tourist shop and a temple. She parked on the curb and walked two blocks to reach the quiet shop. The woody, sweet scents of sandalwood and lotus greeted her as she opened the door, and the tension in her muscles eased. Something about this place always felt like coming home.

"Evening, Cybil." She nodded to the vodouisant manning the cash register.

Cybil tucked a strand of deep-blue hair behind her ear. "Hi, Odette. Natasha's in the back, waiting for you."

She glanced at her watch. The emergency appointment she'd made with her Mambo was set for fifteen minutes ago, but she'd been so distracted that she'd left the office later than planned.

As she stepped through the first threshold, she swept her gaze across the plethora of altars lining the walls, and even more tension slipped from her shoulders. *Vévés* sewn into colorful cloths adorned the spaces set up to honor the loa. Various offerings from tourists and vodouisants alike lay about the altars: keys for Papa Legba, perfume bottles for Erzulie Freda, silver for Damballah, and of course rum and tobacco for Baron Samedi.

She stopped in front of her *met tet's* altar and pulled a cigarette from her purse. Though she'd never smoked one herself, she always carried them to make offerings to the loa. "I could really use some help, Baron." She laid the cigarette next to the skull and closed her eyes, opening her senses in hopes of receiving a message.

But the Baron seemed to be ignoring her. She sighed and shuffled to the back room.

Pushing aside the beaded curtain hanging in the doorway, she found Natasha sitting at her reading table, shuffling a deck of tarot cards. "Sorry I'm late."

"I expected you would be. Sit." The priestess set the cards on the table and folded her hands. "What's so important, child?"

Odette settled in the chair across from her and swallowed the thickness from her throat. She'd had all day to mull over the fact that James might be the one, but saying it out loud, and possibly getting confirmation, had her stomach tied in knots. "I met someone today."

"Oh?" Natasha arched an eyebrow. "Any someone or *the* someone?"

She let out a heavy breath. "I think it might be him. I hope it's not, but there's…something. I feel connected to him somehow, and I shouldn't. I hardly know him; he works for my contractor." She wrapped her arms around herself, clutching her elbows.

"It could be your libido talking. A capable man, who's good with his hands, working on your house. Who wouldn't find that attractive? You've been denying yourself any fun at all for years. Maybe you need to let loose. See where it goes."

"No." She straightened. "I feel this in my bones. Our destinies… our souls are entwined somehow, and if it's because…" Closing her eyes for a long blink, she took a slow breath. "Please, will you do a reading for me? If it's him, I have to make it stop."

"If it's him, I don't think you can." Pursing her lips, the Mambo gave her a sympathetic look. "All right. Let's see if the Spirits will shed any light on it. What's his name?" She slid the stack of cards toward Odette.

"James." The edges of the weathered cards had smoothed from years of use, and a tingle of magic seeped into Odette's fingers as she shuffled them. "James Malveaux."

Natasha reached for the cards but paused, her hand hovering over the center of the table. "The werewolf?"

"Yes. I hired the alpha's construction crew to do the renovations." She slid the deck to the Mambo.

Natasha pressed her lips together and drummed her fingers on the cards.

"What aren't you telling me?" The hollow sensation in her stomach expanded, taking in half her chest.

"Did he mention his readings?"

And there went the rest of her chest, sinking into oblivion. "No. Why? What have you read for him?" Werewolves rarely let their issues leak outside the pack. If James had come to a House of Voodoo for help, it must have been his last resort.

The priestess picked up the cards. "Let's focus on you right now." She turned over the cards, laying out ten in a Celtic cross spread, scrunching her brow, and lightly humming with each addition to the shape.

Tapping a finger on the top card of the deck, Natasha hesitated to turn it over. Odette gripped the sides of her chair, tensing as she waited for her to finish. The look on the priestess's face and her reluctance to display the final card made Odette want to explode with anticipation. This was bad. She could feel it.

Natasha peeked at the final card and locked eyes with Odette. "Remember this card has many meanings, especially for you."

A brick settled in Odette's stomach. She didn't need to look at the card to know what it was, but as she lowered her gaze to the table, a skeleton stared back at her. "Death." Lacing her fingers together, she rested her head on her hands.

"Change." Natasha's voice was firm. "Sit still and give me a minute." The priestess closed her eyes and breathed deeply, swaying from side to side. The energy in the room shifted as she made contact with her Spirit Guides.

Odette held her breath, the hairs on her arms standing on end as the vibration in the air increased. She shivered, and the hollow sensation consumed the rest of her body. She knew the answer as confidently as if it had been ingrained in her soul since birth.

James was the one. The man she was fated to fall in love with and in whose arms she was doomed to die.

Natasha opened her eyes and smiled sadly.

"I knew it." Odette clenched her trembling hands into fists. "I knew it before I came here. I've known since the moment he knocked on my door, but I was hoping…"

"You hoped I'd tell you otherwise."

Her shoulders slumped as the weight of the realization pressed down on her. "And now, there's no hope. I'm going to die a horrific death, and I'm taking him with me. I wonder what it will be this time? A knife to the chest? A slit throat? I don't think I've been fully beheaded yet. I suppose I have that to look forward to."

"You hush your mouth." Natasha rose to her feet and shuffled around the table. "There's always hope." She tapped the death tarot. "It's inverted, which means you're resistant to the change that needs to happen."

"Of course I'm resistant to being murdered."

"My guides tell me your death isn't the change this means. And James… I've felt an unrest in the air ever since I talked to him. What I learned in his reading makes sense now."

"How so?"

"I kept hearing that he's stuck in a cycle that has to be broken. I thought it had something to do with his past, and it does. Not his past in this lifetime though. He's stuck in the same cycle as you, and the two of you have to break it together."

Odette leaned her elbows on the table and dropped her head in her hands. "We haven't been able to break the cycle in how many lifetimes? Why would we be able to stop it now?"

Natasha shuffled to a counter against the wall and lit a white candle in honor of her guides. "Because you're meant to."

"How do you know?" She leaned back in her chair, dragging her hands down her face. "Did a Spirit tell you that?"

"Why did you move here?"

She shrugged. "It's my home. I missed it."

"You moved away when you were twelve years old. Why come back sixteen years later? Did you really miss it? Or did the Baron call you home?"

She sank in her chair. "You know the Baron called me. His distillery was about to go bankrupt, and I had to turn it around. It was part of the deal."

"That was your momma's deal."

"And I'm honoring it." She sat up straight. "I owe Baron Samedi my life."

"Do you think he would have called you back here if it was gonna cut that life short? He gave you a gift, and he's not gonna see it wasted. You're here for a reason, and that reason is to break this cycle. You're a powerful vodouisant in this life, and James is a werewolf. I think the stars have finally aligned for you, and you can end it."

"I'm not powerful anymore."

"You could be. We need to do another past life regression to see if we can figure out why you're holding back. You'll need to use all the power you have to stop this cycle. We can focus on the house this time. See if—"

"No." Odette shot to her feet. She didn't need to delve into any more past lives to know why her own powers terrified her. That incident occurred in *this* lifetime, and no one could ever know what really happened. Not even her Mambo. "The house is… I think I was drawn to it because of the ghost there. He knows me, and he seems to think I should remember him. I probably talked to him when I was a kid. Before I learned to block them out, I saw ghosts everywhere I went. I probably walked by that house with my mom a lot and saw him then. I'm sure that's all it is."

Natasha arched an eyebrow. "You don't think it's possible you lived in that house in a past life?"

"If I did live there…if I knew the ghost when he was alive…it was the early eighteen hundreds, and I do *not* want to relive that. No more regressions."

Natasha eyed her skeptically. She needed to pull herself together before the Mambo figured out that she already knew the reason she held her powers back. Straightening her spine, she held her chin high. "I'll figure something out. If the Baron called me here to meet James and end this cycle, then that's what I'll do…once I figure out how to tell James."

"I suggest you do some digging into your ghost. I have a feeling he's gonna play a role whether you want him to or not."

"I'm one step ahead of you. He told me his name, and I have one of my interns researching his connection to the house. She'll call me as soon as she has some information."

Natasha nodded. "You ain't alone in this, you know? Whatever the Baron tells you, whatever you have to do, I'm here. The whole House will help you."

"Thank you." She couldn't get the entire House involved, though. It may have been her fate to die a gruesome death life after life, but she wouldn't pull anyone else down with her. "What if I made an offering to Erzulie Dantor? She can keep me from falling in love, right? That's what she does. Protects women scorned by their lovers."

Natasha laughed. "You're welcome to try, but you haven't been scorned, and James seems like a good man. I don't think she can help you."

"It's worth a try. If I don't fall in love, I won't be vulnerable."

The Mambo shook her head. "I'm going home. Call me if you need me."

Odette strode into the altar room with new purpose. She wouldn't allow herself to fall in love with James. It was as simple as that. She bought a blood-red rose from the gift shop and laid it on Erzulie Dantor's altar. Clasping her hands over her heart, she closed her eyes and offered her prayer to the loa. "Please, Erzulie Dantor, I'm begging you. Guard my heart. Keep me strong. This man will be the death of me if I fall in love."

CHAPTER SEVEN

"Ms. Allemand?" The intern hesitated in the doorway, clutching a folder to her chest. Her too-long bangs fell across her eyes, and she nervously jerked her head, brushing the blonde locks aside. "I have the information you asked me to find."

Odette held up a finger and finished typing the last sentence of her e-mail with her other hand. *It's about time.* She'd given the job to Kathryn, her most promising intern, because she thought she'd be the fastest. But the research had taken her two days to complete.

Peppering the ghost with questions hadn't helped either. The more she'd talked to Nicolas, the more confused he'd become, until he'd stopped communicating altogether. Sadly, he didn't know he was dead until she'd told him.

Kathryn shrank into the hallway and picked at her fingernails. Odette would have to give the girl a lesson in projecting confidence. Too many sharks lurked in the waters of life, waiting to prey on the weak.

"What do you have for me?" She closed her computer and folded her hands on her desk, giving the intern her full attention, and ignoring the way her heart rate kicked up in anticipation.

Kathryn shuffled through the doorway, sweeping her gaze across the lavender walls before focusing on the mini altar next to Odette's desk. The skulls she used were made of plaster, but word on the company's rumor mill said they belonged to human sacrifice victims. She'd grown accustomed to people fearing her, so she let them believe the rumors.

The intern shivered. "Um…I'm sorry it took so long."

This lack of self-confidence would never do. She'd be doing the girl a disservice if she didn't correct her behavior. "Did I ask for an apology?"

"No, ma'am." Kathryn tightened her grip on the folder, creasing the edge.

"Do I look the slightest bit upset with you?"

She hesitated. "No, ma'am. I'm sorry."

"Don't apologize unless there's a need for it. It makes you seem weak. There are people in this world who prey on weakness. Never allow yourself to be taken advantage of."

"Yes, ma'am. I'm sorry. I mean…" Rather than having her confidence lifted, the poor girl was crumbling.

Odette softened her tone. "Sit down and tell me what you found."

Kathryn nodded and sank into a deep-purple velvet chair across from the desk. "The records are so old they haven't digitized them yet. I had to search through property records and newspapers on microfiche."

"And what did you discover?"

"I found one Nicolas associated with the address you gave me. Nicolas Dubois was a French immigrant and the original owner of the property. He built the house that's there now in 1820."

That partially explained why the ghost was attached to the house, but it didn't account for why the man expected Odette to remember him nor why he didn't cross over when he died. Odette scribbled the name onto a Post-it Note. "Was there any more information on Mr. Dubois?"

Kathryn fought a smile. "Oh, yeah. He was murdered in that house. In his own bedroom."

Odette straightened her spine. Here was the reason his ghost lingered. "Details?"

Opening the folder, Kathryn pulled out a sheet of paper and passed it to Odette. "I found this in the newspaper. His brother, Antoine, had come to visit him one night, and he found him in his bed, decapitated and stabbed in the heart."

Odette cringed. No wonder the poor ghost was stuck. A murder like that would cause anyone to have trouble crossing over. She glanced at the newspaper clipping, but she couldn't bring herself to read the words. "Do they know who did it?"

"Antoine also found Nicolas's house servant, Serafine, in the room. She was hysterical and covered in blood. She came after Antoine with the knife, so he pulled out his own blade and slit her throat."

"I see." A sickening feeling pooled in her stomach. Did the ghost remember any of this? She'd attempted to get more information from him over the past two days, but the poor man had been too confused to answer. Now she understood why. "Thank you for the information, Kathryn. That will be all."

Kathryn scooted to the edge of the chair. "There's more, if you're interested."

She raised her eyebrows. "Oh?"

"It's speculation, passed down by word of mouth, but when the librarian saw whom I was researching, she said there's another story to go along with the newspaper. Rumor has it that Mr. Dubois had taken Serafine as his mistress. She fell in love with him, and when she realized he would have to marry someone else, she murdered him. If she couldn't have him, no one could."

"She loved him." A chill crept through her veins. Was it possible that Nicolas expected her to remember him because *she* was Serafine? No, it wasn't. In her past lives, Odette had always been the one to die first. She died in her lover's arms, at the hands…or claws…of a monster, not a man. And James was to be her lover in this life. A living, breathing man, not a ghost.

Warmth spiraled up her spine at the thought of him. James wouldn't be alive and tempting her if his ghost were haunting her house. Maybe Odette had been another servant for Nicolas. Or perhaps the other woman he'd intended to marry. Who knew?

Armed with the new information, hopefully she could help the ghost to cross over and be done with him. Then, she could focus on the other, much bigger problem.

"Love makes you do crazy things." Kathryn's voice pulled her from her thoughts.

"Is there anything else?"

The intern dropped her gaze for a moment and bit her bottom lip. "I have a question." She briefly looked into Odette's eyes before shifting her gaze to the small purple and black altar. "People say you can talk to ghosts. Is that why you had me research this guy? Did you see his ghost? Is this your house?"

Odette rose and strode around her desk, standing in front of the intern.

Kathryn scrambled to her feet. "I'm sorry. It's none of my business."

Motioning toward the door, Odette paced toward it and gripped the knob. "I appreciate your curiosity, and you're correct, it's none of your business. Thank you for the information. That will be all."

"Yes, ma'am." Kathryn scurried out the door, and Odette closed it behind her.

She turned to her altar and stared at the *vévé* embroidered on the purple flag. Nicolas's mistress had murdered him. She'd been brought to justice…if one could call death justice…so that wasn't the reason his ghost lingered. If he'd been sleeping when she stabbed him, he might not know who killed him.

Maybe that was all he needed—to know the truth about his death—to be able to pass on. She ran her fingers across the soft, purple cloth representing her *met tet.* "Will you take him once he knows the truth?"

Grabbing her purse from her desk drawer, she strode from her office to the parking garage. Excitement tingled in her limbs as she pressed the button on her key fob, and the car chirped. She could finally help the distressed ghost find peace.

James parked on the curb and killed the engine, kneading the steering wheel as he stared at the half-painted mansion. The light-blue Odette had chosen for the exterior fit the Creole style as if it had been blue all along. After spending a few days working inside, he was more than impressed with the structure.

With the crew running ahead of schedule, they'd be finished with the job in two more weeks. James wouldn't be finished with Odette, though. Since he'd met her, his dreams had changed, the sultry vodouisant flitting in and out in place of the nameless woman who'd occupied his mind for too long.

He couldn't bring himself to so much as flirt with another woman —he'd tried…several times—but now it was the image of Odette flashing in his mind that stopped him. He *had* to see her again.

Raking a hand through his hair, he let out his breath in a huff. Leaving his toolbelt in her kitchen was a thinly-veiled excuse to return to her house this evening—he wouldn't need it until morning—but it was all he had.

His wolf had been set on him finding the mystery woman from his dreams, but now the beast didn't know what he wanted. His friends who'd found their fate-bounds made it sound so easy. From the moment they'd met their future mates, they'd…*known*…even if they'd refused to see it at first.

James didn't know. He had too much human blood running through his veins, and his wolf was confused as hell because of it. The beast realized he couldn't claim both women, but that's exactly what it seemed like he was trying to do.

Maybe everything James felt for Odette had come from his human side, and his half-blood nature was what confounded his wolf. "Damn it." The only way to solve this mystery was to spend some time with the woman. He slid from the truck and slammed the door.

The scent of the bougainvillea blooming in the flower beds reminded him of the ones his mom had planted at their own house when he was a kid—that two-year stretch when she'd actually stuck around—and the sweet perfume added to the anxiety churning in his core. He climbed the porch steps and knocked, and a curvy silhouette appeared in the window.

Odette opened the door, and his wolf sprang to attention. She wore a black T-shirt and yoga pants that hugged her curves, flaring slightly at the bottom. She was barefoot, and her purple-painted toenails caused his stomach to tighten, heat pooling in his groin as if he'd gotten a glimpse of way more than her toes. He cleared his throat and forced his gaze to her eyes. "Hi."

She tilted her head. "James. I wasn't expecting you. Is there a problem?" Her own gaze swept the length of him, the corners of her lips tugging upward briefly before she flattened them.

"I think I left my toolbelt inside. Do you mind if I come in and look for it?"

"It's in the kitchen. I can get it for you." She regarded him, narrowing her eyes. Damn it, she saw right through his sad attempt at an excuse to see her, and now she'd probably leave him on the porch and get the belt herself. He should have hidden it.

Opening the door wider, she stepped to the side. "Would you like to come in?" She sounded liked she wasn't sure she should have asked, but he wouldn't waste the opportunity.

"I'd love to." He strode through the door before she could change her mind.

Following her into the kitchen, he made himself take in the surroundings…looking at anything but her tempting curves as her hips swayed. "The job's coming along nicely. At this rate, we'll finish ahead of schedule."

She stopped at the kitchen counter and turned to face him. "That's good to know. Do you want something to drink?"

Holy hell, she'd offered him a drink. That meant she was interested. Did he want her to be interested? His wolf sure seemed to. *Say something, dumbass.* He grabbed his toolbelt and set it on the edge of the counter. "Yeah." *Yeah? That's all you've got, Casanova?*

She held his gaze, the moment stretching into what should have become awkwardness, but it didn't. Looking into her dark-brown eyes, he almost felt as if he were glimpsing her soul. His wolf was restless, a feeling stirring in his own soul that he'd never felt before, and he couldn't blame the primal sensation on his human side.

She didn't move as he took a step toward her; she merely inclined her chin, daring him to come closer. A strange energy charged between them, as if the poles of their soul magnets lined up perfectly, drawing them together.

Her gaze cut to the right, and she furrowed her brow. "Please, not now, Nicolas."

James turned his head in the direction she looked, but he saw nothing. "Your ghost?"

"I've been trying to talk to him all evening, and *now* he decides to make an appearance. He hasn't bothered you, has he?" She glided to the opposite side of the counter.

With the safety of the stationary object between them, the moment they'd shared…or almost shared…dissolved. "No, but I think he follows me. I feel like I'm being watched the whole time I'm here, but I'm sure it's my imagination."

"He probably is following you." She took a glass from a cabinet. "He's confused. I think he knows he's dead now, but I'm not sure he comprehends much else."

"That's sad. Can't you help him?"

She stiffened. "I'm trying. You mentioned you like rum, didn't you?" Grabbing a bottle from a shelf, she didn't wait for his response. "We're releasing a new line of white rum this year. Do you want an advance tasting?"

He grinned. "Hell yeah, I do."

Her lips curved into an almost-smile as she poured a sample into the glass and swirled it. "Give it a taste. If you like it, I'll mix a drink for you."

Taking the glass, he sniffed the liquid. For a white liquor, it had a rich, earthy aroma, almost like a spiced rum. He took a sip, and the smooth liquid glided down his throat like warm honey. "That's amazing. What's in it?"

"That's a secret." She retrieved the glass and mixed more rum with Coke and ice. Then, she grabbed a flavored sparkling water from the fridge and motioned to the table.

He sank into a chair and clutched his glass. "You don't like the rum?"

"I don't drink alcohol."

He laughed, expecting her to at least crack a grin, but she didn't. "You own a rum distillery, and you don't drink alcohol?"

"Alcohol lowers inhibitions and can make you vulnerable. I prefer to keep my wits about me."

"You're quite the contradiction, aren't you?"

"You have no idea."

He sipped his drink, looking at her over the rim of the glass, and she returned his gaze. She had a presence about her, commanding, confident, in charge, but the undercurrent of her magic…of her connection to death…flowed through the energy around her as if she held a key to the gateway of the underworld and could send souls through it at her will. No wonder she intimidated people.

"I remember seeing you in the cemetery when we were kids."

She arched an eyebrow. "You frequented the cemetery?"

"My dad is the caretaker. He took me with him on the weekends when he did the landscape and repaired the tombs. You would come with your mom and leave offerings at the entry. I figured you were visiting a relative, but you were honoring your Baron, weren't you? It's appropriate to leave offerings for him at cemetery gates."

"Someone's done his research."

"I was curious." He chuckled. "My dad always grumbled after you left because he'd have to clean it up. He didn't mind so much when you left the bottles of rum, though."

A genuine smile curved her lips, brightening her eyes, and she laughed. "I bet not." As she relaxed, her magical aura strengthened, buzzing with energy.

Her smile drew him in. Hell, everything about her called to him. *To his wolf.* This was more than a human-level attraction, and he wanted to get to know her. To know Odette and not the Baroness everyone was afraid of.

She sucked in a breath as if she'd realized her guard had slipped, her eyes widening briefly. The smile faded as she sipped her sparkling water and stared off into the distance.

Leaning forward, he rested an arm on the table. "You don't have to do that with me."

"Do what?"

"Hold back. You can be yourself. I'm not afraid of you."

She leaned toward the table, resting her fingertips on the edge. "Maybe you should be. I am a child of death."

He chuckled. "I grew up with death; it doesn't scare me. Neither does your guardian Spirit. I don't know what powers you have, but if you can send me to my grave with your magic, you'd have done it by now if you wanted to."

"Hmm…" She slid her hand forward until her forearm rested on the table.

Placing his hand on hers, he traced his thumb across her soft skin. Her magic seeped into him, sending a jolt straight to his heart. She lowered her gaze to where they touched and drew in a shuddering breath.

"We have rules about dating clients, but after this job is done, would you mind if I asked you out to dinner?"

She lifted her gaze to his eyes, parting her lips to answer. Her jaw trembled for a moment before she clamped her mouth shut and slid her hand from his grasp. "That's not a good idea. It would never work for us."

"Yeah. I guess you're right." He tossed back the rest of his drink and crossed his arms. The first time both he and his wolf had ever felt an inkling of attraction to someone, and she rejected him cold. Who was he kidding? This spark was turning into a full-blown fire. But the bartender was right. A werewolf construction worker had nothing to offer a woman like Odette. Hell, he wasn't even a full werewolf. She deserved someone whole. He gestured to the room. "You can afford to buy a mansion like this, while all I can hope to do is repair it for you."

"No, James. It's not that at all. It's…" She let out a hard breath, and her brow scrunched, confliction tightening her eyes. "If we got together, it wouldn't end well. It never does." Rising, she took his glass and dumped the ice into the sink.

Damn it. He wasn't proud of his reputation with women, but Odette was different… She'd commanded his wolf's attention, and she needed to know *he* could be different too. He strode around the counter. "Who says it has to end?"

"James…" She shook her head and faced him. In her bare feet, she stood four inches shorter than him, and he had to fight the urge to reach for her. The way she looked at him. How her body drifted toward him as he inched a little closer. She felt *something* for him.

"I'll admit I don't have the best track record when it comes to dating, but a man can change when he finds the right woman." He clamped his mouth shut. Those words had come straight from his wolf. It would have been nice if they'd registered in his brain before they'd spilled from his lips, but every one of them had been truth.

Her eyes searched his, and she swallowed. "What makes you think I'm the right woman? Or is that what you say to all the girls?" One corner of her mouth tugged into a grin, making his heart race.

The truth seemed to be working so far. Why not go all in? "I've never said that to anyone. Honestly, I've never been this interested in someone. You're different."

"I'm *very* different, but you've known that since second grade."

"You make me *feel* different." Should he tell her about the dreams? About how his wolf was slowly letting go of the stranger he'd never met because of Odette? He wanted to know more than her body; he wanted to know her mind and her soul.

No. That was too much and way too soon. He was still trying to come to terms with what his wolf was telling him himself.

When he didn't elaborate further, Odette sighed and stepped away from him. "There's a lot you don't know about me. You and I…as tempting as it is, I wouldn't survive the ending. Let's keep it in the friend-zone, okay?"

"Yeah. Okay, I understand. I should get home; I have to work in the morning." He had a couple of weeks to help her change her mind. He grabbed his tool belt from the counter when a pair of glowing red orbs flashed across the window. *What the hell?* "Do you have pets?"

"No." She followed his gaze. "What did you see?"

He strode to the window and peered out the glass, but he couldn't see a damn thing in the dark backyard. "Eyes."

"It could have been an opossum. I seem to attract those." She rested a hand on his shoulder as she looked out the window, her touch sending a flush of warmth through his veins.

An intense urge to protect her grew in his core, and his wolf demanded that he investigate. "The silhouette was too big for an opossum, and the eyes looked red."

She dropped her arm to her side and whispered, "Demon."

"Stay inside. I'll go out the back and check it out."

Following him to the door, she touched his elbow. "Be careful."

He chuckled. "Werewolves were made to hunt demons. I'll be fine."

The porch steps creaked as he descended, and he skirted around a ladder, narrowly missing a stack of paint cans. Adrenaline spiked in his veins, though he wasn't sure if the thrill was for the hunt or for protecting the woman standing in the doorway.

He waved an arm at her and whispered, "Go inside," but she didn't budge. She crossed her arms and leaned against the jamb as if fear didn't exist in her vocabulary.

Though a privacy fence surrounded the yard, he stayed in human form as he scanned the bushes for the fiend. A grunt sounded to his right, and he jerked his head to the side in time to see the squat, black figure barreling toward him. It latched onto his shoulder, sinking its razor-like teeth into his arm.

"Goddammit!" James spun, trying to throw the little shit to the ground, but it hung on with a death grip.

"James!" Odette ran toward him.

"Go back inside. I'm fine." If the damn thing would let go for a second, he could shift and vanquish the bastard. He didn't want to end up with a tooth embedded in his bone if he shifted with it attached to his shoulder.

"You're not fine." Odette grabbed a paintbrush from the ladder and jabbed the wooden handle into the demon's back. With a squeal, the fiend let go and lunged at Odette. She stumbled, tripping over a loose brick and falling to her back.

"I don't think so." James shifted, clamping his jaws on the fiend's leg before it could attack. He yanked it away from her, releasing his hold to bite into its neck. As the demon fell limp in his maw, James dropped it and swiped a claw across its chest, piercing its heart. The minion eroded into a pile of ash.

Odette stood, dusting off her backside, as James returned to human form. She peered at the ash and then looked at him, tilting her head as she studied him. "I've never seen a werewolf shift before. I didn't know you could change form so quickly. Or that your clothes stayed intact."

"The magic absorbs them when I shift. Let's get you inside." With his hand on the small of her back, he guided her through the door. A demon tried to attack her in her own backyard, and she was more concerned about how he shifted. Was the woman afraid of anything? With death as her guardian, he supposed she wasn't.

He locked the door and led her to the kitchen. Turning around, he found her smiling at him. "I'm one of the faster shifters. It's why I hunt demons. I was made for it. You, though…unless you can control creatures from hell like you can control ghosts?"

Her smile faded as she lowered her gaze. "I don't control ghosts, and I have no power over demons."

"You could have been hurt."

"So could you. You're bleeding." She flashed a challenging stare.

He huffed and wiped the wound on his shirt. He didn't need yet another person questioning his strength, especially not her. "I'm going back out to see if there are any more. Please stay inside this time."

"Okay. I will."

Exiting through the back door, James searched the entire property, front yard and back, but he didn't find a sign of any more demons. Like the first one they'd encountered a few days ago, it seemed to be alone. He hung around the yard a bit longer, giving his arm time to heal, before heading up the porch steps.

When he came back in, Odette stood in front of her altar, her eyes closed, and she whispered something too quietly for him to understand. A prayer, maybe? The thought that she could have summoned the thing flashed through his mind, but he dismissed it immediately. Noah had planted that thought, and James didn't buy it for a second.

He stood beside her, and she opened her eyes. "No more, I guess?"

"He was alone, like the other one."

"Other one?"

"We found a demon outside Rusty's a few days ago. This is the second one the pack has come across. Have you encountered anything like it before?"

She shook her head. "What kind of demon is it?"

"It's an imp. Minion to something much bigger and nastier, but I don't know what. With the sightings so sporadic, my guess is whatever is summoning them hasn't fully manifested itself yet. I'll have to check in with the alpha and see if he's found anything."

"There have been two so far, and you've been the one to find them both?"

"Yeah."

Odette nodded, and the first hint of fear finally sparked in her eyes. "I'll talk to my Mambo too. She might be able to ask the Spirits what's going on." Glancing at her watch, she frowned. "I'll call her in the morning. It's getting late. You better go talk to your alpha."

He hesitated. That was his cue to leave, but if any more demons showed up here… "I don't want to leave you unprotected. I can stay the night. I'll sleep on the floor."

She arched an eyebrow. "Are you doubting my powers?"

"No. I don't know what kind of power you have, but you said you can't control demons."

"No evil can get inside this house. Natasha helped me cleanse it, and we put a charm on it. I'm safe. I promise not to go outside until morning."

"Are you sure? I don't mind staying."

"I appreciate your chivalry, but I can take care of myself. Go home, James."

"All right. I'll be here first thing in the morning." Pulling a business card from his wallet, he handed it to her. "My cell number is on there. Call me if you need anything."

"Thank you." She opened the front door and stood to the side, a silent command for him to leave.

He shuffled down the walk to his truck and grumbled as he climbed inside. She may have been safe, but he'd have a wolf watching her house until morning to be safer.

CHAPTER EIGHT

Odette lay in bed, staring at the ceiling, trying to cool the inferno the werewolf had lit in her soul. Her plan to stay away from James, thus ignoring the growing emotions and avoiding the inevitable had failed, like she knew it would. The short time she'd spent with him this evening had sealed her fate. He was her soulmate. Of that she was sure. How she would escape the horrific death awaiting her, she had no clue.

Squeezing her eyes shut, she focused on the image of his handsome features. Dark hair, sky-blue eyes, and from what she could tell with his clothes on, a sexy, muscular body. Oh, to get his clothes off…

Sitting with him, talking to him, looking at him had been a tedious exercise in restraint when all she'd wanted to do was wrap her arms around him and kiss him. But Odette was the queen of restraint. She'd been holding back since she was twelve years old. Losing control was not an option.

Something about James made her want to let her guard down though. It had slipped a little this evening, and her power had intensified briefly. He'd felt it too. The curious look in his eyes as he'd leaned toward her told her he sensed her power, but he could never know what she was capable of. What she'd done before she learned control.

She'd made an offering to Baron Samedi before climbing into bed, all but begging him to visit her in her dreams and give her guidance. If this was the life when she and her soulmate would break the cycle, like Natasha suggested, she'd need all the help she could get.

Focusing on her feet, Odette relaxed each muscle in her body, working her way up to the top of her head as liquid warmth flowed through her limbs. Relaxing even more, she imagined herself floating in a starless night sky until she drifted into a deep sleep.

But Baron Samedi didn't visit her.

As her sleep sank into a dream state, she found James waiting for her in her bed. Dream James wore a light-blue shirt that matched his eyes and dark jeans that hung low on his hips. He rose as she entered the room, and she went to him willingly, allowing him to take her in his arms, giving in to the temptation she'd resisted in life.

He undressed her, and though his calloused hands were rough against her skin, the sensation of his touch was like nothing she'd felt before.

She rolled to her side and hugged a pillow, the ecstasy he gave her in her dream bringing her halfway to consciousness, to a state of awareness that she was in a dream, but she willed herself to stay in the world her subconscious mind had created a little longer.

The dream was so life-like she could have stayed there forever, letting go of her inhibitions, surrendering control like she could never do when awake. In her mind, she lay on her back, looking up into his loving eyes.

As she gazed at him, her vision blurred. His face transformed into another familiar man. Nicolas. Alive and breathing in her dream, he smiled as the pressure of his body on hers held her immobile.

Her stomach fluttered, but the shock of finding another man in her bed didn't send her reeling. Dreams were weird like that. Willing herself to consciousness, she pushed the image from her mind and focused her senses on her surroundings. The feel of the soft cotton sheets against her skin. The soft breeze caressing her cheeks from the ceiling fan whirring above. The presence of a man…

She pried her lids open to find the ghost of Nicolas hovering on the bed as if he lay next to her. Warmth radiated from his form, though he had no body to produce it. She expected to recoil from his close proximity—the dead seemed to draw the life from her whenever they manifested—but Nicolas's presence had an almost comforting effect. She turned toward him. "What are you doing?"

Nicolas smiled and twirled a lock of her hair around his finger. "I've missed you, my sweet Serafine."

"What the..." The woman who murdered him? Sitting up, she clutched the blankets to her chest. "Will you please get out of my bed? This is my private space."

His brow furrowed, confusion clouding his eyes as he faded from the room. Why the hell would he call the murderer his *sweet* Serafine? He couldn't know his mistress was the one who killed him. Odette's assumption had been right. He didn't know the truth about his death, and that was why he was stuck there.

Her stomach sank. She would have to tell him. Explain exactly what happened to him so he could let go. Swinging her legs over the side of the bed, she grabbed her phone from the nightstand and stared at the blank screen. First, she'd have to convince the ghost she wasn't Serafine. Who knew how he'd react to the news of his murder? And if he thought Odette had killed him, he might lash out. Then she'd have to command him to cross over. She shivered.

Running her finger over the screen to wake up her phone, she glanced at the time. Five a.m. No point in going back to sleep now. She texted Natasha to call her as soon as she woke up and made her way to the shower.

When she emerged from the steamy bathroom twenty minutes later, the message light on her phone was blinking. Tugging the towel tighter around her chest, she retrieved the device and returned her Mambo's call. "I've got a problem. Several."

Dishes clanked in the background, followed by the sound of a refrigerator door opening and closing. "I'm listening."

"Where do I start?" Odette sank onto the edge of her bed. "My offering to Erzulie Dantor didn't work. I saw James last night...then I dreamed about him." A shiver ran up her spine at the memory of her dream.

"I didn't figure she'd be much help in your case." Her smile was evident in her voice. "He's a good man."

"I know, and he wanted to ask me out, but I told him it wouldn't end well."

The muffled sound of liquid pouring into a glass filled the silence, and more shuffling ensued before the fridge door opened and closed again. "And what did he say to that?"

"He said that maybe it didn't have to end." A dozen butterfly wings flitted against her abdomen. Under normal circumstances, his words would have thrilled her. "He doesn't have a clue."

"If you're going to be with him, you have to tell him. Did you ask him about his readings? I think he'll understand."

"No, I was too busy trying not to like him. I was hoping if I could avoid falling for him, the monster wouldn't come for us. If we can keep our distance and not start a relationship, maybe we can keep our lives too." She inhaled deeply and blew out a hard breath. "But there was a demon in my backyard last night. James called it an imp. I mean, the monster that's always killed me before is bigger than a man. This one was two feet tall, but..."

All sounds of movement on Natasha's end of the line stopped. The Mambo didn't speak for a moment, and the silence grew heavy and foreboding.

"Are you familiar with imps? He said they're lower-level demons who get summoned by something bigger and nastier." And her fated murderer was both of those. She'd never encountered imps in her past-life regressions, but the moment James had mentioned what summoned them, the first inklings of terror had clawed through her mind.

"He knows what he's talking about. Was it just the one?"

"There was one other, a few days ago. He said he killed it outside Rusty's." Her heart sank. "This is it, isn't it? The beginning of the end?"

"We don't know that. It's possible he has enemies, and the imps are targeting him. It could have nothing to do with you."

The Mambo had a point. James was the common denominator here, not her. Then again, all her friends were at Rusty's the night he killed it. Odette could have been there too. "Or it could have been sent to kill me. I've met my soulmate. Maybe I don't have to fall in love with him to trigger the curse. Maybe it's already happening."

"Where are you?"

"I'm at home."

"Stay there. Work from home today; you're safe inside. I'll prepare a ceremony for this evening, and I'll pick you up at six. We'll contact the Spirits and see if they can guide us."

She rubbed her forehead, closing her eyes for a long blink. "I've been asking for guidance since the moment James walked into my life, but my prayers have gone unanswered."

"You know why. Unless you're ready to let go and embrace your gift, you'll continue to be left to go it alone."

"My powers are not a gift." She bit her tongue to stop herself from continuing. The argument would get her nowhere.

Natasha clucked her tongue. "Don't let the Baron hear you say that. And don't worry. If we gather enough vodouisants, the Spirits are bound to show up."

"I'll see you tonight. Thanks." She pressed end and slid the phone onto her nightstand. Working from home wasn't an issue. She was the boss, after all. But being home all day meant she'd be spending all day with James.

Her stomach fluttered at the thought of seeing him again, and she groaned. She wasn't ready for her life to end.

James parked in front of Odette's house and slid out of his truck. A spark of excitement tingled in his chest at the sight of her car sitting in the driveway, but his anticipation of seeing her again crumbled into worry as he tucked a basket of kitchen towels under his arm and paced up the walk.

He'd watched her house himself most of the night, until Cade showed up insisting the alpha had ordered James to get some sleep. Though he hadn't caught so much as a whiff of demon, his wolf had protested leaving her the whole way home and most of the night.

The few hours of sleep he'd managed were plagued with confusing dreams. His mystery woman appeared as usual, making his heart swell with what he wanted to call love, though he had no experience with the romantic side of the emotion. His heart didn't normally react to women at all, leaving the swelling to his dick instead.

But the mystery woman hadn't stayed in his dream for long. As soon as he'd taken her hand, she'd morphed into Odette, and damn it if the L-word feelings hadn't intensified when he'd looked into her dark-brown eyes.

Now, the sun peeked from behind the mansions on Millionaire's Row, casting the sky in shades of deep pink and orange. The bougainvillea mixed with the scents of fresh paint and sawdust, and he inhaled deeply, letting the familiar aromas calm his nerves.

A werewolf manual laborer had no chance with a woman as polished and professional as Odette Allemand, but his wolf sure seemed to think he did. He glanced at his right hand. Hell, he wasn't even a whole werewolf. He'd spent his entire life trying to hide his slow healing and prove his worth to the pack. Now he was setting himself up to have to prove himself to a woman too. He exhaled a curse and rang the bell.

A tiny smile lighted on Odette's mouth as she opened the door, and she didn't try to hide it this time. Screw it all; he needed to get a taste of those lips.

"You could've let yourself in. You have a key." She stepped aside for him to enter, and he shuffled into the foyer, a smile tugging at his own lips as he took in her outfit. She was barefoot again, and her dark-blue skinny jeans emphasized the length of her legs. Her black silk shirt flowed over her hips, and with the top two buttons undone, it revealed just enough skin to make him yearn to see more.

"This is the first time I've seen you in a color other than black or purple." He gestured to her jeans.

"I'm working from home today." She paused in front of him, holding his gaze as if trying to gauge his reaction.

He arched a brow, his heart rate kicking up at the thought of spending the entire day with her. "Everything okay?"

"Natasha, my Mambo, thinks it's best if I stay home until we figure out where the demon came from." She nodded to the basket under his arm. "What's that?"

"Oh." He clutched it with both hands and held it out to her. "I couldn't get the blood stain out of that towel, so I bought you new ones."

Her smile widened as she took the basket and ran a hand over the lavender cloth. "It was one towel. You didn't have to buy me an entire set."

Heat crept up his neck, and he shoved his hands into his pockets. *Get over yourself, man.* "Consider it a housewarming gift. I thought they'd look good in your kitchen when it's finished."

"Thank you." She lifted her gaze to meet his, and the corners of her eyes tightened in uncertainty for a moment before she straightened her spine. "Do you have time for a cup of coffee before you get started?"

He glanced at his watch. The crew would arrive in fifteen minutes, and he liked to do a sweep of the property before they began work. But he couldn't refuse Odette. He'd make time. "I've got a few minutes to spare."

"Good." She motioned for him to follow her to the kitchen, one of two rooms that had furniture. "Have a seat. I just made a fresh pot."

She'd set up a workstation at the breakfast table, her laptop and notepad occupying one of the spots. James sank into the opposite chair and watched as she took two mugs from the cabinet and filled them with coffee. She had the posture of a ballerina, and she moved as gracefully as if she'd spent years in a dance studio. The woman was alluring, and that was putting it lightly.

She smiled as she glided to the table and set the mugs down. "Do you need cream or sugar?"

"Black is fine." He sipped the coffee, and his admiration of her intensified. Bold and robust, the rich aroma of the coffee went well with her personality. Any woman who took her coffee this strong was a keeper. *Wait.* It was way too soon for thoughts like that. He cleared his throat. "Were you ever a dancer? Ballet or anything?"

She sat next to him. "No. I don't dance. Not even at our ceremonies. Why do you ask?"

"You're built like a dancer. Graceful." He took another sip, eyeing her over the rim of the mug.

Arching an eyebrow, she inclined her chin. "Is that your way of hinting that you like my body?"

He nearly choked on his coffee. A trail of the warm liquid rolled down his chin, and he wiped it with the back of his hand. Setting the mug down, he squared his shoulders. "Who says I like graceful women? Maybe I'd prefer a klutz." With a grin, he took a successful sip from his cup, silently congratulating himself for grabbing control of the conversation before she could turn him into a babbling idiot.

"That's a shame." She traced her finger around the rim of her mug. "I seem to have a thing for men who are good at restoring things. Bringing life back to something nearly lost to time."

He opened his mouth to respond as she held his gaze, but the words didn't come. Something had changed between last night and this morning, and whatever it was, James wasn't about to complain. He also wasn't letting her have the upper hand.

He swept his gaze across the room, doing his best to act like her comment didn't faze him. "I've admired this house since I was a kid, and I've always wondered what it would look like on the inside. Restoring it is a dream come true." He locked eyes with her. "What do you dream about, Odette?"

A blush spread across her cheeks, and she cleared her voice. "Natasha told me I should ask you about your readings. She said you've been into the temple a few times, and she expected to see you again soon."

Heat crept into his ears as he ground his teeth. He had planned to make another appointment, until he met Odette. "So much for her readings being private. What else did she tell you?"

"Nothing." She held up her hands in a show of innocence. "She didn't tell me anything about your reading; she said I should ask you about it. With the ghost here showing so much interest in you, and then the demon last night…I guess she thought it might be related."

He let out a slow breath, quelling his frustration. What would

Odette think about his dream woman and the fact that she herself was now battling for control of his wolf? He'd rather not know. "The ghost hasn't bothered me since the first time. Why do you think he's showing interest in me?"

"Because he's been present since you got here this morning. I think I upset him earlier, and he hasn't shown himself…until you knocked on the door. He's been watching you ever since."

He cut his gaze to the left, following her line of sight, but he couldn't see the ghost. "What's he doing?"

"Staring at you. He looks confused but also…interested." She focused on the empty space in the corner. "Why are you looking at James like that? Do you know him too?" Her shoulders drooped as she picked up her mug. "He disappeared again. Every time I start asking him questions, he vanishes."

"That's weird. Maybe he doesn't want you to know."

She narrowed her eyes and shook her head. "Maybe, but…does the name Serafine sound familiar to you?"

The syllables flowed in his ears like music. Was it the name or the way Odette said it? His chest tightened, and he wracked his brain for the memory that skittered around the edges of his mind. "I feel like it should, but it doesn't ring a bell. It's a pretty name, though. Why?"

She chewed her bottom lip and drummed her manicured nails on the table. "Nicolas, the ghost, mentioned the name. I thought maybe she was someone famous…or infamous…in New Orleans that I hadn't heard of."

"It's possible." The sound of an engine rumbled from outside, followed by doors slamming and the clanking of equipment. "That's my team. I better get to work. Thank you for the coffee."

He rose, but she caught his hand. "What were you looking for in your readings?"

A low growl rumbled in his chest, so quiet she couldn't have heard it, and he lowered himself into the seat. The imploring look in her eyes drew the words from his mouth before he could think twice about telling her. "My wolf is restless. It's time for me to settle down, but…"

She leaned toward him. "But?"

He couldn't tell her about the dreams; they were crazy. *He* was going crazy for having them. "I haven't had good luck in the love department, so I was looking for guidance." *Smooth move, Romeo.* Why didn't he tell her about his broken wolf too? That would really impress her. *Get it together, man.*

He looked into her eyes. "But things have changed since I met you."

She started to speak, but the front door swung open and boots thudded on the wooden floor. "Hey, James. Can we get started?"

Damn you, Noah. "Yeah. We're good to go." He stood and carried his mug to the sink. "That's my cue. We'll try not to make too much noise inside, but I can't make any guarantees."

"Of course." She fumbled for something next to her computer and lifted it in the air. "I've got headphones, so…no worries."

"Good deal. I'll be around if you need me." He turned on his heel and strode out of the kitchen.

Sweet Spirits, that was not what she'd expected to hear. The headphones slipped from her trembling hand as she sank lower in her chair. Things had changed since he'd met her. If he thought meeting her meant his luck in love was getting better, he was in for a rude awakening.

He'd be better off single for the rest of his life than to fall in love with Odette and deal with the tragedy her love would bring.

Natasha wasn't convinced the imps were a sign of things to come, so maybe there was still a chance. Maybe she could convince him she wasn't the one he was looking for. If they never fell in love, maybe…

A clank sounded in the foyer, and she leaned to the side to see James setting up a ladder beneath the chrome light fixture. Two other men held either side of a refurbished nineteenth-century crystal chandelier and waited as he removed the fixture from the ceiling.

As he reached his arms overhead, his dark-blue T-shirt lifted above his waistline, revealing smooth skin and a hint of the delicious V disappearing into his pants.

She bit her lip. How could she convince him she wasn't the one when her insides melted from simply looking at the man?

He caught her gaze and grinned. "The new one's going to look so much better. You've got good taste."

She couldn't help but return the smile. "Thanks."

The rest of the morning crawled by. She couldn't focus on her work when the sexiest werewolf she'd ever laid eyes on kept coming into view. If she didn't know any better, she'd think he was purposely working on little things close to the kitchen so he could steal glances of her the way she'd been doing him.

Nicolas followed him around too. Could the ghost be jealous of the time James was spending with her? With the way Nicolas had looked at her this morning, it made sense. She'd have to find a way to convince him she wasn't his former mistress, but she'd hold off on that conversation until after the ceremony tonight. The loa may have been ignoring Odette, but they wouldn't ignore the whole House.

When James moved to work upstairs, taking the temptation with him, Odette finally focused on her job. She plowed through her inbox, reviewing reports and crunching numbers until her eyes stung. She'd instructed her assistant to call if any emergencies arose at work, but her phone had remained silent all day. Her company ran like a well-oiled machine, both the office end and the distillery.

Why couldn't running companies be her gift? She didn't mind her simple psychic medium powers. Having the ability to see and speak to the dead meant she'd never been afraid of ghosts, even as a child, but she could do without the other magic Baron Samedi had granted her when he'd brought her back to life.

Boots thudded on the staircase, pulling her from her thoughts, and she glanced at the clock. Five p.m. The afternoon had flown by.

"Y'all go ahead." James's deep voice drifted in from the foyer. "I'm going to walk the property with the client to make sure she's happy with the progress."

"I bet you'll make sure she's *real* happy." That voice came from the younger man with auburn hair that she'd heard James call Noah.

Leaning off the edge of her chair so she could see the men, she caught a glimpse of James punching Noah on the shoulder. "Watch yourself," James said.

Noah chuckled. "Sorry, man. Have fun." The men left, and James shuffled into the kitchen.

Odette fought the grin tugging at her lips and folded her hands on the table. "All done for the day?"

"Do you want to do a walk-through? Make sure everything meets your expectations?"

"I've done my own walk-through every day, and I saw you working today. You're exceeding my expectations." In every way imaginable.

He held her gaze with his smoldering blue eyes and cocked his head slightly. "I live about fifteen minutes away. If I run home and take a quick shower, could I come back and take you out to dinner?"

An image of James, naked and dripping wet, formed in her mind, chasing all rational thought from her head. Her body acted before her brain could process a response, and she rose from the table, gliding toward him.

She could have dinner with James...and dessert. Preferably his delectable body covered in chocolate. If she was going to let go and give in to passion, he was the man to do it with. He was supposed to be her soulmate after all. She could trust him, couldn't she? "I thought you had rules against dating clients?"

"It's more of a suggestion, really. I've never been much of a rule-follower."

She couldn't help herself. She drifted a little closer and rested her hand on his shoulder. His muscles were firm, his skin warm beneath his shirt. "As tempting as your offer is, I have to be at the temple in an hour. We're having a ceremony."

"That's cool. Maybe another time." He patted her hand on his shoulder and stepped away. "I'll be back in the morning." He strode to the foyer.

"James..." She followed him to the front door. "You don't take rejection well, do you?"

He stopped and faced her, his eyes narrowing. "I'm not used to being rejected."

"I'm not rejecting *you.* I'm simply not available tonight." She looked into his eyes, willing him to take the hint and ask about another time.

He pressed his mouth into a thin line and lifted his chin. "I see."

Damn it, he didn't take the bait.

She bit her bottom lip. With her poise and the general spooky aura surrounding her, most people backed down instantly when she pressed them. James was the first person not afraid to push back, and that made him all the more intriguing.

She moved closer, placing her hand on his shoulder again. "Will you be watching my house tonight or are you assigning the job to someone else?"

His brow furrowed. "I…How did you know?"

"I could feel your presence, and I saw you across the street. When I woke up around three a.m. someone else was there. I guess you're working in shifts?"

He inhaled deeply, holding her gaze, silently reminding her she couldn't scare him away. "I'm not a stalker. With the demon on your property…we hunt in shifts all night anyway, and I was worried one might try again."

"And the fact that it's *my* house had nothing to do with it?" She inched a little closer until she could feel the heat radiating from his skin.

"This is a high-paying job. Luke would have my ass if something happened to you and you couldn't pay." His gaze flowed between her eyes and her lips.

"Is that the real reason?"

He rested a hand on her hip. "I think you know the real reason. I—"

Tugging him closer, she pressed her lips to his. He stiffened at first, but as she slid her arms around his shoulders, his body relaxed, conforming to hers as if he were made to fit in her embrace.

His lips were soft, his body firm, and as he wrapped his arms around her waist, a growl rumbled up from deep in his chest. She opened for him, brushing her tongue against his, reveling in the way their magic mixed and tingled across her skin.

With a deep, shuddering breath, she pulled away, cupping his face in her hands before stepping back and dropping her arms to her sides. "Natasha is picking me up in a few minutes, so you'd better get going."

He opened his mouth, but he didn't speak.

"She drives a silver Toyota Camry, if you're planning to follow us to the temple. Sometimes these ceremonies last into the early morning, so if you want to send someone to follow me back home, I can't give you an exact time."

"We'll have eyes on you all night. Don't worry."

With Natasha's magic and her own, she wasn't the slightest bit afraid of a little imp. But she couldn't deny that she found James's protective nature appealing. "I won't." She placed a soft kiss on his cheek. "Bye, James."

CHAPTER NINE

Odette held a bag of cornmeal in one hand, the fingers of her free hand lightly tracing the bow of her lips as she replayed the kiss in her mind for the fifteenth time. How could her skin *still* be tingling from his touch?

She shouldn't have kissed him. With the imp showing up at her house, she was all but convinced her demise had begun, but if she could keep her hands to herself and her lips off the sexy werewolf, maybe she could spare him from their horrid fate.

Tell him it was a mistake. That it would never happen again. Shut it down before it began. She could call his boss and ask for a different foreman to finish her house so she wouldn't have to see him anymore. It was the only way to keep James safe.

Then again, with the way he'd reacted to her advances this evening, they'd both boarded a bullet train headed straight for death.

"You bite that lip any harder, and we're going to have a blood offering for Papa Legba." Natasha took the bag from her hand and set it on a table in the corner.

Odette blinked, releasing her bottom lip from the clutch of her teeth and sweeping her gaze across the room. In the ten minutes she'd been internalizing, six vodouisants had entered the room with offerings for the various loa who may or may not grace them with their presence during the ceremony.

Natasha had drawn the *vévé* for Papa Legba, the loa of the crossroads, in cornmeal on the floor. The intricate cross with swirls and stars embellishing each of the corners would act as the gateway, Papa Legba the gatekeeper, allowing the other loa to enter the ritual.

"You've outdone yourself this time, Mambo." Odette gestured to the *vévé*.

Natasha smiled proudly. "My artistic skills are improving."

Pulling a bottle of premium rum from her bag, Odette placed it on the offering table. "I'm sure he's abandoned me, but in case the Baron decides to make an appearance."

"Who abandoned who?" The priestess arched an eyebrow.

"Is anyone else coming?" She didn't need to run down that rabbit hole again. Odette and Baron Samedi had abandoned each other, and she refused to argue about the topic further. It didn't matter who strayed first.

Pressing her lips together, Natasha narrowed her eyes, giving her that *you know I'm right* look. Maybe she was right; maybe she wasn't. The point of this ceremony was to find out where the imps came from, and they didn't need the loa of death to figure that out. Demons didn't die.

"Are we waiting on anyone else?" Natasha scanned the crowd, and when no one spoke up, she lit a black candle and knelt in front of her freshly-drawn *vévé*.

Jackson and Tyrell, two priests-in-training picked up their drums and beat out a melodic rhythm, while Rasheda, Amy, and Darlene, three of the women dressed in all white, began swaying to the cadence. Her voice low, Natasha hummed, slowly increasing her volume as the hum turned from a mumble into a full-blown chant.

Odette recognized few words of the Haitian Creole prayer the priestess recited to the rhythm of the drums, but the message was as clear as if she'd said the chant in English. The Mambo was calling on Papa Legba to open the gates and allow the loa through to deliver their messages.

As the drumbeat changed, the energy in the room shifted, a

buzzing, living electricity dancing through the air, making goose bumps prick on Odette's arms. Darlene spun, taking a bottle of Bacardi from the table and pouring a few drops on the *vévé* as an offering to the loa of the crossroads.

The cadence changed again, and Rasheda and Amy joined Darlene in a dance to honor the Spirits. The pull of energy had Odette leaning toward the dancers, her body betraying her as it swayed in time with the drums. Fisting her hands, she focused on the bite of her nails into her palms, keeping herself firmly grounded in the here and now. Giving in to the rhythm would mean relinquishing control, opening herself up to ritual possession, and *that* was something she'd never do again.

The room buzzed, the vibration increasing as Papa Legba opened the gates, giving the loa permission to visit the Earthly realm. Odette whispered her thanks along with the other vodouisants, and Rasheda placed a coconut on the *vévé*.

"This is intense." Chelsea, a new initiate, wrung her hands as she stepped next to her. "How long have you been a vodouisant?"

Odette unclenched her jaw and glanced at the girl. With her red hair styled into a pixie cut, torn jeans, and Adidas shoes, she didn't look a day over eighteen. "All my life." She tried for a smile, but the corners of her mouth merely twitched.

"Then, why aren't you dancing? I can't wait for my *lavé tet* so I can join in."

Odette focused on her Mambo. "I never dance."

"There's demons after our girl." Natasha sashayed toward her. "Will someone tell us where they came from? Is it her curse?" She stood between Odette and the initiate, carefully eyeing the drummers and dancers for signs of possession.

The atmosphere thickened, the drum cadence quickening, welcoming whatever loa was about to make its presence known. Darlene stiffened, her eyes going wide for a second before they closed and she collapsed into Rasheda's arms.

As she held her breath, Odette clenched her fists tighter, the sensation of her nails cutting into her palms the only thing keeping her in place. The visitor could be any one of the hundreds of loa, and he or she may not even be there to answer her questions. Voodoo Spirits thought for themselves, and they didn't always cooperate.

It was foolish to hope her own *met tet* would arrive to help her. Baron Samedi hadn't shown himself at a ritual Odette attended since the day she turned her back on Voodoo. Even now he rarely visited her in her dreams.

She let out her breath as Darlene regained her footing, righting herself and taking on a posture not her own. Her head held high, she pointed to the perfume and flowers on the table, and Rasheda and Amy draped her in a pink shawl, the color of Erzulie Freda, the loa of love.

"This is the last thing I need," Odette muttered under her breath. If the loa was there to talk about her love life, the demon was most definitely after her. The cycle had begun.

Darlene's gaze locked on Odette, but her smile wasn't her own. She slinked toward her, batting her lashes at Jackson as he softened the beat of his drum. Stopping two feet in front of her, Erzulie Freda smiled sweetly, shaking her head and making a *tsk* sound as she smoothed a strand of Odette's hair back into place. "You found a good one, but you need to work on your presentation if you want to keep him."

She fought the urge to slap Darlene's hand away. This wasn't Darlene; it was Erzulie Freda. "My appearance doesn't seem that important when I'm about to be joining the Baron in the land of the dead."

Resting her hands on her hips, Freda tilted her head and offered a small smile. "The Baron doesn't want you to join him yet."

"I don't think I have a choice."

Freda wrapped an arm around Odette's shoulders and led her away from the others. "What's your beau's name, child?"

"James." She straightened, furrowing her brow as the realization hit. She hadn't hesitated. Didn't argue that he wasn't her boyfriend like she'd expected to. That kiss seemed to have sealed the deal, sealing her fate—and his—along with it.

Closing her eyes, the loa smiled softly, nodding as if receiving messages from the spirit world. "He's a good one. You're lucky."

Odette scoffed. "Until we both end up dead."

Freda stopped and turned to face her. "Maybe you have three more days with him, or maybe you have fifty years. However long you have left, don't you want to make the most of it?"

Odette crossed her arms but quickly dropped them to her sides to avoid showing disrespect to the Ancestral Spirit. "I…" Of course she wanted to make the most of it, but how could she when demons lurked outside her door? "The demon that James killed… It was after me, wasn't it?"

The loa sighed, shaking her head like a disappointed mother. "You were hoping to see your *met tet* tonight?"

"I don't mean to offend, but I already know James is my soulmate. Baron Samedi could help me fight this thing that's coming for me. Whether or not I give in to temptation with James is irrelevant. The cycle has already started."

"The Baron isn't pleased with the way you've been living your life. All work. No fun. Refusing the gifts he blessed you with."

Odette cast her gaze to the floor. "I know."

Freda grinned. "You could start by pleasing that beau of yours." Her husky voice sounded nothing like Darlene's higher-pitched tone. "Let him please you, too, if you know what I mean. Your *met tet* knows that sex and death are part of life. How long has it been for you, child?"

"I really don't want to talk about this."

The loa lifted her chin. "You don't want to talk about your love life with Erzulie Freda? I guess I shouldn't have bothered coming." She turned toward the others who continued the ceremony, dancing and drumming to honor the Spirits.

"Wait." Odette touched her elbow and then let her hand fall to her side. "I mean no disrespect. It's been…a long time."

"How long?"

Not since her past-life regressions with Natasha revealed what would happen when she finally fell in love. "A few years."

Freda let out a low whistle. "That's too long. And with that scrumptious werewolf in your house all day, how do you resist?"

"It hasn't been easy, but I have to. If I give in and bring him into this, he'll die too."

"He's already in it. Like you said, the cycle has started, and he's part of it whether you enjoy him or not."

Enjoy him. She could think of dozens of ways to enjoy James. Her lips curved into an involuntary smile, so she covered her mouth with her fingers.

"Mm-hmm. You haven't completely strayed from your *met tet.* He'd be proud of the thoughts that are probably dancing through your mind right now."

Boy, would he. Odette cleared her throat. "Message received. Thank you, Erzulie Freda."

The loa straightened the shawl on her shoulders, running her fingers over the silk. "I have another message for you."

She sucked in a breath. "From the Baron?"

Ignoring her question, Freda sank into a chair, her playful smile slipping into a frown. "There are things you don't know…things you can't know until the puzzle is solved." She folded her hands in her lap as tears collected on her lower lids.

No. The loa's shift in mood meant her time here was done. Odette wanted to scream. To shake the woman and beg her to answer her questions, but it was no use. Erzulie Freda's possessions always ended in sadness.

"James can help. The two of you have to solve the puzzle so you can break the cycle and have a lifetime of love." Her shoulders shook with her sob. "If you don't, you'll both die, and your love will die too." Lifting her gaze to Odette's, she pleaded with her eyes. "Love is precious. Please don't let it die this time."

Odette's throat thickened, the sight of the loa in tears making her own eyes sting. "I'll do my best."

With a deep, shuddering breath, Freda closed her eyes and slumped in the chair. When she came to, Darlene blinked, her gaze darting about the room. She lifted the shawl from her shoulders and folded it in her lap. "Erzulie Freda?"

Odette nodded. Her friend wouldn't remember a word of the

conversation they'd had. Her consciousness had slipped aside for the loa to take control.

Darlene wiped the tears from her cheeks. "Did you find out what you needed to know?"

"A little." Not nearly enough. Solve the puzzle. What puzzle did she mean?

"Are you banging the Baroness yet?" Cade took a swig of beer and nodded toward the window. "Or is it a coincidence you chose a bar across from the House of Voodoo?"

James narrowed his eyes. "Don't be a dick." He set his empty glass on the bar. "Her name is Odette. Show a little respect."

Cade raised his eyebrows and looked at Noah, who shook his head, chuckling under his breath. James ignored his friends and let his gaze drift across Dumaine Street to the dark-green wooden door covering the entrance to the Voodoo temple. The front third of the establishment acted as a store where practitioners and tourists alike could buy dolls, potions, herbs, and *gris-gris* bags to help with whatever ailed their bodies or souls.

He'd had his cards read several times in the curtained-off corner booths, and he'd glimpsed the middle section of the store, where the altars to the various Spirits were erected in the temple area. He'd never given the area much thought, but now that he'd seen Odette's own altar in her home, curiosity had him itching to go inside.

The green door was locked, no doubt, though. Odette and the other vodouisants were in the back third of the temple, doing whatever it was that Voodoo practitioners did when they summoned their gods.

Cade chugged the rest of his beer and slammed the bottle on the bar. "What the hell's wrong with you, man? You're about as fun as a canker sore lately. Don't tell me you're pining over the Baron—over Odette."

"Pining? Hell no." He wasn't pining. He wanted to make the woman his, but his damn wolf was insane.

Odette wanted him. That kiss she'd planted on him earlier in the evening was all the confirmation he'd needed, but her back and forth behavior raised his hackles. Why did they need to perform a ritual to find out where the imps had come from? The werewolves dealt with the demons in the Quarter; it was the natural way of things. The vodouisants had never gotten involved before.

He cracked his knuckles. "She knows something… She's hiding something from me."

Noah swiveled in his seat. "You starting to think she's summoning them?"

"No, but I think she knows who is. She's protecting someone, and I need to find out who."

CHAPTER TEN

An odd mix of excitement and dread bubbled in Odette's stomach, fizzing up to her chest where it expanded into an anxious sensation that made her want to crawl back into bed and hide under the covers.

She'd steeled herself to pull James aside as soon as he arrived that morning, tell him about the curse and their impending deaths to get it over with, but he'd come in with the rest of the crew, forgoing his usual early arrival.

When she'd asked why he was late, he'd mumbled something about being on the phone with the warehouse, given her an inquisitive look, as if he were about to ask a question, and then his team stomped in with their arms full of cabinet doors, and she hadn't spoken to him since.

She drummed her nails on the folding table she'd set up in the altar room and stared at her watch, counting the seconds until the crew would leave and she could get James alone. She had so much to tell him, but she had no clue where to begin. How could she tell him that because she was falling for him, they'd both be dead within a few weeks? Or days?

"Kitchen cabinets are done if you want to come have a look."

James stood in the doorway wiping his hands on a rag. He half-smiled, but it didn't ease the tightness in his jaw. Whatever his problem was, he needed to get over it. They didn't have time for bruised egos.

He stuffed the rag into his pocket. "They're beautiful."

She rose from her seat and strutted toward him, allowing her power to pool in her core. As her aura tingled with energy, Nicolas, attracted to the magic, appeared behind James, growing more solid as he fed off the energy from the spirit realm passing through Odette. She reined it in, keeping the magic to herself, and lightly touched James's shoulder as she passed. "They better be. That's what I'm paying you for."

He should have felt the void of death as she touched him. The cold emptiness should have made him shiver. That little trick was normally enough to make any grown man cower, and it was the most she ever did with the power the Baron had erroneously gifted her—a tiny boost to remind people she wasn't one to mess with.

But James simply chuckled, catching her hand before she could walk away. "I'm not afraid of you, so if you're trying to get rid of me after last night…"

She squeezed his hand before pulling from his grasp. "I'm not trying to get rid of you. Just having a little fun."

"Is that what you call it?" He closed the distance between them, and taking her hand again, he held it between both of his. "We need to talk."

His magic buzzed on her skin, shimmying up her arm and sparking in her heart. She swallowed the thickness from her throat and gazed into his deep, blue eyes. "I know." He had no idea. "After the crew leaves, okay?"

"Yeah."

He led her into the kitchen, and her breath caught when she saw the transformation. Dark mahogany with elegant scrollwork etched into the trim, the new cabinets deepened the room, giving it an antique yet stylish ambiance. She brought her fingers to her lips as she admired the woodwork.

"Told you they're beautiful." James stood so close his breath tickled her ear. "Classic." He rested a hand on her shoulder. "They're as close to the original cabinetry that we could find. Well, original to the first kitchen that was actually inside the house."

"They're perfect. Thank you." She leaned into him, the warmth of his firm chest against her back making her wish the crew was already gone.

The clank of tools sounded from the foyer, and Noah cleared his throat as he sauntered into the kitchen. James stepped back, taking his warmth with him, and Odette wrapped her arms around herself to rub at the goose bumps on her arms.

"Crew's heading out. You sticking around?" Noah's gazed flicked between James and Odette.

James nodded. "I need to get a few signatures on the paperwork. I'll meet up with you later."

Noah fought a smile and dipped his head at Odette. "Have a good evening, ma'am."

The moment the door clicked shut, James turned to her. "What did you find out at the ceremony?"

"Oh, um…not much, really. I was hoping Baron Samedi would show up, but it seems he's still mad at me." She backed against the counter, gripping the edge. She should say it. Tell him he's her soulmate and they're both going to die because of it. He could handle the truth, couldn't he?

He narrowed his eyes. "Nothing about the imps? You said your loa might be able to tell you where they came from."

Pressing her lips into a hard line, she gripped the counter tighter. If she told him now, he might turn tail and run. That wouldn't help anyone. Death would find him anyway, right after it claimed her.

He stepped toward her and rested his hand on the counter behind her. "Who are you protecting?"

Both of us. "No one. I…" She exhaled a sharp breath. "There are some things you need to know, but it's complicated." Gazing into his eyes, it took every ounce of her willpower not to lean in and kiss him. If he didn't realize they were soulmates yet, he might not believe her. Erzulie Freda said they had to work together if she wanted a chance to break the cycle. She couldn't risk scaring him off. "The loa that spoke to me said there's a puzzle that needs to be solved and you have to help me solve it."

He frowned. "A puzzle?"

"Yes, but she didn't say what, and it's hard to explain." Releasing her grip on the counter, she straightened and brushed a hand down his arm. "I'm free tonight, if you're still interested in having dinner with me. It's going to take a while to explain it all."

He glanced at her fingers where they rested against his and took a deep breath, his gaze roaming from her eyes to her lips and back again. "Now you're asking me out?"

It was either that or push him to the floor and climb on top of him. A date seemed like the more sensible option…for now. "I like you, James. I'd like to get to know you better. Let you get to know me."

Holding her gaze, he purposely hesitated in his reply, drawing it out, trying to get the upper hand. That wouldn't do.

She cocked an eyebrow and slid away from him. "But if your ego is still bruised, then never mind." Pulling her phone from her pocket, she tapped the screen. "I'll have my dinner delivered. Please lock up on your way out."

He yanked the phone from her hand. "Ordering dinner from Instagram? I didn't realize they offered that feature."

Damn it, she should have clicked the Uber Eats app. "I was checking my notifications first."

Stepping toward her, he cupped her cheek in his hand, angling her face toward his. He drifted closer, his nose brushing hers, the warmth of his breath caressing her lips. "I'm going to run home and shower. I'll be back to pick you up in thirty minutes." He paused, his lips an inch from hers, his grin crinkling the corners of his eyes.

Sweet Spirits, if he didn't kiss her, she was going to explode.

His thumb grazed her cheek as he stepped back and dropped his hand. "Stay inside until I get here." With a wink, he turned and strode from the room.

She didn't remember to breathe until the sound of the lock on the front door pulled her from her trance. That man didn't just make her body burn; he lit her soul on fire.

James watched Odette from the corner of his eye as he pretended to be absorbed in the music. A five-piece band sat on a small raised platform in the corner of The Apothecary, a popular hangout for locals and tourists alike to hear live music with a flair only found in New Orleans. Tonight, the music ranged from big band to jazz to the musician's original tunes, and Odette's elusive smile had almost become a permanent fixture throughout the evening.

They'd started with dinner at Chez Jacques. The Tour of New Orleans had included jambalaya, shrimp creole, and a hearty serving of seafood gumbo, and he'd savored every bite of it. Odette's shrimp and grits had smelled divine, and she'd polished off the entire bowl, plus half the loaf of French bread. He admired a woman who wasn't afraid to eat. The more time he spent with her, the more comfortable she became, and the fact he'd helped to put the smile that most people rarely witnessed on her lips made his pulse pound a little harder.

Sitting in this old pharmacy-turned-bar, with the jazz music playing and the rum flowing, was the perfect ending to their first date. Well, with any luck the date wouldn't end until tomorrow morning, but he was still working on that.

He slid his arm across the back of her seat, letting his hand rest on her shoulder. She glanced at him, biting her lower lip and leaning into his side. Damn, this felt right. The evening. The company. The restlessness that had been stirring in his soul had settled, contentment expanding in its place. He kissed the top of her head, and she let out a quiet sigh.

Mine.

The idea shook him to his very core. He could actually spend forever with this woman. He hadn't known her long, but he felt it in his bones. In his soul. Closing his eyes for a long blink, he sat with it, letting it resonate, waiting for his wolf to tell him otherwise. His beast didn't argue.

He couldn't fight his smile. It had finally happened. He'd found his fate-bound.

No sooner had the thought entered his mind when an image of the dream woman flashed behind his eyes.

Also mine.

He held in a groan. Damn his wolf. The *man* had made up his mind. He wanted Odette, but he sure as hell wouldn't take her as his mate unless his wolf was one hundred percent in agreement that she was the *only* one for him.

It would take some convincing, but he was up for the challenge. Hell, he planned on enjoying every minute of it.

The band played a slow, sultry tune, and several couples took to the small dance floor to sway to the rhythm. He grasped Odette's hand and rose to his feet. "Let's dance."

"Oh." Her eyes tightened, and she didn't move from her seat. "I don't dance." Tugging from his grasp, she clutched her hands on the table.

He sank into his chair and covered her hands with his. "What do you mean you don't dance? We live in the Big Easy. The birthplace of Jazz. Everyone dances here."

"I don't." She looked into his eyes, challenging him to argue.

He pried her hands apart and took one in each of his, lowering them to his lap as he scooted closer. "Can I ask why not?"

"Dancing, and music in general, have a hypnotic effect on people. When you surrender to the music…to the rhythm…you are, in a sense, relinquishing control. It takes you to another place."

Which was one of the things he loved about music. A simple tune could transport a person back in time, into a memory he hadn't thought about in ages. "What's wrong with that?"

She squared her shoulders. "I prefer to stay in control of myself. I don't want to relinquish power to anyone or anything. It's safer that way."

He furrowed his brow. "Safer? Did something happen?"

Her eyes widened. "No, I…"

"Prefer to keep your wits about you?" He grinned, trying to lighten the mood. Whatever the reason for her need to be in constant control, she'd share it with him when she was ready. They had all the time in the world to get to know each other.

Her posture relaxed. “Exactly.”

“Do you want to get out of here? Go for a walk or something?”

“I don’t think it’s safe wandering the streets at night with a bunch of imps on the loose, do you? No one has been injured yet, but I’d rather not be the first.”

“Good point.”

“We could go to my place.” She squeezed his hands. “I’d like to talk to you some more.” The sly curve of her lips and the way she trailed her fingers along his thighs as she released his hands said she wanted to do more than talk.

“I like the way you think.”

The moment she closed the front door, James swept Odette into his arms and pressed his lips to hers. They did need to talk, like she’d said. He should press her for more information about the imps; he had no doubt she knew more than she let on. At that moment, though, all he could think about was how perfectly she fit into his arms and how soft her skin felt beneath his fingers.

She snaked her hands behind his neck, leaning into him, parting her lips and slipping out her tongue to tangle with his. A growl rumbled from his chest, and he fought the overwhelming urge to lift her from the ground and carry her to the bedroom. No wonder his friends who’d found their fate-bounds were so happy. If their relationship kept going at this pace, his wolf would have to put all four legs on the train and enjoy the ride.

As if on cue, an ache expanded in his chest. A longing for the woman he’d never met. Damn it, this had to stop.

Odette must have sensed the shift in his energy because she let out a soft sigh and pulled away. “We have an audience.” She nodded to her left.

James followed her gaze, but the house stood empty. “Nicolas?”

“Mm-hmm. Maybe we should get that talk out of the way.” She laced her fingers through his and led him down the hall.

They passed the empty living room, and he glanced through an open doorway at another room devoid of furniture. The one other space in the house that she'd furnished was her bedroom…

Holy hell. What kind of talking did she think was going to happen in there? He could barely keep his hands off her as it was.

"Don't get any ideas." She grinned. "I have a love seat in the bedroom. I thought we'd be more comfortable there than at the kitchen table."

A small television sat on a dresser, and the pale-blue love seat faced it at an angle. A cream-colored duvet covered the bed, and the faint scent of lavender greeted him as he entered the room. She sat on the sofa, curling one leg beneath her, and patted the space next to her.

"I bet you can't wait until the renovation is done. It'll be nice to not be confined to two rooms." He sank onto the cushion and turned to face her, his knee resting against hers.

She glanced at where their legs touched and placed an elbow on the back of the couch. "There's no rush. I kinda like having you around."

His stomach fluttered, a thousand butterflies taking flight and landing in his chest. "I like being around."

She smiled. "There's a reason for that."

He leaned toward her. "I'm positive it's you."

Her lips parted as if she were going to speak, but instead, she narrowed her eyes and chewed her bottom lip. Lowering her gaze, she picked at a loose thread on the cushion.

"Hey." He reached for her, trailing his fingers down her cheek before gently lifting her chin. "What's wrong?"

"This is going to sound crazy. I'm not even sure where to begin."

He dropped his hand to his lap and leaned against the back cushion. "Why don't you start with the imps. You know where they came from, don't you? Who summoned them?"

She sat up straighter and regarded him, studied him as if she were weighing her words. With a deep inhale, she relaxed her shoulders, a sad smile playing on her lips. "The demons are from my past, but I don't know exactly who summoned them."

"You don't know *exactly?*" He relaxed his fist on the back of the couch and traced his finger across the fabric. "Whatever happened in your past, I don't care. If you know where the demons are coming from, the werewolves can take out their boss and keep anyone from getting hurt. Just tell me."

"They're from your past too. That's what I wanted to talk to you about." Her eyes tightened.

"I've never seen those things before." He shook his head, her accusation taking him aback. How could she charge him, a werewolf, the natural-born enemy of demons, of summoning the imps? "I had nothing to do with them showing up."

"I'm not accusing you. Hear me out, okay?" She sighed and took both his hands in hers. "Do you believe in reincarnation?"

He shrugged, her touch taking the edge off his nerves. "Sure. But demons can't die, so they can't be reincarnated, if that's what you're getting at. When we vanquish them, they go back to their hellish dimension until someone summons them again."

She shook her head. "Do you believe in soulmates? That two people can be meant for each other because their destinies are entwined? Because they've been together in every lifetime they've lived?"

His eyes widened, and he fought to keep his expression neutral. Did she feel the same connection he felt to her? Was *that* what she was getting at? "Werewolves use the term fate-bound."

"Because fate binds your hearts. I like that." She smiled and traced her thumbs across the backs of his hands. "This isn't our first life together, James. We're soulmates." She tightened her grip on his hands as if she were afraid he'd run away.

But he wasn't going anywhere. Hearing her confirm what he'd known—at least in the back of his mind—since he first knocked on her door sent electricity running up his spine. He squeezed her hands in return hoping to imply that at least the man in him agreed. Now to convince his wolf. "How do you know?"

"Would you believe me if I said I just do?"

"I'd like to, but I have a feeling there's more to it than that."

"I've done a few past-life regressions with Natasha, trying to… figure things out. When you came into my life, I had a feeling you were the man from my previous lives. The Mambo confirmed it with a reading, and then Erzulie Freda, the loa of love, spoke to me about you at the ceremony. You're my soulmate." She shrugged, not looking at all as happy as she should have.

The corners of her mouth twitched, and she swallowed hard, her gaze darting about, looking at anything but him.

"That's good news, right?" He tried to catch her gaze, but she stared at their joined hands.

"Yes and no. I'm kinda glad to have found you." She finally looked into his eyes. "My feelings for you grow stronger every day."

"Kinda?" If they truly were soulmates, there would be no kinda about it. That type of connection was all or nothing. If she wasn't fully on board, and his wolf wasn't fully on board, maybe it was time he stepped off this train before it headed for certain disaster.

He rubbed his forehead and glanced at the door. The best escape would be honesty. Tell her they should slow things down and then stop seeing her after working hours. Now was the time to stand up and walk away, but he couldn't make himself move.

"Please let me finish." She rested her hand on his knee, the light pressure gluing him to the spot. "We seem to be stuck in a cycle, and it always ends in tragedy. That's why I said kinda. Because I know how this is going to end."

He'd been prepared to bolt, but her mention of being stuck in a cycle drew him back in. "You asked about the readings I've had done? They've told me the same thing. That I have to break the cycle. But no one knows what the cycle is."

"I do." Her brow furrowed, pity filling her eyes. "You said you thought those imps were a precursor to something bigger that hasn't fully formed yet?"

"Yeah?" A sinking sensation formed in the pit of his stomach.

"That *bigger thing* is going to kill us both. First me, and then you. It's happened in every past-life I've visited. I'm going to die in your arms, and I don't know how to stop it from happening."

"Wha—" The words stuck in his throat. *Hell no.* His wolf sprang to attention, the deep need to keep her safe rousing it to the surface.

She couldn't die; he wouldn't let it happen. He'd fought plenty of monsters, vanquished nasty demons that would have sent most wolves running with their tails between their legs. "Come here. I'm not going to let you die. Whatever this monster is, I'll protect you from it." He sidled next to her and wrapped her in his arms.

Resting her head on his shoulder, she draped her legs across his lap and snuggled into his side. "It's going to kill you too. That's the cycle."

Nope. Couldn't happen. The cycle ended now. "There's a hole in your theory."

She lifted her head to look at him. "How so?"

"You said we're both going to die because you've seen it in your past-life regressions. But if you always die in my arms, how can you know that I die too?"

"Because I've researched it. I discovered my name in the regression, then I looked up the records. It's always the same, reported as a double murder or murder-suicide. Two mangled bodies are found with their throats slit or their hearts punctured, but the killer is never discovered."

He held her tighter, letting her words sink in. She'd called the murderer a monster. "Do you know who the killer is? Another reincarnated soul who's out to get us?"

"It's not a human. The memories always grow fuzzy when I recount my death. Probably my brain's way of trying to spare me from the horror. But it's horrible anyway. I'm always with you when it happens. The monster is fast and grotesque. From what I've seen, he looks part-human, but his head has melted onto his shoulders in some way." She shivered.

"I feel teeth and claws. Sometimes I think I see a knife, but it could be a long claw. I don't know if it's a reincarnated beast or if it's the same one, living all these years in seclusion."

"Teeth and claws. Could it be a werewolf?" Could someone in his own pack be out to get him? It wouldn't be the first time a lower-level wolf had challenged for rank, nor the first time a mate had been targeted. James wasn't first-family. He didn't have an ounce of alpha blood in his body, but his solid track record and his friendship with the alpha had raised him in the ranks.

Not high enough to be challenged, though.

"It's possible. I don't know, but whatever it is, our coming together has awakened it."

"Do you know what started it? If it's a cycle, it must have a beginning. Maybe that's the puzzle we need to solve. If we can figure out what started it, then we can stop it."

She shook her head. "The farthest back I've gone is 1897, and I don't think that was the beginning." She rubbed at the goose bumps on her arms. "My death came as a surprise that time. Every time that I've experienced. If we did something in the past to trigger it, to make the monster come for us, I haven't regressed to that life."

"You need to do more then. Keep regressing back until you find what started it, and then we'll stop it together."

She dropped her face into her hands. "I can't."

"Why not?"

"For one, the older the life, the fuzzier the memories. Nothing is clear. The main reason, though…I can't experience another death again. It takes a toll on me. My connection to death is strong as it is, so actually experiencing my own death affects me as if I'm really dying. I need days to recover, and I'm not sure we have that much time."

From what he'd learned about imps, once they showed up, their master wasn't far behind. They couldn't spare days for her to recover. "I'll do it then. We'll call Natasha first thing in the morning and set up an appointment. I'll go back as many times as it takes to figure this out."

"No. You won't just be experiencing your own death. You'll have to watch me die too."

His heart sank. He'd endure his own death as many times as he had to in order to keep her safe. But to watch Odette die again and again? He might not be able to handle that.

He had to, though. "Then I better get it right the first time."

She searched his eyes, the uncertainty in her own transforming into resigned acceptance. "You'd better."

He took her face in his hands, pressing a kiss to her lips. "We'll figure this out together, okay? Solve the puzzle. Stop the cycle. Live to see tomorrow. We've got this."

"We do, don't we?" She smiled and slid her hand halfway up his thigh. "The monster never attacked during the day in the past, so I think it's safe to assume daylight is our friend. And the house is protected, so we're secure inside at night." Her grin turned devilish. "I think it might be best if you stayed here tonight…to be cautious. What do you think?"

His stomach tightened as her fingers inched higher up his leg, his heart pumping a flush of heat through his veins. "I think you might be right. Safety first."

"I'm glad we agree." The words barely escaped her lips before she took his mouth with hers. She kissed him urgently, her right hand squeezing his thigh as she slid her left behind his neck to pull him closer. Her warm vanilla scent tickled his senses, and the feel of her tongue tangling with his was enough to drive him mad.

His jeans grew tight across his groin, and he couldn't hold back the moan that rolled up from his core. He needed this woman. God, he wanted her to be his fate-bound, and at the moment, his wolf seemed to agree.

Sliding a hand behind her back, he leaned into her, hoping to lay her on the couch. She resisted, pushing him back instead and climbing into his lap. Straddling him, she roamed her hands across his chest, down lower…lower, until she reached the waistband of his jeans. Magic shimmied across his stomach as she slipped her fingers beneath his shirt and pressed her palms against his skin.

She broke from his mouth to glide her lips along his jaw, nipping at his earlobe as she tugged his shirt upward. Leaning back, she pulled it over his head and dropped it on the floor. Her pupils dilated, and her tongue slipped out to moisten her lips as her gaze wandered from his eyes down to the bulge in his pants, then back up to his chest. Good lord, the woman was sexy.

"I like your tattoo." She grazed her fingers over his left pec, tracing the pack emblem, a wolf head centered in a fleur-de-lis. "Is it a requirement to be in the pack?"

"No, but it shows our allegiance…"

She dipped her head and licked his nipple, sending a shock of electricity straight to his dick. A groan vibrated in his throat, and she grinned wickedly as she lifted her head and trailed her hands down his stomach.

As she locked eyes with him and popped the button on his jeans, he groaned and reached for her hands. "Are you sure you're ready for this?"

"You're my soulmate; I've always been ready." She tilted her head. "You're the one who's hesitant. Is something wrong?"

"No." His answer came quickly, but his wolf didn't hesitate to show him the image of the dream woman, which he immediately shoved to the back of his mind. "I'm making sure this is really what you want. That was quite a revelation you laid on me."

"Our souls are entwined, and I don't know how much time we have left. Let's not waste a minute of it. I want you, James."

Her sultry words wrapped around him like an electric blanket, filling him with warmth, caressing his skin, stroking his… Nope, that was her hand rubbing his cock through his jeans.

With a deep inhale, he squared his gaze on hers. "I want you too." That much he could honestly confirm.

Her lips curved into a mischievous grin. "Good." She tugged her shirt over her head and dropped it next to his.

Her black lace bra cupped her full breasts, and he glided his hands up her sides to tease her nipples through the fabric. She made an *mmm* sound and tilted her head back, leaning into his touch.

With her hands on his chest, she slid from his lap, lowering to her knees in front of him. His stomach clenched as she reached for his jeans, tugging them over his hips and down his legs. She pulled down his boxer-briefs next, her brow lifting as she licked her lips.

Oh, to have those perfect red lips around his dick…

Lifting from the floor, she leaned into him, taking his mouth in another kiss. The feel of her body pressed to his was enough to send him over the edge, but there was too much fabric between them. That needed to change.

As he reached for the clasp on her bra, she laughed and slid to the floor again. "You first." She ran a single finger down his dick from tip to base, sending a shudder through his body. As she wrapped her hand around him, his ability to form a coherent thought crumbled like cheap mortar on a poorly-made house.

Her tongue felt like velvet against his shaft, and as she took him into her mouth, the sensation of being engulfed in warm, rich honey had him dropping his head back onto the couch and moaning from somewhere deep in his core.

He needed to stop her. She should be the one to come first, but damn it, he'd lost the ability to form words.

She slid her mouth up his cock, rolling her tongue around the tip before taking him in fully again. He wouldn't last five minutes like this, so he lifted his head, placing a hand on her shoulder. But the electricity jolting through his core forced his eyes shut with the ecstasy.

A pounding on the window behind him drew him from his trance as Odette released her hold. Another bang, this time from the one to his left, sounded like it should have shattered the glass. "What the hell?"

She stood and peered through the pane. "There's something out there."

"No kidding." He rose to his feet, but with his pants around his ankles, he stumbled, catching himself on the arm of the loveseat before he could topple to the floor. "Damn it." He fumbled for his pants, yanking them the rest of the way off, and joining her at the window.

A black mass darted into the side yard, but in human form, James couldn't make out its shape in the darkness.

"You're sure nothing can get in?" He wrapped a protective arm around her.

"Positive. The spell is unbreakable." The confidence in her voice didn't mask the worry in her eyes.

"Stay inside this time, okay? I'll take care of it." He strode out of the room toward the back door.

CHAPTER ELEVEN

The moment he shut the door behind him, James shifted and bounded down the porch steps toward the fiend. He paused before he rounded the corner, angling his nose upward to catch its scent. The faint smell of swamp—decomposing foliage and mud—greeted his nostrils, but he didn't detect a trace of the rotting garbage odor that normally clung to demons.

The low growl in his throat was barely audible above the banging on the window. Whatever it was, it wanted inside badly.

James crept around the corner, and the entity whirled around to face him. He barely got a glimpse of the somewhat-human-shaped figure before it sprang from the ground, leaping over him and darting into the backyard.

What the hell? Hackles raised, James spun, ready to give chase.

But the entity had vanished.

Crouching low, he crept into the backyard, his senses on high alert. A shuffling sound emanated from above, and before he could lift his head, the creature dropped onto him, sinking its teeth into his neck.

Dammit, not again. Searing pain tore through his right side, and James yelped, spinning in a circle, jaws snapping until he finally connected with flesh. A garbled squeal—half-animal, half-human—ripped from the beast's throat before it released its hold and leaped over the fence.

James glanced over his shoulder and glimpsed Odette watching through the window, worry furrowing her brow. He hesitated, torn between the instinct to stay and protect her and the need to catch the creature who'd threatened them.

He trusted her magic, but could he trust her to stay put? He took the slight dip of her chin as confirmation she wouldn't leave the house, and blowing out a hard breath, he took off after the beast.

The monster moved faster than anything he'd encountered before, gaining a three-block lead on James before he'd cleared the fence. Even with his enhanced werewolf vision, James could barely make out the silhouette of a humanoid figure with a massive, oddly-shaped head sprinting up Treme Street toward Louis Armstrong Park.

At two a.m, most of the residents were inside their homes, but James kept to the shadows as best he could, running from tree to tree to keep himself hidden. The houses along the way quickly changed from the mansions of Millionaire's Row to small one and two-story cottages in shades of red, purple, and yellow. He ducked behind a parked car as a dilapidated truck ambled through the intersection, losing precious seconds in his chase.

If he continued to keep to the shadows, the monster would be out of sight within the next minute. *Screw it.* James sprinted down the center of the street. Whatever that *thing* was, it would draw more attention than he would. A werewolf sighting could be written off as an enormous dog.

James slowed as he reached St. Philip, where Treme ended and the park began, but movement behind the wrought-iron fence caught his attention. He increased his speed, hurdling the fence and plowing toward the creature.

Damn, this thing was fast. He searched his mind for another wolf to help him. Though they couldn't exactly hear each other's thoughts, werewolves had an almost telepathic connection. He briefly considered calling for Luke, but with Odette involved, this situation was too sticky to contact the alpha yet.

Come on, Cade. Where are you? He focused, feeling his way through the were energy like sifting through the sand to find a shell. When he found his friend, their minds connected, and he relayed the information. He needed help, or the bastard would get away.

With Cade on the move, James followed the creature out of the park and across Basin Street. *Please don't go into the cemetery.*

The beast vaulted over the concrete barrier and entered St. Louis Cemetery Number One. *Shit.*

With a running start, James leaped at the wall, catching it with his front paws and scrambling his back legs up and over. He landed on his side with a *thud*, knocking the breath from his lungs, and pain from his neck wound flashed from his skull to his shoulder.

He lay still for a moment, focusing on the sounds around him: a rat scurrying across the concrete walk, tires turning on the asphalt and the hum of an engine as a car passed, the wind whistling through the rows and rows of above-ground graves that housed the remains of multiple generations of New Orleanians.

Of all the places the beast could have picked to hide… James grunted and rose to his paws. He'd never find the bastard in the city of the dead. The only good thing about this situation was that the cemetery gates locked at dusk, so he didn't have to worry about any humans discovering him.

From massive mausoleums to short, single-family tombs, the graves rose from the ground, creating a labyrinth of twisting paths and dead-ends. Many of the tombs were well-cared for, with new plaster and fresh paint that made them gleam white in the moonlight. Others were crumbling, the plaster decaying to show the brick and mortar beneath.

His chest tightened as the fond memories of his weekends in the cemetery with his dad flooded his mind. Though he'd spent his time in a different cemetery, during the day, something about a graveyard always brought a sense of calmness over him. His dad too. Even through all the turmoil and heartache his mom had caused, James and his father could always find peace in the cemetery.

If he weren't on the trail of a murderous monster, he might have slowed down to enjoy the stillness. Instead, he focused on his senses, searching the darkness for evil.

With no sign of the beast, James wandered amongst the graves, pausing as he reached the end of a row and peering around the corner in hopes of catching the monster off-guard. But with the tombs laid out in no discernable pattern, he soon found himself backtracking, covering the same spaces with no luck.

"James, you still in here?" Noah's hushed voice came from a few rows over, and James searched his mind for Cade.

Connecting with the other wolf, James relayed his location, and the three of them met in front of the famous Voodoo priestess, Marie Laveau's, tomb. Cade's deep-red fur stood in a ridge along his back, and his ears twitched.

Noah looked from wolf to wolf. "What's the plan?" He paused as if they could answer. Because Noah was second-born and couldn't shift, he lacked the telepathic connection that shifting wolves shared. "Let me guess. We split up and scour the place. Yell if we find it?"

What he lacked in ability, Noah made up for in intelligence. James bobbed his head to indicate his agreement, and the men went in different directions, searching for the monster.

Half an hour later, James returned to Marie Laveau's tomb and sat in front of it. Though it had been repainted several times, the small black Xs still showed through. Rumor had it that if a person drew three Xs on the tomb, spun around three times, and left an offering, the Mambo's Spirit would grant his wish.

He'd always thought it hokum, but after spending time with Odette and learning about Baron Samedi, he couldn't help but wonder if there was any truth to the tale. Cade returned in human form, and Noah joined them shortly after.

"What the hell were you chasing?" Cade scanned the area, still on high alert. "The image was fuzzy in your mind."

James rose to all fours. He'd never gotten a clear look at the creature, but it seemed to match Odette's description. When he didn't answer, Cade furrowed his brow.

"C'mon, man. Shift and let's get out of here. This place gives me the creeps."

James growled low in his throat. They'd have to walk ten blocks to get back to Odette's, and he had a slight problem with doing that in human form.

"Do you know what's wrong with him?" Noah asked Cade.

Cade crossed his arms and shook his head. "Are you hurt? There's blood in your fur."

James let out his breath in a huff. Yes, he was hurt, and if he were a full werewolf, it would have healed by now. His injury wasn't the problem, though if his friends tried to coddle him, it would become one—for them.

The corner of Noah's mouth twitched before turning into a full-blown grin. "Wait a minute. You said he was coming from Odette's place, right?"

Cade shrugged. "Yeah."

Noah chuckled. "You're naked, aren't you? You were banging the Baroness when it happened."

Baring his teeth, James let out a menacing growl. Noah needed to show respect for his girlfriend, and if he could form words, he'd tell him so.

Cade guffawed. "Oh, man. This is classic. Give him your pants, Noah."

"No way. You give him yours."

"I don't think he wants mine. I'm commando underneath."

Noah groaned and crossed his arms. "He's not getting my pants. He made it here in wolf form; he can make it back. We'll meet you at Odette's."

At least one of them was making sense. Backing up a few steps, James sprang onto a tomb and then vaulted over the cemetery wall.

Not the smartest move he could have made.

He overshot his target and landed in the road. A horn blared as a car speeding down St. Louis street slammed on its brakes. James scrambled onto the sidewalk, cursing himself for his lack of caution, and the passenger rolled down the window and stared, wide-eyed, as the vehicle crept past. Damn it, he didn't have time for this. He needed to get back to Odette.

Another car passed, and he raced across the road, determined to get his ass out of view. But he wasn't fast enough.

"Holy shit." A police officer with dark hair and a beer belly rounded the corner and nudged his partner, gesturing toward James as he unclipped his gun from its holster.

The taller man stopped and cocked his head, his right hand resting on his firearm. "Is that a wolf?"

Shit. Shit, shit, shit.

Ten more feet and he'd have made it to the public parking lot where he could have hidden amongst the vehicles. Instead, he stood, fully exposed, beneath a street lamp, two cops cautiously approaching with their guns drawn. If he took off now, they'd shoot. Hit him in the heart or head, and he'd be dead.

Sucking in a deep breath, he forced himself to relax to get the ridge of hair running down his back to lay flat. Best to not look menacing to innocent humans with the power to kill him.

"There you are." Noah took off his belt and jogged toward him. "You can't run off like that, buddy." He sweetened his voice, talking to James like he was a dog.

A goddamn dog.

"I told you that leash was a piece of crap." Cade strode up and stopped by Noah. "Snapped in half the first time you used it, didn't it?"

"The leash snapped because you yanked it so hard. Pulled the poor guy's collar right off his neck." Noah held the belt toward James.

James huffed and backed up. No way in hell was he pretending to be a domesticated house pet.

"You don't have much of a choice here, man," Noah whispered under his breath.

One of the officers holstered his gun. Beer belly held his tight by his side. "This your dog?"

"Yes, sir." Noah plastered on a smile and slipped the belt around James's neck. "We're on our way home."

"Why's he bleeding?" The tall guy nodded toward James's shoulder.

"Oh, uh..." Noah squinted at his blood-soaked fur. "He tried to squeeze through a broken fence. Sharp edge of wrought-iron got him. We'll take care of it when we get home."

"Biggest damn dog I've ever seen." Chubby adjusted his grip on his gun, and sweat beaded on his upper lip.

Cade moved to James's other side, flanking him. "He's harmless." He scratched him behind the ear, and James gritted his teeth to stop himself from snapping at his friend.

"Holster your weapon, LeClerc." The taller officer stepped closer, while LeClerc did as he was told. "How'd you domesticate him? He's a wolf, right?"

"He's half-wolf. His domesticated side drains the wild right out of him, doesn't it, buddy?" Cade patted his head, and James held in a growl. "He's not nearly as tough as a full-wolf would be."

James jerked his head from Cade's grasp. That comment better not have been a jab at his lineage. His mom's humanity was common knowledge, but James worked overtime to make up for what he lacked. No one called him a lesser wolf.

"Can I pet him?" The cop reached a hand toward James.

"Uh…" Noah started, but Cade cut him off.

"Sure. He's a sweetheart."

Noah tightened his grip on the belt. He couldn't have held James back if he tried, but the gesture reminded him to play the part in front of the cops. As soon as he was alone with Cade, though…

His friends exchanged a few more words with the officers, and then they headed back toward Odette's. James tugged from Noah's grasp, but his friend clutched the belt again.

"Do you want to draw any more attention? Just a few more blocks."

Cade laughed. "Yeah, buddy. Be a good boy." He rubbed the top of James's head.

He didn't hold back this time. A menacing growl rolled up from his core, and he snapped his jaws, clamping onto Cade's hand, his teeth penetrating to the bone.

"Ow! Damn it, what was that for?" As if he didn't know. Cade tried to pull his hand from James's maw.

Coppery blood oozed into James's mouth, and he tightened his grip, his growl turning into a snarl.

"The half-wolf comment was a low blow," Noah said.

Cade sucked in a breath through his teeth. "I'm sorry, okay? But you knew I was joking."

James released his hand and blew out a hard breath. A sliver of truth laced every so-called joke, and Cade needed to remember his place. James would always out-rank him.

They reached Odette's and searched the perimeter, but they found no sign of the creature. Cade's wound had healed by the time they made it to the front porch, and he lifted his hand to knock as the lock disengaged and Odette opened the door.

She started to speak, but whatever she'd planned to say got stuck in her throat when her eyes met James's. She flicked her gaze to Cade and then Noah before opening the door wider and ushering them all inside.

James narrowed his eyes at his friends, a silent message for them to stay in the foyer, before trotting through the kitchen to Odette's bedroom.

She followed on his heels. "Is everything okay? What happened?"

He shifted to human form and fumbled to right his inside-out jeans. Anger fumed in his chest. Anger at Cade for being an ass. At Noah for the idiotic idea of acting like he was a dog. But most of all at himself for not killing the creature when he had the chance.

"Here. Let me do that." She took his jeans and righted them while he yanked on his underwear. "I take it the demon got away?"

"That was no demon." He shoved his legs into pants, and Odette brushed her fingers across his neck.

"It hurt you."

He touched the wound. Two scratches were all that remained of the gash the creature had torn in his shoulder. He'd healed, but not fast enough to hide it from her or his friends. Then Cade called him harmless because he was only half-wolf… He'd show the jackass harmless.

"I'm fine." He pulled on his shirt and clutched her shoulders. "Did it come back here?"

"I don't think so. It hasn't tried to get in if it did."

Nodding, he took her hand and led her to the foyer. As soon as his gaze met Cade's he dropped her hand and lunged for him, slamming his back against the closed door, his forearm pressing the air from his lungs. "If you *ever* pull a stunt like that again, your ass will be mine. Understood?"

Cade scowled. "What about him?" He gestured with his head toward Noah. "The whole thing was his idea. Aren't you going to bite him too?"

Odette gasped. "You bit him?"

"He was treating me like a dog." He leaned his weight into Cade, showing his dominance.

"We saved your ass and kept the pack's secret safe." Cade's voice strained under the pressure.

"He's right." Noah placed a hand on James's shoulder. "I'm sorry it had to be that way, but the pack does come first."

He glanced at his friend. When did Noah become the voice of reason? "I see your point." He looked into Cade's eyes, holding his gaze, asserting his dominance again. James may have been wrong to challenge his friend, but he wasn't about to lose a fight.

Cade glared at him briefly before lowering his head and dropping his gaze to the floor, ending the confrontation.

Odette clutched his arm, gently tugging until he stepped back, and Cade brushed the front of his shirt as if brushing off the threat.

Wrapping his arms around her, James kissed her forehead and unclenched his jaw. "I'm sorry I didn't end this today."

She leaned into him, resting her hands on his shoulders. "I didn't expect you to. If it's going to end, we have to do it together."

She was right. In his attempt to prove himself capable of protecting her, he'd blown their chance at defeating the monster. They were stuck in this cycle together, so they'd have to work together to end it. No more leaving her behind while he tried to fight the bad guys.

He turned to Cade and offered his hand. "Sorry, man. Thanks for your help out there."

Cade accepted the handshake. "Me too." He glanced at Odette. "Are you going to call Luke?"

James raked a hand through his hair. As the alpha, Luke needed to know what was going on, but as his boss… "Shit. It's complicated. I…"

"You broke the no sleeping with clients rule." Noah failed at hiding his smile.

Odette laughed and slid an arm around James's waist, resting her other hand on his chest. "It's okay. We haven't slept together…yet." She pinched his side as she said the last word, and he jumped.

Noah chuckled. "He still has to explain to the alpha why he was at your house at two a.m…naked."

She laid her head on his shoulder. "I think he'll make an exception in this case. This isn't our first life together. We're soulmates."

Oh, hell. She went there.

"She's your fate-bound?" Cade cracked a smile and slapped James on the shoulder. "Why didn't you say so? Congrats."

James slipped from Odette's hold and ushered his friends toward the door. "We've got it under control here. Why don't you give Luke a preliminary report and tell him I'll call him tomorrow?" He opened the door and shoved them through, following them onto the porch.

"Congratulations." Noah shook his hand. "It's about time."

"Like I said, it's complicated. Just…don't say anything about this, okay?" He gestured to the door. "Tell him about the monster; I'll fill him in on the rest later."

Cade looked at him incredulously. "What could possibly be complicated about finding your fated mate?"

How about the fact that his half-human wolf insisted he needed two mates? He gripped the doorknob. "Thanks for your help tonight. I'll talk to y'all tomorrow."

He went inside to find Odette waiting for him in the foyer, wringing her hands and biting her lower lip. "That was it, wasn't it? The monster that wants to kill us both? It was too big to be an imp."

"I'm afraid so."

Her brow lifted, and for the first time since he'd met her, true fear glinted in her eyes. "What was it?"

"I don't know. It smelled like swamp, so it wasn't a demon. It was human-shaped. Kinda. Its limbs were longer than a person's, and its head was… It's hard to say because it moved so fucking fast, but its head looked like it had melted onto its shoulders like you described. It stayed in the shadows, so I never got a good look at it, but when it bit me, it felt like a wolf bite."

"It sounds like it's the same beast."

He took her in his arms and hugged her tight. "Sure does. What are we going to do?"

"Are you still up for doing a past-life regression? The monster always kills me first, so maybe you'll see more than I do."

His breath hung on her words. Reliving her death and his own wasn't the slightest bit appealing. Could he even handle the trauma? If it would help them fight the thing in this life… "Now?"

She shook her head. "It's three-thirty in the morning. I'll call Natasha tomorrow to set it up."

"Sounds like a plan." He stood still, holding her, memorizing the way she fit in his arms. Like she was made for him. "What should we do until then?"

She slid her hands into his back pockets and gave his ass a squeeze. "How about we finish what we started?"

That he could handle.

CHAPTER TWELVE

The overcast sky blocked the moonlight from illuminating the bedroom, but the hall light filtering in through the open door cast enough glow for Odette to see the seductive smile on James's lips. He removed his shirt for the second time tonight, and she couldn't fight her own smile as she took in his chiseled features. Perfectly defined abs rolled down his stomach, accented by the V disappearing into his jeans.

Oh, that delicious V…

The monster had found them. Death was knocking on their door, but if her time on this Earth was limited, she wanted to get more than a taste of him before she had to go. Slinking toward him, she ran her fingers down his chest, lightly grazing his soft skin. His stomach tightened as she reached his jeans, the muscles becoming even more defined as he held his breath.

When she popped the button and slid down the zipper, a slow hiss escaped his lips. He caught her hands and brought them to his mouth. "This time, you have to get naked too."

"I suppose that's fair." She hadn't begun to have her way with him, but if he wanted to see her, she could afford him that.

She stepped back, peeling her shirt over her head and unclasping her bra, letting it fall to the floor. "Better?"

An appreciative growl rumbled in his chest. "Getting there." He pulled her into an embrace, taking her mouth in a kiss.

Leaning into him, she allowed herself a moment of vulnerability, getting lost in the feel of his strong arms wrapped around her, the warmth of his bare skin against hers and the magic sizzling between them making her shiver with need.

Before she could get too lost, though, she pulled away. "Take off your pants."

James grinned. "My pleasure." He removed the rest of his clothes and stood before her, holding his hands out to his sides. "Your turn."

She let her gaze travel the length of his magnificent body, lingering on his dick, hard and ready, before she stepped toward him and took him in her hand. She stroked him, pressing her lips to his neck and running her tongue up to his ear lobe.

His eyes fluttered shut as a moan slipped from his throat, and he reached for the button on her pants. Stepping away, she pushed him onto the bed. He chuckled and scooted to the center of the mattress. When she didn't move, he arched a brow. "You are planning to join me, aren't you?"

"I have lots of plans for you, James." She unbuttoned her slacks and slid the zipper down. As she worked them over her hips, he rolled onto his side, his blue eyes smoldering in the dim light.

"You are the most beautiful woman I've ever met." His baritone voice wrapped around her, his words encircling her heart, holding it tight. He opened his mouth as if to say more, but his brow furrowed, a look of confusion tightening his eyes briefly before he composed himself.

"Everything okay?"

He blinked. "It would be a lot better if you climbed into bed with me."

She slinked toward him and crawled onto the mattress. He rose onto an elbow, taking her face in his hand and leaning into her as if to put her on her back. When his lips met hers, she clutched his shoulder, pushing him to the sheets and straddling him.

He laughed. "You like to be in control, don't you?"

"Always." She kissed his neck, nipping at his skin as she worked her way down to his shoulder, the taste of him, his intoxicating, warm scent making her blood hum.

"So do I." Faster than should have been possible, he wrapped an arm around her and flipped her onto her back. Clasping a hand in each of his, he raised them above her head, pinning her to the pillow.

She gasped, her first instinct tempting her to wiggle free, to regain control. But she couldn't deny the thrilling quivers shooting through her core, sparking like fireworks inside her. "You're strong."

"I'm a werewolf, and right now, both man and beast want to ravish you." He glided his hands down her arms, across her chest to cup her breasts. As his thumbs teased her nipples, another explosion of sparks ricocheted through her core.

She could do this. She was in control of every aspect of her life. If she were to let go somewhere, here in the bedroom, with her soulmate, was the best place to do it.

He lowered his mouth to her breast and took her nipple between his teeth. Tugging gently, he released her and moved to the other side. He teased her with his tongue, roaming his hands across her body, the roughness of his palms reminding her what a strong, capable man he was. His deep, woodsy scent. The way he touched her. The appreciative growls rolling up from his chest as he caressed her… He was everything she'd dreamed he would be.

"Are you on birth control?" His lips moved against her skin.

"Of course."

"Then we only have one problem." He pressed a kiss between her breasts and rose onto his elbows to look at her.

"We do?"

"You're still not naked." Sitting up, he grasped her panties and slid them down her legs. "I like black lace, but it's time for these to go." He dropped them on the floor and lifted her leg, running his hand from her ankle up to the center of her inner thigh.

Her pulse sprinted as he settled between her legs. She was completely naked, on her back. Vulnerable.

But that was okay. It was her choice to let him take the lead, so she was still in control. She could do this.

He rubbed his cheek against her thigh, the scruff on his skin tickling her. His breath warmed her center, and a war waged between her body and her mind. She wanted him to touch her—to lick her—like she'd never wanted anything in her life. But to allow him to do that to her. To let him take her to the edge, at his pace and not hers, would mean completely letting go.

She was about to die anyway. For once in her life, she could do it. Just this once. With James.

He slipped out his tongue and tasted her, the sensation of warm velvet enveloping her as a moan vibrated across his lips. He licked her again, and a shudder ran through her entire body.

"I can feel your magic getting stronger." His lips moved against her. "It's incredible."

Incredible didn't begin to describe the way he was making her feel, but…

Her heart pounded, icy panic flushing through her veins. She couldn't do this. Couldn't lose control. She'd made a promise to herself. "Please stop."

He froze, his mouth hovering above her center.

"I can't do this." She sat up, scooting back to lean against the headboard.

Confusion contorted his features as he rose onto his knees. "Did I hurt you?"

"No." She shook her head. "I just can't."

Pressing his lips together, he blew out a hard breath. "Should I leave?"

"No. Stay please." She pulled up the sheet, covering herself.

He rubbed his forehead. "If I did something wrong…"

"You didn't do anything wrong. Everything you've done has been amazing. It's…" How could she explain this?

"Wait…are you a virgin?"

She laughed at the dumbfounded expression on his face. "Of course not. Lie down with me. Come here." She pulled back the sheet and patted the space next to her as she lay on her side.

He settled near her, face to face, but not touching. She needed his touch. If she didn't explain her little freak-out quickly, she would ruin the night. Taking his hand, she reached a leg to his, planning to drape it across him. As soon as she touched him, he moved, entwining her leg between his. Holding her.

"What's going on?" Concern filled his eyes, making her heart ache.

She felt like such an idiot. She'd never put herself in this position before. The few men she had slept with had been much more passive than James, allowing her to take the lead. They also didn't have as much interest in her pleasure, none of them protesting when she'd made sure all the focus went to their orgasms and not her own. "I've never let anyone do that to me before."

"Why not?"

She bit her bottom lip and searched his eyes. His puzzled expression morphed into one of compassion, and her reservations dissolved. She could trust this man. It was time to tell him the truth about her past. Some of it anyway. "I'm a bit of a control freak."

He chuckled. "Really? I couldn't tell."

"I have a good reason."

He pressed a kiss to the back of her hand and scooted closer to her. "What does that have to do with what we were just doing?"

"I felt…vulnerable. Exposed. Letting you do that to me…you were in control of my body. That's scary."

Gliding his fingers down her side, he rested a hand on her hip. "I wasn't trying to hurt you. If I did, I'm very sorry."

"You didn't hurt me." She was doing a terrible job of explaining this. *Tell the man. He's not going anywhere.* "Losing control is something I haven't allowed myself to do since I was a kid. Since I moved away."

"What happened when you were a kid?"

She bit her lip, hesitating. "It's a long story."

"I want to know."

Sweet Spirits, she was going to tell him. Lifting her head, she propped it up with her hand. "My dad is Catholic. Completely mundane."

He moved to mirror her posture. "I never would have guessed you didn't have magic from both sides."

"When my mom died, my dad wanted me to continue with Voodoo, but he didn't have a clue how to teach me. So, he sent me to stay with my uncle on the weekends. He had a place out in the swamp." She inhaled deeply to calm her sprinting heart.

"This is your mom's brother?"

She nodded.

"Why did he live in the swamp?" He looked at her intently, his eyes gleaming in the dim light.

"He was a *traiteur*. An extremely powerful faith healer." She stared at their hands entwined on the sheet as the memories came flooding back, and she swallowed the thickness from her throat. "He claimed to be a *traiteur* anyway. Turns out he was much more than a healer, though I didn't know it at the time. My mom had died. I was weak, and he preyed on my weakness, using my powers in ways Baron Samedi never intended them to be used."

"You can do more than communicate with the dead." He continued to hold her gaze, his silence willing her to elaborate.

A normal person, even a werewolf, would turn tail and run if he knew the extent of Odette's power. Her aura alone intimidated most, leaving her with few friends and a distillery full of employees who walked on eggshells.

James was different. He was the first person who wasn't afraid to stand up to her. Even when she'd allowed her power to build, and he'd felt it, he didn't run. She hadn't scared him off yet, and if she planned to spend the rest of her life with him, no matter how short that life may be, he deserved to know her.

"I can control the dead." The words rushed out like a river breaking down a dam, and as the last one left her lips, the constant pressure building inside her for years flooded out with it.

He blinked. "Control?"

"Bend them to my will. Make them do whatever I want them to. My connection to the spirit world is constant. I'm like a conduit. I can channel the energy from that realm and feed it to spirits that are trapped here, giving them abilities dead people shouldn't have. I..."

She inhaled deeply, trying to quell the nausea churning in her stomach. He hadn't recoiled yet. Not that he could have with the vise-grip she had on his hand. She relaxed her fingers and continued, "My uncle was a *bokor*."

"He practiced black magic?"

"Yes, but I didn't know it at the time. I was doing what I was told. I didn't…"

"Hey." He traced his fingertips down her cheek, lifting her chin so she looked at him. "You don't have to defend yourself to me. We've all done things we aren't proud of. You were a kid."

"It's very rare to be crowned by Baron Samedi. If I hadn't died the day I was born, I…" She shook her head. Now wasn't the time for what-ifs. "My uncle recognized my power. He used me to…" She brushed the hair from her forehead, giving James ample time to mull over her words. To get the hell out if he wanted to.

When he didn't move, she continued. "He used black magic to take a piece of a person's soul. But once the soul fragment was severed, he couldn't do anything with it. It would pass on to the spirit realm, and the sick person, who had come to him for help, would die. But I could control the spirit energy. He forced me to put the soul pieces in *ouangas*, jars created to hold spirits. He told me it was for safekeeping. That the people were sick and storing part of their soul would keep them alive."

She lowered her head to the pillow. "I thought it was wrong, but I did it anyway. I mean, they were dying if I didn't store their souls, so why not? And using my power feels so good. It's like a…spiritual orgasm. Stress, worry, all my earthly emotions dissolve, and I feel nothing but bliss."

"I've felt that coming off of you. Why is that?"

"Baron Samedi, and all the loa of the Ghede family, understand that death is the one guarantee in life. All the things we stress about really don't matter, because we're all going to die one day. So we should live life to the fullest. Enjoy every minute of the time we have here because that time is borrowed. When I use my magic, their philosophy fills me, and it's the most amazing thing I've ever felt."

"But you seem to live in opposition to that philosophy."

"Because my uncle wasn't helping the people by storing their souls. He kept them so that when they died, he could control their spirits. He wanted my power, but since Baron Samedi wouldn't grant it to him, he found a loophole. Own a piece of the soul, control the spirit. He was an evil man, and I helped him."

She rolled onto her back and squeezed her eyes shut, the shame of what she'd done raising heat in her cheeks. "But I stopped. Baron Samedi was angry with me, and I stopped. I got away. I…" A shudder ran through her body, and she clamped her mouth shut. He didn't need to know all the gory details.

"How old were you?"

She stared at the ceiling fan whirring above, her gaze latching onto a single blade and following it on its dizzying, circular path. "Twelve."

"That must have been scary." He rested a hand on her shoulder, the warmth of his skin pulling her from the memory and into the present.

"You have no idea. Anyway, I begged my dad to take me away from New Orleans. I wanted nothing to do with Voodoo, my powers, or Baron Samedi ever again."

He scooted closer, pulling her body to his. "So you ran away from everything?"

She'd been on the verge of tears, ready to make a beeline for the bathroom so he wouldn't see her cry, but the warmth and firmness of his embrace grounded her, giving her strength. She didn't need to hide from this man. "I turned my back on my religion and my home, but I couldn't run from myself. My magic follows me wherever I go. Spirits will always be drawn to me."

He kissed her forehead, her cheek, her lips. "I'm glad you came back."

"I had to. The Baron came to me in my dreams. The distillery was about to go under. I owe my life to my *met tet*, and I'd abandoned him. I thought coming back and making his distillery successful again would put me back in his good graces, but I was wrong. He's been appeased, but he's still not happy with me."

"Because you're so uptight?" One corner of his lip tugged into a tentative grin.

She opened her mouth to argue, but what could she say? She was the most uptight person she knew. It was a miracle this rough-around-the-edges werewolf found her attractive at all. "I've been in total control of every aspect of my life for as long as I can remember, and it's worked for me. Then you came along and started chipping away at my façade, restoring the real me that I've kept suppressed all these years. It's terrifying, but I also kinda like it."

And it was time she went with it. She trusted James down to her bones. Relinquishing a little bit of control with him would be good for her; she could control her magic with him. She traced her finger down his nose to his lips, tugging the bottom one down before pressing her mouth to his.

Sliding his hand to her hip, he opened for her, tangling his tongue with hers. He leaned into her, the evidence of his desire pressing against her thigh, sending a flood of warmth through her core. As he broke the kiss, she couldn't stop the moan of protest from escaping her throat.

He twirled a curl around his finger and glided the back of his hand down her cheek. "I would never try to control you or to make you do anything you didn't want to do."

"I know." She kissed him again, trailing her lips across his jaw and down his neck, inhaling his intoxicatingly masculine scent. His pheromones were tuned specifically to her senses, and each inhale brought on a fresh wave of desire. "James?"

"Hmm?" He slid his fingers into her hair and tilted his head, giving her better access to his neck.

That small gesture made her breath catch and pressure build in the back of her eyes. For a werewolf to willingly expose his neck, to make himself even slightly vulnerable, showed a level of trust she would never deserve.

When she didn't move, he pulled back to look into her eyes. "You were going to say something?" Did he even realize what he'd communicated with his body language?

It was time she did the same for him. "Do you think we could try that again? I promise not to freak out this time."

A crooked, kissable grin lit on his lips. "I would like nothing more than to make you come, my dear." He rolled her onto her back, his gaze locking with hers as he ran his hand down her body. If he was looking for signs of fear or panic, he wouldn't find them. She was ready this time.

His eyes smoldered as he settled his shoulders between her legs. "Where were we?" His breath tickled across her center, tightening her core.

She was *so* ready.

As he flicked out his tongue to lick her, she gasped at the electrical sensation pulsing through her core. He paused, giving her plenty of time to change her mind, but there was no turning back now. She was in this, and they were going all the way.

An *mmm* vibrated across his lips as his tension eased, and he licked her again, gently sucking her into his mouth and working her in circles with his tongue. Goose bumps pricked at her skin, every nerve in her body firing on overdrive as she allowed the enthralling sensations to overcome her.

She let go, giving in to the passion as her soulmate took her to the edge. He slipped a finger inside her, and she moaned. When a second finger slid in, she screamed his name. Her orgasm exploded inside her, unraveling her senses, tearing down her walls, making it impossible for her to hide. Her body was his to command, and he was a master. *Sweet Spirits*, was he good.

He slowed his pace, gently bringing her down from the wave of sheer ecstasy. Her breathing under control, she opened her eyes to find him watching her, a hunger in his eyes so palpable she could taste his need.

He growled as he mounted her, and with one swift thrust of his hips, he filled her, sending another explosion of fiery energy flowing through her veins. Nuzzling into her neck, he began moving, slowly at first, the delicious friction sending a shock of electricity through her core.

His pace quickened, and she clutched his shoulders, wrapping her legs around his waist and giving herself to him. His magic caressed her skin, seeping into her core to mingle with her own. For the first time in her life, she didn't hold back. She let her power build, the peaceful emptiness of the spirit world channeling through her, vibrating in her aura.

James moaned and pressed his lips to her ear. "God, this feels so good, Odette."

The thick, raspy tone of his voice sent her over the edge again. As her climax ripped through her, James moved faster, harder, until he found his own release and collapsed on top of her, panting.

They lay there, holding each other, a tangle of pounding hearts and liquid limbs, until their breathing slowed and he rose onto his elbows. "You are one amazing woman, Odette Allemand." He rolled to his side, tugging her body to his. "That was…wow."

"*Wow* is the perfect word to describe it." A bubbly, giddy sensation rose from her stomach to her chest, and she smiled as he moved to his back and held her even closer. She had let go, surrendered control and let James take her to a place she thought she'd never experience in her life. She'd put her trust and faith in him, and he did not disappoint.

Of course he didn't. He belonged with her.

Snuggling into his side, she let his warmth and his woodsy scent envelop her, calming her. They were perfect together, and if they got along this well in the bedroom, surely, they could work together to defeat the monster. She'd been resigned to her tragic fate before, but for the first time, the hope that she could change it lighted in her heart.

CHAPTER THIRTEEN

JAMES LAY ON HIS BACK, NESTLED IN THE CENTER OF ODETTE'S bed, listening to the melodic rhythm of the rain falling against the window panes. With her leg draped across his, her head resting on his shoulder, he could've lain there all day, basking in the afterglow. It was Saturday morning, so he just might. He kissed the top of her head.

Making love to her had been more intense than he'd ever imagined. No doubt they had a soul-deep connection. Once they'd begun, his wolf hadn't interrupted him with visions of the dream woman… until the very end as Odette fell asleep in his arms. He'd pushed the image aside, and he would continue to do so until his wolf relented and would be satisfied with one mate. With Odette.

With a sleepy sigh, she snuggled in closer and pressed a kiss to his chest. Lightly grazing his skin with her fingertips, she tilted her head toward his. "If this is what it's like being mated to a werewolf, I think I'm going to like it."

His heart missed a beat before slamming against his chest. He wasn't ready to *officially* become mates. Not when his wolf's heart was still divided. Scrambling through their conversations, he searched for anything he might have said that would give her an idea like that.

She'd called them soulmates, but he'd been careful not to confirm it. *Shit.* He needed more time.

She propped her head on her hand and smiled. "Normally it would be way too soon for this, but considering the circumstances, I'm going to say it. I love you, James."

He opened his mouth, but he couldn't make a sound pass over the baseball-sized lump in his throat.

Her brow furrowed as her smile twitched and then faded. "You don't have to say it back. I know it's rushed. I just wanted you to know, in case anything happens before…" She shrugged and swallowed hard.

"Um…" He let out a nervous chuckle. "We might not live to see tomorrow. No sense in rushing into anything." Pushing to a sitting position, he leaned his back against the headboard. "Taking a mate is a big step. It's not something to do because you're scared."

"I'm not saying it because I'm scared." Hurt flashed in her eyes before she sat up and pulled the sheet to her chest. "I'm saying it because I mean it, and I wanted you to know."

He chewed his bottom lip and stared at his hands clutched in his lap. He wanted, more than anything, to take her in his arms and tell her he loved her too. That they'd spend the rest of their lives together.

But he couldn't make a promise like that unless he knew he'd be able to keep it.

When he didn't say anything, she slid out of bed and put on a dark-purple satin robe, cinching it at her waist. "I'm not wrong. We are soulmates, and you may not love me yet, but if we have time, you will. It's fate. And what we did last night…that meant something to me. It meant everything."

He groaned and rolled out of bed to pull on his underwear. "I know. It was special to me too, and it's not that I don't love you."

She crossed her arms. "Do you love me?"

"I…" His phone rang from the heap of clothes on the floor, and he cut his gaze toward it.

Odette narrowed her eyes, daring him to answer it. "What is it then? Is there someone else?"

The phone quieted, taking his one hope for a time-out from this conversation with it, and he hesitated. He wanted to tell her no, that she was the only one for him, but she took his immediate silence as confirmation.

Her mouth dropped open, her eyes widening in disbelief. "You're seeing someone else?"

"No." This time the answer came instantly. "I'm not seeing anyone else. My wolf…"

"Your wolf is seeing someone else? What? You've got a girl wolf out in the swamp that you screw when you go hunting?"

"No. That's not it." Frustration grated his nerves. He'd never been good at vocalizing his emotions, and his lack of eloquence wasn't helping this conversation. "There's something—"

His phone rang again, and he rose from the bed. "I need to answer that. It could be the alpha."

"By all means." She gestured toward the sound, her irritation obvious in her jerky movements. Could this situation get any worse?

He pressed the phone to his ear. "Hey, Luke. I was going to call you—"

"We've got a problem. Six people dead. Looks supernatural. Get your ass to the bar. Now." The alpha ended the call. Yep, things got worse.

He raked a hand through his hair and turned to Odette. She stood rigid, her arms crossed over her chest, the power building in her aura causing his neck hairs to stand on end. The pull of death around her hollowed out the space, and for a brief moment, his self-preservation instinct persuaded him to run. But she couldn't scare him into submission.

"That trick doesn't work on me."

She dropped her arms to her sides, her posture relaxing slightly. "I didn't realize I was doing anything."

"That was Luke. I have to go, but this conversation is not over." He had to come clean about his problem, but telling the woman who loved him—who was convinced they were bound by fate—that there could be another would crush her. Hurting Odette was the last thing he wanted to do, but he owed her the truth.

He shoved his legs into his jeans and pulled on his shirt before taking her shoulders in his hands and kissing her cheek. "I will be back as soon as I can, but know this… I am not seeing anyone else. What we did last night was special, and I don't regret a thing. But I do have a problem, and I will tell you all about it when I get back, okay?"

She chewed her bottom lip and nodded.

"Will you be here?"

"I'm not going anywhere."

Sliding his fingers into her hair, he kissed her forehead. "Good. Hopefully this won't take long."

James parked two blocks from O'Malley's and shoved his hands in his pockets as he trekked up the sidewalk to the werewolves' HQ. The rain had stopped, and the morning sun hadn't risen above the buildings, sparing him from its sweltering intensity, but enough humidity hung in the air to make his skin feel like he was walking through a sauna.

A thin layer of water and soap coated the street from its daily early-morning washing from city services, and a mass of dirt-tinged bubbles collected around a storm drain. Situated on St. Philip, O'Malley's sat far enough away from the party end of Bourbon Street to avoid most of the mess and sour smells the tourists deposited overnight, but James welcomed the fresh scent of soap each day, reminding him every morning was a fresh start.

And he'd royally screwed his start to this morning.

A blast of cold air from above mussed his hair as he stepped through the pub door, but he didn't bother smoothing it into place. He hadn't even glanced in a mirror before he left Odette's.

Amber gave him a solemn nod of her head as he stomped past the bar and pushed open the swinging door that led to the back rooms.

Six people dead? If the monster that showed up at Odette's house last night was responsible and he'd missed his chance at stopping it… Damn him and his inadequacies.

Two exposed light bulbs lit the narrow, brick-lined corridor, and his shoes thudded on the concrete floor. He found Luke's office door ajar, the lights inside turned off, and his stomach soured. The people invited to this meeting wouldn't fit inside his office, so he must have summoned the entire demon-hunting team. *Shit.*

He used his shoulder to shove the heavy door to the meeting room open and strode inside. Yep, every werewolf on the team, plus a few extras, filled the folding chairs that sat in a semicircle around a podium. Cade acknowledged him with an eyebrow raise, and Luke nodded as James took a seat next to Macey, the alpha's mate.

"Now that everyone's here, we'll get started." Luke swept his gaze across the pack. "Like you were told on the phone, we've got six bodies with lacerations to the throats and chests that look like teeth and claw marks."

Chase, the pack's second-in-command and James's old hunting buddy, stood next to the alpha. Colorful tattoos sleeved both his arms, and his eyebrow piercing glinted in the overhead light as he stroked his dark-brown beard. "They were all couples, three men and three women. Two couples were found last night and one the night before."

James sank lower in his chair. Had the monster come looking for him and Odette the night before, and the unlucky couple had been its consolation prize when it couldn't find them? No, it was possible the events were unrelated. He hadn't seen hide nor tail of the monster the previous night. Then again, he hadn't spent the night with Odette.

Luke looked at his mate. "Macey, what's happening with the police?"

She stood and strode to the podium. The detective wore her long, blonde hair slicked back into a bun at the nape of her neck, and her bright-green eyes held a fierce determination. Though she was second-born and stood nearly a foot shorter than the alpha, she was a hell of a fighter and as tough as any shifter James knew. "At the moment, we have one witness, though her credibility is in question. The roommate of the second pair of victims claimed to see a deformed man climb in through the living room window and walk right past her to the couple in the back bedroom. She described him as tall and lanky, with longer-than-normal arms and a head that looked like it had melted onto his shoulders."

Oh, hell. James pinched the bridge of his nose and squeezed his eyes shut. This was his fault. Every goddamn bit of it.

"But the markings, if they were teeth marks," Luke said, "didn't come from a human mouth. If the witness really saw what she claims, the demon must have shape-shifting abilities. The teeth marks looked canine."

"The witness had been drinking," Macey added, "so I'm leading the investigation team toward dismissing her claims."

"But it sounds demonic." Chase crossed his arms and looked at Luke for confirmation.

"Agreed. After Cade's report last night, I want to hear the rest of the story." Luke's gaze landed on James, and the hair on the back of his neck pricked. This wasn't the first time he'd been in the hot seat with the alpha, but if he didn't get his act together, it would be the last.

James held Luke's gaze for a brief moment before glancing at Cade. "It's not demonic."

"So you saw it?" Luke crossed his arms. "Cade reported that you were giving chase to a demon, but you lost it in the cemetery. Then Macey told me about the murders, and I put two and two together. Tell me what you saw."

Shit. Shit. Shit. "I saw exactly what the witness described, but it didn't smell like rotting garbage; it smelled like swamp." He described the pursuit through the park and into the cemetery, blaming his inadequacy on the monster's incredible speed and not on the injury that slowed him down. "I should have taken it out last night, but I was sloppy. I'm sorry."

"Do you have any idea where it came from?" Macey returned to the chair next to him. "What it's after?"

He rubbed his sweaty palms on his jeans. "It's after me."

"You?" Luke moved his hands to his hips.

"Me and Odette. It's hard to explain, but we're stuck in this cycle. In every lifetime, when we meet, this monster rises and kills us both. I don't know how or why it happens, just that it does and it's going to keep happening until we're both dead or we kill it first."

Luke held up a hand to quiet the murmur of the pack. "Then I suggest you kill it first."

"I'm working on it. I need to get back to Odette. She's taking me to her Mambo to do a past-life regression to figure out how the cycle started so we can end it." If she'd even speak to him after the mess he made and left behind this morning.

The alpha nodded. "I trust you to do what needs to be done. Bryce and Chase are on first patrol tonight. I'll take Cade on second. You keep me posted."

Luke dismissed the meeting, but as the werewolves filed out the door, he held James back. "Is that scar on your neck from your altercation last night?"

Shit. He couldn't let the alpha know how bad the monster had gotten him, so he instinctively covered it with his hand. "Nah, this is nothing."

"If you need backup with this thing…"

"C'mon, man. You know me. I didn't earn my status in the pack by needing backup." He worked his ass off to prove himself worthy of his position.

"You're right about that." He nodded. "Go find out what you can. We'll discuss the *other* thing that happened last night later."

Did he mean the fact that he was sleeping with a client or that he'd nearly exposed the werewolves and had to act like a domesticated house pet to get out of the predicament? It didn't matter; his ass would be grass for either one.

James ground his teeth and knocked on Odette's door. She didn't say a word when she opened it; she didn't even look at him as she stepped aside for him to enter. Her posture ramrod straight, she closed the door and crossed her arms, the tendons in her neck protruding as she clenched her jaw.

He rubbed the back of his neck and looked into her eyes.

Her posture relaxed, and her eyes softened, her brow furrowing as she dropped her arms to her sides. "What happened?"

He lifted his hands palms up. "Either three other couples are stuck in the same cycle, or they got caught in the crossfire when the monster couldn't get to us."

She covered her mouth. "Six people died?"

"Two couples last night, one the night before. We have to stop this thing."

She nodded and strode past him. "My phone is on the nightstand. I'll call Natasha, and we'll go do that past-life regression."

He followed her into the bedroom. "Hold on. That can wait a few minutes; we need to finish our conversation from before." *If* he could make himself spit it out and tell her the truth. His palms slickened with sweat, and he fisted them at his sides.

She snatched her phone from the nightstand and turned to him. "If people are dying because of us, we need to—"

"We need to talk about us. You said the loa told you we have to fix this together, so let's fix *us* first, okay? Let me explain why I couldn't tell you I love you this morning."

She swallowed hard and gave her head a tiny nod.

Shit. If he wanted to admit his inadequacies to anyone, Odette was the one he could tell. Of course, he'd rather not admit anything, but he didn't have a choice at this point. She deserved to know. He raked a hand through his hair. *Might as well cut to the chase.*

"My wolf is broken. I'm not a full werewolf, so *I'm* broken, and I don't know how to fix it." He dropped onto the sofa, leaning his head back and covering his eyes with his forearm, embarrassment making him wish he could disappear. "I'm sorry."

The cushion next to him compressed as she sat down and rested a hand on his leg. "Don't apologize. You didn't do anything wrong, and you're not broken."

He pressed his arm harder against his eyes. She deserved so much more than he could give her. She deserved someone whole.

"James." She pried his arm from his face and held his hand. "I've seen you shift. You look like a full werewolf to me. Please talk to me."

Lacing his fingers through hers, he chewed the inside of his cheek to keep his mouth closed. A battle raged in his mind, his thoughts volleying between laying it all out, baring his soul…or zipping his lips and keeping his problems to himself where they belonged. The concern in her eyes urged him to spill the truth, but… Where could he even begin?

She cut her gaze to the side. "Not now, Nicolas. Will you give us some privacy?"

"I forgot he was here. Was he around last night?" It hadn't felt like they'd had an audience, but he hadn't been paying attention to much else.

"If he was, he kept himself hidden. He's usually respectful of my privacy, now that we've set up some ground rules." She caught James's gaze. "Please tell me why you think you're broken." She ran her finger over the spot where his pinkie should have been, and the scar tissue tingled.

He stared at their entwined hands. Odette had never asked him what happened to his finger. She'd simply accepted him, flaws and all. She loved him, and…damn it, he had to tell her. "My mom is human."

"So is my dad. Him being mundane doesn't make me any less of a vodouisant."

He blew out a hard breath through his nose. "When only one parent is a were, there's a fifty-fifty chance their firstborn will be a shifter. The chance is even less when one of the parents is human."

"So, you're rare. That doesn't make you broken." She offered a small smile, but he couldn't hold her gaze.

"I don't…" He closed his eyes for a long blink. He trusted Odette to his core, but it didn't make the admission any easier. Opening his eyes, he squared his gaze on her. "I can't heal as fast as the others. You saw the marks where the monster bit me when I came home last night. If I were a full werewolf, they'd have been healed before I reached the cemetery."

Her lips quirked into a smile, and she pressed her fingers to her mouth.

"What?" How could she possibly find this amusing?

She shook her head. "You said when you came *home* last night. You came here."

He'd admitted the one weakness he tried desperately to hide from everyone, and his confession didn't faze her. Her acceptance warmed his heart, tightening his chest, and he chuckled. "I did say that, didn't I? I guess it's starting to feel like home to me."

Her smile widened, and his heart pounded harder. As he looked into her eyes, something unspoken passed between them. She wanted this to be his home as much as he wanted it to be.

Her lips parted on a quick inhale, and she straightened, composing herself. "Do all werewolves heal at the same rate?"

"No, but I might as well be second-born with the way I heal. This." He tightened his grip on her hand and lifted it so she could see his missing finger. "When I lost it on a construction site, I should have been able to reattach it. My body should have stitched it right back on when I touched it to my hand, but it didn't."

He lowered their hands to his lap. "Luke was there, his eyes all full of concern, asking me why it wasn't healing. I couldn't let the would-be alpha see my weakness, so I dropped it in the cement mixer."

She blinked. "You threw away your finger so Luke wouldn't think you weak?"

His ears burned. "I know it's stupid, but yeah, I did. I can't say for sure if it would have healed anyway, so…" He shrugged. "My dad always told me to hide it, not to let anyone know I'm the weakest wolf in the pack. He kept me sheltered when I was a kid so no one ever saw me get injured. When I became an adult, I was tired of hiding, so I did everything I could to prove my strength. I joined the demon hunting team, volunteered for the toughest assignments. I've worked my ass off to prove I'm worthy of my rank, but nothing I do changes who I am. Are you sure you want to be soulmates with a broken werewolf?"

"It wasn't stupid, and you're not broken or weak. I understand not wanting to show weakness. I've spent my entire adult life hiding mine."

"That's not the only way I'm broken." Now for the hard part. The reason he couldn't commit to her, even though every fiber of his human being knew she was the one. "My mom, being human, didn't take the mating bond seriously. Didn't know what she was getting herself into. They weren't fate-bounds, but my dad loved her. He still loves her, and I think somewhere in her twisted heart she loves him too. They're still mates, but she disappears for months, sometimes years, at a time. She wanders. She cheats on him."

"Why doesn't he leave?"

He let out a dry chuckle. "He couldn't if he wanted to. Werewolves mate for life. So I made a promise to myself when I was old enough to understand what was going on that I would never let that happen to me. I would never take a mate unless my wolf was one hundred percent on board. Unless I was certain she was my fate-bound."

"I see." Her jaw tightened, and she inclined her chin. "Because you think you've inherited your mom's wandering eye?"

"I don't want to be that way. I'm not, but…it's the only explanation for…" He lowered his gaze. God, he didn't want to hurt her, but he didn't have a choice.

She pulled from his grasp and folded her hands in her lap. "What's her name?"

"I don't know. I've never met her." He pleaded with his eyes, willing her to understand.

She laughed, unbelieving. "What?"

"About three months ago, I started having dreams about this woman. In my dreams, my wolf has claimed her. My wolf was convinced she was my fate-bound, that I would find her one day… until I knocked on your door. Now he wants you both, and that's not possible. You can't have two fate-bounds, but the stupid beast won't let go of the dream lady."

Silence stretched between them as she processed his confession, her mouth screwing up on the side like she was chewing the inside of her cheek. He scrambled for something else to say, but she finally responded, "Where does that leave us then?"

He took her hands. "Odette, if I were just a man, I'd get down on one knee right now. I do love you. My wolf loves you, but I don't want to hurt you. I can't take you as my mate while my wolf insists there's another. What if I meet her? What if…?" He couldn't finish the sentence. He'd be an idiot to leave Odette. She was meant to be his.

"You can't help him, Nicolas." She shook her head. "Our ghost friend wants to talk to you, but…" She lowered her voice to a whisper.

"He thinks I'm his lover…the one who murdered him, though he doesn't know she did it."

He looked toward the empty space where she'd been speaking. "If he thinks he can help, I'd like to hear what he has to say." He'd take anything he could get at the moment. Hell, it couldn't hurt.

"He can't say much. He's strong, but he's so confused." She narrowed her eyes. "I haven't seen him act this way since the first time you came into the house. He's so frantic."

"What's he saying?"

She shook her head. "'He knows me.'" She looked at James. "He keeps repeating it. He thinks you know him."

"Damn it, I wish I could hear him. If he really can help…" If the ghost had even a sliver of information—a single piece of this massive jigsaw puzzle—James would do anything to learn it. He straightened and glanced from Odette to the place where she stared. "Can't you help him? Give him some of that power you told me about? Be the conduit so he can show himself to me?"

She stood and paced toward the bed. "No. I told you I don't use my powers like that. No one should have that kind of control over the dead."

"You don't have to control him. Just give him a little boost. Open up like when you were trying to scare me the other day." As he rose and moved toward her, an icy emptiness enveloped him. A feeling of familiarity clawed through his chest, making his heart race. A tiny piece of an image flashed through his mind, the scene so recognizable it felt like it had happened yesterday. A woman…the dream woman…stepping out of a horse-drawn carriage.

He jerked to the side, and the cold dissipated, taking the image with it. Warmth slowly returned to his skin, and he rubbed at the goose bumps on his arms.

That image felt nothing like the ones he'd seen before. The recognition made it seem as though it hadn't come from his own mind, but rather it had been waiting for him inside the pocket of cold as if the ghost had generated it. His wolf stirred, hovering near the surface, as anxious for answers as James was himself.

"Did he try to jump me again?"

Odette sank onto the edge of the bed. "No. You walked through him. He won't jump you."

"He won't or he can't because you told him not to? He hasn't bothered me again because you're already controlling him, aren't you?" And if she was controlling him, surely, she could find out what he knew.

She lifted her hands in a show of innocence. "I had no choice. He knocked you out and was trying to get inside you. What was I supposed to do?"

Sitting on the bed beside her, he took her hand and inhaled a slow, deep breath. "Thank you for that." He had to stay calm despite the adrenaline coursing through his veins. The ghost could be the answer to his problems. If Nicolas knew something…*anything* about the dream woman or how he could get his wolf to forget about her, James needed to hear it.

And Odette could make that happen.

"Do you trust me?" He held her gaze, searching for signs of doubt.

"Of course I do."

"Release him. Let him jump me. You don't have to give him any more power, but you have to let him go. I need to know what he has to say."

"No." Fear flashed in her dark-brown eyes. "It's not safe. Ghosts that can get inside people like that…they can make you crazy."

James balanced on the edge of crazy on a daily basis. He'd take his chances. "He won't hurt me."

Her mouth hung open in disbelief before she snapped it shut. "He's already knocked you out. There's no telling what else he might have done to you if I hadn't ordered him to leave you alone."

James dropped to his knees on the floor and faced her. "Because I wasn't ready. This time, I'll be prepared for impact, and I know you won't let him hurt me." Resting his hands on her thighs, he gently squeezed them. "I trust you to keep me safe."

Pressing her lips together, she let out a slow breath through her nose. "You're insane. You know that?"

He rose to his feet. "I've never claimed otherwise."

Standing, she gestured to the bed. "Lie down. You'll probably lose control of your muscles while he's in you."

He crawled onto the bed and lay on his back, fisting his hands at his sides to stop them from trembling. She was right, he was nuts for trying this, especially after what happened the first time. But something deep inside him said he had to.

She rested her fingertips on his shoulder. "The second you show any signs of distress, I'm pulling him out. Whether you've gotten the information you're looking for or not."

He nodded in reply, afraid a tremble in his voice would betray his apprehension.

Turning to face the empty room, Odette pushed her shoulders back. "You be gentle with him. Go ahead and tell him what you need to say."

In less than a second, the temperature around him plummeted. James gasped as the sensation of 220 volts surged through his veins, and his body stiffened like a corpse in rigor mortis before his limbs fell limp at his sides. He tried to move. To fist his hand or open his eyes, but his body was no longer his.

The shock subsided to a mild tingle, and the spirit's energy gathered in his mind, swirling and undulating like a storm on the sea. Emotions not his own rolled through his body—confusion, betrayal, despair—until an image took form behind his eyes.

"Serafine." His mouth formed the word before the thought registered, and her image grounded him, clearing his thoughts and allowing his mind and Nicolas's to join. For that brief moment, for the first time in his life, he felt a sensation he'd never experienced before.

He felt whole.

CHAPTER FOURTEEN

"JAMES?" ODETTE RESTED A HAND ON HIS CHEST AND PATTED his cheek. He didn't move. "Wake up. Come back to me."

She shook his shoulder, and his head lolled to the side, his eyes darting back and forth beneath his lids. "Please wake up." Her throat tightened, and she raked in a ragged breath as tears formed in her eyes.

What had she done? Allowing Nicolas to jump James, even for a minute, was an idiotic move. She'd let the ghost linger too long. She should have pulled him out at the first twitch of James's arm, but the way he'd said, "Serafine," had frozen her.

The name had rolled off his tongue like he'd said it a thousand times, and so much adoration had filled those three syllables, her breath had stilled in her chest. He'd sounded like a man in love.

Now she was paying the price for her hesitation. No, James was paying the price.

"James?" She shook him again, harder this time, but he still didn't respond. The pressure of a hand on her shoulder startled her, and she snapped around to find Nicolas hovering next to the bed. "What did you do to him?" More venom laced her voice than she'd intended, but if James didn't recover, she'd unleash her wrath on the spirit. How dare he harm her soulmate?

"Well?" She shot to her feet, fisting her hands at her sides. "What did you show him? Why won't he wake up?" Her voice hitched on the last word, and she covered her mouth as Nicolas faded away.

"Oh, that's perfect. Run away when things get heated." She would fix this. Her powers had caused enough harm to last twenty lifetimes, and she never should have used them with James. She knew better. *Please, Baron, I can't do this alone.*

Hooking her arms through James's, she tugged him off the bed and dragged him through the house. He was 190 pounds of pure muscle, but she had enough adrenaline coursing through her veins to give her the strength to get him out the door.

Getting him down the back steps proved the problem. His weight shifted as she descended, and her foot missed the second step. She fell backward, taking him down with her, and he landed on her chest, her right arm barely keeping his head from smacking the concrete. Sharp pain shot through her spine, the impact of the slab on her back and the pressure of his weight on top of her making her rib cage feel like it would snap.

She lay still, staring at the sky as the fluffy, white clouds drifted into the shape of a wolf head. Another puff of cumulus started to take the form of a person's body beneath, and she squeezed her eyes shut. She had no time for delirium. As she opened her lids, the shapes her mind had formed vanished, leaving nothing but tufts of cotton candy in the sky.

James moaned, sending her heart into a sprint. Sitting up, she wiggled from beneath him and held his head in her lap. She ran her fingers through his hair, brushing it from his forehead, and he shook his head, his brow furrowing as if he were in pain.

"Come on, love, open your eyes for me." Her insides quivered, her mouth going dry as her fear tipped to panic. He should've been okay by now.

He continued shaking his head, his lids fluttering as if they might open, but he didn't wake up.

Scrambling to her feet, she dragged him to her car and opened the back door. Sliding herself in first, she pulled him onto the back seat and exited the other side. With both doors shut, she climbed into the driver's seat and sped toward the French Quarter.

She called Natasha on the way, and when she arrived at the temple, two vodouisants met her outside and carried James into the back room, laying him on the couch.

The men left, and Odette knelt at James's side, holding his hand and resting her other on his forehead, cursing herself for letting this happen. "Stay with me, James." Her voice cracked.

"What happened?" Natasha gathered an armful of herb jars from a cabinet and set them on the table by her mortar and pestle.

Odette stared at his handsome face. "The ghost. Nicolas wanted to communicate with James, and James…" She sucked in a shaky breath. "He insisted, so I let the ghost jump him." She looked at the Mambo. "James trusted me to keep him safe, and look at him. Look what I did." The tears collecting on her lower lids spilled down her cheeks, her lip trembling as she watched Natasha work.

Natasha ground a mix of herbs in the bowl, and the sharp scent of rosemary filled the air. "You said you let him? You were stopping him from doing it before?"

Biting her bottom lip, Odette nodded. The Mambo didn't say a word, but the expression on her face conveyed her thoughts: *So, you are using your powers.*

"Can you help him?" Her voice sounded tiny, like the helpless little girl sitting in the road by her momma's body.

"Of course." Natasha mixed the herbs with a light blue liquid and poured the concoction into a shot glass. "This will help get him out of his head and into the present."

Tugging on his chin, Odette trickled the potion into James's mouth. As she emptied the container, he swallowed, and a deep moan rumbled from his chest.

Natasha beat a rhythm on a small drum—two slow taps followed by a quick percussion—and chanted a prayer in Haitian Creole. Her magic filled the room, the buzzing electricity prickling across Odette's skin, swirling around her and seeping into James.

Odette pressed her lips to her soulmate's cheek, and his eyes opened.

James gasped as his lids flew open, the cool air raking down his throat like forty-grit sandpaper. "Serafine," he croaked, his heart pounding relentlessly as his mind scrambled to comprehend what he'd seen. The sound of his own name swirled delicately in his ears, and familiar energy vibrated on his skin as soft hands cupped his face.

He squinted through his blurred vision until a figure came into focus. "Odette?" He blinked and then stared into her dark eyes, her presence grounding him, bringing the world into focus.

He glanced about the room, but nothing looked familiar. An old wood and glass cupboard lined one of the walls, and an array of handmade burlap dolls sat upon one of the shelves. Colored glass jars filled the rest of the space, and as he swept his gaze over his surroundings, he took in an old tribal-looking drum set and an altar of some sort against the other wall. "Where are we?" He focused on Odette, and a look of relief smoothed the tight lines in her forehead.

"We're at the temple. Are you okay?"

He stared at her for a moment, and the confusion clouding his thoughts dissipated like a fog burned away by the sun. "I'm fine." He sat up, swinging his legs over the side of the couch and resting his feet on the floor. The room tilted on its axis, and he closed his eyes until the dizzying sensation subsided.

Odette sat next to him, taking his hands in a firm grip. "Do you remember anything?"

He smiled, and his heart filled with joy, making his chest feel like it would explode. He remembered everything. "It all makes sense now."

"What makes sense?" Natasha put a bowl in a cabinet and closed the door. He hadn't noticed her presence before.

"Everything." He looked at the Mambo. "The puzzle. The pieces fit. The woman from my dreams." Turning to Odette, he cupped her cheek in his hand. "She's you. That's why Nicolas called you Serafine. You *are* Serafine."

She shook her head. "That's not possible. You would have to be…" Her eyes widened.

"I was Nicolas, and you were Serafine. It makes perfect sense. I'm connected to the ghost, and when you bought that house, that's when I started seeing Serafine in my dreams. Because Nicolas saw *you.*"

Her mouth hung open, but she didn't speak.

"When he got inside me, for the first time in my life, I didn't feel like a piece of me was missing. My wolf recognized it too. Nicolas is part of me. The logic doesn't make sense, I know. But I feel it in my bones. How can a ghost of my former self be haunting your house when I'm here in the flesh?"

The muscles of her throat worked as she swallowed and glanced at Natasha. "Did you see how you died?"

"I didn't really *see* anything, aside from her face. I felt his emotions: love, betrayal, desperation. As our minds connected, I *knew* things. Like how I know you're Serafine."

"She killed him. That's why he felt betrayal. If a person's death is tragic enough, his soul can fracture." She shook her head. "It's so rare. I've heard of it happening, but I've never met a ghost who had a soul shard before. If you really are Nicolas, then a piece of him stayed behind when he died, and when you reincarnated… James, you've always felt incomplete because the ghost has a piece of your soul."

He stopped breathing mid-inhale as her words settled over him. He'd always felt like a piece of himself was missing, because it was. And that missing piece was the answer to it all. He didn't heal as fast as a normal werewolf, not because his mother was human, but because he himself wasn't complete. And his wolf didn't want two mates. The beast had claimed Serafine because of Nicolas's memories…and Odette *was* Serafine.

Holy hell. He'd finally found his fate-bound.

"James?"

His name on Odette's lips pulled him from his thoughts, and he finished a deep inhale. "This is fantastic." He laughed and pulled her into a hug.

"No, it's not." Her voice was muffled against his chest.

"But it is." Gripping her shoulders, he pushed her far enough away to look at her. "My wolf doesn't want another woman. It's always been you. *You* are my fate-bound."

"That's what I've been trying to tell you." She trailed her fingers down the sides of his face and pressed her lips to his.

Warm and soft, the gentle caress raised goose bumps on his skin and his heart thrummed in his chest. He wrapped his arms around her and coaxed her mouth open with his tongue. Her lips parted for him, and he drank her in, reveling in the overwhelming sensations of love. She was his now, and he would do everything in his power to protect her.

She broke from the kiss, clearing her throat and straightening her shirt as she cast a glance to Natasha, who fought a smile.

"Sorry about that," he said to the Mambo. "Got a little carried away."

"No need to apologize." Natasha's smile faded as she glanced at Odette and gestured with her head to James.

The pained expression on Odette's face popped the bubble of elation in his chest. "What aren't you telling me?"

Odette took a deep breath and blew it out hard. "I am thrilled that you and your wolf got the soulmate issue worked out, but we've got a bigger problem. With a piece of you stuck in limbo like this, the cycle is going to keep repeating forever. And..." She cast her gaze to her lap.

"And?"

"If Serafine killed Nicolas, then she didn't die in his arms. But in every life I've regressed to, I did die in your arms. What if Nicolas is summoning the monster to kill me every time I reincarnate to get even with me?"

"No." The word left his lips before the thought formed in his mind. "Nicolas loves Serafine. He would never do anything like that."

"I don't know James. It would explain—"

"No, he wouldn't. He was inside me. I felt what he felt...nothing less than utter adoration. He's not doing this." And he refused to let Odette even consider it. Her research was wrong.

Natasha pulled a chair next to the couch and sat down. "I think it's time we found out what really happened to Nicolas and Serafine."

Odette squeezed his hand. "Are you still up for that past-life regression? It will be painful."

"Ain't nothing a werewolf can't handle, right?" Natasha winked.

James straightened his spine. He'd relive a thousand deaths before he'd allow anyone to harm his fated mate. "Bring it on."

Natasha instructed James to lie on the sofa, and she scurried to the cupboard and gathered jars of herbs. Odette sat on the edge of the cushion next to him, resting both her hands on his chest.

He placed his hands over hers and squeezed them. "Thank you for making that happen." Tugging a hand to his lips, he kissed her palm. "I'm sorry for not realizing you and the dream woman were the same person. Even though she doesn't look like you, it seems so obvious now."

"There was no way for you to know. Nicolas doesn't look like you either. Souls don't change, but appearances do." Her brow pinched, concern filling her gaze. "Are you sure you want to do this? You'll feel your death…and mine…like it's really happening."

"Death doesn't scare me."

"It doesn't scare me either, but dying sure as hell does. Nicolas was stabbed in the chest and beheaded, and I…Serafine did it."

He chewed the inside of his cheek and studied her, trying to imagine a situation where Odette would be inclined to murder him. She wouldn't. "I don't think she did it."

"But the police report said—"

"We'll soon find out." Natasha handed him a mug of liquid. Rising onto his elbow, he sniffed the contents. "This smells like rum."

"Just a splash to help you relax. The herbs will open your mind. Drink up." The Mambo waved her hand, indicating he should lift the cup to his mouth.

He cringed as he swallowed the bitter liquid. It burned on its way down to his stomach like it was taking a layer of his esophagus with it. "Remind me never to order that in a bar."

Natasha dragged another chair to the end of the couch near his head and ordered Odette to sit. He reached for his fate-bound's hand as she sank into the seat, but she pulled from his grasp.

"My energy could affect your visions. I'll be here, but we can't touch while you're regressing."

"Okay." He smiled, but it probably didn't mask the worry churning in his gut. He was about to watch his fate-bound die.

"I'm not going to leave you, and you'll be in control the whole time." Odette half-smiled, the uncertainty in her eyes disheartening.

He let out a half-hearted chuckle. "I'm not scared."

"You don't have to wear that mask for me. I'd be terrified."

Really reassuring words from the woman he was supposed to spend the rest of his life with. He nodded and swallowed the thickness from his throat.

"If it gets unbearable, you can open your eyes and bring yourself to the present whenever you want. But the longer you can stay under, the more information you'll gather." She kissed his forehead and leaned back in her chair, out of his reach.

Natasha closed her eyes and mumbled something in a language he didn't understand. He tilted his head to look at Odette, and his vision swam. "What's she saying?"

"It's a Haitian Creole prayer to Papa Legba, the guardian of the crossroads. When she's done, she'll guide you through a meditation and into your past life. Close your eyes and relax."

He settled into the cushion and let his lids drift shut. Whatever was in that drink made his limbs feel heavy, and the tension drained from his muscles. As he lay there, listening to the Mambo's rhythmic prayer, he sank deeper and deeper into the couch, until he couldn't tell where his body ended and the fabric began.

The air around him grew heavy, pressing into him as the scents of patchouli and something sharp that he didn't recognize filled the room. Natasha's chanting quieted, and her voice drifted toward him, lightening the pressure on his body. "Clear your mind of everything but the color blue—so dark it's almost black. Let your mind drift into your subconscious and take a deep, cleansing breath with me."

The Mambo inhaled, and James followed her lead, focusing on the color, until liquid warmth flowed through his veins, melting him into an altered state.

"Imagine a pin-prick of light in the corner of the blue." Natasha's voice seemed to come from somewhere inside his mind…all around him, but from nowhere at the same time. "As the light brightens, I want you to focus on Odette's house. Not as it is now, but as it was when you were there long ago."

The scene in his mind brightened into crisp focus. He stood in the foyer of the house on Esplanade. Dark-green paper with intricate gold designs covered the walls, and a crystal chandelier—not unlike the one he'd recently installed—glittered in the rays of the setting sun entering through the open door.

"What do you see, James?" Natasha's voice whispered in his mind.

He worked his jaw, prying his lips apart through the sluggishness in his muscles. "I'm in the house."

"What time period is it? Present day?"

Casting his gaze into the living room, he focused on the brick fireplace. A small clock sat on the mantle, but Odette's altar wasn't there. A pair of intricately-carved, dark-wood chairs with deep-red upholstery faced the hearth, and a chaise lounge sat beneath the window. "No. It's in the past."

"Focus on Serafine, the woman from your dreams. Try to bring her into the picture."

Shuffling sounded at the top of the stairs, and then she appeared, a vision of beauty in a maroon ball gown. She'd swept her hair up into a twist, and shiny, dark curls spiraled from her temples to brush her dark-brown shoulders. A timid smile played on her lips as she descended the steps, and James's chest tightened, so much love filling him he felt like he'd burst from the pressure.

Serafine may have started as his servant, but Nicolas would have moved heaven and Earth for this woman.

"Do you see her?" Natasha asked.

"Yes." His voice cracked.

"Let the scene play out. See what information you can gather."

He took a deep breath and let his thoughts slip away, focusing on the woman in his mind and the emotions intensifying in his heart.

As Serafine reached the bottom floor, he kissed her hand and laced it into the crook of his arm. "We do not want to be late for the party, mon cher."

She hesitated. "I'm still not sure this is the best idea. It will not be good for your reputation."

"I don't give a damn about my reputation." He toyed with the ring on her finger. "You are to be my mate. My wife."

"People will talk."

"Then let them talk, mon cher." He twirled a curl around his finger and brushed her cheek with the back of his hand. "They know better than to cross me."

With Natasha's guidance, James followed the scene as Nicolas and Serafine climbed into a carriage that took them to a mansion down the road. Painted bright blue, with white gingerbread trim, the two-story house boasted a wrap-around porch and a grand gallery on the second floor.

With Serafine on his arm, Nicolas stepped through the doorway, and a hush fell across the crowd. A few dozen people in suits and gowns paused to stare as he led his fated mate deeper into the house.

Serafine tightened her grip on his arm. "They are staring at me."

"Of course they are. You are the most beautiful woman in the room." He picked up two glasses of champagne and offered her one.

"A word, brother." A stocky man with blond hair and deep-blue eyes glared at him and jerked his head to indicate he should follow.

Antoine.

"One moment, mon cher. Let me see what he wants." He kissed her hand, and her eyes widened as she swallowed hard. With a tiny nod, she stepped away from him, and he followed his brother into the next room.

"How dare you bring her here?" Antoine spoke through clenched teeth, the muscles in his neck tight like cords. "Are you trying to ruin everything we have worked for?"

He lifted his chin, narrowing his eyes. "Serafine is my fate-bound. You and everyone else will have to get used to it sooner or later."

Antoine glanced through the doorway and leaned toward him, lowering his voice. "She is your servant."

"She is my fiancée."

His brother narrowed his eyes, and one of them twitched with his agitation. "We are to be the first family in New Orleans. You are to be alpha. You cannot take her as your mate."

Nicolas downed his champagne in one gulp and set the glass on a table. "Her father was a were. I will not taint the bloodline."

Antoine stepped closer, taking him by the arm. "Her mother was a slave."

He jerked from his brother's grip, a low growl rumbling in his chest. "I am aware of her lineage." He turned to leave the room.

"You will ruin us, bringing attention to yourself like this. The alpha cannot afford to be in the human spotlight."

Nicolas stopped and looked over his shoulder. "I don't care the cost. The full moon is tomorrow, and we will become mates. You cannot stop this."

James gasped. "Nicolas was alpha." His lids fluttered, his head shaking as he tried to open his eyes.

"Stay under." Odette's voice calmed him, caressing his temples, and sending a wave of relaxation through his body. "Try to go to the night of their deaths. We need to know what happened."

With a long exhale, James let his mind drift back in time.

A bedroom. Serafine in a long, white nightgown. He lay next to her, his mind spinning with thoughts. His brother was right, but Nicolas didn't care the consequence. Serafine was his fate-bound; they would make this work.

Nicolas slipped into a dream, rolling onto his back as the sound of boot heels thudding on the floor echoed somewhere in his mind. Serafine gasped, and as the bed jerked, Nicolas awoke.

His fate-bound's scream ripped through the night, dragging him into full consciousness, and he sat up, shock not allowing him to comprehend what was happening. Antoine stood over Serafine, his bloody dagger raising and lowering into her heart.

Bright-red blood pooled from her chest, staining her gown as life drained from the wound. Searing pain tore through Nicolas's heart, shredding him.

Agony. Betrayal.

He scooped her into his arms as Antoine backed against the wall, his chest heaving. "My sweet Serafine." A sob lodged in his throat, and he swept the matted hair from her face. Blood trickled from the corner of her mouth, taking her life force with it. Her head fell back, her eyes wide, the light in them gone. His entire world shattered into nothingness, and hot tears trailed down his cheeks as he lifted his gaze to his treacherous brother.

Numb with grief, he pushed the question through the thickness in his throat. "Why?"

"I will not have you ruining our lives over a woman." Fear flashed in

Antoine's eyes, and he gripped the dagger tighter. "You will thank me for this when the pack is formed."

"Thank you?" Laying his fate-bound onto the mattress, he focused on the single spark of anger burning in his soul. The only sensation palpable through the emptiness of his despair. He stoked the flame until his rage consumed him, vengeance his sole focus.

He rose from the bed, a growl rolling up from his chest as he called on his beast. His brother would pay for what he had done. But in his grief, he'd grown numb. As he leaped toward Antoine, he failed to shift. His brother plunged the dagger into his chest, piercing his heart.

Falling backward onto the bed, he gasped for breath, but the fatal puncture refused to give him air. Searing pain spread through his body, and he choked on his own blood as Antoine jerked the knife from his chest and brought it down on his throat.

"Serafine!" James shot up, raking in a ragged breath and grasping for his fate-bound. His vision swam, and nausea lurched in his stomach, making him double over.

"James." Odette sat next to him and wrapped her arms around his shoulders, running her hand across his back. "Breathe, honey. Just breathe."

Squeezing his eyes shut, he sucked in a breath, then another, until his head stopped spinning and he straightened. Blinking his gaze into focus, he found Natasha across the room, grinding herbs into another drink.

He looked at Odette, and cool relief flooded his veins, spiraling up his chest and coming out as something between a sob and a laugh.

Holding his face in her hands, she wiped the dampness from his cheeks and kissed his forehead. "Are you okay?"

He rubbed his chest where the knife had been, and a faint burning sensation spread across his skin. "I'm…fine. Are you…? That was intense."

Natasha handed him a cup. "This will help with the nausea and the fog in your brain."

He sipped the warm licorice-flavored liquid and leaned into Odette's side. Her presence grounded him, bringing him fully back to the present as the drink eased the physical strain the regression had put on his body. He drained the cup, and Natasha returned it to the counter.

Odette rested her hand on his thigh. "Did you see the monster?"

"It wasn't a monster. It was his brother. Antoine killed both of them." He explained what he'd seen in his vision.

"You were right then." She shook her head. "Serafine was innocent, yet she was blamed for it all. Typical."

"There's got to be more to the story, though." James rubbed his throat, trying to relieve the burning sensation left over from his regression. "The Dubois didn't become the first family. The Masons did."

She frowned. "If Nicolas was the shifter, Antoine couldn't have become alpha, could he? A second-born alpha? Is that possible?"

James raked a hand through his hair. "If a first-born dies prematurely, the shifter magic in the second-born is triggered. Antoine should have inherited the ability when Nicolas died, and he should have become alpha. They were the first werewolves to inhabit New Orleans."

Odette's eyes widened. "But Nicolas's soul fractured. Part of him has been stuck in the house since his murder."

"And that could have kept Antoine from inheriting the ability to shift." It made sense, but it didn't explain the murders recurring in every life. "What happened to Antoine afterward? Did you find anything in your research?"

"There was nothing about Antoine after that. He seemed to have disappeared."

"Werewolves aren't immortal, so we know he's not still alive. Could his ghost be doing this?"

She shook her head. "In my regressions, the killer was always solid. A ghost can't strangle someone unless it's getting help from the living."

"So someone living is involved?"

"You know who could answer these questions." Natasha crossed her arms and lifted a brow at Odette. "I'll set up another ceremony for tonight, but you're gonna have to get right with your *met tet* if you want him to show."

Odette groaned and leaned into James's side.

"Unless you're both ready to join the Baron on the other side, you've got work to do."

James cut his gaze between the women. "How do you get right with Baron Samedi?"

Odette took in a deep breath and blew it out hard. "I'm going to need your help."

CHAPTER FIFTEEN

"HEY." JAMES REACHED ACROSS THE CONSOLE AND PRIED Odette's hand from its death-grip on the steering wheel. His skin was warm, a stark contrast to her ice-cold fingers. "You're going to be okay. I don't think Baron Samedi would give you powers he didn't think you could control."

"I know." Her voice was a whisper over the lump in her throat. How many times had the Mambo said those same words? She chewed her bottom lip and stared out the windshield at the cemetery across the street. Growing up, her mom brought her here every Saturday to show their respects for the Baron and leave him offerings at the gate. As an adult, she'd paid tribute here once, the day she moved back to the city, and she hadn't returned since.

She'd been gone for far too long. Scared for too long too. Not just scared of her powers and what she was capable of doing with them, but afraid of life. She was living on borrowed time, and she'd spent so much of it trying to control everything that she'd forgotten what a gift life was. Especially her life.

It was time she made amends with the giver.

She looked at her fingers entwined with James's and focused on the magic seeping from his skin. Magic that blended so well with her own it felt as if her soul connected to his. With this man, she was whole, and she would do whatever it took to make him whole too.

Her stomach soured at the thought of what she would probably have to do. Only with the Baron could she mend the fracture in James's soul, and to do that, he'd…

"Are you ready?" James squeezed her hand and rested his fingers on the door latch. He caught her gaze, and the deep blue of his eyes grounded her. She could do this.

They could do it together.

"As I'll ever be." She slid out of the car.

Slinging her bag over her shoulder, she took his hand, and they darted across the street. James strolled toward the weathered concrete walls and nearly crossed the threshold, but she held him back.

"We can't go in yet. The Baron is a gatekeeper, so we start at the entrance to honor him." Setting her bag near the wall, she took a deep breath to calm her sprinting heart.

"Right. I saw you do this when we were kids. Sorry." James shoved his hands into his pockets and gave her a sheepish grin.

"Don't apologize." She knelt on the sidewalk and dug through her bag to find a thick piece of purple chalk. Settling in the entryway, she pressed the chalk into the concrete and dragged down and to the right. It made a scraping sound as the fine powder marked the ground, and Odette let down her carefully constructed walls, allowing her powers to manifest.

Her arm hairs stood on end, goose bumps pricking at her skin as the cross and coffins of Baron Samedi's *vévé* took shape. Her *met tet's* presence surrounded her, the emptiness of death overpowering the natural humming energy of life.

"Is it just me, or is it getting colder?" James knelt beside her and rubbed his arms. "I've never felt this happen around you before."

She exchanged the chalk for a bottle of spiced rum from her bag and twisted the cap. "The Baron hasn't come this close in a long time." A shiver ran up her spine. "He's listening." She held the bottle in both hands and ran her thumb across the label. "I was stupid to think the distillery was a fair trade for my life. It's a small tribute for the gift you've given me, Baron, and I'm here to make amends."

Pressing the bottle to her lips, she took in a mouthful of rum. The warm undercurrents of cinnamon and nutmeg danced on her tongue, and James's eyes widened as she leaned forward and spit the alcohol across the *vévé*.

"I never saw you do *that* when we were kids."

She handed him the bottle. "My mother did it on special occasions. Your turn."

He gave her a wary look. "Spit it?"

"As an offering for the Baron. We aren't going to make it without his help." Facing the monster wasn't optional. They would either kill it, or it would kill them, but they couldn't let another couple die in their place.

Gazing at the bottle, he chuckled. "Normally, I'd say that's a waste of good rum, but in this case, I suppose it's the best use of it." He took a swig and spit it on the ground before offering the bottle to her.

She shook her head. "Now take a drink for us."

Locking his gaze with hers, he drank deeply and put the bottle in her hands. His eyes held her still, calming the sprint of her heart as she raised the container to her lips. She took a gulp, and the rum burned its way down to her stomach. It had been years since she'd swallowed a sip of alcohol. Too many to count.

Capping the bottle, she picked up her bag and rose, leading James across the threshold into the cemetery. Then, she set the bottle by the wall along with an expensive cigar and a top hat she'd bought at a party store. "We offer you rum and tobacco for listening to our prayers."

James stood next to her and rested his hand on the small of her back. "What now?"

She stared out into the cemetery, at row after row of above-ground tombs. Dingy white plaster covered many of the graves, while others had worn away until the brick beneath was all that remained. Stone urns filled with colorful flowers adorned many of the tombs, a symbol that though the dead may be gone, they were not forgotten by the living.

A weeping angel sat atop a 150-year-old tomb, watching over the remains of its inhabitants. Did the loa ever weep for her?

She looked at James. "Now I beg for forgiveness."

Running her fingers along the sectioned graves in the wall, she traced the names engraved on the plaques, stopping at a recent burial. While the standing graves within the cemetery housed the remains of generations of family members, the law stated a new body could only be entombed at least a year and a day after the previous one. If a family member passed away within the year, his body was housed in a temporary grave in the wall until enough time had passed to move him to the family plot.

No one in Odette's family had died since her mom. Not on her father's side anyway. Their family tomb was ready to receive, and hopefully she wouldn't be its next inhabitant.

"I've made it a point to never say 'I'm sorry' unless an apology is actually warranted." She stood in front of her offerings and gazed at the shiny, black top hat. "In this case, I can't say 'I'm sorry' enough to make up for what I've done. You gave me life and some powerful gifts, and I've squandered them. After…everything that happened…I thought if I denied my powers and lived in contrast to the Ghede way I could control not just my life, but everyone's around me."

Pressure built in the back of her eyes. "But there are some things that are beyond my control, and I've got to learn to accept them. I *will* learn. This man…" She took James's hand. "He's teaching me. I know you know him. He spent a lot of time here as a kid, he and his dad honoring you without even realizing it. His life is in danger because of me, and if I…"

A sob lodged in her throat, and she swallowed it down. "If I don't change my ways, we're both going to die, and for that, I am deeply sorry." She looked into James's eyes. "I'm so sorry I dragged you into this. I was supposed to die as a baby. If my mom hadn't made a deal with death, we never would have met and we wouldn't have awoken whatever it is that's after us. I'm so sorry, James."

The first tear trailed down her cheek, and he wiped it away with his thumb. "I'd take a single day in love with you over a lifetime of having never met. We're soulmates."

Something between a laugh and a sob rolled up from her chest. "Yes, we are." She sniffled and wiped another tear from her cheek. "I'm sorry, Baron. I'm sorry for abandoning my faith, and I'm sorry for not living in your image. Today, I'm offering my apology, this rum and tobacco…and I'm offering my life. If you will help us, come to the ceremony tonight and speak to us, guide us, tell us how to fix this, I swear on my mother's grave that I will start living. I will embrace my magic, and damn it, I'll learn how to have fun."

"I'll make sure she follows through on the fun part." James slid an arm around her waist. "Oh, shit. Is it okay if I address him too? Or did I ruin your prayer?"

She laughed. "It's fine. I have a feeling he's been watching over you too."

She looked at James, and the pressure of all the emotion, all the built-up magic and energy that she'd been suppressing for years exploded in her chest like a water balloon bursting on the pavement. The floodgates opened, and tears streamed down her cheeks as she buried her face in his shirt.

He held her as she sobbed, and a weight seemed to lift from her chest as she let go. She didn't have to hold it in anymore. Didn't have to always be in control. For the first time in as long as she could remember, she was relinquishing the wheel, letting the loa and fate steer her life.

She pulled back to look at James. "First thing I want to do when this is all over is go dancing."

He grinned. "You got it."

A frigid wind kicked up, swirling around them before settling into stillness. The Baron's way of letting her know her prayer had been heard. Tonight, she'd learn if she'd been forgiven.

"Thank you for not being afraid of my powers."

"Fate knows better than to bind you to a scaredy-cat. Lucky for you, there isn't much that scares me." He pressed his lips to hers.

She expected a quick kiss, but he lingered, his sweet breath warming her skin. Snaking her arms behind his neck, she pulled him closer, pressing her body to his and deepening the kiss. With James by her side, she could do anything.

He pulled away and chuckled. "We probably shouldn't be making out in a cemetery."

"Want to head home? The ceremony doesn't start for another two hours."

A tour guide's voice drifted on the air, "That's a *vévé* for the god of death. It's a symbol a Voodoo practitioner draws on the ground to summon the god. We better be careful in here and stick together…" The guide flashed a mischievous grin. "Unless you want to end up hexed."

"Oh, please." Odette rolled her eyes and strode toward the exit. "I hate it when they get things wrong on these tours. I wish they'd do a little more research. Maybe *ask* someone before they start spreading rumors."

James chuckled. "I'm not sure they could handle the truth."

"You're probably right." As she slung her bag over her shoulder a chill formed in the air behind her. Contrary to popular belief, ghosts didn't tend to congregate in cemeteries; they generally followed people or objects. With this group of twenty shadowing the tour guide, the spirit probably belonged to one of them.

She turned and took in the spectral form—an eighty-something-year-old man with hunched shoulders and dark-brown eyes. From the looks of him, he had to be recently deceased. Long-dead ghosts usually showed themselves as they appeared in the primes of their lives.

James looked at her quizzically, and she sighed. As much as she wanted to spend what little time she had left with her soulmate, this ghost appearing now could be a test from the Baron. "Give me a minute?" she said to James. "I think I need to help someone."

He looked toward the spirit, though he probably saw an empty space. "Ghost?"

She nodded. "Do you need help, sir?"

The ghost gazed out over the crowd of tourists.

"Is someone you know out there? A loved one?"

The spirit nodded and drifted toward the crowd. Odette followed, with James on her heels, and joined the group as the guide explained the history of the cemetery.

"Has anyone here ever had any experiences with ghosts?" the guide asked.

A few hands went up, and people described various experiences of things moving, as well as hearing voices.

"I wish my grandpa would pay me a visit," a woman in an LSU T-shirt muttered. "Or at least tell me where he hid his stash."

The ghost's eyes brightened, and he looked at Odette. She hung back as the crowd moved on, and she whispered, "Is that who you're here for?"

He opened his mouth to speak, but no sound formed.

Odette closed her eyes and rubbed her forehead. This had to be a test. Make a promise to the Baron, and be ready to pay up. She let out her breath in a long exhale.

James rested his hand on her back, grounding her again, and she had to wonder if he realized how calming his touch was for her. He must have, because he always did it at just the right moment. "He needs more energy?"

"How'd you know?"

"Call it a hunch." Stepping behind her, he rested both hands on her shoulders. "You've got this. I'm right here if you need me."

Nodding, she closed her eyes and opened up the channel. Weightless, empty energy from the underworld flowed through her, chilling her veins and making her shiver. James wrapped his arms around her, pressing his front to her back, grounding her even more.

She pushed the energy outward toward the spirit, and it grew solid. She could have given the ghost enough energy for all the tourists to see—wouldn't that have made their day—but she reined it in, only giving as much as was needed for him to speak. "I can pass on a message if you have one."

The ghost told her about his death, and a little too much about his life. He'd never trusted the banks, so his entire life savings, cash and gold coins, lay hidden inside his home.

The ghost followed Odette as she approached the woman, his granddaughter, his energy fading as she closed the channel along the way.

"Excuse me, Elizabeth." She touched the woman's arm.

Elizabeth's eyes widened. "Do I know you?"

"Your grandfather says his savings is in a safe in the Northwest corner of the attic, behind the framed map of the Gulf."

Her mouth dropped open. "Who are you?"

Odette smiled. "No one important. Have a nice day."

Taking James's hand, she strolled toward the exit, and the woman pressed her phone to her ear.

"Yes!" The excited voice echoed off the cemetery walls, and Odette smiled. She'd passed the test.

"I'm curious." James followed Odette up the front steps and into the foyer. "If Baron Samedi shows up at the ceremony, will he be in ghost form? Will everyone be able to see him or only you?"

With the ghost approaching her in the cemetery as a test, the loa's appearance at the ceremony seemed likely, and his mind had been churning with questions ever since.

She took his hand and led him toward the bedroom. "No one will be able to *see* him. He'll communicate through ritual possession."

"Possession?" He stopped in the hallway. Plenty of rumors about what went on at Voodoo rituals circulated through New Orleans, and that was one he'd hoped wasn't true. "You mean he'll do like Nicolas did to me? Get inside your head and show you things?"

Stepping toward him, she smiled softly and cupped his face in her hand. "He, and any other Spirit that makes an appearance, will get inside someone and take over their body, moving and speaking through the host." She laughed softly. "We call the host a horse, and the loa is the rider."

His eyes widened. No way in hell was a Spirit getting inside him. He opened his mouth to suggest he wait outside while the vodouisants did their thing, but she caught his lips in a kiss instead.

Her magic shimmied across his skin, and warmth bloomed in his chest, chasing away his fear. As she moved closer, pressing her soft curves into his body and slipping her arms around his waist, all logical thought dissolved from his brain.

"Don't worry." She kissed his jaw, trailing her lips up to his ear. "The loa won't ride you unless you're open to it, and you haven't been initiated. You'll be a spectator." Sliding her hands beneath his shirt, she nipped at his lobe.

His knees nearly buckled with the sensation. "Good, because the only person I want riding me is *you.*"

"I can make that happen." Running her hands up his chest, she pulled his shirt over his head and stepped back, admiring him. Her eyes filled with hunger, and she licked her lips as her gaze traveled up and down his form.

His stomach tightened, blood rushing to his groin. "Saddle up, sweetheart."

"Hmm…" She unbuttoned his jeans, letting them fall around his ankles before pushing him against the wall and reaching into his boxer-briefs to grip his dick. "I prefer bareback if you don't mind."

He held her gaze for a moment, trying for a witty comeback, but the feel of her soft fingers wrapped around his cock scattered his thoughts like sawdust in a summer wind. She stroked him, and electricity shot through his core. He leaned his head back against the wall and closed his eyes as she explored his body with her mouth.

Gliding her lips along his neck, she moved down to kiss his chest, her warm breath raising goose bumps on his skin. As she flicked out her tongue to lick his nipple, a shudder ran through his entire body, a possessive growl rumbling in his chest.

This was his woman. His fate-bound. And his wolf finally agreed she was the *only* one for him. Forever. He belonged to her, body, mind, and soul, and it was time he gave himself to her fully. No more holding back on his emotions. On anything.

He was hers to do with as she pleased, and as she straightened and stepped back, the mischievous look in her eyes said there was plenty of pleasure to come.

"Bedroom. Now." Not waiting for a response, she strutted through the doorway, dropping her clothes to the floor on her way to the bed.

"Yes, ma'am." He toed off his shoes and stumbled out of his jeans before going to her and running his hands along her curves. "You are so beautiful." He kissed her, sucking her bottom lip into his mouth as he unclasped her bra.

A soft moan escaped her throat, and she leaned into him, her body molding to his. This woman was made for him, and he intended to spend the rest of his life showing her how perfect she was.

She grinned and pulled down his underwear before removing her own. Then, she tugged him toward the loveseat and gently pushed him down onto a cushion. She straddled him, sandwiching his dick between his stomach and her center, and kissing him like this was their last moment together.

Running his hands up her back, he drank her in, the thrilling sensation of her growing magic enveloping him, heightening his senses. She rocked her hips, and her soft folds rubbed against his cock, sending a shock of passion rocketing through his core.

He broke the kiss to press his lips into her ear. "I want you, Odette." He needed her like he needed air to breathe.

"Tell me what you want, James." She moved her hips again, teasing him, igniting a desire so deep within him he could think of nothing else.

"You." His voice rumbled in his throat. "I want you." He trembled as she took his length in her hand and rose onto her knees.

"Is this what you want?" She lowered onto him until his tip slipped between her folds.

"Yes. God, yes." Gripping her hips, he pulled her down, lifting his own until their bodies met and he filled her completely, her wet warmth squeezing him, fire shooting through his veins.

He drew out slightly, and she gasped. Folding forward, she gripped his shoulders and leaned into him, following him down as he settled onto the cushion. Then he leaned back and let her take control.

And man, was she good at being in control.

She lifted her hips, sliding up his shaft until only his tip remained inside her luscious folds. Then she took him back in, her heat wrapping around him, enveloping him in rapture. He couldn't help but match her thrusts with his own.

With his hands on her hips, he slid his thumb between her legs to find her clit. She moaned as he circled the sensitive flesh, and her rhythm shifted, her movements growing shorter and harder until his climax coiled inside him like a tightly-wound spring.

"Oh, James." She threw her head back as she tightened around him, her orgasm making her entire body shudder.

The breathy sound of his name on her lips pushed him over the edge. His release ricocheted through his core, shattering his senses until he and Odette were the only people left in the world.

Wrapping his arms around her, he held her tight to his chest, showering her in kisses until she laughed and sat up. Her dark curls spiraled down to her shoulders, and he coiled one around his finger and watched it unravel as he caressed her soft cheek.

"I love you." The words tumbled from his lips without a second thought. Pure truth. Every bit of it.

"Took you long enough to figure it out." She smiled and gave him a quick kiss. "I love you too."

"Cut me a little slack." He gazed out into the empty room. "There's a piece of my soul floating around in here somewhere."

She moved to sit sideways in his lap and snuggled into him. "And I am going to figure out how to put you back together. If the Baron makes an appearance at the ceremony, I'll ask him for help. Whatever the price."

"What should I expect tonight? Will he be possessing you?"

She drew in a quick breath and slid from his lap. "No. I won't be possessed." Rising from the couch, she shuffled about the room, gathering her discarded clothes.

He seemed to have hit a nerve. She disappeared into the hallway and returned with his jeans and T-shirt, laying them on the bed. Without making eye contact, she dressed, and he rose and picked up his pants.

"Have you ever been possessed?"

Her hard swallow was audible as she clutched her shirt to her chest. As she lifted her gaze to his, her eyes tightened with concern. "That's a long story."

He shoved his legs into his jeans. "Will you tell me on the way?"

Pressing her lips together, she studied him, but what was she looking for? Wondering if he could handle the truth? How bad could it be?

He took her hand. "Whatever it is, I want to know. I can take it."

She glanced at their hands and then into his eyes. "You're right. You deserve to know."

CHAPTER SIXTEEN

"I'd like to know what happened to you before we go in there." James shifted into park and looked at Odette. His deep blue eyes held concern and compassion, and she couldn't blame him for the hint of apprehension emanating from his aura.

Fear of the unknown could be the worst kind of fear.

She glanced at her watch; they had twenty minutes to spare. A fluttering formed in her stomach but not the usual butterflies that took flight when James was near. This felt more like a swarm of angry wasps. "No time like the present." Clearing her throat, she took a deep breath and blew it out hard. "Remember when I told you about my uncle and the pieces of souls he was keeping in *ouangas*?"

He shifted in his seat to face her. "I remember." His eyes widened. "Wait. You put them in the containers. If you can force a soul into a jar, you can force one into a person, can't you? My body is a container for my soul."

The hopefulness in his voice tore at her heart. "I can't. That part of you is attached to the house. It's trapped there, and only Baron Samedi can mend a broken soul."

"Oh." His posture deflated. "Well, a guy can hope. Anyway, what happened with the *ouangas*?"

She took his hand. "When Baron Samedi found out about my uncle's soul collection, he was furious. He insisted the souls be set free so they could rejoin with their rightful owners, but like I said, I don't have that power. I can help spirit energy cross over, but I can't mend an actual soul. Since these souls were residing in *ouangas,* Baron Samedi had to cross over into our world, and in order to do that, he had to act through a conduit. Through me." Her voice trailed off, her will to tell this story crumbling. What would James think of her if he knew the entire truth?

He placed his free hand on top of hers. "He possessed you when you were twelve years old?"

She nodded. "It was the only way. I had to give up control of my body, let Baron Samedi take over. Things got out of hand. Jars were shattering. The spirits I'd trapped were angry with me. My uncle was livid." Her lip trembled, and she blinked back the tears collecting on her lower lids.

"That must have been scary for you."

"Most of the time, during a ritual possession, the horse doesn't remember the ride. When a loa takes over, the host loses consciousness along with their control." She held his gaze. "I remember everything, and it was terrifying. I was there, but my body wasn't my own. I couldn't move. Couldn't speak. But I was acting. Moving. Destroying the *ouangas.* Releasing the souls."

Her heart sprinted in her chest, and she took a few slow breaths to calm herself. That was all he needed to know. Only two other living beings knew the rest of the story. Her father would never utter a word, and she would never see her cousin again. No need to add a third to the mix. "When it was over I swore I would never let it happen again." She laughed. "Now you see why I have control issues."

He shook his head. "I can imagine, but…" His eyes narrowed, and she could practically see the questions forming in his mind. He could tell she was holding back.

Time to change the subject. "What about when you're in wolf form? Does the animal ever take over? Do you lose control?" She pressed her lips into a tight smile and prayed the deflection would work.

"Never. My wolf and I are the same being. Whether we're in his form or mine, we work together. That's why I couldn't commit to you at first, before I knew the other woman he'd claimed was also you. When fate binds a werewolf's heart, there is no fighting it, so I was confused as hell as to how I could be bound to two women."

She grinned. "Bound to two mates. Sounds like a sexy romance novel."

He chuckled. "Well, this is real life, sweetheart, and you are the only woman for me."

"That's good to know." She cupped his face in her hand and ran her thumb across the dark stubble that was turning into a beard. "I like this look. Very rugged, handsome."

Holding her hand to his face, he turned his head, rubbing the softening hairs against her palm before kissing it. "Maybe I'll stop shaving then."

She held his gaze, and the corners of his eyes crinkled with his smile. His sky-blue irises held little flecks of gold, like treasure in an infinite sea she wanted to swim through for the rest of her life. Her stomach tightened, a feeling of elation expanding in her core, slowly making its way into her chest. How could she get so much satisfaction from staring into someone's eyes?

She could have sat in the car all afternoon simply looking at this man, but if she wanted more afternoons with him to come, they had work to do. "Are you ready to go in now?"

"I was born ready."

"Such a tough guy." She mussed his hair and climbed out of the truck.

The smell of burning incense greeted her nose as they entered the Voodoo temple. Taking James's hand, she led him through the front of the shop into the altar room, where she stopped in front of Papa Legba's dais.

"Please allow Baron Samedi to cross over today, Papa. I need to speak with him." Tugging an old house key from her pocket, she kissed it and dropped it in a bowl next to a walking stick.

"Do I need to do anything? Say a special prayer or…" He rested his hand on her back tentatively. Nervousness rolled from his aura, and she slid an arm around his waist.

"Get right in your head. Outsiders like to write these rituals off as hokum, but I assure you everything you're about to see is real. No one is faking."

"You realize you're asking a man who turns into a wolf to believe in magic, right?"

She smiled. "You'd be surprised how easy it is for your brain to convince you something isn't real."

"I'm a believer." He pressed a kiss to her temple.

She tightened her arm around him. "Understand that these are Ancestral Spirits, and we must hold them in reverence. Show them respect at all times. Follow my lead. I'll let you know if you need to do something specific."

"I'll follow you anywhere, sweetheart."

The conviction in his voice would have melted her doubts, but she didn't have them anymore. He would follow her into certain death. Now it was up to her not to lead him there.

As they entered the ritual room, Natasha knelt on the ground, drawing a *vévé* to Papa Legba. Never lifting her gaze from her creation, she said, "Welcome back, you two," and continued with her masterpiece.

"How'd she know it was us without looking?" James's voice was a whisper, his eyes tight with worry as he glanced about the room at the other vodouisants.

"She knows things." Odette rubbed his back, trying to ease his fear the way his presence always soothed her own.

The same drummers and dancers from the previous ceremony were preparing to begin, and three more female members of the house had joined them this time. A sour sensation churned in her stomach. She'd rather the entire Voodoo community *not* know about her situation, but there was strength in numbers, and the Baron did enjoy the women when they danced. If this didn't entice the loa to pay her a visit she…

No. Don't even think like that. This would work. They were out of options.

"Are we waiting on anyone else?" Natasha scanned the crowd, and the vodouisants shook their heads. "Alrighty then. Let's get this party started." The Mambo began her chant, and the drummers, Jackson and Tyrell, joined in, matching her rhythm.

"She's going to ask Papa Legba to allow the loa to cross over, and then we're going to pray that Baron Samedi will come." She caught James's gaze. "Keep him in your thoughts, and stay beside me, no matter what happens."

His lips quirked into a hesitant smile. "I won't leave your side."

He had no idea how much strength that simple sentence gave to her. She hadn't spoken to the Baron in person since the incident, and a brick settled in her stomach at the thought of all the things he might have to say. Things she deserved to hear.

As the beat continued, the dancers congregated in the center of the floor and moved along with the rhythm. The melodic cadence called to Odette, her body swaying before she realized what was happening. Instinct stiffened her, the usual fear of losing control taking over and bringing her mind into sharp focus. She had to keep it together. Panicking would do no good for anyone.

Natasha knelt again, grabbing a handful of cornmeal and drawing Baron Samedi's *vévé* on the floor in front of Odette.

A flitting sensation bubbled in her stomach, reaching up to her throat, but she swallowed it down. She'd made a promise to her *met tet*, and she had to keep it. Slipping her hand into James's, she relaxed her mind, allowing the music to penetrate her soul. As she swayed, her thoughts cleared, and she drifted into a semi-meditative state.

The energy around her shifted, an emptiness in the vibrational field increasing in strength. Was it her own magic intensifying with the ritual, or was her *met tet* joining the party? The darkness contracted, deepening and gathering into a cantaloupe-sized sphere.

The Baron was here.

Pressure built in Odette's chest as her heart sprinted and her palms slickened with sweat. An electrical current pulsed up and down her spine. Though she'd only experienced it once, she would never forget the feeling of being ridden by a loa.

Panic tightened her throat, and her stomach turned. This couldn't happen. Not now. She wasn't ready. The last thing she wanted to do was renege on her promise to the Baron, but agreeing to live her life in his image and allowing the Spirit complete control over her body were nowhere near the same thing.

Tightening her grip on James's hand, she turned her head toward him. He looked into her eyes, and she focused on the deep-blue color, the tiny flecks of gold glittering in the light. His aura, his presence, sharpened her mind and gave her the strength to let the loa know, in no uncertain terms, that she was not a horse to be ridden.

"I need to talk to you, Baron," she whispered. "I can't be your host."

James raised his eyebrows, silently asking if she was okay.

She nodded, letting out a breath of relief as the loa's presence dissipated, but a pang of regret flashed through her chest the moment his energy left. She may have ruined her one chance to receive Baron Samedi's help.

Tyrell stopped drumming, his face falling slack and his shoulders slumping. The Mambo dashed toward him as his body stiffened, and she caught him before he collapsed on the floor.

"Is he okay?" James squeezed her hand tighter.

"He's being possessed." *Please let it be the Baron.* She'd never forgive herself if her irrational fear had screwed up their one shot.

Odette held her breath as Tyrell regained his footing. Slipping the strap over his head, he set the drum on the floor and rolled his shoulders, stretching his neck from side to side. He ran his hands down his stomach to lift his shirt and peer at his abs.

"Not bad." He gave his wash-board stomach an appreciative nod and straightened, sweeping his gaze across the room. He paused on James for a split second, a look of recognition flashing in his dark-brown eyes, before focusing on Odette.

She gasped, and his lips curled into an un-Tyrell-like grin. Her pulse sprinted, and her lunch threatened to make a reappearance. Her prayer had been answered, but it didn't make facing her *met tet* any easier.

He looked at Natasha and spread his arms, speaking in a thick Haitian accent. "What have you got for your Baron, Mambo?"

Natasha bowed her head and presented him with a bowl of white powder. He dipped his fingers in the substance and smeared it on his skin, making circles around his eyes and mouth until his face took on a skull-like appearance. Strutting toward a table, he picked up a pair of round sunglasses, popped out one of the lenses, and settled them on his nose. Then, he placed a silk top hat on his head and ran his fingers across the brim.

"He looks like the guy on the rum bottle," James whispered, but no one responded.

Every vodouisant in the room had stopped to stare as Tyrell transformed into Baron Samedi, and the loa lifted his hands, palms up. "Why did the music stop? You know I love a party."

Natasha picked up Tyrell's drum, and she and Jackson played an upbeat rhythm.

Baron Samedi smiled, gyrating his hips and grinding on each of the dancers in turn as he made his way toward Odette. Stopping in front of her, the Baron pointed and then crooked his finger, indicating she should join him. Heat crept up her neck, and a low growl rumbled from James's chest. Her werewolf didn't want her to dance any more than she did, but she didn't have a choice.

She leaned into James's side. "Remember, he's not Tyrell right now. I'm dancing with an Ancestral Spirit."

He released his grip on her hand, but his gaze bore into her back as she stepped toward Baron Samedi and swayed her shoulders from side to side. Dancing with him was no different than an offering of rum or tobacco. She did it to honor her *met tet.* She needed to remember that.

"You call that dancing?" The Baron gripped her butt and pulled her body to his, circling his hips until she had no choice but to move along with him.

"I'm trying." She rested her hands on his shoulders and forced a smile. "I promise I am."

He laughed and released her, and James put his hand on the small of her back, reminding her he was with her no matter what.

"Your promise ain't gonna be an easy one to keep, is it?" Baron

Samedi arched a brow, and the white powder creased in the lines on his forehead.

She straightened. "Nothing worthwhile is easy. I brought you an offering." She handed him a bottle of her newest white rum. "I hope you'll accept it, along with my sincerest apology."

The Baron uncapped the bottle and pressed it to his lips. Tipping his head back, he gulped down half the contents before handing it back to her. "Not bad."

James's mouth dropped open as he eyed the half-empty bottle. "Tyrell's not gonna know what hit him."

Baron Samedi grinned, snatched the bottle, and drank three more gulps. "I like this guy." He gestured to James. "He's good for you. Let's talk." Draping his arms over their shoulders, he led Odette and James to some chairs in the back of the room. He gestured for them to sit, so she sank into a seat between her *met tet* and her soulmate.

The ceremony continued across the room, and Baron Samedi moved his shoulders, dancing along to the drumbeat. "You need my help."

She clutched her hands in her lap. "Yes. Something is trying to kill us, and it happens in every life cycle."

The loa nodded. "I know. I've seen it every time. Happens when you two meet." He looked at James. "I almost hated seeing you reborn, knowing what would happen to you."

"But…" She let out an exasperated sigh. "If you knew this would happen, why didn't you take me the first time I died? Why let me live, only to curse him too?"

"Because, child, you were a baby. Even the loa of death doesn't like to take the souls of children. And your mother made such a tempting offer." He took another swig of rum. "An entire distillery dedicated to me? I had to save you. Besides…" He patted her shoulder. "Your other half had already been born. This was willed by fate."

"So, our fate is to die?" Irritation edged James's voice, but he cleared his throat, lowering his gaze and keeping it under control.

The Baron grinned. "Not necessarily. You have the power to stop him this time. You've been second-born in every life between then and now, and it takes a shifting werewolf to defeat the Rougarou."

"You can't be serious," Odette said.

"He can't shift?"

"Yes, he can, but..." Everyone knew the Rougarou was nothing but a legend. Some centuries-old folklore from the bayou passed down through the ages. She gaped at the loa, expecting him to laugh at the preposterous idea. When he kept a straight face, she looked at James.

He rubbed at the scruff on his chin. "Maybe it's something different in Voodoo, but for werewolves, the Rougarou is the equivalent to the boogeyman. It's a story parents tell their kids to keep them in line."

Baron Samedi shrugged. "Eh, call him what you want, mon. The Rougarou is real, and he's fully awake."

Skepticism snaked into her mind, but she knew better than to doubt the word of a loa. At least out loud. But this cycle started with a power-hungry man. "Why is it after us? It must have something to do with Antoine, the one who killed Nicolas and Serafine. Did he make a deal with the monster?"

"Antoine *is* the Rougarou." He looked at them both, holding eye contact with her and then with James as his words sank in. "He's cursed."

She sucked in a breath. Why didn't she think of this before? "Serafine was a vodouisant."

"Now you're catching on." He straightened his shoulders as if her statement made him proud. It was just like a loa to make a vodouisant find her own answers to her questions.

Odette wasn't about to complain, though. She was lucky he'd shown up at all. Glancing at James, she chewed her bottom lip as the pieces of the puzzle clicked into place. "She didn't curse him, though; she wouldn't have had time. A family member did it."

The loa looked at his hand and rubbed his fingers together as if rolling something between them. More answers would require more offerings.

She patted James's leg. "Will you get the cigar out of my bag?"

"I'm on it." He strode to her bag and returned with the cigar and a lighter. Handing the smoke to the Baron, he held out the lighter and lit the end as the loa puffed away.

Returning to his chair, James leaned forward, resting his elbows on his knees. "How did it happen? And more importantly, what can we do to stop him?"

Baron Samedi examined the cigar and nodded, seemingly satisfied with the quality. "You were supposed to be the first alpha, yeah?"

James rubbed the back of his neck, his unease at the statement apparent in his pinched expression. "According to the past-life regression, I was, yes."

"With Nicolas out of the picture, Antoine should have inherited the ability to shift, but he didn't." Odette cut her gaze between the Baron and James.

James scratched his head. "That's how it usually works."

Odette's eyes widened. The puzzle was nearly complete. "Antoine didn't realize he'd fractured Nicolas's soul. When he didn't inherit the ability, he went to a *bokor*, didn't he?"

Baron Samedi nodded, tapping a finger to his nose.

"You mean like your uncle?" James asked.

Her breath caught, and she lowered her gaze to her lap. She glanced at the Baron, and his smile faded. "Yes." She forced out the answer, her heart pounding against her breast. "But the *bokor* was related to Serafine, wasn't he? Her uncle?" She nearly choked on the last word.

"He may have served the loa with both hands," Baron Samedi puffed on the cigar. "But he did love his niece."

Her chest ached at the memory of what happened with her own uncle, and she couldn't help but wonder if the Baron's statement was meant for both. "I'm sorry." Her whisper was barely audible, but James heard it. He rubbed his hand across her back, comforting her, but she could never change what had happened that day. If it were possible to go back in time and undo all the damage she'd done, she'd go in a heartbeat. Instead, her sins would weigh heavy on her shoulders for the rest of her life.

"Doesn't mean he didn't get what he deserved in the end." Baron Samedi winked, implying the double-edge of that statement as well. "Antoine went to the *bokor* to have the wolf gene activated, and he did get what he asked for. But the curse that came as the price was far higher than poor old Antoine ever imagined."

"He became the Rougarou." She reached for James's hand.

"That he did." The Baron extinguished the cigar and dropped it into the nearly-empty rum bottle. "Stuck somewhere mid-shift, he can't take on a complete human form, but he can't become a full wolf either. His body is in limbo, along with his soul."

"Damn." James shook his head. "I'll never tell that story to scare the pack kids again."

Baron Samedi rose to his feet. "Now the Rougarou sleeps somewhere in the swamp until the two of you meet. Then, he wakes up with nothing but revenge on his mind. As his power builds, demons feed on it and rise up from the underworld to come after you, weaken you."

"Shit." James leaned back in his chair. "But I can kill him? In wolf form, I can take him out for good?"

"There's a Spirit guardian in the swamp that watches over the Rougarou, does his best to keep him sedated after his revenge is exacted. But the Spirit ain't strong enough to make him sleep forever. The Rougarou's hatred for the ones he feels are responsible for his condition is powerful. When you're together, he knows, and he will kill you. Unless…"

James stood eye to eye with the loa. "Unless what?"

Baron Samedi's eyes fluttered and began rolling up—a sure sign the loa was done with the conversation and taking his leave. Odette stood and motioned for Natasha to help catch Tyrell when he fell.

"Work together, and you can kill the Rougarou. You'll need *L'Acallemon.* The *traiteur* in the swamp can lead you to him." Tyrell collapsed, and James caught him by the shoulders.

Natasha helped them settle him in a chair and wiped the white chalk from his face with a damp rag.

Odette's stomach soured, and she ground her teeth until sharp pain shot through her temple. *Please don't let it be the traiteur I think it is.*

"Who's *L'Acallemon?*" James asked.

Odette scrunched her brow. "The Gator Man. Another myth."

"He's no myth." Natasha held Tyrell's face as his eyes fluttered open.

"Who?" Tyrell tugged the glasses from his nose and took off the top hat. A grin tugged at the corners of his mouth as he examined the articles. "Baron Samedi?"

Odette nodded.

Tyrell chuckled. "That's a first."

"How you feeling?" James gestured to the nearly-empty rum bottle.

Tyrell held it up, his eyes wide. "The Baron drank all that?"

"With your body. Can you stand?" James tugged him to his feet and held his arm until he stood steady.

"Huh." Tyrell looked at the bottle again. "He must've taken it all with him. I feel fine."

James gave her a quizzical look, and Odette shrugged. "It happens," she said.

"I hope you got what you were looking for." Tyrell hugged Odette and returned to his drum.

She turned to Natasha. "What do you mean the Gator Man is no myth? He's a story told to tourists along with the Rougarou."

"If Baron Samedi says they're real, then they are." Natasha leaned in, her voice hushed. "Don't doubt your *met tet.*"

"Then which *traiteur* in the swamp is he talking about? There must be dozens." There had to be. This situation was a mess as it was. If they had to seek help from the *traiteur* her gut told her the Baron meant, they were screwed.

"Twenty years ago, maybe, but times have changed. There's one *traiteur* left near New Orleans, and it's Emile."

The name pulled the breath from Odette's lungs. She struggled to inhale, but a vise-grip held her chest, squeezing until her lungs felt like they would collapse. Not Emile.

Anyone but Emile.

A gasp from across the room drew her attention, and one of the dancers collapsed as a loa possessed her.

"Good luck." Natasha squeezed Odette's shoulder and scurried back to the ritual.

"Who's Emile?" James furrowed his brow, concern dancing in his gaze.

"He's..." Her cousin. The one other living being who knew the truth about the day she turned her back on Voodoo. She hadn't dared speak to him since it happened.

Her head spun, and she blinked rapidly as thoughts tumbled through her mind. She might as well seek out the Rougarou and offer herself to him now. Her cousin wouldn't help her. Hell, he probably wanted to kill her. Raised by a *bokor*...no telling what the man was capable of.

Was this Baron Samedi's way of punishing her? Sending her back to the place where she ruined everything?

"Talk to me, sweetheart." James cupped her cheek in his hand, lifting her gaze to his. "We're in this together, remember?"

She swallowed the bitter bile creeping up her throat and nodded. "Let's go somewhere quiet. It's not an easy story to tell."

CHAPTER SEVENTEEN

JAMES SHIELDED HIS EYES FROM THE SUMMER SUN AS HE followed Odette out the door and onto Dumaine Street. Humid heat enveloped him, coaxing sweat from his pores the moment he stepped out of the shade. A bicycle bell rang, and he jumped back to avoid being run over by a grubby-looking guy with a scraggly beard, riding an old Schwinn. The scents of body odor and weed trailed behind him like the tail of a kite, and James wrinkled his nose as he jogged to catch up with Odette.

She stared straight ahead, her determined strides propelling her to her destination at a fast clip. Her fluid dancer's posture tightened, her shoulders drawing toward her ears as she clenched and unclenched her fists.

Catching up to her, he matched her pace. "Why don't we find somewhere to sit, so we can talk." He rested his hand on the small of her back, and she slowed, blinking at him as if she'd forgotten he was there.

"Let's walk and talk. I need to keep moving or I'll…" She shook her head. "This is bad, James. Emile is… I don't even know where to begin."

"Take your time." He slipped his hand into hers and strolled beside her. His presence seemed to calm her like it usually did, bringing her down from the steep cliff she teetered on, but he'd never seen her this worried.

Her palm slickened, and she chewed her bottom lip, glancing at him occasionally as she composed her thoughts. Whoever this Emile guy was, Odette was afraid of him…and her fear commanded his wolf's attention. If Emile had done something to hurt her…

"He's my cousin." Her voice was thin, but as she relaxed her shoulders, it grew stronger. "The *bokor's* son. He was there when Baron Samedi set the souls free, and when I killed his father."

"You—?" James stopped, tightening his grip on her hand and tugging her to face him. "You killed him?"

She held his gaze for a moment, and a five-piece street band started up a brassy rendition of "When the Saints Go Marching In."

"Come on." She pulled him around the corner onto Royal Street.

"When you were twelve?" His childhood memory of her battled with this new information. Odette wasn't a murderer. There was no way. She may have lived with one foot in the spirit realm, but she'd never send someone there intentionally. She didn't have it in her. Not now and especially not as a kid.

She drew in a deep breath and blew it out hard. "I've told you my uncle was livid when Baron Samedi released his souls."

"Yeah?"

"Once the souls were free to return to the bodies of the living, the Baron took his leave. I collapsed from the possession…like Tyrell did at the ceremony." She rubbed at her throat. "I was weak and vulnerable, and when I came to, my uncle was on top of me, choking me. A few of the souls belonged to people who had already died, so their spirit energy lingered. They were as mad at me for trapping them as my uncle was for setting them free."

She shivered. "Emile helped me. He dragged my uncle off of me, and then the asshole turned on him. He was in a fit of rage, going after his own son. I don't think Emile even knew the souls had been trapped."

James pulled her to his side. "What happened then?"

She hesitated, pressing her lips together, the muscles in her mouth working like she was chewing the inside of her cheek. "I used my magic. I was terrified, and I didn't know what else to do. He was going to kill both of us, so I commanded the spirits. I gave them the energy to act and ordered them to attack him." She stared straight ahead, her gaze growing distant. "The ghosts grew so strong they turned solid. They bombarded him, and one of them broke his neck. He was lying there dead, and the ghosts floated above him, waiting for their next command."

She stopped and faced him. "They were like mindless soldiers. I could have made them do anything I wanted. It was the most terrifying thing I've ever done. I was trembling and crying, and Emile lay there, his eyes as wide as dinner plates, staring at me. I was scared, James, but it felt so good. All that power running through me."

Shaking her head, she took both his hands in hers. "I crossed them over. No matter how good the power felt, I knew it was wrong, and I sent them to the Baron. To the other side. Emile didn't say a word. We carried his dad's body to the swamp and sank it with some cinder blocks. I tried to talk to him, but he wouldn't even look at me. I left, told my dad what happened, and we packed up and moved away."

And she'd been harboring that secret for nearly twenty years. No wonder her powers terrified her. He couldn't imagine the pain she'd endured. The guilt. The suffering. He brought her fingers to his lips and kissed them. "Sounds like you did what you had to do. You saved Emile's life."

"By killing his father. I haven't spoken to him since the day it happened. How can I go to him for help after all these years? Why would he want to help *me?*"

"It looks like we don't have a choice. If we don't stop the Rougarou tonight, someone else will die. He won't be just helping you; he'll be helping everyone in New Orleans."

She huffed. "If he's anything like his dad, he doesn't care about anyone but himself." She laughed, but there was no humor in it. "Natasha convinced me to do these past-life regressions to help me figure out why I was afraid of my powers. Of course, *I* knew what the problem was, but I couldn't let the Mambo know I'd killed a man. I went through a few regressions to humor her, but when the pattern of death started emerging, I quit."

He kissed her cheek. "It's a good thing you did them. Otherwise, we'd both be dead by now and neither of us would have seen it coming." He couldn't fault her for not telling him before. He'd thought his wolf's issues were too tragic to share, but this… He couldn't imagine going through that at twelve years old.

Wrapping his arms around her, he inhaled the warm, sweet scent of her hair. A scent he wanted to experience every day for the rest of his life. "This is all going to work out. I've got your back with Emile… and after we kill this thing, we'll go home, and I'll have your front too."

Her laugh vibrated in his chest, and she pulled away to look at him. The tension around her eyes eased, the worry lines on her forehead smoothing. "If we make it through this, you can have any side of me that you want."

He cocked an eyebrow. "Whenever I want?"

"Forever." She gestured to a wooden sign hanging from the gallery above. "Have you been inside the Voodoo museum?"

He peered at the *vévé* carved into the plaque. A series of stars and swirls embellished two straight lines intersecting at a ninety-degree angle, much like the one Natasha had drawn in cornmeal to start the ceremony. "Can't say that I have."

"Come with me. I want to show you something." Taking his hand, she led him through the door and handed a ten-dollar bill to the attendant for the entrance fee.

They paused at the entry as a line of tourists exited the narrow hallway, and then they continued into the museum. On the right, a row of portraits hung, each one representing a famous Mambo from the past. A twenty by thirty-inch frame contained a painting of Marie Laveau herself, with a white scarf wrapped around her head, a snake draped over her shoulders.

He shuddered. The only animals not afraid of werewolves, snakes didn't hesitate to bite his legs when he got too close in the swamp. Their venom didn't slow him down, but it burned like hell until his body expunged it. "What is it with Voodoo and snakes?"

She slipped an arm around his bicep. "The snake represents Damballa, the creator of all life."

The beady, red eyes of the snake in the portrait stared back at him, and its forked tongue protruded between its fangs. "Ah, so kinda important then."

"There's a live one in the back. A python. Would you like to see it?" Her lips quirked into an adorable, kissable grin.

"No thanks. I see enough snakes when I'm hunting."

She wandered down the hall, and he followed her into a small room filled with life-size portrayals of various loa. A science class skeleton wearing a top hat, black jacket, and sunglasses with a lens missing stood in the corner. They'd spoken to the guy in person; why did they need to look at a replica? "Why does Baron Samedi have cotton in his nose?"

"It's a Haitian funeral tradition, but he's not who we're here to see. Look." She pointed to two figures standing side by side.

He moved closer to the statues. "Wolf head, human body, red eyes. That's the Rougarou my dad used to tell me about when I wouldn't go to bed." The same boogeyman he'd warned little Emma about when she'd thrown a fit in the bar a week ago.

The fake wolf's lips drew back in a snarl, and its hunched posture and pained expression in its eyes almost made James feel sorry for the guy. Almost. "Hard to believe I'm related to that thing."

He studied the other figure. An alligator head with a red mohawk sat atop a moss-stuffed mannequin wearing white coveralls. A small placard read, *"The Gator Man (L'Acallemon) protects people from the Rougarou (werewolves)."*

James huffed. "The Rougarou is *not* a werewolf. Nobody needs protection from us."

Odette chuckled. "Relax. No one believes any of this is real, werewolves included. When you live in secrecy, outsiders make up their own stories."

"But these." He gestured to the statues. "These aren't stories."

"Apparently not." She glanced at her watch. "We've got three hours of daylight left. We'd better pay Emile a visit."

Nausea churned in Odette's stomach on the twenty-minute drive out of the city. Curiosity had led her to research Emile when she'd returned to New Orleans a few years ago. That and her desire to avoid running into him by chance.

His website proclaimed him a *traiteur*, which was odd in itself. Faith healers usually didn't advertise their services. Then again, word of mouth traveled mostly online these days. Maybe it wasn't so odd after all.

His list of services didn't include anything that alluded to black magic, but that didn't mean anything. His father had kept his dark side hidden unless the price was right.

"Make a right here." She pointed to a narrow dirt road, and James turned, his truck bumping along the uneven path.

Cypress and pine trees rose on either side of them, creating a canopy over the road, their needles filtering the soft sunlight, making it appear darker than it should have at six-thirty in the evening in July.

James rolled down the windows and inhaled deeply. "I love the smell of the bayou in the summertime. Don't you?"

The earthy aromas of moss, mud, and arbor took her back to her childhood. To the tragedy she was about to return to. "My nose isn't as sensitive as yours."

"You're missing out." He reached across the seat and took her hand, trying to lighten the mood, to calm her, and his presence did help.

But nothing could tame the hurricane-strength anxiety blowing through her mind that returning to the scene of her crime had induced.

"There it is." She pointed ahead as the house came into view.

The wooden cottage looked exactly like she remembered it. Thick coats of white paint, applied over the peeling layers beneath, gave the panels a bumpy, mottled appearance. The corrugated-tin roof had rusted, and a blue tarp covered one corner to stop it from leaking.

An herb garden took up twenty square feet of the front yard, the rich, green plants overflowing the railroad tie barriers to take in another two feet. Emile had inherited his father's green thumb.

James parked the truck on the side of the road and looked at her with raised eyebrows, his silent question giving her pause.

Was she ready for this? Not really. Not at all.

She climbed out of the truck and walked hand-in-hand with James up the front steps. He reached for the screen door, but she tugged him along the porch to the side of the house.

"Always enter a *traiteur's* house through the back door. It's considered rude to go in through the front."

"Interesting." James rubbed at the scruff on his chin. "I'd have thought the opposite."

"I think it's safe to let go of everything we *thought* from here on out."

A wooden "open" sign hung on the door, so she twisted the knob and gave it a push. A set of chimes hanging from the ceiling jingled, announcing their presence.

She peered up at the wood and metal instrument. "Chicken bones."

"What?" James slid past her into the room and followed her gaze to the ceiling.

"When my uncle lived here, those were chicken bones. They rattled when the door opened." Her uncle had said the rattle of bones was significant because the people who came to him for help were on their deathbeds.

She knew better now.

"Have a sit. I'll be out in a minute." The man's voice was deeper than she remembered Emile's, but he was seventeen the last time she saw him.

Odette's heart slammed against her breast before crawling into her throat. James gestured to the worn sofa beneath the window, and she sank onto the edge, her back straight, muscles tense and ready to flee. What was she doing here? No good could come from this.

James rested a hand on her knee. "We've got this."

"I know." She scanned the room, searching for signs of black magic. A shelf filled with books on herbalism and healing lined one wall, and a lush array of herbs, too delicate for the Louisiana heat, filled an assortment of clay pots on the windowsill. No animal bones. No signs of blood sacrifice. Even the energy in the room felt lighter than she remembered.

Had Emile moved, taking her only chance of survival with him?

A woman in a pale-yellow dress entered the waiting area from a side door. Her shiny black hair flowed to her shoulders, and a white daisy pinned near her temple matched her necklace and bracelet. She smiled warmly. "Can I help you?"

Odette stood, the quick movement more aggressive than she'd intended. "We're here to see Emile. Does he still live here?"

The woman took a step back, her smile faltering before she composed herself. "Yes, he does. I'm his wife, Brooke. Do you have an appointment?"

"No, we don't." She tried to relax her posture, to tone down the off-putting aura of death that usually scared people away.

Unfazed, Brooke took a tablet from a shelf. "Would you like to make one?"

"This is an emergency." James stood next to Odette, so close his shoulder brushed hers.

Brooke's smile widened as she glanced at James and then looked at Odette. "Let me guess, you need a fertility spell?"

Odette glowered at the woman.

"I'm James, and this is Odette." He held out his hand, and Brooke shook it. "She's human," he said, as if assuring her the woman was harmless.

Brooke raised her eyebrows. "I take it you aren't?"

"Just a few more sessions, and it should be cleared up." Emile's voice drifted through the door first. Then his patient stepped through, a woman in her eighties with silver hair and bright blue eyes.

"I still think you should charge a fee for your services," the woman said. "Donations aren't a stable income. You can't count on people's generosity."

Emile smiled. "It's worked so far. See you next week."

As the woman shuffled out the door, Emile's gaze landed on Odette. His smile slipped into a frown, and he cut his gaze to James and then to his wife before looking back at Odette. "What are you doing here?"

The fear and guilt she'd kept bottled inside all these years erupted in her gut like someone dropped a Mentos into a bottle of Diet Coke. The little girl in her screamed to run, to leave New Orleans, her past, and everything behind. Running away had worked before; it could work again.

But the Rougarou would keep killing until it found her.

She straightened her spine and drew upon her magic, letting it build, gathering a static charge in the air, reminding her cousin of her power. "I need your help."

Emile crossed his arms. "Death isn't welcome in my clinic, and I've got bigger things to worry about. You need to leave."

"I'm not here to bring death. I want to stop it."

He scoffed. "Like you stopped my father?"

Brooke gasped and covered her mouth. "She's the one?"

"She is, and she's leaving. I've worked too hard to rid myself of my father's *bokor* legacy for you to come in and ruin everything. And to bring a werewolf with you?" He shook his head and ushered them toward the door. "Out you go. Scoot. And don't come back."

James crossed his arms, refusing to budge. "Tell us where to find the Gator Man, and we'll be happy to leave."

Emile narrowed his eyes. "What do you know about *L'Acallemon?*"

"We know he's the only one who can stop the Rougarou," James said.

"And that he can't do it on his own." She reached toward her cousin and touched his elbow. His magic vibrated up her arm before he jerked away. "Please, Emile. Will you help us?"

Her cousin's fingers curled into his palms as he ground his teeth. "My father took you in when the House didn't want you. He taught you how to use your magic, how to control it so you didn't bring death everywhere you went. He may have served the loa with both hands, but he…"

He clamped his mouth shut and took in a deep breath. "Yes, my father practiced black magic, and while he may not have been the most honorable man, he loved you…more than he loved me."

Odette blinked, scrambling for something to say. Emile had no clue what she'd suffered at the hands of his father. Crossing her arms, she inclined her chin. "If that's what you believe, then why didn't you turn me in?"

"No one missed the crazy old man from the swamp. Anyway, the magical community takes care of their own problems." He cut his gaze to James. "I bet your *boyfriend* can tell you some stories. I've heard about werewolf justice."

James stiffened, taking a step toward Emile, but Odette caught his hand.

"You could have turned me in to the House since you say they didn't want me anyway. Why'd you let me get away with it?"

"Your dad paid me for my silence." He crossed his arms to mirror her posture. "But, since there's no statute of limitations on murder, maybe I should call the police."

A growl rumbled in James's chest. "She was defending herself."

"He was attacking *me* when she killed him." Emile jabbed a finger at his own chest.

"Okay, let's all take a deep breath." Brooke put up her hands to stop the argument, but a sharp look from Emile had her backing up.

"He loved my magic, not me," Odette said. "I had enough bruises to prove it, but I hid them. So, go ahead and call the police. Are you going to tell them a twelve-year-old broke your dad's neck or that a bunch of ghosts did it? Which do you think they'll believe?"

Emile's mouth opened and closed a few times, his eyes losing focus as he processed her words. "Bruises?"

Her chin trembled, so she snapped her teeth together. "He beat me into submission whenever you weren't around because he wanted my power. He thought if he could control a child of Baron Samedi that he could control the dead." Her own uncle. Her *family.* Pressure built in the back of her eyes as the knife of betrayal twisted in her chest. A knife she'd thought she'd gotten rid of but had apparently just been ignoring.

This argument was pointless. No matter how justified she'd been, she did kill Emile's father. She didn't deserve his forgiveness, nor did she need it. Asking for his help had been a mistake. She tightened her grip on James's hand and stepped toward the door. "You know what, Emile? Never mind. If I could survive two years under your father's thumb, I can survive anything. Come on, James. We'll figure something else out."

She tugged James out the back door and rounded the corner, stopping on the side of the house. Her head spun, and what little she'd eaten today threatened to make a reappearance as she leaned against the porch railing. That confrontation had gone about as well as she'd expected it to.

"Are you okay?" James faced her, resting his hands on her hips.

She sucked in a trembling breath, shaking her head. "I knew he wouldn't help us. He'll never forgive me for what I did."

"He might if you ask him to. Have you ever apologized?"

"I…" she dropped her gaze to the ground. "I guess I haven't. I've been too busy defending myself, making sure nothing like that could ever happen again."

He tucked a spiral curl behind her ear. "Maybe you should. According to Baron Samedi, *L'Acallemon* is our last hope for defeating this thing. Without him, we're screwed."

She chewed her bottom lip as she held his gaze. Funny how James had turned into the sensible one. "I'll try. But I don't think it will help."

"Odette." Emile trotted around the corner, stopping when his gaze locked with hers. "Good. You're still here."

She pushed from the railing and faced him. "You've got access to *L'Acallemon*, and we're offering to help him defeat the Rougarou. If you really want to end your family's black magic legacy, this is your chance." It wasn't exactly an apology, but it was the best she could do at the moment.

James cleared his throat. "I think what she's trying to say is…"

"I know what she's saying. I heard every word, and you're right."

Of course she was right. He may have cleansed himself of his father's black magic, but she was offering him the means to stop a two-hundred-year-old curse.

"Give us the Gator Man, and we'll put an end to the reign of the Rougarou."

Emile let out a dry laugh as Brooke stepped onto the porch. "You don't know what you're offering. You'll die trying to defeat him."

James put his hand on her shoulder. "We'll die if we don't. We're the reason he's awake."

Emile's eyes widened as Brooke squeezed his arm. "I'll get some tea. You all better come inside." She scurried to the kitchen, and Emile led them to his living room. As they settled onto the sofa, Brooke returned with four tall glasses of sweet tea.

Emile sat in a teal accent chair, and Brooke perched on the arm beside him. "So you're his target this time." He chuckled and rubbed his mouth as if to rub the humor away. "No wonder it's taking so long. He's up against a shifter and child of Baron Samedi. How did you figure it out?"

She told him about her past-life regressions, James's dreams, the imps, and the ghost. "And Natasha said you're the keeper of *L'Acallemon*. That your family has been since the beginning."

"We have been because we're the ones who made him." He pressed his lips together, eyeing her as if he wasn't sure he should divulge the information. "We made the Rougarou too."

Emile paused, but if he was waiting for her to act shocked, he'd be sorely disappointed. She was in this mess up to her eyeballs, so it made sense that her cousin's side of the family would be too.

"Curses are made with black magic, which is unstable in itself," Emile continued. "From what I've read, the *bokor* who cursed the man into the Rougarou had a grudge, and adding negative emotions into the mix makes it even less predictable."

Odette nodded. "He killed the *bokor's* niece."

Surprise flashed in his eyes before he shook his head. "The Rougarou wasn't supposed to live forever. The curse was meant to make him hideous so he would have to spend the rest of his days in hiding, not quite a wolf but not a man either, and never able to claim New Orleans to start a pack. Unfortunately, with black magic, side effects occur and his strength multiplied, the curse binding his soul to the earth, making him impossible for an earthly-realm being to kill."

James put his hand on Odette's knee. "Has he ever gone up against a werewolf? We slay demons like piñatas. Maybe we don't even need the Gator Man's help."

"Many have tried." Emile's eyes darkened. "The Rougarou went on a killing spree when the curse was complete. Rogue werewolves from the bayou tried to stop him, but he tore them to pieces like *they* were the piñatas."

Emile arched a brow as James leaned back into the seat. Odette took her soulmate's hand and squeezed it. Now was not the time for a battle of egos. "So your family created *L'Acallemon* to fight him?"

"Our ancestors created *L'Acallemon* to defeat him, but their dealings with the black arts made the loa reluctant to help. Their magic wasn't strong enough to create an entity that could kill the Rougarou —only subdue him. Without a body, *L'Acallemon* is no match for the rage inside the monster. The rage that awakens him when the target couple meets."

Emile took a long drink of his tea. "I'm surprised you've lasted this long, even with your power."

Did he not remember what she was capable of? She took a slow, deep breath. Now was not the time for rivalry either. "I have a charm on the house, and we haven't been out after dark since the killings started. He's found us though. James has already fought him once and injured him. With *L'Acallemon's* help, we can—"

He set his glass on the coffee table with a *thunk*. "*L'Acallemon* can't do anything without a host. He has to ride someone."

Her heart dropped into her stomach to swim around with the churning, nauseating mess of emotions she'd been trying to keep down since they walked through the door. Before she could utter a word, James cut in.

"I'll do it. He can ride me."

"No, James. You're not even initiated. You can't…"

"I can initiate him." Emile looked at his wife as she lovingly rubbed her hand across his back. "I'm a *houngan*, so that's not the issue."

"It's settled then." James leaned back on the sofa. "With my fighting abilities and whatever magic the Gator Man brings to the table, the Rougarou won't stand a chance."

"Maybe not." Sadness filled Emile's eyes. "But *L'Acallemon* isn't really a loa. He can't move in and out of beings without harming them, because he was created for a single purpose. If you allow him to ride you, he'll probably sever your soul; it's what he was made to do. The priestess who created him died in the process."

Her stomach, heart, and every other organ in her body plummeted to the floor. *L'Acallemon* required the ultimate offering in exchange for his help—a life. With her hand on James's leg, she squeezed until her knuckles turned white.

"What are you trying to say?" He patted her hand, but she couldn't release her grip.

The one and only way to defeat the plague that had been following them through countless lives would kill the man she loved. She ground her teeth, cursing fate for its sick sense of humor.

Closing her eyes, she blew out a slow breath and swallowed the dryness from her mouth. "He's saying you'll die."

CHAPTER EIGHTEEN

"So, if I let *L'Acallemon* possess me, you're sure I can beat the Rougarou?" James pried Odette's fingers from his leg and held her hand in both of his. Her fingers had turned to ice, so he sandwiched them between his palms.

"According to the notes left behind, yes." Emile looked at his wife. "Get the book, will you?"

Brooke disappeared through a door and returned with a worn, leather-bound volume filled with yellowing paper. It creaked as she opened it and laid it in his lap, and the deteriorating pages looked so brittle they might fall out of the binding.

Emile turned to a bookmarked page and pointed to an entry. "They used a lock of Antoine's hair in the ritual when they created *L'Acallemon.* The Spirit is tied to the beast, they share energy, so he should be able to defeat it."

The warmth returned to Odette's fingers, so he laced his own through hers and swallowed the thickness from his throat. "And why haven't I tried this before in any of my past lives?" Besides the fact that he'd be facing certain death, because death was coming for him either way.

Flipping a few pages, Emile scanned the documents. "I don't think you knew what was happening before. Normally, when the Rougarou wakes up, he finds his target the same night and returns to the swamp where *L'Acallemon* puts him back to sleep."

It made sense. Baron Samedi said James had been second-born in every life since the cycle started. He wouldn't have been involved with hunting the demons that preceded the attack. He'd never had a clue… until now.

Odette's fingers tightened on his hand as she slowly shook her head. "You can't do this, James; I can't lose you. There has to be another way." Her eyes were wide with fear.

"I'm open to ideas."

"We can move away. Go to London or Australia. Somewhere the Rougarou could never get to us." Her brow pinched, the reality that the idea would never work draining the hope from her voice.

"He'll never stop killing."

"Until we're dead." Her expression blanked, a mask of resolve covering her fear as she looked into his eyes. "We have to stop him. People are dying because of our love."

"Not our love, sweetheart." He trailed his fingers down her cheek. "Because of the ridiculous standards of an outdated society and one man's hunger for power. Hate and greed created this monster. Love will take it down."

Emile handed Brooke the volume, and she took it to the other room, returning with a small yellow suitcase. "I'll be back in the morning, love." She blew a kiss to Emile, and he rose and hugged her. "Be careful."

"Always."

"It was nice meeting you two." She waved and shuffled out the door.

Emile took the tea glasses to the sink. "She's been spending the night with her sister two hours away since it started. The beast is looking for couples, and I've been casting locator spells and begging the loa for help. If I'd known who he was after…" He shook his head.

"We'll stop him." James rose and cracked his knuckles. No one else would die because of his twisted fate. "Tell me what to do."

Emile nodded. "Come with me. We'll need to perform a *lavé tet.*"

"It's a head-washing ceremony." Odette took James's hand and guided him into another room. "A spiritual cleansing to make you ready to receive a loa in possession."

He sat in the chair Odette gestured to. A row of cabinets with shelves full of herbs lined one wall, and a table holding equipment similar to what he'd seen in Natasha's temple sat next to it. "But the Gator Man isn't a loa."

"Which is why the short version of this ceremony should be enough to make the possession tolerable for you." Emile filled a bucket with water and sprinkled in herbs from the jars. Pressing his palms together, he said a prayer over the mixture, blessing it.

Odette sat next to James, her death grip on his hand letting him know how much she disliked what he was doing. Hell, he didn't like it any more than she did, but what choice did he have?

Emile set the bucket on the floor and pulled up a chair. "Take off your shirt and tilt your head back."

James tugged his shirt over his head, and Odette put her hand on his chest.

Her fingers felt like icicles again. "Wait. What if I carry *L'Acallemon*? You can subdue the creature, and the Gator Man can use me to kill him. Then at least you'll have a chance to survive."

Her lips paled as she spoke, her fear of relinquishing all control causing her shoulders to draw up toward her ears. No way would he let her go through something so traumatic to spare his life.

Holding her hand to his chest, he kissed her temple. "I don't want to survive if it means living without you."

Tears collected on her lower lids. "That sentiment works both ways, you know."

He draped his shirt across his knee and took her face in his hands. "I'm not afraid of being possessed. I'm not afraid of death or of dying. I was made for this."

"The only thing that scares me is losing you." A tear dripped down her cheek, and he wiped it away with his thumb.

"I've got this."

"But I can—"

"No, Odette. You can't." Emile dipped a wooden spoon into the bucket and stirred the contents.

"Yes, I can." She shot to her feet. "Voodoo created the curse, so a vodouisant should be sacrificed to end it. I won't let James die over something *my* ancestor caused."

While James admired her determination, there was no way in hell he would let her die. "Odette." He reached for her hand, but she jerked away.

"Put your shirt back on. I'm hosting *L'Acallemon*."

Emile carried the bucket to James's chair. "You've put up a block; I can feel it in your aura. Baron Samedi himself couldn't ride you in this condition, much less a home-grown Spirit like *L'Acallemon.*"

"I can handle it, Emile. I'll do whatever needs to be done."

James reached for her hand again, and this time she let him take it. He pried her fingers from her palm and gave her hand a squeeze. She relaxed a little with his touch, but she was riled up and ready to fight. God, he loved this woman.

"Regardless of what you can or can't handle, it has to be James. You said yourself that Baron Samedi told you only a shifting wolf can kill the Rougarou, and I understand why." Emile dropped the spoon into the bucket and glanced at James, hesitating to continue. "*L'Acallemon* was conjured using werewolf blood."

"Son of a bitch." No wonder this situation was so royally fucked. Blood magic, especially the kind involving werewolf blood, was extremely volatile and always came with a price.

Emile raised his hands. "I didn't write the spell. I read about it in the family journals." He laughed dryly and looked at Odette. "I've been studying this for the past sixteen years, trying to figure out the secret, and then you come along, chat with your *met tet*, and suddenly you've got all the answers. Loa don't lie. If the Baron said it has to be a werewolf, then it *has* to be a werewolf."

"You have no idea what it took to get Baron Samedi to help me. It sure as hell wasn't a simple chat."

Her cousin raised his hands. "Whatever it took, you got the answers. Unless your dad is secretly a werewolf, you know as well as I do that you can't be the host for *L'Acallemon.*"

Her breath released in a hiss as she lowered into the chair, the expression on her face one of pure determination. She wasn't going to let *L'Acallemon* take him without a fight.

James leaned back in the chair, and Emile dumped cup after cup of seasoned water over his head, saying both Catholic prayers and Haitian Creole chants. He wiped at the room-temperature liquid to stop it from getting in his eyes, but it ran in rivulets down the back of his neck, soaking his shoulders and half his torso.

The magic in the room intensified, the vibration of the air increasing, raising the hairs on his arms. When Emile used up the last of the water, he wrapped James's head in a white towel and took the bucket to the sink.

Odette clutched her hands in her lap and smiled weakly. "Normally we'd dress you in all white and have you lie down for the rest of the day." She glanced at her watch. "But we've got to get going if we're going to make it home before dark."

"We're not doing this at your house. You've got neighbors." He took the towel Emile offered, and he patted himself dry. Bits of crushed rosemary and sage clung to his skin, making him smell like a Thanksgiving turkey waiting to go in the oven.

"The neighbors won't see a thing. I'll lift the charm; the Rougarou will come inside to find us." She took the white towel from his head and gave it to Emile.

"We'll tear the place apart." He pulled his shirt over his head, slipping his arms through the sleeves and running a hand through his wet hair.

She straightened her spine. "It's a sacrifice I'm willing to make. If you're going to…" Her voice hitched, and she swallowed. "If you're going to die, it needs to happen in the house. I think I can…" She dropped her gaze to the floor, and a sob caused her shoulders to bounce.

James pulled her into a hug and kissed the top of her head, his heart breaking at the sadness in her voice.

"If you die, I think I can make Nicolas cross over with you. If he sees his brother pay for his crimes, he'll be able to move on too. You'll be whole again."

Emile handed him a preserved alligator head, its snout nearly the length of his entire arm. "*L'Acallemon* is tied to this. It's the gator that was sacrificed to create the Spirit, preserved with magic and formaldehyde. For the Spirit to possess you, you'll have to put it on your head. *L'Acallemon* will travel down through your crown and into your body."

James lifted the mummified head toward his own.

"Not yet." Emile put his hand on the gator. "The possession will happen quickly. Wait until the Rougarou is in sight."

"Thank you." James shook his hand.

"Yes, thank you, Emile." Odette clasped her hands together. "I wanted to tell you that I'm sorry about everything that happened. I didn't use any black magic that day. It was the power Baron Samedi gifted me, but I abused it. I am so, so sorry."

Emile pressed his lips together and nodded. "You saved my life, and you kept my father's secret. I should have thanked you a long time ago." He held out his hand, and Odette accepted it. "Good luck. I hope you can end this cycle."

"We will." James shook his hand once more and led Odette out the back door.

Odette sat quietly in the passenger seat as James maneuvered along the bumpy dirt road and back out onto the highway. A tornado of emotions swirled through her body, and she focused on them one at a time, so they didn't overwhelm her.

The easiest emotion to pluck from the storm was her relief that Emile didn't hold a grudge. She'd hoped for forgiveness, but to receive his thanks after all these years of turmoil was like opening a pressure valve on her soul.

She'd made right by her *met tet* and made amends with her last living relative on her mother's side. If not for the impending death of the man sitting next to her, she'd have said things were looking up.

The despair of losing her soulmate tore open her chest, fracturing her heart, and causing a sob to bubble up from her throat. James glanced at her, and she coughed to cover it up. *He* was the one about to die, and no tears streamed from his eyes. If he could be strong, so could she.

She stared out the window as the blur of trees made way for buildings as they approached the city. Who was she kidding? Her strength was a façade. It always had been. Ritual possession was nothing for a seasoned vodouisant like herself to be afraid of. She'd seen it happen to her friends countless times, and none of them were harmed in the process.

Now the one Spirit that would harm its host was about to possess her boyfriend, and there wasn't a damn thing she could do about it. Or maybe there was…

She remained silent as he spoke with his alpha on the phone. Her attempt at protesting his desire to ask the pack for help fell flat when he reminded her that wolves were pack animals. If he was going to die in this fight, she'd let it happen on his terms.

If she let it happen at all.

He tossed his phone into a cupholder and reached across the console to rub the back of her neck. "Luke's gathering a few weres to meet us at the house. If I fight the Rougarou with the pack's help, it will be over faster. Less damage to your home."

She nodded and fought the tremble in her voice. "You didn't tell him you wouldn't be surviving the fight."

The corner of his mouth twitched. "If he knew that, he'd never agree to the plan. You and I both know this is the only way to end the cycle. Sacrificing my life will stop anyone else from dying at the hands of the Rougarou."

"Sometimes I wish you weren't so damn noble."

James chuckled. "You wouldn't have me any other way."

He stopped in the driveway, and they both watched in silence as the sun sank behind the house. The orange and pink of the sky morphed into a deep purply-blue, and an early cricket chirped, its ominous song a harbinger of tragedy.

A ten-ton weight pressed into Odette's chest, squeezing the air from her lungs. She held her eyes wide, but try as she might, she couldn't stop the tears from falling. Turning her head, she slid out of the truck and paced toward the front door.

James caught up to her on the porch, and balancing the gator head on the railing, he pulled her into his arms, wiping the tears from her cheeks. "Hey." He hooked a finger under her chin, lifting her gaze to his. "This isn't goodbye, you know. I'll find you in our next life, and then we'll have our happily ever after, okay? I promise."

She nuzzled her face into his chest, breathing in his woodsy, masculine scent. A scent she'd come to associate with comfort. With home. James had done more than restore this old house; he'd restored *her*. He had chipped away the plaster of her carefully constructed façade and found the woman beneath, bringing her to the surface and reminding her how to live.

James was right; this wasn't goodbye. Emile had said the Gator Man would drain James's life force and *probably* sever his soul. That qualifier was her ray of hope, and she planned to hold onto it until the end.

Pulling herself together, she faced the front door and whispered a banishing spell, asking Papa Legba for help opening the gateway to her home, breaking the protection charm. Magic vibrated in the air, gathering in front of the door, condensing and expanding until the pressure popped like a bubble and dissipated into the air. "It's done. The Rougarou, and anything else for that matter, can get inside." The fact sat heavy in her stomach like a block of dried-up mashed potatoes.

"Then we'd better get ourselves in and get ready."

As if she could prepare for the impending death of her soulmate. Living the rest of this life without James would be unbearable, and she refused to continue living alone.

A sense of resolve washed over her as she stepped through the threshold. If defeating the Rougarou, breaking the cycle, meant ending James's life, she knew what she'd have to do. James wasn't afraid of death. Neither was she.

James paused on the porch as Luke, Cade, Noah, and a woman with a blonde pixie cut and bright-green eyes strode up the walk.

Luke shook James's hand. "Chase and Bryce are leading a patrol in case your beast tries to make any pitstops on the way."

James nodded and gestured for them to enter. Odette chewed the inside of her cheek as James set the gator head on a table, and they gathered in the foyer. The woman hesitated to close the door. She looked outside and glanced at Luke before lowering her gaze.

"We need you here."

At the alpha's words, she closed the door and nodded.

James rested a hand on Odette's back and whispered, "Her mate is on patrol. They haven't been together long."

Odette recognized the worried expression. Her own face probably looked the same.

"This is Alexis," Luke said. "She's our healer."

"Healer?" Her eyebrows raised as the tiny ray of hope she clung to grew a little brighter, but James rolled his neck, his back stiffening.

"She'll help us fight, but if anyone gets hurt in the crossfire, she can use her enhanced healing ability on others." Luke flashed a small smile, focusing on Odette. "We'll keep you safe."

James's tension eased, but she hadn't been the slightest bit worried about herself. She'd been caught up in the soul-severing fear and hadn't stopped to think about how the confrontation had gone down in her previous lives. The Rougarou would come after her first.

Luke held a hand above the gator head, but he didn't touch it. "There's a Voodoo Spirit attached to this thing?"

"*L'Acallemon.*" James picked it up and looked into its glassy eyes. Cocking his head, he squinted, studying the object as if he were looking for the Spirit, but even Odette couldn't see the Gator Man.

Was it even attached to it? What if Emile hadn't forgiven her and this was a cruel attempt at getting even? She had killed his father, a man that he loved. Maybe her cousin had infused them with the false hope that they could defeat the Rougarou, when his true intention had been ensuring their timely deaths. Bile crept up the back of her throat, but she swallowed it down. Her cousin's intent didn't matter at this point. The beast would be there soon, and the house was unprotected.

Cade shoved his hands first in his front pockets and then his back before crossing his arms. "You're sure you want to let it possess you?"

"It's the only way to end this." James looked at Odette, and pressure built in the back of her eyes again, so she lowered her gaze. She would not cry in front of his pack.

"Are you sure it's safe?" Alexis peered at the head and curled her lip.

"He can handle it." Noah clapped James on his shoulder. "This'll be over before midnight, and I'll buy the first round of beers when we're through."

She dared another glance at James, and when his eyes met hers, time seemed to freeze. Her lungs betrayed her, not allowing her breath to pass in nor out, and the force of gravity multiplied, threatening to crumbled her. She would not live a single day without this man, and she had all the ingredients she needed to make sure she wouldn't have to in her cupboard. Now, she had to convince Baron Samedi to cooperate.

Shaking herself to break the trance James's gaze had put upon her, she cleared her throat. "We should prepare."

"She's right." James carried the gator head beneath his arm and stood by her side. "Luke, I think it's best if y'all hide. Odette and I will wait in the bedroom since that's where it likes to find its victims. Stay in the laundry room across the hall. There are no windows, so it can't see you, and when you hear the fight starting, then come in. Not before. I don't want the Rougarou to take off before the Gator Man has a chance to take hold."

The alpha squared his gaze on Odette. "Are you sure this is safe for him?"

"It's the only way." James slipped his hand into hers. "I trust her with my life, and I trust that if anything happens to me, the pack won't seek retaliation. I'm doing this voluntarily, and I'm aware of all the risks."

Luke cut his gaze between them and nodded. "Agreed."

"I'll prepare the *vévés.*" She shuffled into the kitchen, with James on her heels, as the alpha called his pack into a huddle. "I'll be right back." She kissed James on the cheek and glanced out the window at the final rays of light disappearing behind the horizon.

He clutched her hand. "We're out of time."

Out of time before the Rougarou arrived, before their lives ended, their love lost. "I'll be fast."

Taking a sack of cornmeal from a cabinet, she hurried to the bedroom and drew Papa Legba's *vévé* in the entrance.

"Please, Papa, allow *L'Acallemon* to enter our world and take James as his host." She glanced over her shoulder to be sure she was alone. "And please allow Baron Samedi to cross over, should he so desire."

Nicolas appeared before her, a confused expression pinching his ghostly brow.

"Stay with me. You'll be free from this place soon." She returned to the hallway as the werewolves headed to the laundry room to hide, and James gave her a questioning look. "One more minute. I need a word with the Baron."

James nodded, and she rushed to her altar room. Pausing to take a deep breath and center herself, she dropped to her knees and drew her *met tet's vévé* in cornmeal on the floor in front of his altar. "Please Baron Samedi, name your terms. I'll pay any price if you'll allow me to be with James, if not in this world, then in yours."

His pack mates squeezed into the laundry room, and James tapped Noah on the arm. "A word?"

"What's up?" Noah followed him into the hallway, his excitement at being included in the fight evident in his casual smile. Hopefully the pack would continue to include him after James was gone.

He guided his friend out of the alpha's earshot and lowered his voice to a whisper. "There's a ninety-nine percent chance I'm not going to make it out of this alive."

Noah's expression fell. "Wha—"

"Shut up, man. This is between you and me." Odette returned from her prayer to Baron Samedi, and he pulled her to his side. "This Spirit is probably going to kill me, and I'm well aware of it. I need you…"

Noah shifted from side to side, opening and closing his mouth like he wanted to protest.

James held up a hand to keep him quiet. "I need you to keep your mouth shut, first of all. Second, when this is over, I need you to make sure she's taken care of. If anyone holds my death against her, you set them straight. Understood?" He stared his friend hard in the eyes, willing him to understand. James didn't want to die any more than the next person, but if it meant Odette would be safe and no one else would fall victim to the Rougarou again, he'd gladly make the sacrifice.

He squeezed Noah's shoulder. "I'm telling you this because I trust you. Will you do this for me? Consider it my dying wish."

Noah blinked a few times, his mouth hanging open like his mind couldn't comprehend. "Yeah. Of course, but…damn, James. Are you sure?"

"If one more person asks me if I'm sure, I'm going to punch him." He jerked his head toward Odette. "Whatever she needs, you get it for her. No matter how weird her request."

"Got it. I…" His eyes softened, his brow pinching.

"Don't you dare say you're gonna miss me or any bullshit like that." He was having a hard enough time keeping it together for Odette. If his friend started blubbering, he might lose it right there in front of her. "Get in there and be quiet."

Noah nodded and shuffled to the laundry room to join the pack, and James followed Odette into the bedroom, setting the alligator head on the dresser.

She paused by the bed and ran her hand across the cream-colored duvet. "Now that I've had you in this bed, I won't be able to sleep in it without you."

"Come here." He hugged her tight and caught her mouth in a tender kiss. He started slow, gently brushing her lips with his, but as the reality that this would be their last kiss settled in, he tangled his hands in her hair and drank her in.

Her fingers dug into his back as she held him, and she leaned into him, returning his passion with an unbridled heat like nothing he'd ever felt before. He'd barely scraped the surface of her cool and refined shell. If he'd had more time with her, he could imagine the ecstasy they could have shared.

Her sweet scent. The warmth of her body. The softness of her curves. She was built to be in his arms, and this was the most wonderful, painful moment he'd felt in his entire life. "I love you, Odette."

"I love you too." Her lips moved against his, her sweet breath sending shivers down his spine.

What he would have given to make this moment last forever.

But a bang sounded against the window, the pane rattling with the impact. James spun around, shoving Odette behind his back and widening his stance. The silhouette of a hand with elongated fingers slammed against the glass, and the piercing screech of claws dragging down the pane resonated in his ears. He reached for the gator head, ready to let *L'Acallemon* kill the bastard, but Odette stopped him with a hand on his arm.

"Let him come inside first. If he senses the Gator Man, he might run."

His heart pounding in his throat, James clutched her hand and lowered his arm to his side. His wolf howled inside him, begging to be released, but James held on to his humanity a little longer. His human side had to be fully in control in order to accept the Voodoo Spirit into his body.

The creature outside grunted and shattered the glass with a fist. Uncurling its claws, it gripped the windowsill and hauled itself into the opening. Squatting on the ledge, its legs resembled canine haunches, the knees bending backward with an extra joint below the hip jutting forward. Its fingers extended into sharp, black claws, and its face… Good God, its face.

The skin appeared half-melted, while the bone structure looked stuck mid-shift between human and wolf. Its nose and mouth jutted forward in a short, malformed muzzle, and its pointed human ears sat too high on its head—above the temple, but not quite where a wolf's would be.

Odette gasped, and the beast jerked its head toward them, a menacing sneer curving what was left of its lips over canine teeth. It lowered itself into the bedroom and straightened to its full six-and-a-half-foot height.

"The bitch dies first." Its gravelly voice sounded more like a growl.

James released Odette's hand and stepped forward. "Not a

chance." He reached for the alligator head and shouted, "Now, Odette."

She began the ritual, asking the Spirit for help, and the beast snarled as its head morphed into a wolf with glowing red eyes and razor-sharp teeth. The Rougarou lunged, swiping the gator head from James's hands, and it slid across the room, slamming into the wall with a *thud.*

"Damn it. Noah! Luke!" He was no match for this beast in his human form, but he needed that head before he shifted. With his arms stretched wide, he backed Odette into the hall.

But the beast moved like lightning, gripping James's shoulders and tossing him aside as if he were weightless. His head slammed into the hardwood floor, and his vision spun as he scrambled to his feet. He righted himself, and the room tilted on its side. *Not now.* He couldn't afford to black out.

Odette screamed, and his heart stopped for a beat or two before pounding against his ribs. He would not let that thing hurt his fate-bound. Grabbing the gator head, he placed it on his own and raced into the hallway.

Luke howled, and the other wolves joined in, charging the Rougarou as it advanced on Odette. Luke swiped a paw across its back, and it reeled, spinning and running into the foyer. Odette locked eyes with him and quickly called on the Spirit, her magic intensifying, filling the room with a static charge.

Noah glanced between them, rubbing the goose bumps from his arms. "I'm going to miss you, buddy, but I know you've got this."

James closed his eyes and invited *L'Acallemon* inside him, relinquishing control and giving himself over to the Spirit. The top of his head heated, and vibrating magic bore into his skull, filling first his head, and then his entire body with Spirit energy.

He looked at Odette and opened his mouth to tell her goodbye, but the Spirit took over, using James's magic to transform him into his wolf, absorbing the gator head into his form.

As his paws hit the ground, James darted down the hall toward the fray. Odette started to follow the sounds of snarling beasts, but Noah stopped her with a hand on her arm.

He jerked it away and rubbed his palm on his jeans. "Is he possessed now? Like, that's not James anymore?"

"The Gator Man is inside him. I don't know how much control he has. If *L'Acallemon* were a loa, James would have no control." And a little dizziness would be the only symptom he'd experience when it was done.

She paced toward the fight, keeping Nicolas in her peripheral vision. The ghost needed to see what was about to happen if he was ever to be free from this realm.

"And it's going to kill him?" Noah followed on her heels.

"*Probably* going to kill him. It might not." *I hope it won't.*

She rounded the corner as a sandy-colored wolf and a light-brown one sprang toward the Rougarou, each one clamping onto a shoulder. The beast cried out, hurling its lanky arms in circles, throwing the wolves to the ground. Damn, that thing was strong.

The Rougarou lunged for James, biting into his back as it clung to his gray fur. James spun, snapping his jaws at the beast, but he couldn't reach. Dark-red blood soaked his coat around the puncture, and he stumbled.

Odette gripped the doorjamb to stop herself from running into the fight. Would he heal instantly if his soul were whole? They hadn't mentioned his problem to Emile. How much would his weakness hinder his ability to stop the monster?

The beast snarled, wrapping its arms around James's chest, and he let out a pained yelp. Odette's heart raced at a hummingbird's pace. The Gator Man Spirit was supposed to make James stronger. He was supposed to kill the Rougarou. She had to do something.

Fisting her hands, she inhaled a deep breath and called upon her power. Her energy built, emptying the room of its buzzing life energy, filling it with the static emptiness of the spirit world.

The Rougarou hesitated, glancing at her, and the reddish wolf rammed into the beast and knocked it to the ground before sinking its teeth into the creature's malformed leg. It cried out in pain, and the two other wolves gripped its upper arms, spreading it out on the floor as James loomed over it, one paw pressing down on its chest.

James growled, peeling his lips back over his teeth, and positioned his head to strike the killing blow.

"Wait." Odette poured her magic into Nicolas, filling the ghost with energy until he became as solid as a living being.

"Holy shit." Noah stood next to her, his eyes wide as he stared at the specter. "Is that a ghost? Has he been here the whole time?"

She ignored him, focusing her attention on Nicolas. The spirit's brow lifted, his expression becoming even more confused. "Serafine?"

"This is who killed Serafine. Look at him, Nicolas. He's your brother. He killed you too."

The ghost floated toward the creature and peered down at it. "Antoine?"

The Rougarou shifted, a sickening sloshing sound filling the room as its face transformed into the half-human abomination it was when it broke in. James growled again, shifting his weight forward, onto the beast.

Turning its head toward Nicolas, the Rougarou winced in pain before its eyes widened. "Brother, have mercy," it croaked.

Nicolas shook, a rage filling his ghostly form as he gathered more of Odette's energy. "You don't deserve mercy." Gripping the table in the foyer, Nicolas flung it across the room. It hit the wall with a crash, the wood splitting and falling to pieces on the floor.

"That's enough, Nicolas." Odette reined in her power, the high of opening herself to the other realm dissipating as the spirit grew transparent.

Nicolas grasped at a broken table leg, but his hand passed through the wood. He grunted and whirled to face Odette. "He must pay for his crimes."

"He will, but his curse has bound his soul to the earth. *L'Acallemon* can break the bond and end his life."

The Rougarou struggled, yanking its leg from the red wolf's grasp. James snarled and delivered the killing blow, clamping his maw on the creature's throat. He held on, his wolf form convulsing as *L'Acallemon* ripped the curse from the creature's body, scattering the dark magic into the universe.

The Rougarou gasped, a gurgling sound emanating from its throat as its face finally made the full transformation back to human, and the life in its eyes dimmed. Antoine's soul lifted from his body, and Odette called on her power again to force him to cross over.

The spirit disappeared, whisked away to the underworld, where he could never harm a living being. They had broken the cycle. She'd never have to die in her lover's arms again.

She allowed herself a single breath of relief, but no more. Killing the Rougarou had been the easy part.

The wolves released the body and backed away, their gazes locked on Antoine's lifeless form. Seemingly satisfied that the creature was dead, Luke shifted, a mist gathering around his fur, elongating his body until he stood erect, and then disappearing into his human form.

The other wolves followed their alpha's lead, shifting to human form, their faces bright with satisfaction that they'd rid the world of such a terror.

But Odette's nightmare had just begun.

James shifted, rising to his feet as *L'Acallemon* ripped from his body. The mummified alligator head tumbled to the floor, shattering into dust on impact. The Gator Man had been created for a single purpose: to fight the Rougarou. With the threat extinguished, the magic holding the Spirit together dissipated into the atmosphere, leaving James drained and dying.

He collapsed into her arms, and she lowered him to the floor, her heart beating a frantic rhythm in her throat as she held him tight to her chest. "Please, Baron, don't take him yet." If her *met tet* took James, he'd have to take her too.

"What's wrong with him?" Luke dropped to his knees beside them. "Alexis, heal him."

Alexis knelt and put her hand on the bite mark on his back. "Unless that thing was venomous, this wound shouldn't be fatal." She closed her eyes for a long blink and opened them with a confused expression. "The wound is healed. I don't sense any poison, but he's slipping. His heart…it's not beating."

Odette loosened her grip, letting James slide from her lap, and gently laid him on the floor. Sitting back on her heels, she focused on his lifeless body, waiting for his soul to ascend, and a sob lodged in her throat. Or was that her heart wrenching from her chest?

This was not the end. She would be with him forever—one way or another. "Please, Baron Samedi, I need your help. I'll keep my promise; name the price."

She dropped her walls, opening herself to every ounce of magic the loa had blessed her with. No more restraint. No more self-imposed blocks on her power. Rising to her feet, she let it all go and focused on her connection to the spirit realm. She wasn't merely a conduit; she became a portal, an open doorway to the other side, the energy flowing through her like the river Styx through Hades.

"Jesus Christ, it's getting cold in here." Cade rubbed at his arms.

"Well?" Luke gave Alexis a pointed look, but their conversation barely registered. Odette stood with one foot in the spirit world.

"I can't heal him. Nothing is broken." Alexis's tone raised an octave with her panic.

"Start CPR." Luke began chest compressions, and Odette wandered into her altar room.

James and Nicolas stood side-by-side, two parts of a single soul, and Odette's chest ached at the sight of the spirits. Her magic had solidified them, but the werewolves were too concerned with his body to notice his soul. The commotion in the other room dulled to a hum as James drifted toward her.

A sad smile curved his lips, and the love in his eyes made her breath catch. "I told you I wouldn't let you die in my arms."

"Yeah, but you weren't supposed to die in mine." Something between a laugh and another sob bubbled up from her chest. Where was Baron Samedi?

James ran his fingers down her face leaving a trail of warmth on her skin and giving her hope. The heat meant his soul remained, not just his spirit energy. "Why can I touch you? Is your magic doing this?"

She nodded. "I'm giving you everything I've got."

"That's all I ever wanted."

Like it or not, he was about to get more. Holding her arms to her sides in the most open posture she could manage, she lifted her chin and made one final plea to her *met tet.* "Baron Samedi, grant me the power to mend this fractured soul. My body is yours. I open myself to your magic." She absorbed the deep blue of her soulmate's eyes. "I refuse to live without him."

Baron Samedi's presence pressed on her shoulders, building in intensity as the temperature in the room plummeted. She exhaled a breath of fog, and her body hummed with new power. Magic so pure and white that her fear crumbled, her core filling with warm light. The magic to heal a soul.

Holding her arms in front of her, she motioned for the spirits to come toward her. As they approached, she took James's face in her left hand and Nicolas's in her right. Both men were warm and soft to the touch, almost as if they were alive.

"Breathe, dammit," Luke shouted behind her, as the werewolves continued CPR, trying in vain to bring James back to life.

Odette stroked her thumb across her soulmate's cheek and gently pushed the spirits together. "What hate and greed fractured, let love mend."

The spirits glowed, bright golden light surrounding them both as they joined into one. As the light subsided, only James remained, a complete soul, ready to be reborn whole.

"Thank you, sweetheart. I promise I'll find you in the next life."

Odette shook her head. "I'm not living another minute without you by my side."

"What?" He reached for her, but she withdrew her magic, and his arm passed through her. "Odette."

"I'm ready, Baron Samedi. Take me."

"You can't… He won't let you die." Panic creased James's forehead. "Noah! Cade, stop her!" His friends couldn't hear his screams.

Odette swayed, letting an imaginary rhythm guide her movements as if she were dancing at a ritual. She spun and stomped, lifting her hands to the sky and clapping out a beat. Calling on her *met tet* to take her.

"Are you okay?" Noah hesitated in the doorway, his arched brow and concerned gaze indicating he thought she'd clearly gone insane.

"Are you going to keep your promise? Do anything I ask?" Her rhythm increased with the vibrating energy pulsing through her. Baron Samedi's presence pressed harder on her shoulders, giving her one last chance to change her mind, but she was doing this. Fear was no longer an option, and the block she had created all those years ago dissolved with her determination.

"Yeah." Noah shuffled into the room. "What do you need?"

"Get ready to catch me." She took a deep breath and invited the loa inside her.

An electric shock ricocheted through her body, paralyzing her. She collapsed into Noah's arms, and he guided her to a chair.

"What's wrong? What's happening?" He straightened her head and situated her feet flat on the floor.

She tried to speak. To tell him her *met tet* had possessed her, but she had no control of her body. Instead, her eyes opened wide, and her lips curved into what felt like a Cheshire grin. Her body rose against her will, Baron Samedi in complete control, and she sauntered toward the altar.

Picking up the small bottle of rum, she uncapped it and tossed back the contents. The liquor warmed her throat, and she expected a light-headed sensation to form, but she felt no effects from the drink.

Her gaze locked on the top hat sitting atop the fabricated skull, and her hand reached toward it, her finger brushing the brim. All of her senses remained intact. She was like a puppet, the master residing in her own head.

Her hands trailed down her sides and up her stomach to cup her breasts. "Nice," her voice said aloud. "If I had access to a body like this, I'd never leave the bedroom." She glanced at James's ghost. "You're a lucky man," the Baron made her say with his Haitian accent.

She put on the hat and sunglasses and took a cigar from the mantel. "Tell your friends to stop. Whether he lives or dies is up to me."

"Uh, guys." Noah waved a hand, his brow creased in concern. "She said to stop."

"Bullshit." Luke continued the chest compressions.

"I said stop!" Her commanding voice rose above the noise, and Luke froze with his hands on James's chest. Though it was impossible to tell where her magic ended and Baron Samedi's began, that power had felt like her own. "Not bad," the Baron made her say, clearly impressed with her ability.

James's spirit floated in front of her. "Baron Samedi." He bowed his head and pressed his hands together in prayer. "Please don't take Odette. She deserves to live a full life."

"I gave her this life. Don't you think I know that, son?" He made her head turn. "Noah, go to the kitchen and get me a decent-sized bottle of rum. This flask ain't gonna do it. And I need a sprig of rosemary, some betel nut, anise seed, and henbane. And a cup of water."

Had she been in control of her body, her heart would have been racing. Not only could Baron Samedi move and speak through her, but he had access to her knowledge, her memories too. And the combination of herbs he'd requested would be lethal for anyone to ingest.

"Yes, ma'am." Noah scurried to the kitchen.

"Bring his body in here by my altar." She stepped aside, and Luke and Cade obeyed, carrying James into the room and laying him on the floor.

Alexis followed, and the Baron sidled next to her. "Hey there, sweet thing."

"What the hell?" Alexis stared into her eyes, squinting her own as the realization hit. "Guys, I don't think Odette is here right now." She snapped her fingers in front of Odette's face, and Baron Samedi made her grin widen. "Who are you?"

"I'm Death, of course. Who did you expect?" Baron Samedi laughed and settled Odette's form on the floor next to James's body, James's spirit hovering by her side.

"Here's everything you asked for." Noah put the ingredients on the floor next to her.

James covered the herbs with his hands. "That combination will kill her. You can't drink that."

The Baron reached her hand through the spirit and picked up the henbane. "The woman wants to spend forever by your side, man. Stop complaining." Breaking the root apart, she dropped it into the cup of water. "Where's my rum?"

"It's here." Noah handed it to her. "I couldn't carry it all."

"When you're in the presence of a Ghede, boy, the rum always comes first." She unscrewed the cap and sucked down a third of the bottle. Surely now she'd feel the effects. If she'd been the one doing the swallowing, she'd have gagged. Thrown up all over the floor. Instead, she wiped her mouth and set the bottle down, feeling nothing but a tingle on her tongue. "That's more like it."

Closing her eyes, she took a deep breath, and the room vibrated with energy. The werewolves moved closer, encroaching on the sacred space Baron Samedi was creating, so she opened one eye and flicked a hand. "Go stand by the wall, all of you."

So much power filled her words not even the alpha argued. They all shuffled to the wall and stood obediently, their gazes trained on James's body lying on the floor.

She settled back into a trance, and her mouth began forming words she didn't understand. A chant in Haitian Creole flowed from her lips, but she didn't need to comprehend the syllables. The power building in her core was unmistakable.

Her body swaying from side to side, she rubbed her hands together, the friction building a heat almost unbearable on her skin. Pressing her hands to James's forehead, the ancient energy flowed through her arms and into his body, a connection forming between them as thick and strong as an iron cable running from her heart to his.

As the heat on her skin subsided, she crushed the remaining herbs and dropped them into the water before placing a piece of betel nut over both of James's eyes. Another Haitian prayer rolled off her tongue, more magic building in her core.

The calmness Baron Samedi exuded over her body was killing her. She needed her heart to race, her hands to tremble, her lungs to expel a scream. Anything to release the pressure inside her. If the Baron called on another ounce of magic, she would explode.

Reaching a steady hand to the cup, she picked it up, and James's spirit tried in vain to knock it from her grip.

Ghostly tears filled his eyes as he clutched his hands in front of his chest. "Please, Baron, I'm begging you. Spare her life."

A wry smile curved her lips, and she tossed the contents onto James's lifeless face. As the mixture splashed across his skin, a searing sensation ripped through her body, Baron Samedi taking his leave. Her stomach lurched as she collapsed onto her back, her vision tunneling until darkness consumed her.

CHAPTER NINETEEN

James gasped, his quick inhale sucking the Voodoo concoction into his nostrils. The mixture burned and rolled to the back of his throat, causing a coughing fit to wrack his chest. A commotion ensued around him, and the sound of shoes shuffling on the wood and his name being called repeatedly grated in his ears, making his head pound.

He rolled to his side and sputtered the last of the liquid from his orifices before opening his eyes. Odette lay next to him, her arm draped across her forehead, her eyes closed.

The pounding in his head subsided, and he registered the activity around him. Noah knelt by his side, resting his hand on his shoulder. "James? Are you okay? Is that…are you *you?*"

He blinked and turned his head toward his friend, squinting through his blurred vision. He was breathing, wasn't he? And awake. Why the hell were they so concerned with him when Odette lay unconscious on the floor?

Turning back to his fate-bound, he cupped her face in his hand, running his thumb across her soft cheek. Was she herself? *That* was the obvious question his friends should have been asking, and he'd tell them so if he could find his voice.

Odette stirred beneath his touch, nuzzling into his hand, a tiny smile playing on her lips. A very Odette-like smile. Cool relief flushed through his chest. Baron Samedi wouldn't nuzzle against him like this.

"James." Concern filled the alpha's voice, but James didn't miss the irritation edging his tone. Luke would want answers, though he'd probably figured most of it out by now.

He braced his forearm against the floor, propping himself up.

Luke rushed toward him. "Lie down for a while. You were dead for a good ten minutes."

"I'm fine." He pushed to sitting and rubbed a hand across his chest. He was better than fine. More life surged through his veins than he'd ever felt before. He held his hand up, and the collective gasp added to his own astonishment. He held the other hand up and turned them both over several times. He had all ten fingers. "How the hell?"

Odette really had made him whole, just like she'd promised.

A soft *mmm* emanated from her throat, and she rolled to her side, blinking her eyes open. With a small gasp, she sat up, clutching her head as she swayed. "James." She threw herself into his arms, climbing into his lap and burying her face in his neck.

Her magic danced across his skin, mingling with his with an intensity he'd never felt before. A shared connection, like she was actually a part of him now. He tightened his arms around her, soaking her in, the emotions compressing in his chest, expanding into an ache that consumed him. *Mine*, his wolf said with a penetrating fierceness. As if the man needed to be reminded.

He kissed her forehead and stroked her hair before glancing up at his alpha, silently telling him they were okay.

Luke nodded. "Cade, Alexis, take care of the body. Noah, clean up the mess and make note of what repairs are needed."

Noah clapped James on the shoulder as he rose to his feet. "I'm glad you're back, man."

"Me too." Cade nodded.

"I'd have been fine without you." Alexis grinned before heading into the foyer with Cade.

James pressed his lips to Odette's ear. "You scared me. I thought you were going to kill yourself."

Lifting her head, she brushed her lips to his. "I told Baron Samedi I'd pay any price to be with you. How that happened was up to him."

He pulled her close, nuzzling into her hair, the overwhelming feeling of sheer joy bringing tears to his eyes, tightening his throat. "And I asked him not to let you die."

"I guess he had no choice but to bring you back, then."

He tried to laugh, but it came out as a muffled sob. "We owe your *met tet* big time."

"We have the rest of our lives to pay him back, and I plan to enjoy every minute of it." She kissed him, and the magical connection flared, fire shooting through his veins.

He held her closer, sliding his fingers into her hair and kissing her harder. He owed his life to this woman. She'd mended his soul, her love making him whole.

Pressing his forehead to hers, he held her face in his hands. "Thank you for saving my life…and for this." He held up his hand, wiggling his new finger.

"That was a gift from Baron Samedi. I didn't know he could do that." Taking his hand in hers, she trailed her lips from the base of his pinkie to the top, sucking the tip into her mouth. Her dark eyes bore into his soul, and an inferno ignited in his core.

He leaned in, taking her mouth with his again, unable to stop the possessive growl from rolling through his chest. *Mine. Forever.*

Luke cleared his voice, and James reluctantly broke the kiss to address his alpha. "I know you need answers." He glanced into his eyes and lowered his gaze, his silent admission that he'd done wrong by the pack, not telling them…or at least Luke…the truth about *L'Acallemon.*

"I expect you in my office tomorrow afternoon with a full report. You both deserve some rest after that ordeal. If you want to call it rest." A smile tugged at his lips, but he flattened it. "But I do have a rule about my crew sleeping with clients. You remember that, right?"

James fought a grin. "Sure do, boss. That's one rule I intend to follow."

Luke nodded. "I'll leave you to it then."

Odette stood, pulling James up with her. "Thank you for your help and for cooperating with Baron Samedi." She offered her hand to shake, and Luke accepted.

"You…*he* didn't give us much choice." Luke crossed his arms.

"I hope you know that I had no ill intent in any of this. We were only trying to stop the Rougarou."

The alpha narrowed his eyes at her and cut his gaze to James. "He trusts you. I trust his judgment. James, my office tomorrow at noon."

"Got it." James shook his hand. Luke knew better than anyone that when fate chose a werewolf's mate, there was no use fighting it. Fate would never match a were with anyone less than perfect for him.

The alpha sauntered through the foyer and out the front door, closing it behind him. Silence enveloped the home as James eyed the mess left behind. The dented, cracked drywall would have to be replaced, and the small table was toast. Dark-red blood stained the wood floor where the body had lain, and he bent to get a closer look. "I think we can sand this out. The repairs will add another three days onto the timeline, but we were ahead of schedule anyway."

"And the bedroom window?" Odette stood next to him, and he ran his hands up her shapely legs as he rose to his feet.

With his arms around her waist, he pressed a kiss to the curve where her neck met her shoulder. "We'll fix that too. Everything will be perfect," he whispered against her skin.

"Mmm… You are so good at scattering my thoughts and turning my knees to jelly." She pulled from his embrace and picked some dried herbs from his forehead. "But we need to get that window covered so no critters get in tonight."

He didn't hide the disappointment in his sigh. "Always the responsible one." She was right though, and the sooner they took care of the mess, the sooner he could take care of her.

She laughed. "One of us has to be. I'll set up a temporary protection spell, and you cover the window with plastic."

He let out another overdramatic sigh and slumped his shoulders, fighting a grin. "Yes, ma'am."

"And when you're done with that, you're going to make up for dying on me." She crossed her arms, lifting her chin as if daring him to challenge her order.

"How am I going to do that?" He placed his hands on her hips.

She gripped his wrists, pulling his arms together and pressing them into his chest. "However you see fit, as long as you make me scream your name."

Oh, he'd make her scream. Again and again. "Deal."

James cleaned up the glass and covered the window in fifteen minutes flat, thoughts of how he would make amends with Odette making his dick harder than a lead pipe. He adjusted his jeans and shuffled into the kitchen to find her leaning against the counter, sipping a glass of spiced rum.

He stopped in the entry, resting his hand against the jamb and admiring his fate-bound. Her dark jeans hugged her curvy hips, and the V-neck of her black shirt revealed enough of her delicate collarbone to make his mouth water in anticipation of exploring the rest of her soft, dark skin.

She smiled as he sauntered toward her, and she picked up another glass of rum. "Have a drink."

"I'd rather have you." Gripping her hip, he closed the distance between them. Her warm vanilla scent mixed with the spices of the rum, and he leaned in, gliding his tongue along her lip. She opened for him, deepening the kiss for a moment before pulling back and offering him the glass.

"You'll have me in time." She grinned. "We have plenty of that now."

"That we do." He took the glass and clinked it against hers before taking a long sip. "You didn't get enough of this stuff earlier? I think you downed half a fifth."

"Baron Samedi took it with him. This one." She gently rocked her glass. "Is for us." She drained the contents and set it on the counter. "The Baron also took what was left of Nicolas's spirit energy. Your soul is complete, and the ghost has crossed over. This is the first time we've been truly alone in this house."

"And all I can think about is making you scream my name, yet here you stand, cool as a popsicle." He sipped the rum and set his glass next to hers.

"Oh, I'm plenty hot, James. Don't worry about that. But I've been thinking."

The intensity in her gaze made his throat thicken, and he swallowed the dryness from his mouth. "I'm thinking about getting you naked."

She suppressed a chuckle. "Take off your shirt."

"With pleasure." Finally, he was going to get this woman into bed. He yanked his shirt over his head and went straight for the button on his jeans.

"Uh-uh." She shook her head. "Just the shirt for now." Biting her bottom lip, she swept her heated gaze down his chest, the gesture feeling so much like a caress his stomach tightened.

"Your turn." He motioned with his hands toward her shirt. Whatever game she had planned, he'd be happy to play as long as they both ended up naked in the end.

With a sly grin, she tugged her shirt off and dropped it on the counter. "My entire life has been a practice in self-control. While I fully intend to fulfill my promise to Baron Samedi and live in his image, giving up my old ways isn't going to be easy."

He stepped toward her, but she put up a hand to stop him, and he froze. "I can help you with that."

"I don't think I need to completely give up my control issues, though." Her grin widened. "Self-control can be quite erotic."

He chuckled. "How so?"

"Put your hands behind your back." She unclasped her bra and let it fall to the floor. "No touching."

Though his fingers twitched with the need to feel her supple breasts, he did as he was told. She slinked toward him, stopping a scant inch away, so close her breath warmed his neck as she moved her lips along his skin, not touching, but leaving a trail of fire in her wake.

She stepped away, the intensity of the moment pulling his breath out in a rush. His skin turned to gooseflesh, and a shiver ran up his spine. "What kind of magic are you using on me?"

"None at all, love. This is the power of desire." Unbuttoning her pants, she worked them over her hips and slipped them off her ankles, a thin strip of black satin the only thing left covering her.

His heart thrummed, and he reached for her, but she raised her hands again. "I said no touching. Not yet. Take off your pants."

"Your self-control is admirable, but mine is lacking. I'm not sure how much more of this I can take." He toed off his shoes and removed his pants, kicking them aside.

She arched a brow. "You'll take however much I want to give you."

A growl rolled up from his chest. Damn, this woman was hot. He'd never been keen on taking orders from anyone but the alpha, but Odette had him wrapped around her finger. He'd move the Earth for this woman.

He took an involuntary step toward her, and she laughed. "Control yourself. Let the anticipation build, and the release will be that much sweeter."

Straightening, he fisted his hands at his sides to stop them from reaching for her again. If she kept this up, he'd be releasing in his boxer-briefs.

"Take off your underwear." She shimmied hers down her legs and stepped out of them, standing before him magnificently naked, her warm, soft skin beckoning him.

With a shuddering inhale, he removed the rest of his clothes, his dick springing free from its constraints. Her gaze locked on his cock, and she slipped the tip of her tongue out to moisten her lips.

That tiny flash of pink nearly crumbled him. His dick ached to fill her. His hands twitched to feel her. If any more blood rushed from his head to his groin, he'd pass out. He ground his teeth, forcing his growl into words. "I need you, Odette."

"I need you too, James." She closed the distance between them, her tight nipples almost brushing his chest as she hovered her mouth near his, still not touching, building the heat between them. "So bad."

Good God, he wanted to touch her. To bend her over the counter and sink his cock deep inside her. This little game of control had him hotter than hellfire, his core trembling with a need like nothing he'd felt before.

She hovered her lips above his skin, trailing down his neck, his chest, his stomach, her breath the only thing touching him. It was a painfully wonderful, erotic sensation, and as a bead of moisture gathered on the end of his cock, she paused and licked her lips.

"I'd like to taste." She glanced up at him with fire in her eyes. "Do you want me to taste it?"

He fought to find his voice. "Yes. God, yes. Please." He was breathless, and the woman hadn't even touched him yet.

She flicked out her tongue, licking his tip, the warm velvet sensation sending a shudder through his body. He held his breath, waiting for more, but she straightened, moving so close his dick rested against her stomach.

The sensation of her soft skin against his tightened his balls, and searing electricity shot through his veins. His hands trembled, so he clenched them into fists behind his back. Raw, primal need churned in his core, and his wolf howled in his head, begging him to take her.

"You're doing very well." Her lips tickled his ear. "Are you thoroughly turned on yet?"

"I'm a Roman candle with a very short fuse, sweetheart." Every nerve in his body was firing on overdrive. The heat from her skin against his felt as good as anything she could have done with her hands. Well, not quite *as* good, but pretty damn close.

She smiled. "So I've proved my point?"

"Clear as day."

She finally touched him. Her fingertips glided across his shoulders and down his arms like liquid fire. "All right, James. Make me scream."

He didn't give her a chance to change her mind. Pouncing like a predator, he wrapped her in a tight embrace and planted his mouth on hers. Her lips parted on a gasp as he gripped her ass and lifted her from the ground, setting her on the countertop.

She parted her legs, and he dove to her center, lapping at her clit and reveling in the sweet taste of her as she tangled her fingers in his hair. Sucking her sensitive nub into his mouth, he slid two fingers inside. Her wet warmth clenched around them, her lustful moan melting in his ears like salted chocolate.

The taste of her on his tongue made him shiver. He wanted to savor her. To take his time pleasuring her, but she'd awakened a passion inside him that he couldn't hold back any longer. They had the rest of their lives for savoring each other. Right now, he needed to be inside her.

Sliding her from the counter, he gently pushed her against the wall, covering her body with his, their magic entwining so he couldn't tell where hers ended and his began.

Mine. Possessiveness clenched in his chest, his wolf reminding him of his claim.

Grabbing her thigh, he lifted her leg to his hip and pressed against her opening. She gripped the back of his neck and held his gaze with fiery passion in her eyes. In one swift thrust, he filled her, and her gasp danced in his ears.

He lifted her other leg, wrapping it around his waist, and she leaned back against the wall for leverage, matching his thrusts as he slid in and out of her, maddening friction igniting every nerve in his body.

His climax coiled tight in his core, and he held her ass with one hand, stroking her clit with his thumb.

She clutched his shoulders, her nails digging into his skin as a beautiful, erotic moan flowed up from her chest. "Oh, James." She shuddered, her center contracting around him as he thrust faster and harder.

His release unfurled in his groin, and he leaned into her, his knees nearly buckling beneath him. His orgasm overtook him, slicing through his soul and mending the broken pieces, making him stronger than ever before. As his breathing slowed, he slipped out of her, lowering one of her legs to the floor.

"I'm not sure I can stand up after that." She laughed, clutching his shoulders with trembling arms. "Sweet Spirits, that was intense."

"I've got you, sweetheart." Slipping an arm behind her knees, he cradled her against his chest and carried her to the bedroom. He snuggled under the covers next to her, holding his fate-bound in his arms. "You weren't kidding about that control thing. That was the hottest sex in…the history of sex."

"Finding balance is important. I don't have to change who I am to embrace my wilder side." She rested her head on his shoulder and draped her leg across his waist.

"You don't need to change a thing. You're sheer perfection." His need satiated, he drifted in and out of sleep, comfortable, but unwilling to give in to slumber just yet. Spending every single day with this woman for the rest of his life wouldn't be enough, and closing his eyes seemed like a waste of the time they had left. Even if it was forever.

"James." She lifted her head to look at him. "You told Luke you intended to follow his rule about not sleeping with clients."

He brushed a curl from her forehead. "Yes, I did."

"You haven't broken that rule; you've shattered it to pieces. What will you tell him?" She rested a hand on his chest, and he covered it with his own.

"There's a caveat to that rule: don't sleep with a client, unless you plan on taking her as your mate."

Grinning, she propped her head on her hand. "I see. Well, I wouldn't want you to get in trouble with your boss."

"I don't plan to." He returned her smile. "Odette, will you be my mate?"

"I always have been, James, and I always will be. In this life and every one that comes. Forever."

EPILOGUE

Odette signed off on the catering order and turned to scan the scene. Twinkling lights draping from massive oaks illuminated the park, and a jazz band occupied the stage, tuning their instruments in preparation for the party. The October air had an early fall bite, and she pulled her lavender shawl up around her shoulders to chase away the chill.

James stood in the back of the VIP tasting tent, nervously turning the bottles so all the labels faced forward. The pack had lent some of their members to help, and Amber, the owner of O'Malley's, slapped at James's hand and shooed him away.

After Odette's comment about liking his facial hair, James had let his beard grow in fully, giving her already-rough-around-the-edges werewolf a rugged, even more masculine look. He bent over to hide a power cord beneath a table, and she admired the view of his backside. She'd spent every day with the man for the last four months, and she still couldn't get enough of him.

She strode toward him and slipped a hand beneath the back of his shirt. "They have placards. It's okay if the bottles are turned."

"I know." He grinned and pulled her to his side. "I'm just trying to make everything perfect for the first-annual Baron Samedi Festival."

"You can't call it annual unless it happens more than once, and this will only happen again if it's a success."

"It will be. You'll see."

Loosening the reins at the distillery had been the hardest part of her promise to the Baron. She'd found balance in every aspect of her life, James making sure she took a break to enjoy herself whenever she got too uptight. She went out with friends—his and hers—went dancing, communicated with the dead who approached her for help, and enjoyed life in general…something she hadn't done since she was a kid.

When she started playing music at the distillery, her employees had looked at her like she'd gone insane. When she had her intern plan the first company happy hour, they thought she'd been abducted and replaced with an alien replica.

The people around her were slowly starting to accept her new attitude toward life, and everyone from the distillery and the House of Voodoo had pitched in to make this tribute to Baron Samedi happen. If all went well, it would be an annual party to celebrate her *met tet* and all that he had done for her and James, and hopefully enlighten the attendees about the mystery of Voodoo in the process.

She took James's hand and guided him out of the tent. "Gates open in ten minutes."

"You've got this, sweetheart. I won't leave your side."

She leaned into him and took one last moment to appreciate everyone's efforts. They had a children's section with inflatable bounce houses and an obstacle course. In addition to the VIP tasting tent, several booths with offerings of food and drinks were stationed around the festival grounds, and the Voodoo museum had an informative display set up across from the main stage.

Five vodouisants sat at tables beneath the trees, and Natasha waved her over. "Tyrell caught a stomach bug, so we're short one reader. Will five be enough?"

"If not, I can fill in as a medium. I'm sure there will be plenty of people who'd like to talk to lost loved ones." A familiar flutter beat in her stomach, but it died down as quickly as it had begun. Her powers weren't nearly as scary as they used to be.

Natasha shuffled her tarot cards. "Then who will run the show?"

"I'll take care of it," James said.

Natasha nodded. "You got yourself a good man right there."

"He's the best." She pressed a kiss to his cheek and waved as Noah approached.

"Hey, y'all. Sorry I'm late." Noah hugged Odette and shook James's hand. "Where do you need me?"

James glanced over his shoulder, a sly grin curving his lips. "I think Amber might need some help in the tasting tent."

"Dude." Noah's shoulders slumped, but his gaze drifted toward the tent as he shook his head. "I'd be better off selling tickets or something."

Odette cut her gaze between the two men. "What am I missing here?"

"He's had a thing for Amber since high school, but he's too chicken to do anything about it."

Noah's jaw tightened.

"She's nice." Odette followed his gaze toward the tent, where Amber stood, straightening her apron. "It doesn't hurt to talk to her, does it?"

"She's the alpha's sister." Noah shoved his hands in his pockets.

"So?" She looked at James for explanation.

"He's second-born, so he thinks he's not good enough to date someone with alpha blood."

She cocked her head. "Isn't the alpha's mate second-born? If she's good enough…"

"It's not the same." Noah pleaded with his gaze. "What else do you need help with?"

James slapped him on the shoulder. "Just the tasting tent. Hey, Amber?" He lifted a hand to get her attention. "Your help is here."

A genuine smile lit up her features, and something sparked in her bright-blue eyes. "Send him over."

"Ah, hell," Noah groaned.

"You'll survive." James gave him a push and laughed as Noah shuffled to the tent.

"That's the smile of a woman who is happy to see a man." She looked at James. "Can't he see that?"

"What we think about ourselves sometimes gets in the way of what we see right before our eyes."

She wrapped her arms around him. "I guess we know that better than anyone."

"We learned our lesson." He kissed her cheek. "He will too. Eventually."

A SONG TO REMEMBER

CARRIE PULKINEN

CHAPTER ONE

Shane Anderson clutched the steering wheel and peeled out of the hotel parking lot, merging onto the highway and narrowly avoiding a collision with a pickup truck. He jerked the wheel right, and the rumble of reflectors beneath his tires reminded him to focus on the road.

What have those bloody witches done this time?

Ricardo's voice over the phone had sounded frantic. He'd mumbled something about Cammie botching a spell to release Shane from their idiotic plan and passing out. They needed him there to complete the incantation and keep Cammie from slipping into a magic-induced coma.

Something was off, though, and skepticism clawed through his chest, his wolf growling a warning in his mind. If this was some kind of joke or their way of getting even after he'd left the band…

"Bloody hell." He'd met his fate-bound tonight. Witches couldn't fathom the connection a werewolf felt when he met his soulmate. They probably thought they were being funny, dragging him out of bed and away from the woman he was meant to spend the rest of his life with.

But if Cammie really was hurt, he had to help her. He'd do whatever he needed to and be done with the witches for good. Then he'd get his ass back to Bekah and convince her the night they'd shared was the beginning of forever.

He'd pack his bags and move to New Orleans tomorrow. Hell, he'd follow his fate-bound anywhere; his wolf wouldn't have it any other way.

Pulling into the apartment parking lot, he cut the engine and ran his hand across the worn leather of his saxophone case in the passenger seat. The brass nameplate felt cool against his fingers, and the engraving of his name had smoothed so much it barely registered on his skin.

Looking into Bekah's eyes tonight, every broken piece of his world converged, snapping back together. Her presence filled in the blank spots, making him whole, and it all made sense now. Leaving his home in London, his dad disowning him so he couldn't go back, following a doomed relationship on a tour of the United States, being dumped in Florida…it all led him to today.

To his fate-bound.

He drummed his fingers on the sax case. New Orleans was the perfect place for him to settle down and open his music school. At least his mum would've been proud of him if she were still here.

A balmy Florida breeze mussed his hair as he climbed out of his Jeep and slammed the door. He hit the lock button on his key fob and jogged across the parking lot to Ricardo's apartment. As he lifted his hand to knock, the door swung open and Ricardo ushered him inside.

A dozen black candles illuminated the room in flickering firelight, and the overwhelming aroma of incense and herbs assaulted his nose, stinging his eyes. The furniture had been pushed against the walls, and a pentagram drawn in white powder took up most of the living room floor.

Shane's heart thrummed, his wolf's warning growl growing louder in his mind. "What the hell is going on, mate? Where's Cammie?"

Regret flashed in Ricardo's eyes. "I'm sorry, buddy. If you're not with us, you're a liability."

Cammie stepped into the room wearing a black, hooded robe. The moment she lifted her arms toward Shane, a wall of magic slammed into him, knocking the breath from his lungs. He called on his wolf, his fight instinct kicking into high gear, and his body hummed with magic as he shifted form.

Ears flat against his head, he bared his teeth and growled, cutting his gaze between Ricardo and Cammie.

Ricardo squealed and jumped over the couch. "You said he wouldn't be able to shift, Cam. Change him back."

"Give me a second." She fisted her hands and then splayed her fingers, sending another blast of dark magic toward Shane, neutralizing his own.

A quivering sensation ran through his entire body as he lost hold of his wolf and transformed to human.

"What are you doing?" Panic surged, a thrumming, vibrating urgency turning his blood to liquid fire. He tried to run, but his muscles seized, the room pressing down on him, the unbearable heaviness bringing him to his knees.

Cammie's eyes rolled back as a string of Latin words flowed from her blood-red lips, and dark magic pricked at Shane's skin, clawing at the base of his skull. He tried to stand, to get the hell out of there, but his body betrayed him. He was paralyzed, the pressure and pain making his stomach churn and his vision swim.

Ricardo clutched his wrist, holding it against his chest as he dragged a cursed blade across Shane's forearm. Searing pain exploded across his skin, and blood dripped into a bowl before his were magic sealed the wound.

His wolf howled in his head, but Shane didn't need to be reminded of the consequences. Were blood held powerful magic that no witch should ever have access to. He tried to speak, but his jaw clenched tight, his teeth grinding together until sharp pain shot through his temple.

Ricardo shoved him to the floor, and he landed on his side, his cheek pressing into the rough carpet. Cammie stopped chanting, and the pressure lifted, but his body felt like a lump of rock.

She knelt to run her fingers through Shane's hair. "It would be easier to kill him. We have his blood. That's all we need."

"He's our friend, Cam. I can't have that on my conscience."

Ricardo set the bowl on a table. "Just wipe his mind, and we'll dump him down the road like we agreed."

Shane groaned, trying to force words through his thickening throat, but they wouldn't come. The witches were the closest he had to family, and sadly, their betrayal was far from surprising.

"Roll him onto his back." Cammie dipped a spoon into the bowl of blood and added a single drop to a glass of purple liquid. As soon as the drop hit the surface, the mixture flashed bright pink and steam rose from the container. "He's got to swallow this for the spell to work."

Ricardo shoved his shoulder, and his muscles screamed as he rolled to his back. "Our plans require a blood sacrifice from everyone involved. You were already in it, so you can't back out." He patted his shoulder. "Don't worry man, in a few minutes, you won't remember anything."

With his thumb on Shane's chin, Ricardo pried his lips apart and poured the steaming mixture into his mouth. The sickly-sweet liquid burned his tongue and the back of his throat, but he refused to swallow. These witches would not steal his memory, nor would he play a role in their black magic scheme. This paralyzing spell would wear off eventually, and then they'd pay.

Ricardo looked at Cammie. "He's not swallowing."

The witch let out a dramatic sigh and bent over Shane, pinching his nose so he couldn't breathe. He tried to shake his head, to curl his hands into fists, to move *anything* on his body, but he was frozen. His lungs ached for air, pressure building in his chest like a stack of cinder blocks sat atop him.

Instinct took over, and he gasped for breath, sucking the magic concoction down his throat. He choked, sputtering the liquid and inhaling it again as a coughing fit wracked his body. The potion singed his sinuses, scorching from the back of his throat up to his watering eyes. Ricardo rolled him onto his side, and purple splattered across the floor as he expelled the last of the contents from his throat.

"He didn't swallow it all." Ricardo hauled him up, and his legs wobbled as the paralyzing spell began to lose its hold.

"He got enough," Cammie said. "Put him in his car and drive. I'll follow you."

His vision tunneled into darkness, and he squeezed his eyes shut. When he opened them, a woman in a black robe lowered her hood to reveal long, blonde hair. Where had she come from?

She looked familiar, and he wracked his brain, but her name eluded him. "Who are you?"

The woman smiled. "It's already working. Let's dump him before he gets all his strength back. Take his phone and wallet. We don't want him finding us later."

The man emptied his pockets and dragged him out the door. Shane tried to pull from his grasp, but he stumbled, and the man shoved him into the back seat of a car. His muscles ached, and his head spun as they sped down the highway. On a secluded section of road, the driver pulled over and hauled him out of the back seat, settling him behind the wheel.

He took in the man's dark hair and eyes, and familiarity pricked in his mind. "I know you, don't I?"

"Not anymore." The man slammed the door and jogged toward a van.

He watched as the van disappeared down the road, and he ran his hands over the leather steering wheel in front of him. He'd gotten in this car for a reason, but he couldn't recall what it was. He was going…somewhere. He needed to see someone, but…

Panic surged ice-cold through his veins. A million thoughts danced around the outskirts of his memory, swirling in a tornado of muddled perplexity, but he couldn't grab onto any of them. He didn't know where he was nor where he was going. *Bloody hell.* He didn't even know *who* he was.

New Orleans.

Through the jumbled, incomprehensible blankness of his mind, that one name was a lighthouse in the fog. A beacon of hope. Whatever happened to his memory, he would find it in New Orleans.

CHAPTER TWO

Nine Hours Earlier

"In what universe is summoning a demon ever a good idea?" Shane sat his saxophone case on the floor and clenched his fists at his sides, sucking in a gulp of air. The mere mention of getting help from a fiend raised his hackles, and his wolf hovered dangerously near the surface.

Ricardo was insane. That was the only explanation.

"It's not *a* demon. We're making a deal with Amdusias. He's a duke of hell, and he rules over music." Ricardo palmed his shoulder. "He can make our dreams come true."

"*Your* dreams." Shane shrugged off the witch's hand and marched toward Cammie, who sat with her legs curled beneath her on a brown sofa. "Are you in on this too?"

The blue-eyed witch twirled a drumstick in her fingers and blew a pale-pink bubble the size of her face. The gum popped, and she worked it back into her mouth before answering. "We're *all* in on this. The initial connection has been made. We have to finish the ritual beneath the full moon tomorrow night, and fame and fortune will be ours." Her bright-red lips curved into a smile, and she tucked a blonde curl behind her ear. "Relax, wolfman. We aren't going to summon him into the flesh. We'll bring him close enough to the surface for his energy to pass into us, and then we'll shut the gates."

The gates. The witches were planning to open the gates of hell as casually as a barn door…and they didn't see the problem with it.

"How did you make the initial connection? How are we *all* in this already?"

Cammie glanced toward Ricardo and lifted one shoulder. "It was just a bit of hair. Ricardo picked it up from the floor when you guys had your little bro date and got your hair cut together."

"You took my hair?" He glared at the lead singer.

Ricardo raised his hands. "It was going in the trash anyway."

"You're part of this, Shane." Cammie smiled and popped her gum.

"Jesus Christ." Raking a hand through his hair, he glared at his other bandmates. "You'll sell your souls for a chance at success?"

"Souls are overrated." Ricardo laughed. "Anyway, man, we're not going to promise our souls. We're going to give him our lives right now, let Amdusias run our careers. He'll be our manager. Cammie's agreed to let him speak to her through her dreams."

Shane took another deep breath and focused on the twenty-by-thirty landscape painting hanging above Cammie's head. Snow clung to the ground and trees in the image, a far cry from the humid Florida weather he'd gotten used to. He hadn't seen a white Christmas in five years, and if he had his way, he never would again.

The kind of success his friends wanted would require touring. A different city every night. Different weather. No stability. He'd been there, done that, and experienced the fall-out when things didn't work out.

"You're all crazy. You know that?" Any Witch Way consisted of five members: four American witches and Shane, the token werewolf. The only Brit. While his friends' musical ability was decent enough to land gigs at weddings, small venues, and hotel bars, like the one they were about to play, they would never achieve stardom with their mediocre talent.

Shane was counting on that.

"C'mon, dude. You're the only one of us who's had a taste of fame, and we want to sample that deliciously sweet stardom too," Ricardo said.

"And that went swimmingly for me, didn't it?"

"You could have moved back to jolly old London, mate," Ricardo mocked Shane's accent, "but you stayed. Don't tell me you wouldn't do anything to get that back."

"I won't sell my soul." There was no use arguing with them. All creative types had egos, and convincing them stardom wasn't all they imagined it would be was impossible. He'd been in their position once. The lure of fame was hard to ignore.

Of course, he'd been more interested in the woman that came with the package. Being in a famous rock band was never his dream; it just happened to be part of the deal.

But that was over now.

"I want out. I'll play tonight's show, and then I'm done."

"We need you, Shane." Cammie rose to her feet. "You're the most talented member of the band, and your songs are killer."

"No one wants to hear original music at the gigs we've been booking," Ricardo said. "If we don't do this, we'll be stuck playing crappy covers to small crowds who are more interested in getting drunk than hearing good music. It's time to expand our horizons."

Shane tried to hold back his groan, but it came out as a heavy sigh. "I get it, okay? I really do." And while he didn't share his mates' desire to make the band any bigger than it was, he didn't want to hold his friends back. "But asking a demon for help will only lead to trouble. Black magic is nothing to play with."

Cammie scoffed. "As if a werewolf knows more about magic than a witch."

He gritted his teeth. "I know plenty about demons." In London, the werewolves acted as the supernatural police force of the city. They were the demons' sworn enemies. Their job was to keep London safe from the fiends and the idiots who summoned them.

"My dad taught me all I need to know, but..." Cammie cut her gaze to Ricardo again, a silent agreement passing between them. "If you want out, we'll let you out. Finish the gig tonight. Sleep on it, and if you're still not convinced in the morning, you're free. You just have to promise not to spill our secret when we become famous."

Cammie clutched Ricardo's bicep, resting her other hand on his shoulder before kissing him on the cheek. They were a perfectly matched couple now, but being in the spotlight tended to tear people apart.

"Think about it, old friend." Ricardo squeezed his shoulder. "That's all we ask."

Shane didn't have to think about it. Communing with demons went against his very nature. If he were a pack member, he'd be obliged to report the witches' intended activity to the alpha. Being rogue, he answered to no one, but he'd be damned if he'd let them turn a demon loose on Pensacola.

"All right, mate. I can give you that much." He'd let them think he was considering their scheme, anyway. "But for the record, I happen to enjoy the crappy covers. People appreciate familiarity."

"And when our album goes platinum, bands will be doing covers of our stuff. We'll be the familiar ones." Cammie clutched her drumsticks and strutted toward the door. "The stage is waiting, boys."

Shane picked up his sax case and slung his guitar over his shoulder. This was what he got for joining a band of witches.

Bekah Beauchamp stopped at the hotel bar and ordered a glass of rosé. Sectioned off from the restaurant, the spacious bar had elegant, modern lighting. Multiple nooks with tables and deep-blue upholstered chairs surrounded a small dance floor where a band had set up their instruments on the adjacent stage.

She sipped her wine, savoring the way the blend managed to be fruity and slightly dry at the same time, and scanned the crowd for her new friend. Tambra, a witch she'd met at the restauranteur conference in Pensacola, had convinced her to listen to the band playing in the bar on the last night of the symposium.

Her first instinct had been to decline the invitation. She needed to organize her notes from the day, plus she planned to drive home to

New Orleans first thing in the morning. She hadn't seen Emma in three days, and though she'd spoken to her daughter on the phone every night at bedtime, a constant ache had formed in her chest from missing the little squirt.

Emma was in good hands with her grandma, though, and it wasn't like Bekah could make the drive home safely tonight. Still, a pang of guilt flashed through her chest every time she sipped her drink.

"Bekah!" Tambra waved, and six gold bangle bracelets slid up to her elbow. A matching gold flower hairpin adorned her short, blonde curls, and dark-gray, shimmery shadow created a smoky effect around her blue eyes.

A knot released in Bekah's chest as she strode toward the table Tambra had claimed on the edge of the dance floor. Though her own makeup was a far cry from the smoky-eyed vixen look of Tambra's palette, Bekah had applied a little extra shadow and a darker-than-normal shade of lipstick. But her attempt at making herself feel alive again had gifted her with a weighty dose of self-consciousness instead.

"Hey, Tambra. Thanks for inviting me." Bekah slid into the seat next to the witch.

"Thank you for coming. My cousin, Cammie, is the drummer, and she'd kill me if she knew I was in town and didn't see her show." She clinked her glass to Bekah's. "A woman sitting alone in a bar always attracts the weirdos who assume she's looking for a date. You saved me from deflecting all the beer-breathed come-ons tonight."

Bekah laughed. "It's been so long since I've had a night out, I wouldn't recognize a come-on if the beer breath stared me in the face." Nor would she know how to react. She hadn't attempted to flirt with anyone since the day she found out she was pregnant with Emma.

"A beautiful, successful woman like you? C'mon, you've probably got all your male packmates falling over themselves to get to you." Tambra lifted the chardonnay to her lips.

Drumming her nails on the table, Bekah shook her head. "I haven't had a date in eight years."

Tambra choked, sputtering wine across the table. "Girl." She swiped the cocktail napkin on the surface, absorbing the mess. "Eight years?"

"Not since Emma's dad left." She shrugged. "I'm a single mom. Most men tuck tail and run as soon as they find that out."

"Even werewolves? The men seem like such protectors."

"Especially werewolves. Emma's father is a witch, so we won't know if she'll be a shifting wolf or have witch powers until she comes into her magic. Only first-born weres can shift, so if Emma has that ability, whatever mate I ended up with wouldn't have shifting offspring of his own. No one wants to take that chance."

Tambra's brow furrowed. "Werewolves are assholes."

Bekah laughed. "So are witches."

"Isn't everyone? Well, if werewolves are out, you can still date humans, can't you?"

"I could, but I've been so busy between raising Emma, finishing college, and then opening my café. I haven't thought about it much." She traced her fingers across the wood pattern on the table. That was a lie. She *had* thought about it. Taking care of an eight-year-old on her own, she rarely got a moment alone, but lately, she'd never felt lonelier.

Tambra waved the waiter over and ordered another round of wine. "Maybe it's time you started."

"Maybe it is. I feel guilty though. I mean, I'm a mom first, and Emma…"

The witch held up a finger. "You're a woman first, and your daughter would benefit from seeing her mother happy and modeling healthy relationships."

She opened her mouth to argue, but she couldn't form a rebuttal. "Jeez, Tambra, forget restaurants. You should go into therapy."

"Ten years as a bartender, and you learn how to talk to people about their problems." She held up her glass in a toast. "To your first night out and the start of finding Bekah, the woman, again. She's in there somewhere."

"I'll drink to that." Bekah sipped her rosé, and a weight lifted from her shoulders. Tambra was right; she was a woman first, and she'd lost herself along the way.

Things were different now, though. Emma was in school and wise beyond her years. Bekah was done with college, and her café was running smoothly. She had a bit of free time, a luxury she could never afford before. Maybe she should focus some of her energy on herself for a change. It was time she found the woman she'd lost, and she would start by letting go of her mom guilt and enjoying herself tonight.

A side door opened, and the band shuffled through. Tambra waved and shouted, "Cammie," and a young woman with long blonde hair and bright-red lips waved, her eyes lighting up with her smile.

Drumsticks in hand, Cammie trotted toward their table and hugged Tambra. "I'm so glad you came."

"I wouldn't miss my baby cousin's show. I even brought a friend. This is Bekah."

"Hi." Bekah shook Cammie's hand, and the witch's magical signature shimmied up her arm along with her emotions. Wiping her palm on her jeans, Bekah tried to keep her expression neutral. She'd learned to control her empathic ability as a teen, and she rarely picked up on anyone's feelings unless she wanted to.

But Cammie's emotions undulated through her, their intensity making them impossible to ignore. The natural excitement and anticipation for her upcoming performance paled in comparison to another type of eagerness spiked with fear.

"Nice to meet you." Cammie turned to Tambra. "Will you be around after the show?"

"You know it." Tambra smiled fondly as Cammie mounted the stage and settled behind the drum set.

Bekah shivered as the last of Cammie's emotions dissipated from her consciousness. "Is she okay? She seems a little…nervous."

"Oh, she's fine." Tambra waved off her concern. "She's always been high-strung."

"She must've been a handful as a kid."

As the rest of the band members set up their instruments, Bekah's gaze locked on a tall, dark-haired man beside the keyboard. He set a black acoustic guitar on a stand and knelt to open an instrument case.

"Who is that?" Bekah pointed at the tall drink of water and knocked her empty wine glass over on the table. She caught it before it could roll off the edge, but she made enough of a commotion to capture the handsome musician's attention.

He glanced up from his case and looked at her with the most piercing set of sea-green eyes she'd ever seen. A short, dark beard accentuated his strong jaw, and as one corner of his mouth tugged into a crooked grin, her heart lost count of its rhythm.

"Close your mouth, hon, you're gaping at the man." Tambra snatched the empty glass from her hand and set it on the table behind them. "That's Shane."

Bekah snapped her mouth shut and leaned back in her chair, reminding herself to breathe. If a simple smile from a stranger could send her pulse racing like this, she definitely needed to get out more.

Shane pulled a saxophone from the case and set it on another stand next to the guitar. As he attached the mouthpiece, he flicked his gaze to Bekah again and nodded a hello.

Dammit, she was still staring at him. Biting her lip, she lifted her fingers in a pathetic attempt at a wave and shifted in her chair to face Tambra. "What…umm…What does he play?"

Tambra grinned. "Everything. Keyboard, guitar, sax. He's good with his hands and his mouth, if that's what you're wondering."

Her laugh came out as a snort, and she covered her mouth. "I was not wondering that."

"If a guy like Shane looked at me the way he's been looking at you, that's exactly what I'd be wondering." She nudged her with an elbow. "I'm pretty sure he's single too."

Her body warmed, and though she was tempted to fan herself with a napkin, she refrained. Instead, she took a few slow, deep breaths to calm the raging hormones that had finally broken the dam.

The band opened the set with an Imagine Dragons cover, and Shane's fingers flew across the keyboard so effortlessly he could have played it with his eyes closed. At times he did, and when he opened them again, he glanced at Bekah, almost as if to be sure she was watching.

As the set went on, Tambra ordered another glass of wine, but Bekah had no need for alcohol. The way her body reacted to watching the sexy musician was better than any buzz the wine could have provided.

"What else do you know about Shane?" She glanced at Tambra before focusing on the man.

"Well…he's a werewolf, but don't let that discourage you. He's the most mature one of the bunch."

Her heart sank. She'd suspected as much based on his looks and the confident way he carried himself, but the only way to truly know a magical being's nature was through touch. The buzzing, electrical signature emanating from their skin was like a supernatural calling card.

Oh, well. Better to find out now so she could temper the hormones surging through her core. Shane was nice to look at, but that's all he could be, which was fine. At least she knew she could still be attracted to a man.

As the set ended, Tambra jumped from her seat and sashayed to the stage to talk to her cousin, leaving Bekah alone at the small table. Shane set his guitar in the stand and made a beeline for the bar, not sparing a single glance for her as he laughed with the bartender and ordered a beer.

Her chest deflated with her sigh. A man like that would never be interested in someone like her. Even with the extra coat of makeup, her hair and her clothes screamed, "mom." An attractive artist with those long, dexterous fingers, he probably had a different woman in his bed every night, and not one of them had stretchmarks across her hips.

She dug in her purse for her phone to check the time. Heading back to her room now would mean she'd be ready for an early start in the morning. With her gaze cast downward, she caught a glimpse of a pair of black leather boots stopping near her table. Her phone slipped back into her purse as she lifted her head and found Shane standing in front of her. His leather jacket hung open over a dark-gray V-neck T-shirt, and his torn jeans hung low on his hips in typical rock star fashion.

That same crooked, kissable grin tugged on his lips, making heat bloom below her navel. "Hello." He slipped around the side of the table and settled into the empty chair. "I hope I'm not being too forward, but the bartender said you were drinking rosé." A delectable accent lilted his speech as he set the glass of wine in front of her. "I'm Shane."

"You're British." She clamped her mouth shut as heat flushed her cheeks. *Way to go, Captain Obvious. Why don't you tell him he's male too?*

"Guilty." He chuckled. "I'm also a musician, in case you hadn't noticed."

She gazed into his eyes, trying to remember how to form a coherent sentence. A thread of yellow encircled his pupils, shattering in a starburst pattern to blend with the deep green of his irises. The fine lines on the outer edge of his eyes crinkled, deepening as his smile widened.

Swallowing the dryness from her mouth, she pulled herself together. "I'm Bekah."

"Bekah. That's a pretty name." In typical English fashion, he added an imaginary *R* sound to the end of her name, and in typical American girl fashion, her heart fluttered at the sound of his accent. "Is it short for Rebekah?"

"No, it's just Bekah."

"Well, it's nice to meet you, Bekah." If he didn't stop saying her name like that she might start running a fever.

He reached a hand toward her to shake, and she paused, making sure she had her empathic ability in check before accepting the gesture. His magical signature registered on her skin, but nothing more. She'd rather not know his true emotions at the moment.

"Hmm. Are you…?" He held onto her hand a beat longer than necessary.

Her stomach fluttered as she slipped from his grasp. "Second-born. Yes." First-born wolves had a strong signature, but those that couldn't shift gave off a more muddled magic and were often mistaken for witches.

He rubbed his beard and let out an unbelieving chuckle. "Beautiful woman, beautiful name, and a werewolf too. It's no wonder you've piqued my interest."

She ran her finger around the rim of the glass. "Oh, I've piqued your interest, have I?" It had been ages since she'd been the object of anyone's flirtation, but this sure did seem like flirting. A buzzing sensation spread beneath her skin, curving her lips into a smile she couldn't have fought if her life depended on it.

He leaned toward her, resting a forearm on the table. "Very much." He had a warm, woodsy scent mixed with leather and a hint of the sea, and she found herself drifting toward him, drawn in by his presence.

"Yo, Shane. Two minutes," the lead singer called from the stage.

"Bloody hell." He closed his eyes for a long blink and let out an exasperated sigh.

Bekah stifled her giggle, clearing her throat to cover it.

He arched a brow. "Something funny?"

"That's such a British thing to say. 'Bloody hell.' I can't imagine hell being anything but bloody."

"You're making fun of me?" He straightened and took a long drink from his beer, watching her with an amused expression over the bottle as he held it to his lips.

"Not making fun. It's cute."

"Cute?"

"Oh, come on. With your looks alone, you're a ten. Then you open your mouth, and that deep voice with the sexy accent comes out, and women's clothes probably fall off on their own."

He narrowed his eyes, his gaze smoldering as he swept it up and down the length of her. "Yours are still on."

They wouldn't be for long if he kept looking at her like that, and maybe that wasn't such a bad thing. In the ten minutes she'd known the man, he was doing a damn good job of finding the woman in her she'd lost. A sexy musician, one night of passion, and then she'd go home and be a mom again. A little fun wouldn't hurt her.

With her elbow on the table, she rested her chin on her hand. "I guess you'll have to try a little harder if you want them off."

Passion sparked in his eyes so primal it pulled the breath from her lungs. She'd never been so drawn to a man in her entire life, and the temptation to touch him, to use her ability to see if he felt the same, had her fisting her hands in her lap. She wouldn't intrude in his emotions when hers were running so high. She might not be able to separate his from her own.

He slid his arm across the back of her chair and leaned in, his breath warming her ear. "If that's a challenge, love, consider it accepted."

Oh, lord, what have I done? Her body hummed in anticipation as she turned her face toward his. "Good luck."

His gaze drifted to her lips. "Won't need it."

"Let's go, Shane. Last set," the drummer called.

He rose and whisked his beer from the table. "You'll stay to the end." The last word didn't lift in a question. "I'm not done talking to you."

"I planned to. I'm not done with you either." She held her breath as his gaze bore into her…hot, steady, strong. His raw sex appeal had her trembling on the inside, but she straightened her spine, congratulating herself for projecting way more confidence than she felt.

"This is our last set. Any requests?"

She glanced at the instruments on the stage. A dozen different jazz tunes flitted through her mind, but their repertoire seemed to be rock and pop, so she dismissed them. "I haven't heard you play the sax yet. Can you do 'Careless Whisper?'"

He arched a brow with an *are you serious?* expression.

"That sax solo has got to be the sexiest piece of music ever written, but if you can't, that's okay."

His heated gaze danced between her eyes and her lips. "Anything for you, love. Consider it done."

CHAPTER THREE

Shane picked up his guitar and strummed the rhythm of the first song of their set. If Bekah wanted "Careless Whisper," he'd play it for her, but he'd save it for the end to make sure she didn't get any ideas about leaving early.

The moment he'd looked into her bright, hazel eyes, he'd been mesmerized. Something deep in his soul began to stir, filling him with a longing he'd never felt before. She'd commanded his wolf's attention, and to satiate his beast, he'd have to get to know her.

As the set went on, Bekah sipped the wine he'd bought her, the intensity of her gaze boring deeper into his soul with each song. She was the only person in the room, and every note he played belonged to her.

He signaled to Cammie to start the beat for Bekah's requested song, and Bekah straightened, a smile lifting her pink lips, lighting her entire face. Dark hair fell across her shoulders as she leaned forward on the table, and as he played the solo, her words rang in his ears: *the sexiest piece of music ever written.* In her modest pink blouse and knee-length skirt, Bekah's sex appeal topped it all. She looked polished and professional. Like a woman who had her shit together and wouldn't drop a man on his ass when he couldn't keep up with her partying.

Bekah's outfit left plenty to the imagination, and man, could he imagine.

His eyes usually closed on instinct as he melded with the music, his body becoming part of the song, but he fought to keep them open as he played, his gaze locked on the gorgeous muse sitting before him. Her eyes wandered from his face to his hands, and she bit her bottom lip as she focused on his fingers splaying across the keys.

As the song came to an end, Ricardo thanked the crowd and concluded the show. Bekah hugged Cammie's cousin and strolled toward the stage, clasping her hands behind her back as she eyed him.

"You're very good. You should do more songs that require the saxophone."

So she liked the sax better than the guitar or keyboard. That said a lot about her taste in music, particularly that it was in line with his own. "I've tried to get them to include a few jazz numbers, but they aren't having it."

"I love jazz."

"Do you?" This woman kept getting better. He tugged the strap from around his neck and put the sax in its case.

She shrugged. "I'm from New Orleans. It's ingrained in my soul."

"That must be an exciting place to live. I've always wanted to go there." He lifted the keyboard from the stand and shoved it in the case, breaking apart his setup as fast as he could.

Bekah crossed her arms and drummed her lavender nails against her bicep. "You play sax, you like jazz, and you've never been to New Orleans? You're missing out."

He paused and regarded her, taking in her beauty. She'd brushed her dark-brown hair behind her shoulders, revealing the elegant sweep of her neck, and a magnetic energy buzzed around her, drawing him to her and making him want nothing more than to take her in his arms and plant his lips on hers. "It seems I'm missing out on more than music in the Big Easy. Maybe I should visit some time."

The muscles in her throat worked as she swallowed, and a hint of uncertainty sparked in her eyes, her confidence slipping briefly before she composed herself. "Maybe you should."

"Maybe I will." He stared into her eyes, enchanted by the little gold and brown flecks shimmering in her irises. He could get lost in eyes like those.

A warm palm slapped his shoulder, breaking the trance. "Load up your gear, man. Let's jet."

Shane jumped from the stage and closed the distance between him and Bekah. When she didn't move away, he couldn't help himself; he had to touch her. Gliding his fingertips down her shoulder, he lightly grasped her elbow and leaned toward her. She smelled like heaven, the light floral fragrance of her shampoo mixing with her pheromones to create an intoxicatingly feminine scent that he wanted to wrap himself up in. "I need to put my things in the van so my mates can leave, but if you have a few minutes, I'd love to buy you another drink."

"Oh." She pressed her lips together, glancing toward the exit, her senses seeming to get the better of her. "I have to drive home in the morning. I don't need to drink anymore."

"Coffee then?" He couldn't let her get away. He needed to get to know her, to see if the message his wolf seemed to be sending was what he thought—he hoped—it was.

"I…" She swept her gaze down the length of him, her nostrils flaring as a mask of determination set in her features. "I suppose I have time for coffee. Decaf."

"Brilliant." He flagged down a waitress and ordered two cups. "I'll be right back. Don't go anywhere."

"I'll be here." Bekah slid into a seat, and he set his sax case on the floor by the empty chair.

Shane hauled his gear to the van and shoved it inside before turning back to the hotel.

Ricardo grabbed his arm. "We're leaving. You with us?"

"I'm not missing this opportunity."

"You're supposed to be considering our deal." Cammie put her hands on her hips. "The full moon is tomorrow. We have to do it then."

He inhaled deeply, furrowing his brow like he was considering their offer. "It's going to be a no for me." Not that saying *yes* had ever crossed his mind. "That woman in there…" He glanced at the door.

"She could be the one, and she doesn't look like the touring type. I wish you all the success you deserve, but that life isn't for me."

Cammie rolled her eyes. "Love at first sight doesn't exist."

"It does for werewolves, and I'm not wasting this chance."

"Yeah?" Ricardo crossed his arms. "Well, we started the spell with you in it. We still need—"

"It's fine." Cammie gripped Ricardo's arm. "We'll figure it out without him."

Shane strode across the sidewalk and reached for the doorknob. "Sorry, guys. I hate to let you down, but I think I just found my fate-bound."

"What am I doing?" Bekah clutched her coffee mug and stared at the exit Shane had disappeared through. Emma was at home waiting for her. She should've been in bed resting so she could make the drive home first thing in the morning and get back to her life. Back to being a mom.

A light breeze swept in through the door as Shane opened it, and his green eyes glinted with his smile. Her heart thrummed, her stomach fluttering like a teenager who'd caught the eye of the cutest boy in school. His jeans clung to his muscular thighs as he strode toward her, and he slipped off his jacket to reveal a pair of equally muscular arms.

Emma did have school tomorrow, so she wouldn't be able to see her until the afternoon anyway. Having coffee with the man wouldn't hurt anything.

"Thanks for waiting." Shane slipped into the seat next to her, angling his body so his knee brushed hers.

That innocent touch flipped a switch inside her, sending white-hot electricity buzzing in her core. *Holy crap.* She'd be an idiot to fight an attraction this strong. No way in hell was she going home tomorrow without seeing how things played out tonight with Shane. It had been way too long since anyone had touched her—looked at her—the way he was doing right then.

Play it cool, Bek. Maybe he just wants to talk. "You forgot to take your saxophone."

He reached down and ran his hand along the worn, leather case. "This one stays with me. My mum gave it to me when I was seventeen." A look of surprise flashed in his eyes like he hadn't meant to divulge so much.

"That's sweet." She rested a forearm on the table, tracing the wood pattern with her finger. "Do your parents still live in the UK?"

"London." He placed his arm on the table next to hers, so close she could feel the heat radiating from his skin. "My dad does. My mum died when I was eighteen."

"I'm sorry."

"It was a long time ago." His eyes smoldered as he leaned toward her, his gaze wandering around her face, lingering on her lips as if he were memorizing her features. No one—not even Tommy—had ever looked at her this way. Shane's expression wavered somewhere between wanting to worship her and needing to consume her, and being the object of this delectable werewolf's attention lit a fire inside her that might burn her to ash.

A man like Shane could easily have any woman he wanted, and here he was, sitting in a hotel bar with *her*, caressing her with his eyes and making her feel things she'd wondered if she'd ever feel again.

Words, Bekah. Talk to the man. She cleared her throat. "I guess you came here for your music? Following your dreams?"

He lowered his gaze before looking into her eyes. "I was following something. What about you? What brings you to the sunny state of Florida?"

"Restauranteur conference. I own the Blue Moon Café in the French Quarter, and I was hoping to pick up some tips. Learn some new insights into the business."

"Tell me more." He leaned in, listening intently as she told him about her waitressing jobs and how she eventually moved up to a management position. She'd always dreamed of owning her own place, so she moved in with her brother and went to college to get her degree in restaurant management. She talked about how she'd opened the place and her trusted manager that was watching over the business while she was here, learning more about the trade.

She told him everything. Well, everything except that she had a daughter. This was a one-night-only performance, and she planned to milk it for all it was worth. She'd never see the man again after tonight. No need to complicate things, so she ignored the pinch of guilt in her chest and laid out the rest of her life for him.

He seemed to hang on her every word, listening to her like he was actually interested as she droned on about her café. She couldn't remember a time she'd ever felt so…heard.

The lights behind the bar dimmed before the stage lights blinked out, and she sucked in a sharp breath. "I've talked the bar into closing time. You must think I'm so self-centered, but really I'm not used to someone listening to me."

He took her hand on the table. "I think you're a fascinating, inspirational woman, who is drilling her way into my heart as we speak."

His words held such sincerity, she nearly dropped her shields and let his emotions in, just to see if it could be true.

But it didn't matter if he was telling the truth. She wasn't looking for a relationship. She simply wanted to feel like a woman again, and he was exactly the kind of man who could get her there.

The lights above them dimmed, and moonlight spilling in through the windows cast the room in a silvery glow.

"I guess that's our cue to leave," she said.

"I suppose it is." But he didn't make a move to get up. Instead, he held her gaze with that smoldering intensity and traced his thumb across her hand.

It appeared he didn't want the night to end any more than she did. *Why not?* "Walk me to my room?"

His gaze nearly set her on fire. "My pleasure."

CHAPTER FOUR

As the elevator door slid open and the maid who had joined them on the ride hung a sharp left down the hallway, Bekah took Shane's hand and turned right toward her room. They'd both been silent on the ride up, the maid's presence stopping her from wrapping herself up in his strong embrace like she wanted to.

He'd put his jacket back on, covering those delectable biceps, but she remembered what they looked like, stretching and flexing beneath his T-shirt as he moved. Her pulse raced as they neared her door. She couldn't wait to touch him, to experience the hard sinew beneath his soft skin. To feel his hands on her body, his tongue on her…

A shiver ran up her spine as she pressed the keycard against the lock. "It's just one night."

He brushed her hair behind her shoulder, running the backs of his fingers along her neck. "Did you say something, love?"

She hadn't meant to say that out loud. "Nothing. Damn keycard's giving me trouble." She shoved the door open and turned to face him, swallowing the dryness from her mouth. "Do you want to come in?"

He inhaled deeply, looking her hard in the eyes, as if trying to decipher her question. It wasn't difficult. Either he wanted her like she wanted him, or he didn't.

Stepping into the room, she tossed her purse on the dresser. "I wouldn't have asked you in if I didn't want you to come." She slipped off her shoes and threw them under a chair. "Your move."

He crossed the threshold in two strides and shut the door behind him. "You're smart, strong, insanely gorgeous, and you know exactly what you want. You're a woman after my own heart, Bekah."

Her stomach fluttered. That was the second time he'd mentioned his heart, and they hadn't even kissed yet. *It's just one night.* He probably said these things to all the women he slept with, and that was fine. They were both consenting adults. She didn't mind being another notch in his bedpost.

But the way he looked at her…like she was the only woman in the world… That fire in his gaze came from somewhere deep inside him, and tiny sparks electrified her heart at the idea that his wolf might want her as much as the man did.

When she didn't respond, he hesitated, flicking his gaze from her to the bed to a chair, and then back to her before clearing his throat.

"You should kiss me now."

He nodded. "Right." Closing the distance between them, he took her face in his hand, gliding his fingers into her hair along her temple and running his thumb over her skin. The intensity in his gaze held her, coaxing open her soul and penetrating to the depths of her being.

She felt naked, exposed, as if he'd reached inside and plucked every thought from her mind and wrapped himself in every emotion she'd ever felt.

As he leaned in and brushed his lips to hers, liquid heat rolled through her veins, converging in her chest as her heart went up in flames. His lips were soft, the coarse hair around his mouth tickling her skin as he cupped the back of her head and slid his other hand to her hip.

Running her hands up his chest, she gripped his shoulders, her head spinning as she parted her lips and brushed her tongue against his.

A possessive growl rumbled in his chest, and he pulled her body to his, enveloping her in his strong embrace and kissing her like there was no tomorrow.

With another growl, he broke the kiss, inhaling deeply as he pulled back to look at her. His eyes narrowed, studying her with an expression of disbelief mixed with pure lust. "Tell me you feel that too."

"I'm feeling a lot of things." Number one being that she needed to get this man naked before she exploded.

She tugged his jacket from his shoulders, and he shrugged out of it, letting it fall to the floor. Then he gripped the fabric at the back of his neck and pulled his shirt over his head, dropping it by the jacket.

Bekah's lips parted on an involuntary gasp as her gaze swept across his magnificent chest. Perfectly-sculpted muscles rippled down his stomach, and his low-hung jeans provided a glimpse of the tantalizing V disappearing into the denim.

He chuckled. "Like what you see, love?"

"Very much." Starting at his stomach, she traced her fingers up his body to cup the back of his neck. The softness of his skin and the tingling magic seeping into her hands sent her pulse racing. The way he held her to his chest, dipping his tongue into her mouth, his hands roaming her body, gripping her like he couldn't hold her close enough… She'd never felt so wanted in her entire life.

And there was entirely too much fabric between them.

Never breaking contact with his body, she pressed her hips into his, arching her back and lifting her shirt over her head.

An appreciative grunt sounded from his throat as he lowered his gaze to her chest and cupped her breasts in his hands. His hooded gaze bore into her as he teased her nipples through her bra, and she reached behind her back to snap open the clasp.

The straps slid off her shoulders, and he tossed the garment aside. "Magnificent."

Dipping his head, he flicked out his tongue, bathing her nipple in wet heat. As he sucked it into his mouth, his teeth grazing the sensitive flesh, electricity zinged to her middle, tightening her stomach, her body aching with desire.

He moved to her other breast, taking the nipple between his lips and circling his tongue over the hardened tip. The sensation was maddening, and she tangled her fingers in his dark hair as a moan emanated from her throat.

As he glided his lips up her chest to nip at her neck, he reached behind her, tugging at her zipper and working her skirt over her hips. The garment fell to the floor, and he stepped back, taking in the length of her with his eyes.

She cringed inwardly, fighting the urge to cover her stomach, expecting his gaze to linger on the pooch of baby weight she'd never lost or for the desire in his eyes to fizzle out as he took in the stretch marks arcing over her hips.

But the longing intensified as he moved toward her, wrapping her in a consuming embrace and kissing her like she *belonged* to him.

Like his wolf was claiming her.

Her blood fizzed at the thought, her entire body lighting up like a Fourth of July fireworks display.

She fumbled with the button on his jeans, and he stilled her hands, leaning back just far enough to look into her eyes.

"Are you on birth control?"

"Yes."

"Is this what you want?"

Her heart pounded in her throat. His warm, woodsy scent filled her senses, and her need for this man occupied every thought her mind would form. "I want you, Shane."

"Then you'll have me, love." He toed off his boots and pulled down his jeans, kicking them aside before removing the rest of his clothes. As he stood before her, naked and rock hard all over, he spread his arms to his sides. "I'm yours."

"Yes, you are." She snaked her hands behind his neck and took his mouth in a kiss. The feel of his warm body pressed to hers was almost too much to bear, achingly intimate, yet she couldn't seem to get close enough to him.

Sensing her urgency, he grabbed her ass, lifting her from the floor, and she cinched her legs around his waist as they fell to the bed. He showered her face and neck in kisses, rocking his hips and rubbing his cock against her center, but her cotton panties blocked him, dulling the sensation she so desperately needed to feel.

"You are so beautiful, Bekah." The imaginary *R* he added at the end of her name made her shiver, and he trailed his lips across her collar bone, down between her breasts and toward her stomach as he slowly slid to his knees on the floor.

Resting his chin near her navel, he gazed up at her, roaming his hands over her body, caressing every inch of her bare skin. He circled his tongue around her belly button, gliding it down to the edge of her panties, leaving a trail of fire everywhere he touched.

She held her breath as he slipped her underwear off, tossing them aside before running his hands up the insides of her thighs. Clutching her hips, he tugged her toward the edge of the bed and draped her legs over his shoulders.

Her body trembled, anticipation coiling in her core as his warm breath danced across her skin. He slipped out his tongue, bathing her sensitive nub in wet warmth, sending a shock of electricity ricocheting through her body.

She gasped, and a sensual moan rumbled in his throat as he gripped her hips, diving into her center and lapping at her as if his sole purpose in life were to pleasure her. He knew exactly what to do, where to touch, the perfect pressure and rhythm to drive her wild.

She clutched the sheets, arching her back as her climax built, crying out as her orgasm crested like a wave, crashing into her, drowning her in passion.

As he slowed his pace, he lightened the pressure of his tongue, bringing her down slowly before rising and pressing a kiss to her stomach, between her breasts, and to her mouth. "The sounds you make when I pleasure you are more beautiful than any music I've ever heard."

Heat crept up her neck, and she pulled him down for another kiss, reaching her hand between them to grip his dick. "I need you inside me, Shane."

He rose onto his hands, pinning her with a heated gaze that said he wanted to consume her…and she couldn't wait to be devoured.

She scooted from the edge of the bed to lie in the center, and he moved with her, covering her with his body, his gaze never straying from hers. As she stroked his cock, his eyelids fluttered, and with a long exhale, he settled his hips between her legs.

He pressed against her, his tip barely penetrating her folds as he held his weight on his arms. She needed him. God, she ached to feel him inside her, filling her. He pushed in a little farther, so torturously, wonderfully slow she wanted to scream. He wasn't hesitating…rather savoring each delicious inch he took.

The intensity in his gaze grew heavier the deeper he slid inside her, making this moment feel like something…more. "This is it, love."

As his hips met hers and he filled her completely, a sense of wholeness fell over her. He lowered his body to hers, sliding his hands beneath her shoulders to hold her, clutching her to his chest as he moved.

He slid in and out, slowly at first, but increasing in both speed and intensity as the passion overtook them. She gripped his back, clinging to him, wrapping her legs around his waist as another climax coiled inside her, and he growled, burying his face in her neck as he pumped his hips furiously.

Lightning surged in her core, releasing a storm of emotion as her orgasm ripped through her body, her muscles shuddering beneath his weight, and her shields slipped. Shane's emotions seeped into her, flooding her heart with passion, ecstasy, and… *No, it couldn't be.*

There, in the mix of desire and lust, she felt his wolf, and the beast had one word on its mind: *Mine.*

Shane groaned, pressing into her as his own climax consumed him, before relaxing on top of her, his fingers slowly releasing their grip on her shoulders. He nuzzled into her, a feeling of utter happiness emanating from his skin, filling her with a sense of unfounded joy.

This wasn't happening. His wolf was not claiming her.

She slid her shields back into place, blocking Shane's emotions from her consciousness. She knew better than to try to read someone she was close to like this. When her own emotions ran high, her senses were easily clouded. She hadn't actually felt his wolf claiming her. That was a product of her imagination.

In the couple of hours she'd known Shane, he'd made her feel more important, more wanted, more needed than she'd felt in her entire life. She'd be thrilled if a man like him wanted to claim her. Who wouldn't be?

Her own fanciful desires were muddling her perception, so she would forget her shields had ever slipped.

He was enjoying the night with her like she was enjoying it with him, and tonight was all they would ever have.

She'd made the mistake of confusing her own emotions with her boyfriend's in the past. She wouldn't let it happen again.

Shane's muscles felt like jelly as he rolled onto his back and pulled Bekah to his side. She laid her head on his pec, draping her leg over his hips and resting her hand on his opposite shoulder, her body conforming to his like the final piece of a puzzle clicking into place.

She was made for him. Made to fit in his arms, to be in his life. He kissed the top of her head and breathed in the sweet, clean fragrance of her shampoo, the warm undercurrent that was uniquely Bekah awakening his wolf, bringing the beast to the surface.

Mine.

There was no sense in fighting this. The timing couldn't have been more perfect, but such was the nature of fate. The stars had aligned and were shining down on him, sending the message loud and clear.

He'd found his fate-bound.

He tightened his arms around her, memorizing the way her body felt wrapped up in his embrace. She belonged with him, and based on the way they'd made love, she felt it too.

She lifted her head to look at him, a sleepy smile tugging at her lips as she pressed a kiss to the corner of his mouth. Propping her head on her hand, she glided her fingers across his chest. "You never told me what brought you to Florida. Following the music?"

He placed his hand on top of hers, holding it to his chest. "I was following a girl."

Surprise flashed in her eyes. "All the way from the UK? She must have been pretty special."

He chuckled. "She thought she was."

"What happened?"

What the hell? His wolf had already claimed her, and he planned to eventually take her as his mate. He might as well lay it all out for her. "About five years ago, I fell in love with a human." He held her gaze, gauging her reaction to decide if he should hold back.

When she didn't flinch, he continued, "Let me rephrase that. I *thought* I was in love with a human, but I was young and dumb, and my wolf wasn't the slightest bit interested in her, but…"

"Been there." She laughed. "Not with a human, but the young and dumb part. So she moved here, and you followed her?"

"Worse than that. I played in her band."

She lifted her eyebrows, urging him to continue.

"She got an American recording contract, so she moved to LA. I came with her and played lead guitar. We toured all over the US, sleeping in a different hotel room every night, never really calling anywhere home."

"That sounds exciting."

"It gets old fast, believe me. The parties, the drinking, the drugs. She was living the rock star lifestyle, but all I wanted to do was stay in one place more than a few days at a time. She tired of me quickly when I stopped partying with her."

"Couldn't keep up?" She flashed a teasing smile.

"I'm a werewolf. I could drink her under the table, and it drove her mad when I'd be up at dawn the next day while she nursed her hangover until midafternoon. Anyway, after a while, she fell *in* love with those white, powdery lines, and fell *out* of love with me. We played a show in Orlando, and she dumped me straight after. Kicked me out of the band and left me there with nothing but my saxophone for company."

"Ouch. That sucks."

He shrugged. "It did for a while, but I got over it. I met Ricardo and Cammie and joined their band. We do local shows, all in-state. It's a slower pace, but it suits me."

"Do you ever think about going home to London? Back to your pack and your family?"

He started to tell her he'd never been in a pack, that his parents had always been rogues, but he thought better of it. Bekah had mentioned that her brother was second in command of the New Orleans pack when she'd told him her life story in the bar, and he had no idea how she felt about rogues. Better to let her get to know him before she had the chance to form judgments.

"If my mum were alive, I might consider it."

"What happened to her? I mean…if you don't mind telling me." Her eyes held so much compassion he couldn't fathom holding anything else back.

"She was in the wrong place at the wrong time. Got caught in a convenience shop robbery and was shot in the heart." His throat thickened, and he pushed the memory aside. Now was not the time for reminiscing about his past. Not when he held his future in his arms.

"I'm so sorry, Shane." She bit her bottom lip.

"It's okay, love. Like I said, it was a long time ago. Anyway, my father disowned me when I left for America, so there's no point in going back." Maybe he shouldn't have told her that part, but it was out there now, and she didn't pull away.

"Why would he do that?"

He searched her eyes for judgment, but all he found was concern. Usually, people only wanted to hear about his time on tour. When the conversation shifted to his personal life, most women got bored, their eyes glazing if they couldn't steer the subject back to Shane the rocker.

Bekah was actually interested in the man. *Of course she is, wanker. She's your fate-bound.* "My mum was a music teacher. She taught me everything I know; I can play any instrument I get my hands on. Music is ingrained in my soul, but my father wanted me to pick a more 'useful' profession."

"It was okay with him for your mom to teach music, but not for you to perform?"

"He's a…" The word rogue almost slipped out, but he bit it back. "He's independent. Thinks music is for women and… I won't use his words, but not for masculine men, you know?"

"Gotcha. Well, I think musicians can be very masculine." She kissed him, lingering near his lips until he couldn't help but kiss her again. He dipped his tongue into the wet warmth of her mouth, and a shiver ran down his spine. Oh, yes. This woman belonged with him.

She pulled back, her gaze dancing around his face. "Our alpha can play piano, believe it or not."

"Considering it's New Orleans, I believe it." Which was another reason the stars were shining on him tonight. His fate-bound lived in the birthplace of jazz. He couldn't think of a better place to settle down and live his dream. "In answer to your question, no, I never think about going back to London, but I am planning to see New Orleans soon."

Her expression darkened, her brow furrowing as she chewed her bottom lip. Not the reaction he was expecting, but maybe she didn't understand what he was saying.

He cupped her cheek in his hand. "I have to see you again."

She shook her head and sat up, clutching a pillow in her lap. "Shane, you and I both know what this was, so you don't have to make promises you don't intend to keep. I'm not delusional. I know I'm never going to see you again."

He sat up too. "You are delusional if you think a one-night stand is all I want from you. Bekah, this is the start of something, not the end."

She studied him, narrowing her eyes as if trying to decide if she should believe him.

"Earlier, when I said 'this is it,' I meant this is *it*. The beginning of a relationship. I have to see you again, and if that means going to New Orleans, then that's what I'll do."

She smiled and loosened her grip on the pillow. "I'd like that."

"Yeah?" His heart pounded in his chest.

"Yeah."

"Good." His phone rang from somewhere in the heap of clothes on the floor, but he ignored it.

Confliction clouded her eyes as she scooted to the edge of the bed. "If you're sure about this…about coming to New Orleans to see me…"

"I've never been more sure of anything in my life."

The corners of her mouth twitched like she wanted to smile again.

"There's something you need to know about me. I..." She blew out a hard breath. "I have a kid."

His heart took a nosedive into his stomach. *Oh, hell.* Had his wolf claimed someone who was spoken for? "Do you have a boyfriend?"

"No." She shook her head adamantly. "It's a long story, but I got pregnant when I was nineteen. Emma's father is a witch, but he left as soon as he found out, and I haven't seen him since. I'm not... I just wanted you to know, in case you want to change your mind."

He tucked a strand of hair behind her ear. "Why would I want to change my mind?"

She drew her shoulders up. "She's my first-born. She's only eight, so I don't know if she'll be a shifter yet or not. Before you start making plans to see where this goes with you and me, you need to know what you're getting into. What it could mean for...the future. Your lineage."

He sucked in a breath as the realization dawned on him. She was trying to tell him his first-born wouldn't be her first-born, so he may not have a shifting child of his own. "I don't give a damn about my lineage. Do you want to know what I want out of life?"

She nodded.

"I don't think I've ever told anyone this before, but..." He chuckled. "I want to settle down someday and have my own music school like my mum. I want to teach kids the love of music, and I want to have a few kids of my own. Whether or not they can shift isn't important to me." He simply wanted to love them. To be everything his father never was for him. To be dependable.

"Are you sure?"

"I—" The phone rang again, and he glanced toward his pants.

"You can answer. It could be your pack."

He hesitated, glancing between the ringtone and Bekah, but she motioned with her hand for him to take the call. Rolling out of bed, he dug in his pocket and checked the screen. Ricardo. "Bloody hell." He pressed the device to his ear. "It's three a.m."

"Cammie's passed out."

He crept into the bathroom and lowered his voice. "That happens when she drinks too much."

"No, man." Ricardo's voice sounded frantic. "It's the spell. She was working on it, and…we need you. She was trying to continue it without you, but she can't remove you from it without you here." A muffled *bang* sounded in the distance. "Something happened to her, and she blacked out. Can you get over here? I think I can revive her if we're all present. The guys are on their way."

Damn it, these witches had the worst timing. "All right, mate. I'll come, you'll remove me from the whole ordeal, and then I'm done. Got it?"

"Yeah, yeah. Just get here as fast as you can." Ricardo ended the call, and Shane fought the urge to hurl his phone across the room. *Stupid witches.*

He shuffled into the bedroom and found Bekah picking up his clothes, turning them right side out. "I have to go."

She shrugged and smiled. "I figured as much. When the pack calls, we answer, right?"

"Right." No need to explain the predicament he was in. He'd be done with the witches soon enough. "What time are you leaving tomorrow?"

She handed him his pants and picked up his shirt, righting it as she spoke. "I was planning to leave first thing in the morning, but I could stick around a little longer if…"

"Good. Get some rest, and I'll be back at ten a.m. We'll have a late breakfast and figure out a plan for when I can see you again." He took his shirt from her hands and slipped it over her head. "And you can wear this while I'm gone, so you don't forget about me."

She laughed and put her arms through the sleeves. "I don't think I could ever forget about you." She lifted the fabric to her nose and inhaled deeply, closing her eyes as if reveling in the scent.

His stomach tightened, his dick hardening at the thought of her reveling in him. He put his jacket on and stepped into his boots before pulling her into a tight embrace. "I'll be back before you know it, love."

"Here." She slipped a ring of dark-gray beads around his wrist. A lighter gray, iridescent marble pattern ran through the polished stones, glinting in the lamplight. "So you don't forget about *me* while you're gone."

He examined the bracelet, holding onto Bekah with his free hand. His wolf didn't want to let her go. Neither did the man. "This is pretty."

"It's a clarity bracelet that my sister-in-law made for me. It's supposed to help you focus on the most important things in your life."

His chest tightened. He didn't need a bracelet to tell him what he wanted out of life, and he was finally on his way to having it all. He pressed a kiss to her lips and reluctantly let her go. "I'll see you soon, Bekah."

CHAPTER FIVE

Bekah sat on the edge of the bed, clutching her keys in her hands and watching the little red numbers on the clock face flip from ten forty-five to forty-six, forty-seven. Her nostrils flared as she let out a slow breath, the reality of the situation pressing on her shoulders, shame making heat creep up her neck and bloom across her cheeks.

She should have seen this coming. Hot guys like Shane weren't looking to settle down, especially not with a single mom who lived in another state. As if he'd follow her to New Orleans.

In her defense, he did say he followed a girl here all the way from the UK. What were a few hundred miles when he'd crossed an entire ocean before? Especially after what she'd thought she felt from him…

She picked up his shirt and pressed it to her nose, inhaling his woodsy, masculine scent. It still made her stomach flutter, even though he'd stood her up. She groaned and shoved the shirt into her suitcase.

Everything had been fine until he started filling her head with false promises, making her believe what she felt in him had been real. She was prepared for a one-night stand. She'd *wanted* it to be a one-night stand. All she'd needed was for him to help her feel like a woman again, and he'd done a bang-up job of that.

She shivered at the memory of his hands on her body, and the way he worked his tongue. But then, in the heat of passion, the emotions she'd felt in him were beyond her wildest expectations. Strong, primal, possessive.

She'd felt something similar when she read her brother after he met his fate-bound, and then when she felt it coming from Shane…

Well, she *thought* she'd felt the emotions from Shane. Obviously, her own desires had overpowered his actual emotions, and that was no surprise. She hadn't had a clue when Tommy freaked out about Emma. When she'd told him she was pregnant, he'd acted happy, which had made her happy in return.

And even when she'd attempted to read the bastard, her own emotions had clouded her ability, making it impossible to tell what he was really feeling. That Tommy had planned to disappear as soon as she fell asleep.

She couldn't trust her ability when her own emotions were involved. She *knew* that, but it didn't ease the stabbing pain in her heart. Zipping her suitcase, she rose to her feet and wheeled it out the door. Check-out ended at eleven, and she was out of time.

She hit the button for the elevator and ground her teeth. Shane left without asking for her number. That should have been a red flag, but she'd been so high on the stupid fated mates idea she hadn't even considered that she had no way to contact him.

The doors slid open, and she held her breath, hoping maybe…

The space stood empty. She blew out a breath and stepped into the elevator, determined to put Shane and all his beautiful, empty promises out of her mind.

Bekah picked up Emma from her grandma's house that afternoon, and after three days, life in New Orleans returned to normal. She ran her café, slowly implementing the new techniques she'd learned at the conference, and though it took her a few days, she was able to forgive the befuddled ending to her night with Shane and relish the memory of feeling alive again for the first time in years.

He'd merely proven himself the asshole she'd expected him to be. No reason to hold a grudge against a man she'd never see again. No harm was done, and it had been plenty of fun at the time.

"Bekah." Dani, the head server, knocked on the office door, pulling her from her thoughts. "Oooh, what are you grinning about? I wanna see." She pranced around the desk, scowling as she glimpsed the spreadsheet on the computer screen. "That's nothing to smile at."

Bekah laughed. "Sorry to disappoint. What's up?"

"Oh." Dani adjusted her ponytail and stepped around the desk. "There's a guy out on the patio; he's been here about an hour but hasn't ordered anything. He looks like he might be homeless, and he seems pretty confused too. Do you want me to send him away or call the cops?"

Bekah cringed. Most of the homeless knew the rules: if they didn't order something, they didn't get to occupy the tables. But if he was new in town, he might need to be clued in to the way things worked. "Don't call the cops yet. I'll come out and talk to him."

"You got it, boss." Dani gave her a mock salute. "He could be a hottie if he cleaned himself up and got off whatever he's taking that makes him so spaced out."

She sighed, rising to her feet, and followed her employee through the dining room and out onto the patio. Dani thought any man with eyes and a heartbeat could be a hottie, so Bekah wasn't expecting much.

The man sat at a table near the edge of the patio, looking out across the street. His black leather jacket and mop of dark hair stopped Bekah in her tracks. Her heart dipped into her stomach before lodging into her throat as Dani tapped him on his shoulder.

"This is Bekah, the café owner. She'd like to speak to you." Dani gestured toward her, and the man turned around as Dani scurried off to clean up the coffee a customer spilled on the floor.

His sea-green eyes pierced her soul like the first time they'd met, and for a moment, the fact that he'd stood her up didn't matter, and her heart filled with hope. Shane had come to New Orleans.

"Shane?" Her body lightened, and she rose onto her toes as she drifted toward him. "What are you doing here?"

His brow pinched, a strange look clouding his eyes as he blinked at her and glanced at his saxophone case. "You're Bekah?"

The bubble of hope in her chest sprang a leak, and she put her hands on her hips. "Who else would I be?"

"Bekah," he muttered and studied the menu on the table. "Blue Moon Café."

"What's going on?" A sense of unease washed over her, souring her stomach.

He lifted his gaze to hers and tilted his head. "I'm sorry, love. Do I know you?"

Her jaw dropped open, her eyes going wide as he twisted a knife in her heart. "Are you kidding me? Is this some kind of joke?" A couple at a table across the patio looked at her, and she took a deep breath to compose herself, lowering her voice to a whisper. "What are you doing, Shane?"

He shook his head, acting like he seriously didn't remember her, a cocky smile lighting on his lips. "Bekah. Blue Moon Café."

Resting a hand on the table, she leaned in closer to him, a spark of anger igniting in her core. He smelled like he hadn't showered since she'd seen him three days ago, but that warm, woodsy undercurrent peeked through, his pheromones still calling to her, making her body react against her will.

She bent to his eye level. "Yes, I'm Bekah from the Blue Moon Café. The woman you slept with and made beautiful promises of beginnings and things to come." She fisted her hands to stop herself from grabbing a handful of his jacket and shoving him off the patio. "I was fine with a one-night stand. You didn't have to say all those things, you sick bastard."

His lips parted on a quick inhale, but she wasn't about to let him get another word in.

"You've been sitting here for an hour. Either order something or stop taking up space in my café." She straightened and crossed her arms over her chest. "What's it going to be?"

He glanced about the café before clearing his throat. "I seem to have misplaced my wallet." His smile returned, fueling the fire of her anger.

"Get out, Shane."

"I don't have any money, love. I'm not sure where to go."

She fought her eye-roll. "You have the gall to come to my café, pretend like you don't remember me, and then tell me you have nowhere to go? What? You think I'm going to take you in? Give you money?" Her body shook with anger. "Why don't you take your saxophone and go play 'Careless Whisper' on the street? I'm sure the tourists will help you out with some cash."

He blinked, flinching as if he'd been slapped. "The sexiest piece of music ever written."

Her blood boiled. "Get. Out."

He hesitated, his mouth hanging open.

"Leave, Shane. Don't come back."

He grabbed his sax case and rose to his feet, shaking his head and muttering, "Bekah. Blue Moon Café," still pretending like he had no idea who she was.

What an ass. As he crossed the sidewalk into the street, Bekah turned on her heel and marched into the dining room.

A tiny voice in the back of her mind screamed at her to stop him. Damn it, even after that tenacious display of assholery, she was still attracted to him. *Get a grip.*

She shook her hands, trying to rid herself of the lightning sparking inside her. *He's an asshole, just like you thought he'd be. Deal with it.*

"Aw. You got rid of Hottie Homeless Guy?" Dani stopped in front of her, carrying a tray of empty coffee mugs. "Did you notice he was shirtless beneath that sexy leather jacket? Six pack and everything."

No, she did not notice that. She'd been too focused on all the ridiculous emotions swirling through her own body, tunneling her vision. She hadn't paid attention to anything but his eyes at the time, but now that Dani mentioned it, he seemed to be wearing the same clothes he'd had on when he left her hotel room. There was no telling what a guy like that could've gotten himself into.

It didn't matter. She was done with Shane. "If he comes back, call the cops. I'm not dealing with him again."

Shane knew her.

She was important somehow, but every time a fuzzy memory began to form, it dissolved into mist. *This is bloody frustrating.* He raked a hand through his hair, pulling it at the roots as he crossed the street, moving away from the café.

The Blue Moon Café.

The place was important too, but he couldn't for the life of him remember why. He hung a left and paced up the sidewalk, wracking his brain for a memory of…anything. Hell, the only reason he knew his name was Shane was because of the engraved plate on the saxophone case. Even then, he wasn't sure the name belonged to him until Bekah said it.

Other than his name and the fact that he apparently slept with the beautiful café owner, he couldn't remember a bloody thing. He'd learned from the address on the menu that he was in New Orleans. That seemed important too, but he had no idea how he got there, if he lived there…or if he didn't, where he came from.

Nothing.

But the memories were there. They danced around his consciousness, teasing him with blurry images and feelings of recognition before darting away the moment he tried to grab onto one.

Bekah was there, somewhere in the void of his mind, but she also ran deeper, into his soul. Something about her resonated with him. His wolf recognized her. Though the beast's memories were as clouded as his own, the moment their eyes had met, his wolf had stirred. The animal became restless, and the urge to take her in his arms, to protect her from…something…had overwhelmed him.

He paused on a street corner and held the sax case in both hands. When Bekah mentioned that song…"Careless Whisper"…it jarred loose a memory. Her teasing smile. A passionate gaze. The words *"the sexiest piece of music ever written"* had come from somewhere.

He needed to take stock. Figure out what he did know, and then he could work on recalling what he'd lost. He knew how to play the instrument, of that he was sure. And Bekah…

A shudder ran through his body at the thought of her. She was the key to everything; he could feel it in his bones. Remembering her was his top priority.

He closed his eyes and focused on the sliver of memory her mention of the song had provided. He saw her face, her smile. That song meant something to them, and he had to figure out what it was.

Two women stopped in front of a shop window, the brunette taking her phone from her purse and swiping at the screen. Shane zipped his jacket closed—finding a shirt should be his next priority—and strolled toward them, putting on his most charming smile. "Excuse me, I wonder if you could help a bloke out."

The woman's brows shot up, a slight wariness tightening her eyes before she relaxed into a smile. "You're British."

The flush of irritation in his chest told him he probably got that response a lot. "I seem to have misplaced my phone, and I got a request for a song I'm unfamiliar with. I was hoping you could look it up for me."

She tapped her screen. "Sure, what's it called?"

"The song is 'Careless Whisper.' I'm not sure of the artist."

The woman laughed and glanced at her friend. "Are you yanking my chain? You're British, and you're *unfamiliar* with Wham!?" She made air quotes with her fingers.

He bit back his frustration and forced a smile. "I'm afraid I'm not a big fan of pop music."

The woman shook her head. "George Michael? You must know him."

Clenching his teeth, he let out a slow breath. Perhaps there was a music store nearby. He'd find another way to hear the song. "Thank you for your time. I'm sorry to bother you." He nodded and turned to walk away.

"Wait," the woman called. "Here it is." She held her phone toward him, and a man's voice drifted through the air.

Shane focused on the rhythm, closing his eyes and allowing the music to seep into his soul. Familiarity buzzed around his senses, the tune becoming more recognizable as the singer crooned on. When the saxophone solo played, something in his mind snapped. Another memory wiggled free from its confines, presenting itself to him like a movie.

In his mind, Shane stood on stage playing this same riff. He'd fought to keep his eyes open while he played because Bekah watched him from the audience, a sultry smile and a look of longing in her eyes.

That was it. He'd played the song for *her*. Maybe if he played it for her again…

He opened his eyes and nodded at the woman. "Thank you, so very much."

Shane darted across the street, and a car slammed on its brakes, laying on the horn as he narrowly missed being flattened by the front end. He tapped the hood and waved an apology before stepping onto the sidewalk and heading back to the café. To Bekah.

He stopped outside the entrance, set the case on the ground, and slipped the strap on his saxophone over his head. Attaching the mouthpiece, he positioned the reed, tightening it into place before drumming his fingers across the keys. The instrument felt so natural in his hands, like he'd played it a thousand times, though he couldn't remember any of them.

Any but one. Playing for Bekah.

He ran the tune through his mind, fingering the keys as he thought about the melody. He remembered how to form every note, yet he couldn't recall where he'd slept last night. A glance through the café window showed Bekah behind the counter, handing a takeaway order to a customer. She didn't want him inside her restaurant, but the sidewalk outside was a public area.

He brought the reed to his lips and blew into the instrument, belting out the song flawlessly. He didn't have to think about the music; it was as natural to him as breathing. As he played, the fog in his mind began to lift, his night with Bekah coming into clear view.

Their flirtatious banter at a bar had turned into a passionate night between the sheets. With his eyes closed, the image of Bekah filled his mind, stirring in his heart and awakening a feeling so strong it was a wonder how it had been buried with his memories.

He burned for her, and being with her had made him feel like his life was complete. His wolf hovered near the surface as he played, and a single word echoed in his head.

Mine.

CHAPTER SIX

As a customer opened the café door, a familiar song drifted inside, making Bekah's breath catch. She finished ringing up a to-go order and padded around the counter to the window.

Her pulse thrummed. Shane stood outside, "Careless Whisper" flowing from his saxophone with the same soulful intensity she remembered from the night they met. *What kind of game is he playing?* Her hands curled into fists, and her emotions battled over swooning for the man all over again and wanting to wring his neck for putting her through this.

She focused on the anger and marched out the door, intent on giving him a piece of her mind. But as she stood in front of him, watching him play, his eyes closed, his body moving as if the music were a part of him, the urge to swoon clawed its way to the top.

She forced the ridiculous emotions down and crossed her arms, waiting for the song to end. "What do you think you're doing?"

Shane opened his eyes. "I played that song for you the night we met."

"Oh, you remember now? Isn't that nice?" She tapped her foot.

"I do, Bekah." He stepped toward her, but she stepped back. His shoulders slumped, and he swallowed hard. "Can we talk somewhere private?"

"I've got nothing to say to you."

"Then listen, please." He reached for her, and her bracelet peeked from his sleeve.

Her throat thickened as she raked her gaze over his disheveled form. She'd been so caught up in her anger at being stood up, she hadn't stopped to consider his side of the story. From the way he looked, something had happened to him between then and now. "Please tell me what's going on. Why did you act like you didn't remember me?"

"Because I didn't." His green eyes held her gaze, pleading with her to understand. "I don't…I *didn't* remember anything. My mind…" He waved his hand around his head. "I've lost my memory, Bekah." As the crowd that had formed around him while he played dispersed, he tried again to move closer to her, and this time she let him.

"What happened? Where have you been?"

"I don't know. I don't…" He let out a frustrated sigh. "I don't know who I am. I can't remember where I'm from nor how I got here. All I know is that I found your café. I found you. Somewhere in the void of my mind, you were there, and I found you. And seeing you again, it didn't register at first, until you mentioned the song. Then an image broke free, and that image was of you, smiling at me, and I knew you were important."

He raked a hand through his hair and shook his head. "Playing the music helped me, but the only thing I can remember is you. Do you know why that is?"

"I don't…no." A hummingbird took flight in her stomach.

"You're my fate-bound, Bekah. My wolf has claimed you, and I think you feel it too. I know you do."

She sucked in a sharp breath, her fingers covering her lips as she searched his eyes. What she was looking for, she wasn't sure. She did feel it too. She'd felt it the moment they'd met, but she'd blamed it on her hormones and the fact that she hadn't been with a man since Emma was born.

Reaching a trembling hand toward him, she gripped his wrist, opening her sixth sense and letting his emotions flow into her. Confusion, despair, and determination swirled through his psyche, but in the middle of it all, steady and strong as iron, she felt his wolf…and his wolf *had* claimed her.

"Wait here." She pushed open the door but paused and looked at him. "Don't leave."

He smiled. "I'm not going anywhere without you, love."

The hummingbird wings beating against her stomach multiplied into a swarm as she rushed through the dining room and into the office. She grabbed her purse from her desk drawer and found her assistant manager in the kitchen. "I have to cut out early today. Can you hold down the fort?"

"No problem. Everything okay?"

"It will be." She turned on her heel and flew through the front door, finally slowing down to breathe when she found Shane leaning against the wall, the sax case at his feet.

"Come with me." She took his hand and led him away from the café.

"Where are we going?" He strode beside her, a sense of relief loosening the tension in his broad shoulders.

"To my place so we can talk." They walked in silence toward her house as Bekah attempted to corral her thoughts. A brisk breeze blew down the street, mussing her hair, and she rubbed at the goose bumps on her arms.

Shane's gaze flitted around at the scenery, his expression ranging from confusion to the wide-eyed look of awe at his surroundings. As they passed through Jackson Square, he stared at the massive St. Louis Cathedral, with its off-white façade and triple steeples, until a street performer juggling fire batons drew his attention.

She guided him out of the square, deeper into the French Quarter, toward the residential area. A three-piece band struck up a jazzy tune on a street corner, and Shane paused, tilting his head as he watched them play.

"Almost there." Bekah tugged him around the corner, onto a street lined with one and two-story Creole cottages painted in shades ranging from gray to bright purple. Her mind raced as they approached her house, a deep brown, shotgun-style home with dark-blue trim.

She unlocked the front door, ushering him inside. "What's the last thing you remember?"

He set his case down and swept his gaze around her open living room and kitchen area. "I remember you. Not much else."

"Do you remember your bandmates? Your family? Anything?"

He squeezed his eyes shut and pinched the bridge of his nose. "I don't, but I know I should. I can feel the memories. They're in my mind, but I can't access them."

"I don't know what happened to you, but I'm going to help you figure it out. First, though, you need to clean yourself up. I don't think you've showered since we met." She guided him through the kitchen and pointed out the bathroom. "There's an extra toothbrush in the drawer. I'll wash your clothes while you're in the shower."

He looked around at the bathroom before pinning her with his gaze. "Thank you, Bekah, for believing me. I don't know who I can trust right now, except for you." He shrugged out of his jacket and popped the button on his jeans.

His body was as sculpted as she remembered, and heat pooled below her navel as she stepped into the hallway and pulled the door halfway shut. "Just…toss your clothes out here and I'll throw them in the wash. Towels are in the linen closet." She couldn't handle seeing him naked right now. *Focus on what's important.*

He reached his hands through the open space in the doorway, offering her the pile of clothes. "I appreciate your hospitality."

Oh boy. She took the clothes and padded to the laundry room as the bathroom door clicked shut. His pockets were empty, so she shoved his clothes into the machine and set it on the quick-wash cycle before shuffling to the living room.

Think, Bekah. Focus. At the rate werewolves could heal, even a massive blow to the head wouldn't cause complete amnesia. If he'd gotten in a car accident when he left her hotel room, he wouldn't have made it all the way to New Orleans. Unless he hitchhiked. An accident didn't feel right though. Someone did this to him, and she was going to find out who.

She paced a line from the kitchen to the living room, wringing her hands and trying to concentrate on the situation, but she couldn't focus. Sinking onto the couch, she smiled. Shane's wolf had claimed her; she hadn't imagined it.

Giddy laughter bubbled from her chest, and she covered her mouth to muffle it. She'd found her soulmate. He couldn't remember a single thing about his life, but he remembered her. He belonged to her.

A wave of dizziness forced her to squeeze her eyes shut. She hadn't seen this coming. Had she known her attempt at a one-night stand would turn into a lifelong, soul-deep connection, she would have…

Well, what would you have done, Bek? Fate hadn't given her a choice in the matter and she had Emma to consider. Her daughter may not take to Shane, and what then? Surely fate wouldn't bind her heart to someone her daughter wouldn't like. That's if fate even considered other people when bringing two souls together.

The washing machine buzzed, signaling the end of the cycle, and she moved his clothes to the dryer. A few minutes later, Shane emerged from the bathroom, wearing nothing but a dark-blue towel wrapped around his waist.

Her fingers twitched, the memory of his soft skin and hard… everything…awakening a feral desire deep inside her. She wanted to go to him. To take him in her arms and tell him everything would be okay and kiss away the worry etching canyons into his forehead.

She bit the inside of her cheek to keep herself grounded. He was in a dangerous situation. They had no clue who had wiped his memory nor why, and him being here…while everything about him being here felt so right, he may have brought the danger into her pack, into her home.

"Your clothes should be dry in about twenty minutes."

"Thank you." He ran a hand through his damp hair, brushing it away from his face, and his biceps bunched, flexing with the movement.

Her gaze wandered from his muscular arms, down his stomach, toward his… She had to get some clothes on this man before she lost control.

"Just a second." She marched into her bedroom and dug some garments from her dresser. "You can put these on while you wait." She handed him the stack of clothes, and he followed her into the living room.

"Whose are these?" He tugged the shirt over his head and stepped into the sweat pants, pulling them up beneath the towel before uncinching it from his waist and laying it across the back of a chair.

There. That was better. At least he was covered now. "The shirt is yours. The pants my brother left here when he babysat Emma."

His brow scrunched as he ran his hands down his chest, examining the shirt. "I gave this to you."

She moved toward him. "You said it was so I—"

"Wouldn't forget about me while I was away." He looked into her eyes, and she drifted closer to him, like metal to a magnet...or a mosquito to a bug zapper.

Be careful. You don't know what he's gotten into. "Where did you go that night?"

He paused, his eyes searching hers as if he could find the answer inside her. "I don't know. I can't remember anything unless it involves you."

She took his hand and ran her thumb across the bracelet on his wrist. "I gave this to you. It's a clarity bracelet, so that might be why." She sucked in a sharp breath. "Rain can help. My sister-in-law is a powerful witch. I bet she can write a spell to undo whatever was done to you."

He laced his fingers through hers and kissed the back of her hand. "Do you think it will be that easy?"

Her stomach fluttered. "Witchcraft is never easy, but it's worth a shot. I think I might know how to get in touch with your band. Maybe they can shed some light on what happened."

He rubbed his forehead. "I wish I could remember. I don't recall being in a band." A rumbling sounded from his stomach.

"You must be starving. When was the last time you ate?"

He lifted his hands palms up. "I don't even know where I slept last night."

Poor thing. Her heart ached for him, and the desire to take him in her arms and kiss away the pain surge through her again. "Sit down. I'll get you something to eat."

She could handle this situation if she kept herself busy. Focus on one thing at a time, and she could get through it. This was how she got through college and opened a café while raising her daughter. Tackle the issues as they come and don't get overwhelmed with the big picture.

Of course, the big picture here was that her heart was bound to a man she hardly knew. She gripped the fridge door and blew out a hard breath. *I can handle this.*

She fixed him a turkey sandwich and set it in front of him before retrieving his clothes from the dryer. When she returned to the kitchen, he'd already finished the food, and she handed him his pants. "Go get dressed. The first thing we need to do is get you registered. You're on Crescent City territory, and we don't want to start any issues between the packs."

He wrapped his strong arms around her, pulling her to his chest. "Thank you, Bekah. For everything."

The mix of her soap and his own woodsy scent filled her senses, and she couldn't help but melt into his embrace. There was no doubt in her mind that she was bound to this man, but she'd have to pick Emma up from school soon. She had to figure out a way to keep her family safe and hope her daughter would be okay with having a new person in their lives.

She cleared her throat and pulled from his embrace. "Okay. Let's get you taken care of."

CHAPTER SEVEN

Shane fought the urge to take Bekah's hand as they strode toward her pack's headquarters, and he focused on the scenery instead. As they crossed the street, the small, brightly-colored cottages gave way to two- and three-story buildings in shades of beige, yellow, and blue. Potted plants adorned the wrought-iron-trimmed galleries, and colorful beads and purple-and-green wreaths added to the embellishments.

She followed his gaze toward a lavishly decorated balcony. "It'll be Mardi Gras soon."

He smiled, but her lips merely twitched in return. She was holding back, and he honestly couldn't blame her. She had explained the details of their relationship, and as the blanks were filled in, he realized his mistake.

What kind of wanker tells a woman his wolf has claimed her after one date?

The kind who doesn't remember they've only had one date.

He'd overwhelmed her, and he was lucky she'd offered to help him at all. As much as he needed to take her in his arms and make the woman his, he'd dial it back. Give her time to process. Her wolf was dormant, so she might not even feel the strong connection tethering his heart to hers.

She would eventually, and he could wait.

"This is it." She pointed to a dark blue building nestled between two taller structures. A wooden sign above the door read O'Malley's Pub, and a curtain of cool air blasted his skin from above as he followed her inside.

Shaded lights hung from exposed wood beams, and a woman with light-brown hair and bright blue eyes stood behind the bar. She slid the drink she was mixing to a patron and nodded a hello. "Luke and Chase are in the office waiting for you. Head on back."

"Thanks, Amber." Bekah motioned for him to follow and padded toward a side door that had a cardboard sign with *Employees and Werewolves Only* written in black marker.

Shane paused and scratched his head. He may not remember much about his own life, but there was no way the existence of werewolves was out in the open, even in New Orleans. "Is this…?"

Bekah stepped through the door and held it open. "It's a joke. Human customers used to say the old alpha looked like a wolfman, so he went with it."

"I see. What happened to him?" He followed her down a short set of stone steps and through the brick-lined corridor, wracking his brain for a memory of his own alpha—or at least his pack or his family. He found nothing but a void where his memories should have been.

She paused outside an office door and squeezed his hand. "He retired, and his son took over. We're a peaceful pack. Don't worry."

Another sliver of memory from his night with Bekah crept into his mind. "And your brother is his second?"

Her eyes brightened with her smile. "You're remembering."

"Only because it has to do with you."

"It's a start." She dropped his hand and smoothed her hair from her face before knocking on the door.

"It's open," a man called from inside.

Shane straightened his spine and strode through the door, refusing to let the alpha see how lost he felt. A dark-haired man with tattoos and a beard leaned against the massive oak desk, and as Shane stepped through the door, another man rose to his feet and stepped around toward him. This guy was taller, with a barrel of a chest and light-brown hair tied back in a band.

Shane instinctively lowered his gaze, his wolf recognizing the alpha before the man even spoke.

"Hey, guys. This is Shane." Bekah lightly touched his back, ushering him farther into the room. "This is my brother, Chase, and the alpha, Luke."

Shane shook Luke's hand, and the alpha's intense power rolled through his skin. "Pleasure to meet you." He shook Chase's hand, and the man narrowed his eyes, cutting his gaze between Shane and Bekah.

Bekah cleared her throat and settled into a chair, patting the one next to her, indicating Shane should sit too. He reluctantly lowered into the seat, his wolf protesting the submissive position.

Luke strode around his desk and opened a laptop before addressing Bekah. "Chase explained what you told him on the phone, but I need you to go over it again. What's going on?"

"Shane's memory has been wiped. All we know is that he's a British musician who lives in Florida and plays in a local band. He's lived in the States for five years, but he doesn't remember what pack he belongs to or why anyone would do this to him."

The alpha focused on Shane. "How did you end up here?"

He bristled, his body involuntarily reacting to the dominant wolf. "I have no idea how I got here, but I'm positive I came looking for Bekah."

Chase crossed his arms. "Why would you be looking for Bekah?"

She straightened. "He had my clarity bracelet on. Rain's magic probably led him here."

Her brother scowled. "Why did he have your bracelet?"

Pressing her lips together, she flashed Shane an apologetic look. "Now isn't the time to play protective older brother, Chase. I gave it to him, and that's all you need to know."

Shane's chest tightened. He shouldn't have been surprised she didn't want her family to know he'd claimed her. He'd sprung it on her without giving her a chance to get to know him. To fall in love with him. It was wrong of him to expect her to be certain of him the way he was of her.

"That must be what it was." He looked at Chase and then Luke. "This bracelet must be the only thing keeping me grounded, and since it was a gift from Bekah, my subconscious brought me here."

Luke nodded, seemingly satisfied with his answer. "And you have no idea who would have done this to you? Did you get into trouble with a neighboring pack?"

"I honestly have no clue. Bekah said a witch named Rain might be able to help."

Chase stiffened. "You're not bringing my mate into this. This whole situation smells like trouble, and that's the last thing our pack needs."

"I've already called her." Bekah's tone was indignant. "We're heading to the bakery as soon as we're done here."

Chase glared at his sister, and she returned his challenging stare.

"Well?" She crossed her arms to mirror his posture. "Are we done here?"

"You're done. I've still got a few words for your friend."

She dropped her arms by her sides and looked at the alpha. "I can help him, Luke. I think I can get in contact with someone who knows his band. They might be able to fill in the missing pieces of his memory…at least point us to his pack."

Luke shook his head. "It's too dangerous. If whoever did this to him finds out he's here, they might turn on us for harboring him. You can talk to Rain, but don't try to contact anyone he knows. I won't put my pack in harm's way for an outsider."

She lowered her gaze, clasping her hands over her heart. "I understand. The pack comes first. Are we dismissed?"

"Let me know what you find out."

Shane stood and turned to follow Bekah out the door, but Chase put a heavy hand on his shoulder. "A word."

He fought the urge to shrug off Chase's hand, and he touched Bekah on the elbow. "I'll just be a minute."

She nodded, a look of wariness pinching her brow as she shuffled toward the bar.

Chase rubbed at his beard. "I don't know what's going on between you and my sister, but you need to watch yourself."

"I would never do anything to put her in danger." Hell, he'd sacrifice his life for her.

"You being here puts her in danger. She's got a kid, too, and—"

"Emma. She's eight years old. I know." The memory of when Bekah told him skittered through his mind. She'd been afraid he'd lose interest if his lineage were threatened, but he didn't give a damn about lineage. There was a reason he didn't care. Pack status didn't matter either. In fact, having to answer to this alpha and his second sat sour in his stomach like expired milk.

Chase blinked the surprise from his expression. "She's a special little girl, and if anything were to happen to her, your ass would be mine."

"Enough." The alpha's commanding tone put his second in his place.

Chase's posture relaxed, and he took a step back. "If you care about them, you'll leave town. Solve your problems on your own and leave them out of it. They've been through enough already."

The alpha didn't contradict him. "If you do stay in town, keep me posted on your situation. The safety of my pack is my number one priority."

"Understood." Shane strode out the door and shut it behind him.

Bloody hell, Chase was right. Whatever had happened to him, putting his fate-bound in danger was the last thing he wanted to do. He should leave. He could head back to Florida and hope something there would jog his memory. If Bekah could put him in touch with his bandmates, maybe they could help. He could fix his situation and return when he could ensure Bekah's safety… Assuming this ordeal *could* be fixed.

If he couldn't extinguish the threat—whatever it was—he couldn't come back. Ever. The mere thought of never looking into his fate-bound's bright, hazel eyes again tore a gaping hole in his heart.

He paused in the hallway, rubbing his chest. Life without Bekah would be torturous, but he would endure a mountain of suffering to guarantee her safety.

Squaring his shoulders, he paced into the bar and found Bekah sitting on a stool, waiting for him.

"What did my brother say?"

"He said I should leave town. My being here is putting you and your daughter in danger, and he's right. I should go."

"What?" Her eyes widened. "No, Shane, I can help you. We'll figure this out together."

"Bekah." He took her shoulders in his hands. "The last thing I want to do is endanger you or your family. I have a feeling I've been doing things on my own for a while, so let me fix this, and I'll come back to you. I promise."

"No. Absolutely not. Sit your ass on that chair and wait. I'm going to talk to my brother, and when I get done, we are going to see Rain."

"Bekah…"

"No, Shane. You found your way to me. I'm not losing you again. Stay put." She jabbed a finger at him before spinning around and marching through the door.

Leave town? These men were insane if they thought she was going to watch her fate-bound walk away. Her hurried strides slowed as her emotions sank in. She'd been hesitant before they'd come here, worrying about what trouble his predicament might bring.

But the thought of him leaving, of having to face this on his own, tore a hole in her chest big enough to swallow her entire world. Meeting Shane when she did was no accident. Fate didn't make mistakes.

He'd found his way to her because he needed her, and she'd be damned if she was going to let anyone take him away.

She stopped herself from shoving the door open. If her brother had been in the office alone, she'd have barged right in, but she knew better than to disrespect Luke. She knocked, and as Chase opened it, she grabbed his arm and yanked him into the hallway.

"You told him to leave?" Her teeth made an audible click as she clenched her jaw. "Why would you do that?"

He narrowed his eyes. "Your life's not worth risking over some guy you met at a bar." He gripped her shoulder, softening his gaze. "It's better if he goes. If not for your sake, then for Emma's."

She fisted her hands by her sides to stop them from trembling. "If he were *some guy* I met at a bar, I would agree, but he's not." She inclined her chin. "I'm his fate-bound."

Her brother's eyes widened, his mouth dropping open as he gaped at her. "He… How…? He has no memory. How can you be his fate-bound?"

"His memory was fine when I met him. I felt it in him when it happened, and I feel it in him now. That's why he came to New Orleans. He's lost everything, but he managed to find me, and I am not letting him go. If you don't want to help him, that's fine, but Rain has already agreed."

"Why didn't he say so when we questioned him?"

She crossed her arms. "He was respectful to the alpha, and you were looming over him, playing the overprotective big brother and threatening him."

His mouth opened and closed a few times before he spoke. "I was not threatening him."

"Yes, you were, and you owe him an apology."

"I'm sorry, Bekah. If I'd known…"

"Well, now you do, so make it right. He's here to stay." She stormed through the door into the bar, and her heart dropped when she spied the empty seat where Shane had been.

Amber raised her hands. "I tried to get him to stay, but he insisted he had to take care of it on his own."

"Christ. Where does he think he's going to go?" She darted out of the bar, stopping on the sidewalk and looking right and left. Instinct pulled her right, and she rounded the corner to find Shane leaning against the wall, pinching the bridge of his nose as he squeezed his eyes shut.

She ran to him, taking his shoulders in her hands. "What are you doing?"

"I want to fix this. I thought I could go to Florida, but I don't have a car. I don't have any money… I have nothing."

The pain in his eyes shattered her heart, and she wrapped her arms around him. As he slid his arms to her waist, she cupped his face in her hands, pressing her lips to his. He opened for her, deepening the kiss as he tightened his embrace. She fit in his arms like she was made for him to hold, and she refused to fight the magnetic pull his wolf had on her. Fate had a plan for them, and she was ready to follow it.

As the kiss slowed, she touched her forehead to his. "You have me, Shane."

"You have us." Chase stepped toward them, and though skepticism tightened his eyes, he offered his hand to Shane. "You should have told me she was your fate-bound."

Shane accepted the handshake. "I didn't know it would make a difference."

"It makes all the difference. You're with my sister, you're one of us. Let's go see Rain."

Bekah rested her head on Shane's shoulder and smiled at her brother. Chase had been willing to run to hell and back when his fate-bound was in trouble. He understood the bond of fated mates, even as she was still adjusting to it.

CHAPTER EIGHT

Shane held Bekah's hand as they paced down Royal Street toward a bright-yellow building. Tourists meandered along the sidewalk, pausing to look into the shop windows, and the mid-afternoon sun hung high in the sky, warming his face like the woman next to him warmed his soul.

A deep sense of gratitude settled in his heart. The way Bekah, and now her brother and his mate, had dropped everything to help him felt foreign, and he couldn't tell if it was because *everything* felt new to him or if he'd never had this kind of support before.

He gazed up at the nineteenth-century buildings—old structures by American standards—their decorative wrought-iron railings swirling across the galleries lined with ferns, and he smiled. He could get used to living in this city.

A bell chimed as Chase opened a wooden door, and the scents of cinnamon and vanilla wafted to Shane's senses as he entered Spellbound Sweets bakery. To his left stood a glass case filled with cookies and other delicacies, and two women laughed behind the counter.

The tall, platinum blonde lifted a hand to wave. "Hey, guys." She looked at Shane. "I'm Snow."

He nodded. "Nice to meet you."

The other woman, with long, dark curls and stormy gray eyes, shuffled around the counter and stepped into Chase's arms, placing a kiss on his lips. "I didn't expect you to come. Is everything okay?"

Chase brushed a curl from her face, his love for his mate evident in his eyes. "It seems my sister has bonded with a Brit. It's pack business now."

Bekah squeezed Shane's hand before releasing it and sliding an arm around his waist. Damn, it felt good for her to touch him, to slip into his embrace like they'd been together their entire lives. "This is Shane." She paused and looked into his eyes. "My fate-bound."

Her lips curled into a smile as she said it, and his heart pounded harder. Maybe he didn't need his memory back. Whatever happened to him between his life in London and finding his way here didn't matter as long as he had Bekah by his side.

He shook Rain's hand, and her magical signature buzzed across his skin, revealing her immense power.

She pursed her lips and studied him, her gaze shifting to the area around him. "His powers aren't bound, which is a good thing. Unbinding spells are a bitch. But there's a current of dark magic running through his aura. He's definitely been cursed."

Bekah's arm tightened around him, and his heart sank. Whatever trouble he'd gotten into, he didn't want to bring it to New Orleans… to Bekah. "Can you break the curse?"

"Come back to the kitchen, and I'll mix something up." Rain padded around the counter, and he followed, slipping his hand into Bekah's as she released her hold of his waist.

Stainless steel countertops gleamed in the overhead lights, and the heat from an oven warmed the space as he stepped deeper into the room. A fresh batch of cookies sat on a cooling rack, and Rain pulled a chocolate cake from the oven before dropping her mitts and standing in front of him.

She placed her hands on either side of his head, closing her eyes and swaying slightly. She shivered and dropped her arms. "Black magic. Whoever did this to you was incredibly powerful, but I can undo it. The spell will take time to work, though."

"How much time, *cher*?" Chase grabbed a cookie from the rack. "We have no idea what kind of danger he's in."

Rain gathered herbs from a cabinet, dumping them into a bowl and grinding them with a pestle, wafting the savory scent of rosemary into the air. "Could be a few days. Maybe a week."

That was a long time to go without his memory. Without anything. He could play his sax on the street for money. The tourists had dropped seven dollars in his case for the one song he'd played outside Bekah's café. He could shift and sleep in the woods until he earned enough for a room.

"Emma can stay with us." Chase's voice pulled him from his thoughts. "And we'll patrol your house to make sure nothing tries to sneak in while he's recovering."

"I don't think we need the patrol, but I agree about Emma…just to be safe." Bekah flashed him a small smile.

They were talking like he was part of their pack. As if there were no question where he would stay or how he'd get along while he waited for the spell to break. Gratitude ballooned in his chest again, along with a sense of disbelief, making him wonder how his trust had been damaged before. That was something he'd rather not remember.

"I'm sure I'll be fine on my own. I apparently made it three days and several hundred miles with no memory. No need to worry about me."

Bekah looked at him as if he were crazy. "You're staying with me."

Chase nodded. "We take care of our own."

Their own. As if Shane were one of them. A memory buzzed in the back of his mind, and a feeling of abandonment attempted to form. But it flitted away the moment he tried to bring it into focus.

"Here, drink this." Rain handed him a cup of bright-blue liquid.

Little flecks of silver sparkled in the mixture, and he hesitated, casting a glance at Bekah.

"It's safe." She smiled and nodded, gesturing for him to drink.

He swallowed the liquid, and a sweet, bubblegum flavor filled his mouth as a cooling sensation crept down his throat.

Rain took the glass, setting it on the counter. "Is that Bekah's clarity bracelet?"

"It is."

"May I?" She held out her hand, so he slipped off the bracelet and gave it to her. Holding it between her palms, she whispered a spell before carrying it to her cupboard and sprinkling it with herbs. "Here you go." She handed it back to him, and he put it on. "I recharged the clarity spell. It should help the potion bring your memories back, so keep it on at all times."

"Thanks, Rain." Bekah took Shane's hand before looking at her brother. "Will you pick Emma up from school? I'll pack a bag for her, and you can pick it up on your way."

Chase glanced between them. "I think Emma should meet him."

"Maybe better to wait until we figure out what happened," Bekah said.

"Emma is intuitive. She might be able to give us a new perspective on the situation." He cleared his throat. "Not that I don't believe you two are fate-bound, but…he's under a spell, and you've been wrong before."

Rain put her hand on Chase's shoulder. "I don't—"

"Emma was right about us before I even figured it out." Chase arched an eyebrow at his mate. "It can't hurt."

A look passed between the three of them, and Shane tempered his curiosity. Something had happened in the past for this cryptic conversation to make sense to everyone except him, but he'd wait until he had Bekah alone to ask for an explanation.

"Y'all head home," Chase said, "and I'll swing by with Emma as soon as school lets out."

Bekah sat on the couch next to Shane and fired up her laptop. "Your band's name had witch in the title. Witch Ways or something like that. We can probably do a Google search to figure out who they are."

She opened a web browser and glanced at Shane. "I met a witch at the conference named Tambra, and her cousin is the drummer. Blonde hair, blue eyes? Does any of this ring a bell?"

He rubbed his forehead as if searching for the memories pained him. "Not a bit of it."

She put her hand on his knee, and he immediately covered it with his own. "Rain said it will take a few days. We'll do some research in the meantime and see if we can at least figure out your last name."

Shane chuckled. "We probably should have exchanged full names before hopping into bed. I can't say for sure, but it doesn't feel like that's the kind of thing I normally do."

"I've never done anything like that, but it doesn't matter. If we really are fate-bound…"

"What do you mean *if?*"

She lowered her gaze, chewing her bottom lip as her brother's words rolled through her mind. *He's under a spell, and you've been wrong before.*

"Bekah?" He cupped her cheek in his hand, turning her head toward him to catch her gaze. "Are you having doubts? Does this have anything to do with what Chase said?"

She licked her lips, unable to force the words from her throat. *What if I'm wrong again?*

"Have you thought someone's wolf claimed you before?" The hurt in his eyes tugged at her heart.

"No. He was talking about Emma's father. When Tommy left, I should have seen it coming. My ability, since I'm second-born, is empathy. When I touch people, I can feel their emotions. I should have felt Tommy recoiling when he found out I was pregnant, but my own emotions overpowered my ability."

She laced her fingers through his, opening her senses to Shane's emotions. So many feelings swirled through him it was a wonder he could sit upright, but the same strong undercurrent provided a foundation to it all. His wolf wanted her…unless the emotions were fabricated with a spell.

"I felt your wolf claim me the night we met, but when you stood me up, I assumed it had been wishful thinking on my part. But I felt it again this morning outside the café, and I still feel it in you now."

"What's the problem then? I know it happened fast, but that's the nature of fate."

She set the computer on the coffee table and turned to face him. "Before Rain met Chase, she was under a spell that made her think she was in love with someone. It had a messy, bloody ending, and I worry…with the spell that wiped your memory…what if that's not the only spell you're under?"

He took both her hands in his. "I wasn't under a spell the night we met, love, and that's when my wolf claimed you. This is real."

"What if it isn't? You were in a band of witches. One of them could have…"

He laughed. "I hope I'm smart enough not to associate with people who would put a spell on me."

"Maybe someone they know did it. I don't know, Shane, but I've been burned before." Emma had never met her father, but she was about to meet Shane. What if she bonded with him, and once the spells cleared, he left? She couldn't put her daughter through that.

"I understand, but I also know what I feel in my soul, and we belong to each other. What can I do to prove it to you?"

"Let's give it some time. See what happens when your memories return before we start planning a mating ceremony." It was the logical thing to do. Every fiber of her being may have been telling her to make the man hers, but like Chase said…she'd been wrong before.

Shane brought her fingers to his lips and kissed them. "Take all the time you need, love. I'm not going anywhere without you."

A knock sounded on the door, and she shot to her feet, thankful for the distraction from Shane's intense gaze. "That'll be Emma." A glance through the peephole confirmed her daughter was home, so she threw open the door and scooped the little girl into her arms. "Hi, sweetheart. How was your day?"

Emma gave her neck a squeeze before wiggling from her embrace. "Good. Is this Shane?" She narrowed her eyes at him as Chase slipped in behind her.

"Be polite, Emma," Bekah said. "Say 'hello.'"

"Hi. Uncle Chase is skepi…skept…ical of you." She stepped in front of him, assessing him with her gaze.

At eight years old, Emma hadn't fully come into her powers yet, but she had an uncanny ability to detect relationships between people. She was also an excellent judge of character.

"I'd be concerned if he wasn't." Shane smiled, holding out his hand to shake, and Emma accepted. "Hello, Emma. It's nice to meet you."

She gripped his hand, holding on longer than politely necessary, studying him. With a deep inhale, she cut her gaze between Shane and Bekah before looking over her shoulder at her uncle. "He's cool."

"That's good to know." The tension in Chase's shoulders eased, and Bekah's own posture relaxed with her daughter's confirmation.

With her free hand, Emma took her mom's hand, holding onto both Bekah and Shane for a moment before placing Bekah's hand in his and stepping back. "I approve." She strolled to the recliner and grabbed the overnight bag Bekah had packed for her.

Slinging it over her shoulder, she paused and eyed Shane's saxophone case sitting by the couch. "What's that?"

His eyes brightened. "It's my saxophone. Would you like to see it?" Shane dropped to his knees and opened the case, offering the instrument to Emma.

Bekah's throat thickened as her daughter moved toward him, running her hand along the brass. The smile lighting up Emma's face made her heart ache.

"Will you teach me to play it?"

Shane grinned, returning the instrument to its case. "I would love to." He tapped his temple. "As soon as my mind is working right, yeah?"

"I hope you're better soon." Emma shuffled to the door and took Chase's hand. "When his memory comes back, will we be moving to England, or will he live here?"

Bekah blinked, her daughter's words wrapping around her heart and squeezing it tight. While her own emotions could hinder her ability, she'd never known Emma to be wrong about anyone.

"I'm never going back to England." Shane's brow shot up as if he'd surprised himself with the declaration.

"Was that a memory?" She squeezed his hand, fighting the urge to throw her arms around him.

He blinked a few times, his mouth screwing up to the side as he searched his mind. "More like a feeling."

"It's a start."

"It certainly is."

She squatted to eye-level with Emma and put her hands on her shoulders. "You'll be okay spending a few days with Aunt Rain and Uncle Chase? It's just until we know you'll be safe."

Emma smiled. "Aunt Rain's going to make chocolate muffins for breakfast every morning, and Uncle Chase promised to take me to the park this weekend."

"Sounds like you're going to have a great time. I'll see you soon." She hugged her daughter, and they said their goodbyes. As Chase led Emma down the front steps, Bekah turned to Shane.

God, he was a beautiful man, with his chiseled features and soulful eyes. She couldn't stop herself from stepping into his inviting embrace, and as the protective cage of his arms closed around her, she wanted nothing more than to give herself to him. To feel his hands on her body, his lips setting fire to her skin.

But if Rain, the most powerful witch she'd ever met, could be fooled by a spell, it was possible Emma's judgment could be clouded too. Unlikely, but the possibility remained, so she would keep her guard up, at least for a little while.

CHAPTER NINE

Over the next week, Bekah spent every spare moment she had helping Shane recover his memory. Through her Internet searches, she discovered his band and found their Facebook page. Photos of Shane playing and lounging with the members should have jogged his mind, but he couldn't recall a single moment with any of them.

Bekah cleared the dishes from a café table, handing the tray to a waitress on her way to the kitchen. At least some of Shane's other memories were returning. The process seemed painful for him, but reversing black magic was never easy.

The music had never left him, though. With the patio doors wide open, Bekah stood in her café watching Shane play his saxophone for the customers outside. He'd been nervous at first, but he borrowed her phone to look up the requested songs he couldn't remember, and as soon as he heard the tune, his fingers flew across the keys like the song had been ingrained in his being.

He spent the days entertaining the patrons while Bekah worked in the café, and when she had lunch with Emma at school each afternoon, he wandered the French Quarter, familiarizing himself with the city. It was a routine she could get used to.

As he finished his instrumental rendition of "Shape of You" by Ed

Sheeran, he glanced inside and caught her gaze. With a wink, he started "Careless Whisper," and the familiar hummingbirds took flight in her stomach as her lips curved into a goofy grin. She could never get enough of this man.

Dani stepped out of the kitchen, tying an apron around her waist, and picked up a serving tray. "Jeez. I go visit family for a few days, and when I come back to work, Hottie Homeless Guy is now our live entertainment. What did I miss?"

Bekah tore her gaze away from Shane's sexy mouth caressing the sax and tucked a strand of hair behind her ear. "His name is Shane, and I know him. We had a misunderstanding before, but we've worked it out." Her gaze drifted back to the patio.

"So, he's here to stay? You two are…"

"He's a great guy." And she was an idiot for insisting they keep their distance from each other. His memories were slowly coming back. He could recall his family now, and he remembered his mom teaching him the love of music. In fact, the more he played, the more he seemed to remember.

And while his confusion was clearing, his emotions stabilizing, the solid sentiment that fate had bound their hearts was unwavering. If his feelings for her were fabricated by a spell, it would have cracked by now, wouldn't it? It was time she consulted a witch to be sure.

Dani held the tray to her chest and drummed her nails on it. "He's a great guy and a talented musician, but are you shacking up?" She wiggled her eyebrows. "Is he your beau?"

Bekah grinned. "If I say yes, will you get to work and wait on some customers?"

The waitress nodded.

"Yes. We're a couple. Now go." She pointed to the dining room. "I have to make a phone call."

"I'll keep an eye on him for you." Dani winked and sashayed toward a table.

Bekah ducked into the office and dialed Rain's number on the office phone. Her sister-in-law picked up on the third ring. "Thank you for calling Spellbound Sweets. This is Rain. How can I help you?"

"Is it possible this fate-bound thing is because of the spell Shane is under?"

Shuffling sounded in the receiver as the background noise quieted. "There's not a spell in existence that can mimic the werewolf mating bond. That's something that runs soul-deep, and if you'll stop second-guessing yourself, you'll realize that. Even Emma sees it."

She chewed her lip, trying desperately to rid her mind of the doubt. "But if it were a spell, couldn't it fool Emma too? You were fooled."

Rain let out a heavy sigh. "That was different. Isaac wasn't a werewolf, and what I thought I felt for him was a speck of dust. Chase is my whole world. I know it's scary, but you've got the real deal with Shane. That potion I gave him was an all-inclusive banishing spell. The only curse I sensed in him was the memory wipe, but if he was being affected by anything else, it's gone now."

"Are you sure?" Of course Rain was sure. Bekah was sure deep in her soul. She was letting her thoughts consume her, hold her back from her fate.

"I'm positive, but I can come by and have another look at him if you want. His aura was strong, though. If his memories are returning, and you still feel the bond, it's safe to say he's yours."

"Thanks, Rain. You're the best." Her chest expanded like a can of store-bought biscuits popping open in her heart. She hung up the phone and grabbed her purse from the drawer.

Whatever danger he was in, they would face it together, because together was where they belonged. She was done holding back with Shane, and he was done sleeping on the couch.

Shane sat on Bekah's sofa, staring at the picture of him and his bandmates on her laptop screen. Over the past week, the potion Rain gave him had knocked loose most of his memories. They came in chunks, mostly returning while he was playing his sax, which made sense now that he remembered his history with his mum and how much music had meant to him throughout his life.

He blew out a hard breath and closed the computer. When it came to his most recent band, he couldn't remember a bloody thing. Their faces weren't familiar. He couldn't recall what kind of music they played. Hell, he wouldn't believe they existed at all if Bekah hadn't seen him play with them.

He could see in his mind the night he played "Careless Whisper" for Bekah. Could see her sweet smile and the spark of lust in her eyes as she watched him. But as he tried to expand his vision, to see where he was or who was around him, he saw nothing but inky blackness.

The band had to be involved in his curse, but he couldn't fathom a reason why.

His life before the curse grew clearer by the hour. His night with Bekah was as vivid in his mind as if it happened yesterday. But the days…or possibly years…leading up to the moment he met her were empty.

He remembered his girlfriend dumping him in Florida. The feelings of betrayal gnawed in his gut, but he also remembered not being surprised when it happened. He'd been on his own most of his life, and his father had taught him from a young age that he couldn't depend on anyone…and that no one should rely on him.

He'd been raised a rogue, his dad insisting packs existed to control people. That werewolves were better off on their own, and no one could be trusted. The old man had proven that himself when he told Shane if he chose music, not to come back to London.

Raking a hand through his hair, he watched the beautiful woman putting away the dishes in the kitchen. He'd offered to help, but she'd insisted he sit down and rest, his quietness at dinner making her worry…about *him*.

He could depend on Bekah. She'd proven herself again and again, not that she'd needed to. His wolf knew, and that was good enough for him. Her pack was nothing like what his father had claimed. They treated him like he belonged.

Shane had never belonged anywhere.

"Almost done. You okay?" Bekah raised her brows as she gazed at him from the kitchen, her hazel eyes holding more concern than he was used to seeing. She cared deeply for him, but how would she feel when he told her he was a rogue?

"Fine, love. No rush."

Bekah's brother was second in command, which gave her pack status. When she'd talked casually about Shane's past, she'd assumed he was in a pack too. She might revolt at the idea of mating with a man who'd grown up a rogue. Her pack might not even allow them to be mates.

His stomach turned at the idea of losing her over a past he'd have been fine not remembering.

She smiled as she shuffled into the living room and sank onto the sofa next to him. Resting her hand on his knee, she pressed a kiss to his temple, and his chest gave a squeeze. "You remembered a lot today, didn't you? Too much to process?"

This woman could read him like a book. Even when she wasn't using her empathic powers, she seemed to sense his moods. "Quite a bit, yeah."

"Anything you want to talk about?"

All of it. None of it. If he could, he'd whisk her away in the night. Take her and Emma to Australia or somewhere far away from whatever trouble he was in. But Bekah was rooted in this pack. Her daughter had friends here. If he wanted to be with her, he had to face it all. No running this time.

"I still don't remember the band. It's like they don't exist, and those photos are fabricated."

Bekah nodded. "They're all witches, but who knows if any of them are powerful enough to do this to you. It would be a lot easier if we could contact them, but Luke forbade it." She squeezed his knee and folded her hands in her lap. "We have a meeting with him tomorrow to talk about what you remember, and maybe he'll let us contact them then."

His father's words rang in his mind. *Packs exist to control.*

Maybe. Or perhaps their purpose was to protect. "I understand his reasoning. If the band is responsible…" He rubbed his forehead. Forcing the memories made his head ache.

Bekah took his hand. "We'll figure it out. In the meantime, I wanted to talk to you about something."

"There's something else I need to tell you too." And the sooner he got it off his chest, the better. He couldn't hide it from her.

"Just let me say this, okay? I think it will help you feel better."

He clamped his mouth shut and nodded.

"I've been holding back because I've been scared. I feel the mating bond with you…in my own heart and in yours, but my brother…" She huffed. "Chase is skeptical of everyone at first, and I let his ideas burrow into my brain, even though I know better. I *know* this bond we share is real, and I'm sorry for doubting you. I want to be with you, Shane, and from this point forward, I'm all in."

"Oh, Bekah." He leaned back on the couch and squeezed his eyes shut. Her words coiled around his heart, squeezing it until he thought it would burst. It was precisely what he wanted to hear, but she didn't know his past. He'd lured her in under false pretenses, assuming he'd been a pack man because she wanted him to be.

"That's not the reaction I was expecting." She tucked her hair behind her ears. "What's going on? You've been quiet since we got home."

There was no use in sugar-coating it. He just needed to tell her. *Well, go on then, mate. Spit it out.* Opening his eyes, he turned to look at her. "I'm a rogue. I always have been." He braced himself for her recoil, but she didn't even flinch.

"Okay?" An amused grin curved her lips. "Is that what's been bothering you all evening? You remembered you're a rogue, and you thought I would object?"

"Well, yeah. You're an integral part of your pack. Your whole family is. I'll bring shame to your bloodline."

She laughed a deep, musical belly laugh. "Shane…" She sucked in a breath and clutched his hands, attempting to get her amusement under control. "My parents were rogues. My dad died when I was little, and my mom joined this pack because my brother was so wild she couldn't handle him. I got pregnant when I was nineteen by a man who never wanted to be my mate, and the only reason my brother has the status he does is that his best friend is the alpha."

She scooted closer to him, wrapping her arms around his shoulders and kissing his cheek. "And after all that, we've never been shamed. This is a good, peaceful pack. We take care of our own, and we leave no one behind."

Leaning back, she looked into his eyes. "The only problem that could come from you being a rogue is if you intend to stay that way. Are you willing to settle down and join us? Sleep in the same bed every night?"

Settle down. Stay in one place. It was exactly what he wanted. Being part of a pack would take some getting used to, but he was up for the challenge. "Bekah, as long as that bed has you in it, I will gladly settle down."

"That can be arranged." She held his gaze, the green and gold in her hazel irises shimmering with her smile. "We'll figure out everything about your missing memories tomorrow. Tonight, I want to be with you."

She leaned into him, taking his mouth in a kiss as she pushed him onto his back. With his head resting on the arm of the sofa, he held her tight, parting his lips and dipping his tongue into her warm, sweet mouth.

Slipping her hand beneath his shirt, she ran her palm up his stomach, gripping his chest as a moan vibrated across her lips. She broke the kiss to sit up, tugging his shirt over his head and tossing it to the floor before removing her own.

With a fire in her eyes that set his soul ablaze, she dragged her hands down his chest, her tongue slipping out to moisten her lips as she popped the button on his jeans and tugged at the zipper. She worked the fabric over his hips, rising to her feet to pull his clothes from his legs, stepping out of her own pants before diving on top of him and kissing him again.

She was a goddess wrapped in pink satin, and the feel of her supple body pressed to his was enough to drive him mad. He stroked his hands up and down her back, gripping her ass and grinding his hips against hers, her quick intake of breath and the goose bumps running down her arms his reward.

With a mischievous grin, she inched downward, pressing her lips to his neck, grazing his nipples with her teeth, her mouth growing nearer and nearer to his dick. He held his breath as she kissed down to his hip, his stomach tightening as she lifted her head, and her warm breath blew across his cock.

Taking his length in her hand, she stroked it with her tongue from base to tip, circling around the head and flicking her gaze to his. She watched him intently as she took him into her mouth, sliding up until only the tip remained between her lips.

He groaned, the sensation of being enveloped in warm, wet velvet forcing his lids closed. He wouldn't last long at all like this, so he opened his eyes and put a hand on her head to still her. "I need to be inside you, Bekah. Make love to me."

She smiled wickedly, rising onto her knees and tossing her bra aside before shimmying out of her panties. Straddling him, she used her hand to guide him to her folds, lowering herself onto him slowly, until their bodies joined as one.

He paused, clutching her hips to hold her still and memorizing the way they fit together. "This…" He glided his hands up her sides to cup her breasts. "Is the most beautiful sight I've ever seen."

As he teased her nipples, she slid up and down his dick, the sensuous friction sending an electric current buzzing through his muscles. Her magic mingled with his, dancing across his skin, setting every nerve in his body on fire.

His climax coiled in his core, but there was no way he'd come before she did. He licked his thumb and pressed it to her clit, working the sensitive nub in circles until she cried out, tossing her head back as she rode him through her orgasm.

As her rhythm slowed, he grabbed her ass and flipped her onto her back, never breaking their intimate union as he covered her body with his and took her. He thrust deep inside her, hooking his arms behind her shoulders and burying his face in her neck. He was in her, a part of her, but he still felt like he couldn't get close enough.

She couldn't possibly realize the level of his devotion. He'd stop the world from spinning if she asked him to. "Feel me, Bekah."

"It feels so good, Shane." She clutched his back, wrapping her legs around his waist as he pumped his hips.

"Use your power. Feel what I feel. I want you to know."

She flattened her palms on his back and sucked in a sharp breath. "I feel you." Her whisper against his ear nearly sent him over the edge.

"Do you understand?"

"You belong to me. Like I belong to you."

His orgasm exploded through his body, a rippling wave of ecstasy crashing into him, shattering his senses.

"Oh my God, Shane." Still connected to his emotions, Bekah rode the crest of his orgasm, her body trembling as if it were her own.

He collapsed on top of her, panting, showering her face and neck in kisses as his heart rate slowed. Still gripping his waist with her legs, she relaxed her arms, sliding her hands to his shoulders as he rose onto his elbows to look at her.

She was a vision of beauty with tousled, dark hair and passion-drunk eyes looking up at him like he was the only man in the world. To him, she was the only woman.

"No more doubts about us, yeah?" He kissed her forehead, her nose, her mouth. "We're meant to be."

She smiled. "No doubts. We're fate-bound."

CHAPTER TEN

Bekah lay nestled in the crook of Shane's arm, her head resting on his shoulder. After their intense lovemaking on the couch, they eventually made it to the bedroom, where they did it all over again.

And again.

She couldn't fight her smile. Emma would finally have a full-time father in her life, and Shane seemed excited at the prospect. This afternoon, he'd be joining them at Emma's school for lunch.

With the help of the pack, she had no doubt they'd figure out what happened to Shane's memory. They'd end the threat—whatever it was—and she'd get her happily ever after.

Shane stirred, turning onto his side and pulling her into his arms. This was exactly where she belonged; all the pieces of her life were finally clicking into place. She snuggled into his chest and breathed in his intoxicating scent, reveling in the protectiveness of his embrace.

With a gasp, he jerked, flopping onto his back and clutching the sheets, dragging the corner off the edge of the bed. She sat up, placing her hand on his shoulder and trying to soothe him, but he squeezed his eyes shut in a pained expression.

"Shane?" She shook him gently. He'd had similar episodes several times during the night, his restless movements rousing Bekah from sleep before he'd roll over and settle down.

This time, his lids flew open, and he gasped, shooting upright and dragging the sheets from the bed. "Oh, God, I remember." He looked at her, eyes wild, and jabbed his fingers into his hair, pulling it at the roots. "I remember everything."

Her phone rang from the nightstand, and she glanced at the screen as the café's landline number lit up the device. She let the call go to voicemail and rubbed Shane's back. "What do you remember?"

He sucked in a shaky breath. "It was Cammie. The drummer. Damn it, and Ricardo helped her. They wanted me out of the way."

"Out of the way of what?" Her phone rang again, and she snatched it from the nightstand, holding up a finger to Shane. "Hello?"

"Bekah, I'm sorry to bother you on your day off," her manager said, "but this woman left eight messages on the recorder before I got in this morning. Someone named Tambra. She sounded frantic, so I thought you might want to know."

"Did she leave a number?" With a trembling hand, she scribbled the digits onto a notepad and ended the call. "Tambra is trying to reach me."

"That's Cammie's cousin. Bloody hell, what did she do?" Shane marched down the hallway and returned with their discarded clothes. He shoved his legs into his jeans and paced in front of the bed.

"What *did* she do, Shane? Why did she wipe your memory?"

He groaned. "A stupid plan. The most idiotic thing she could have done. I wanted nothing to do with it, so they ambushed me." He stopped pacing and dropped his arms to his sides. "Ricardo called me that night in your hotel room. I left you there because he said Cammie was in trouble. I should have known better than to trust them."

"Let me call Tambra and see what's going on."

He sat on the edge of the bed. "Don't tell her I'm with you. Cammie wanted to kill me."

"Jesus, Shane." She dialed the number, and Tambra answered on the second ring.

"Hey, it's Bekah. I got a message that you called."

The sound of a car engine emanated through the headset, and a horn blared in the background. "Are you still seeing Shane? Do you know where he is?"

"What's going on? Why are you breathless?" She put the phone on speaker and held it up so Shane could hear.

"Cammie's dead." Tambra sucked in a breath. "They're all dead, and it's going after the ones they love."

Shane's face paled, his jaw going slack.

"What are you talking about, Tambra? Who's going after them?"

She lowered her voice to a whisper. "They summoned a demon. I told her she was crazy when she told me the plan, but she did it anyway. It's linked to all of them, and Bekah…she completed the spell with werewolf blood. It had to be Shane's. Something went wrong. There was more magic in his blood than she could control, and a demon broke through the veil. They couldn't appease it, so it killed them all. They've found all the bodies, except Shane's."

"Oh my God." Bekah's eyes widened.

Shane shot to his feet, clenching and unclenching his hands.

"If you know where he is, you have to warn him. It's coming for him, and Bekah, if you're with him…it's coming for you too. I got out of town before it could find me, but if someone doesn't stop it…"

Shane threw on the rest of his clothes and stuffed his feet into his boots. He marched toward the front door, and Bekah followed, catching him by the arm before he could open it.

"Why would it be coming for me?"

"It got inside their minds. It killed the other band members and their girlfriends before it came after Cammie and Ricardo. She called me, warned me to get out of town. It's not going to stop until it kills them all and everyone they love."

Shane tried to move toward the door, but she tightened her grip on his arm. "Take care of yourself. If I see Shane, I'll let him know."

"Be careful." Tambra ended the call.

"Where do you think you're going?" Bekah tossed the phone on the coffee table.

"I have to stop it."

"Shane." She clutched his shoulders, staring him hard in the eyes. "It's six o'clock in the morning. Demons only act at night, and you don't have to face it alone. Let me get dressed, and we'll talk to Luke. The pack will handle it. They'll help you."

Her phone rang again, her brother's name illuminating the screen this time, and she pressed the device to her ear.

"Are y'all safe?"

Her pulse thrummed. "We're okay. What's going on?"

"Two musicians were murdered outside a club on Frenchman around four a.m. It looks demonic," Chase said.

Her blood ran cold. "Shit."

"What do you know?"

"Call Mom and have her take Emma away for a few days. Meet us at the bar, and we'll explain."

"They ambushed me." Shane ground his teeth as he paced in front of the alpha's desk. "My mind was…elsewhere." He glanced at Bekah sitting in a chair, and then at Rain. "They told me they were going to remove me from the spell, but they bound me to it even tighter."

A flush of anger heated his chest. He'd trusted his bandmates, and now his misjudgment had put Bekah and her pack in danger. He was an idiot.

"Blood magic is tricky." Rain leaned into Chase's side. "If your friends made a blood sacrifice to the demon for his help, adding were blood into the mix would have made the offering volatile at best. If she was powerful enough to paralyze a werewolf, I'm not surprised a fiend was able to escape through the rift she tore in the veil."

"I read the reports from the pack in charge of the area." Luke tapped a few keys on the laptop. "It appears the demon went in through the nasal cavity, accessed their memories, and then scrambled their brains. Aside from a few scrapes and bruises from the struggle, that's the only injury. Same for the two we found on Frenchman last night."

Shane let out his breath in a hiss. "Bastard was recharging, and then the sun came up."

"Probably," Chase said. "He felt the power in your blood and knew you wouldn't be as easy of a target as the others, and with the distance he traveled in one night…he needed an energy boost."

"What's the plan?" Bekah clutched Shane's arm to stop his pacing. "We can sit here and speculate the why and how all day, but what are we going to do to stop it before anyone else gets killed?" She tightened her grip on his arm, her icy fingers digging into his flesh, betraying the fear that her confident voice hid.

The alpha closed his computer and folded his arms on the desk. "Chase, contact James and Cade. Fill them in on the details. We'll need their help."

Chase nodded, and Luke focused on Shane, his heavy gaze making the hairs on the back of his neck stand on end. "You'll be the bait. Before sunset, we'll take you to our hunting grounds, away from the city. The demon will follow, and then we'll attack. I don't care how powerful the fiend is; it won't stand a chance against the five of us."

The five of *us*. The alpha lumped him in with the pack as if he were one of them. From the moment they'd discovered he was bound to Bekah, they'd taken him in, treated him like he belonged.

We take care of our own. He'd heard their mantra several times since he arrived, but he wasn't one of them. Not yet. He couldn't let them risk their lives for the trouble he'd brought to their territory.

He should have left when Chase first told him to. Battled the demon on his own once it found him. Then, if he'd lost the fight, he wouldn't have had any memories for the fiend to use to find his loved ones.

Except for Bekah.

His hands curled into fists. He could slip away this afternoon and fight the demon by himself, but if he lost… He couldn't take the risk of it coming after Bekah and Emma.

"Right." He nodded at Luke. "That sounds like a plan, then." Not a plan that would ever come to fruition, but he knew better than to try negotiating with an alpha. He'd handle this problem on his own like he'd been doing his entire life. Then, if he survived, he'd find his way back to his fate-bound.

Shane spent the rest of the morning and into the early afternoon holed up in Bekah's house. She made him lunch and tried her best to soothe his frazzled nerves, but his beast couldn't be quieted.

Luke's plan was too risky. Rain was right; if Cammie were powerful enough to paralyze a werewolf, take his blood, and wipe his memory, she would have been able to defeat any mid to lower-level demon that came after her. Her death meant whatever she'd turned loose was stronger than anything he—or Bekah's pack—had ever dealt with.

If they couldn't defeat it…if it got into his head and went after Bekah…

He couldn't let that happen, and there was only one way he knew to ensure it wouldn't.

Bekah's phone rang, and her entire face lit up as she answered it. "Hey, pumpkin! Did you and grandma make it to Shreveport?"

She paused to let Emma speak, and Shane's chest tightened at the joy in her voice. He was supposed to make their family complete. Damn Cammie and Ricardo…and the whole bloody band for messing with his fate.

"You have fun, and I'll see you in a couple of days. Oh, okay." She held the phone toward him. "She wants to talk to you."

His heart racing, he took the device and pressed it to his ear. "Hey, Emma. How are you?"

"My mom loves you, and I know you love her too." She said it like it was a matter of fact, the most obvious thing in the world. "So take care of her while I'm gone, okay?"

He swallowed the lump from his throat. "Yeah. Of course. Everything's going to be fine."

"And when I get back, you'll be safe, right? And we can all be a family?"

"Umm… How do you know we'll be a family? Did your mum tell you that?" He glanced at Bekah, and she smiled, shaking her head.

Emma sighed. "A girl just knows these things. I don't know why I have to keep telling people that. You can't fight fate."

"You're right. No one can." It was his fate to be a part of this family, and he would do everything he could to fix what Cammie broke. "I'll see you soon."

"Bye, Shane." Emma ended the call, and he handed the phone to Bekah.

"I told you she's intuitive," Bekah said.

"She's a special girl." He pulled her into a hug, pressing his lips to her temple, closing his eyes and memorizing the way she felt in his arms.

This would not be the last time he held her. If he found her before, he could do it again. "I'm going to go for a walk, yeah? I need to get out of the house and clear my head before tonight."

"I can imagine you must be getting cabin fever. Do you want me to come with you?" She held his gaze, and his will nearly crumbled. But he had to do this. It was the only way.

"Give me a little time. I just…need to be alone for a bit. It's a lot to process."

"Promise you'll come back to me?" She said it in a joking way, but uneasiness underscored her humor.

"Always." He picked up his sax case, and she gave him a curious look.

"You are coming back, right?" She glanced at the case, concern creasing her forehead. "You're not taking your most prized possession with you because you're planning on running away, are you?"

"Music helps me focus." He tucked a strand of hair behind her ear. "Nothing can keep me away from you." She was as much a part of him as the heart in his chest.

Bekah nodded. "I'll be here."

He twisted the doorknob but hesitated. "Listen, Bekah, whatever happens, I want you to know…"

She closed the distance between them in two strides and took his mouth in a kiss. He gripped the back of her neck, holding her close and drinking her in like it was their last. Her magic tingled on his lips, but if she felt his emotions—if she had any clue what he was planning—she didn't let on.

Resting her hands on his chest, she looked into his eyes. "I know. I do too."

He nodded and stepped onto the porch, closing the door between them.

CHAPTER ELEVEN

BEKAH PACED IN FRONT OF THE DOOR, WRINGING HER HANDS and cursing herself for not giving Shane her phone. He'd been gone three hours, and Chase was due to pick him up in twenty minutes to head out to the swamp.

"How long does it take to clear your mind?" He didn't run away. He promised he'd be back.

Maybe he'd lost track of time, but the sinking sun should have clued him in that night would fall soon. After three hours, he could be anywhere in the city. He could be lost or hurt. Maybe the return of his memory had been temporary. If confusion set in and he was miles away from home, there was no telling where he could have gone.

She stepped onto the front porch and peered down the road, but there was no sign of Shane. In a few more minutes, the sun would dip behind the buildings, and the pinks and blues of the sky would morph to deep purples and reds.

She started down the steps, but her ringtone sounded from inside the house, and she darted to the kitchen, whisking her phone from the table. "Hello?"

"Where is Shane?" The wariness in Rain's voice made her stomach drop.

"I don't know. He went for a walk, and he hasn't come back. Is Chase on his way?"

"I'm with Rain," Chase said into the phone.

"You need to come to the bakery now. I just got a call from the high priestess. A werewolf stopped by the coven looking for an amnesia spell. He didn't have any money, so he traded a saxophone for the potion."

"He didn't." She picked up her purse and headed out the door before she realized her feet were moving.

"He did." Irritation edged her brother's voice. "The witches didn't recognize him, so they reported it to Rain. They're going to return the sax, but dammit, Bekah. If he—"

"Thank the goddess the coven is trying to get along with the pack or we may have never known," Rain said. "How fast can you get here?"

"I'm on my way."

When Bekah entered the bakery, Chase locked the door and ushered her to the kitchen. Rain had filled a large copper bowl with water and set it on the counter, where she peered into it, whispering a rhyming verse.

"She put a locator spell on the bracelet you gave him, and she's trying to find it." Chase crossed his arms. "Does he think he can just forget any of this ever happened and the threat will cease to exist? That's not how demons work."

"Found him." Rain sprinkled an herb into the bowl and stirred it with her finger. "He's in the nature preserve to the west."

Chase growled. "What the hell is he doing out there?"

Bekah's stomach turned. "He's going to fight it on his own. The potion was to erase me from his memory in case the demon wins."

She leaned against the counter and tipped her head back. How could she have been so stupid? She'd felt it in him. His apprehension, determination along with a sickening feeling of imminent doom. She'd chalked the emotions up to nerves. Hell, she'd be scared to death if she had to fight a demon, even with the help of four of the pack's strongest wolves.

She'd tried to give him space to work it out, when she should have called bullshit the moment he picked up his saxophone. "I should have known he'd do this."

"You're an empath, not a clairvoyant. And look…" Rain wrapped her arm around Bekah's shoulders and held up a vial of pink powder. "I made a remedy, but…"

"I don't like the sound of that but."

"The witch he found is powerful, but she's an idiot. She's been known to…" She closed her eyes and shook her head. "She botched the spell."

Nausea churned in her stomach. "What are you trying to say?"

"She didn't cast an amnesia spell. I had her explain what she did, and he'll lose his memories like he asked…but if we don't get to him in time, he'll lose his ability to think at all." She sucked in a deep breath and blew it out hard. "She cast a mind deterioration spell. He'll lose everything: his memories, his personality, his ability to make decisions. It could be permanent."

Rain's words crashed into her like a tidal wave, hollowing out her chest. "How could…? Why…?"

"I don't know. Those spells are forbidden, and the high priestess herself is taking care of the witch who cast it. But Bekah…if his memory has completely faded when we find him, this remedy won't bring it back. All it will do is stop the deterioration. What's gone will be gone for good."

She tried to swallow, but her throat had formed into a knot. "So, he may never remember me?"

"He might not."

"Either way, we need to get to him before the demon does, or his memories won't matter. Let's go." Chase gestured toward the door, and they followed him outside, piling into Rain's car.

Bekah's fear tipped toward panic as she buckled her seatbelt and closed her eyes, her quick, shallow breaths making her head spin. Letting the demon get to him wasn't an option. Her soul was bound to Shane's, and losing him would tear her life apart.

"It's barely dark. We'll get there in time." Rain flashed a small smile as she peered over the back of the seat.

"What if we don't?" The words felt like sandpaper on her throat.

"He's got a powerful aura. Have some faith."

Chase grunted into his phone. "Yeah. See you there." He glanced at her in the rearview mirror. "Luke and the others are on their way. You two stay in the car until the demon is vanquished."

Bekah glared at him. "I'm not afraid of a demon."

He clenched his teeth. "You're defenseless."

Rain put her hand on his knee. "We'll be fine, dear. I'll strike it with a bolt of lightning if it gets anywhere near her."

He blew out a hard breath and took Rain's hand. "Both of you be careful, please."

As the sun sank behind the horizon, Shane followed a trail deeper into the woods. Spanish moss hung like drapes from cypress trees, creating a canopy over the path and making the hiking trail appear more like a tunnel into the ominous night.

The dirt path veered left, so Shane went right, twigs and dry leaves crunching beneath his boots as he ventured farther into the swamp. As he neared the water, the ground turned soft, the mud clinging to his shoes and making a sucking sound with each step he took.

"This is far enough away from civilization, I guess." He found a dry patch of ground and leaned against a tree, uncapping the potion bottle he'd gotten from the witch. The sickly-sweet cotton candy scent singed his nostrils, and nausea churned in his gut.

Leaning his head back against the tree trunk, he closed his eyes and offered a prayer to whatever god might be listening. "If I make it through this, please help me find my way back to Bekah."

He tossed back the potion like a shot of whiskey, cringing as the syrupy liquid coated his throat, burning its way down to his stomach. His pulse thrummed as he shoved the empty bottle into his pocket. A spinning sensation in his head forced his eyes shut, and he gripped the tree to steady himself.

An image of Bekah formed behind his lids, her hazel eyes crinkling with her sexy smile, but he forced it from his mind. She was the first thing he needed to forget.

"I'm here you wanker, come and get me." With his blood link to the demon, it wouldn't take the bastard long to find him.

Pushing from the trunk, he stumbled forward, his vision blurring for a moment before coming into focus. The scents of mud, cypress, and decaying foliage filled his senses, and he blinked, taking in his surroundings.

Why was he in the swamp?

If he'd come to hunt, he'd have shifted by now. He spun in a circle, trying to get his bearings, wracking his brain for the reason he'd come here, but his mind felt like a void. Confusion pinched his brow, and a flush of icy panic raced through his veins.

He couldn't remember anything.

A rustling in the brush drew his attention, and the putrid scent of rancid garbage assaulted his senses before the creature stepped into view. Standing nearly seven feet tall, the demon had slick, maroon skin and a set of short, wicked-sharp horns atop its head. One hundred pointed teeth filled its lipless maw, and elongated fingers curled into talons that could gut a werewolf with one swipe.

The demon snarled, and Shane's wolf took over, his body vibrating as it transformed into his beast. Crouching low, he backpedaled, the ridge of hair on his back standing on end as he assessed the fiend for a weak spot.

A vein pulsed on the monster's neck, and Shane locked his focus on the heartbeat, peeling his lips back in a growl. He shifted onto his haunches and sprang.

As his teeth latched onto the demon's neck, it spun, flinging him into a tree. The impact cracked the thin trunk, forcing the breath from Shane's lungs, and he hit the ground with a smack. The sharp, coppery taste of demon blood filled his mouth, and the thick, black-red substance trailed down the fiend's shoulder.

Grunting, Shane scrambled to his feet and lunged again, latching onto the monster's leg and dragging it to the ground. The fiend wailed and gripped him by the scruff of his neck like a pup, tossing him aside as if he were merely a mild inconvenience.

Shane rolled through the leaves, his nails gripping the dirt as he righted himself, adrenaline pooling in his muscles as he sprang toward the demon again.

The fiend caught him by the throat and lifted him into the air.

His legs flailing, Shane rotated his torso, trying to break from the demon's clutches. It merely tightened its grip on his throat. Shane gasped for breath that wouldn't come. Darkness tunneled his vision.

Turning its free hand palm up, the demon reached a claw toward Shane's nostril. The sharp tip burrowed into his snout, and fiery heat consumed his head, his senses thickening until they ceased to register anything but the pain. Intense pressure pushed on his skull from the inside out as the inferno of his brain threatened to explode.

Thunder clapped from above, and an electric jolt zipped through his body as he crashed to the ground. He sucked a ragged breath into his starving lungs and lifted his head. The world spun, and he lay his head in the dirt, giving himself time to heal from the attack.

His senses returning, the snarling, grunting sounds of a battle registered in his ears. A female shouted, "Shane!" and he stumbled to his paws to find a pack of werewolves fighting the demon.

A chocolate-colored wolf lunged toward it, clamping onto its arm before it tossed him aside. A gray wolf went for its chest, but it knocked him aside before he could make contact. The alpha of the pack, an enormous light-brown wolf, attacked, gripping the demon's injured neck and dragging it to the ground.

Shane growled. This was his demon. He couldn't recall why, but he was connected to this atrocity, and it was his duty to vanquish it.

The wolves continued attacking, the demon deflecting their advances as it moved toward Shane. He stalked forward and joined the fray, sinking his teeth into leathery flesh before being knocked to the ground.

The alpha howled, and his pack responded, lunging in unison, four maws clamping onto the demon's soft spots from behind. Shane growled and leaped toward it, swiping his claws across the fiend's chest, piercing its heart.

It exploded into a cloud of ash, leaving Shane face-to-face with a pack of angry werewolves.

Bekah hid behind the bushes, Rain's fingers digging into her arm the only thing keeping her from running into the middle of the standoff. Through the bramble, she glimpsed the deep-brown fur standing in a ridge down Shane's back. His eyes were wild, his posture defensive as Luke and the others fanned out around him in a semicircle.

"He's scared." She tugged from Rain's grip. "He doesn't recognize them. They're making it worse."

Bekah darted into the clearing behind Shane. "You need to shift, Luke. He feels threatened."

Shane snapped his head around at the sound of her voice and snarled.

Her stomach plummeted to her feet as she scrambled backward into a tree. "It's me, Shane. It's Bekah." She slipped a trembling hand into her pocket, closing her fingers around the vial of powder.

Shane turned back to the wolves, a defensive growl rumbling in his throat.

Luke's nostrils flared as he blew out a hard breath and jerked his head upward. His body shimmered, his human form taking shape as he stood on two feet. Chase and the others followed his lead, shifting and moving closer to the alpha.

The tension in Shane's haunches loosened, but he hesitated to shift.

"We're not going to hurt you, buddy." Luke raised his hands. "We just want to talk."

As Luke moved toward him, Shane took two cautious steps back, his lips peeling back to bare his teeth.

Her muscles trembling, Bekah crept toward Shane, one arm outstretched, her other hand gripping the possible remedy for his amnesia. He glanced between Luke and her, blinking and tilting his head as she finally held his gaze.

"You know me, Shane." She reached for him, running her hand along the soft fur of his neck. Opening her senses to him, she felt his confusion and fear. He was lost and on the verge of bolting. "Please shift so we can talk. I want to help you."

Rain shuffled to her side. "He needs to be in human form for the spell to work…*if* it's going to work."

"Please, Shane." She leaned in, her face dangerously close to his razor-sharp teeth, and Chase let out a disapproving grunt.

Slowly, she drifted closer, pressing her lips to his forehead and clutching his fur as tears gathered on her lower lids. She was his fate-bound, damn it. She shouldn't be so easily erased from his mind. A sob bubbled up from her chest, and she released him, allowing the tears to drip onto her cheeks. His wolf should have recognized her.

If this remedy didn't work… If the amnesia was permanent this time, she might have to spend the rest of her life bound to a man who wasn't bound to her. Shane had stolen her heart the day she met him, and it had been beating inside him ever since. She couldn't lose him.

"You know me." She clenched her teeth, fisting her hands at her sides. "Damn it, Shane, your wolf knows me. *Remember*."

He stepped back, his gaze darting between Bekah and her pack-mates as a deep whimper emanated from his throat. Locking eyes with her, he sucked in a deep breath and shifted to his human form.

His brow furrowed over his sea-green eyes, and he took two cautious steps toward her. "Where are we?"

She swallowed the baseball-sized lump from her throat. "The Louisiana swamp, near New Orleans."

He blinked, his face scrunching like it did before when he couldn't access a memory. "How did I get here?"

Her heart sank, and she cursed the witch who gave him a botched spell. The woman's stupidity had wrenched Bekah's soulmate from her grasp, tearing a gaping hole in her heart. Spending the rest of her life in love with a man who couldn't remember he loved her back was unimaginable.

She dumped the remedy powder into her palm. He may not remember her, but at least Rain's spell would stop him from losing any more of himself. "You walked here to fight a demon. You were trying to protect me."

He met her gaze, and a look of recognition smoothed his features. "I know you, don't I?"

Her blood felt fizzy, hope blooming in her heart as she moved toward him. "You do know me."

"You… Are we…?" He squeezed his eyes shut and shook his head. "Why do I get the feeling I'm in love with you?"

"Because you are." She blew the remedy into his face, and he coughed, fanning it away. "And I'm in love with you too."

As the cloud of shimmering powder dissipated, Shane smiled. Pink crystals clung to his lashes, drifting onto his cheeks as he blinked.

Sweet relief flushed her system as she returned the smile. Even if his other memories never returned, their soul-deep connection remained intact. He may have lost his past, but his future was here with her. "Do you remember me?"

He stepped toward her, placing a hand on her hip and cupping her face in his other, running his thumb over her cheek. "You're my fatebound, Bekah. I could never forget you." He brushed his lips to hers. "Well, not for long anyway."

EPILOGUE

SHANE STOOD IN THE WING, WATCHING HIS STUDENT FINISH HIS piano solo. As the audience clapped, the boy stood and bowed, and Shane strode onto the stage.

He shook the kid's hand and addressed the audience. "Let's hear another round for Jacob. Wasn't he brilliant?"

The little boy beamed with pride and hurried down the steps to his mother's waiting arms.

"Last up is Emma on saxophone." He motioned for her to join him on stage, and his heart swelled with love as she shuffled toward him. His old sax was nearly as big as her, and she cradled it to her chest as she turned toward the audience.

"Knock 'em dead, sweetheart." He kissed the top of her head and descended the steps to join Bekah in the front row.

His music school had been in business for six months, and though he only had fifteen students performing, their first recital had drawn a crowd. Half the pack had shown up, filling the small auditorium to the brim, and the kids were thrilled to be playing for more than their own parents.

Emma played her version of "You are my Sunshine," and he slipped his hand into Bekah's. "She's good."

Bekah rested her head on his shoulder. "She has a good teacher."

She finished the song, and the pack rose to their feet, giving her a standing ovation. Emma's smile lit up the room, and he joined her on the stage to wrap up the show.

As the parents left with their kids, the pack hung around, congratulating Emma and shaking Shane's hand one by one, showing their support. His throat tightened as the alpha clapped him on the shoulder and told him he did a great job. Moving to New Orleans, being with Bekah, and joining the pack was the best decision he'd ever made.

For the first time in his life, he belonged somewhere. Being a part of a pack…part of a family…was everything he'd ever wanted. And the beautiful woman standing before him had made that happen.

The botched spell the witch gave him had clouded his memories, which turned out to be a blessing. It had been easy to dismiss his preconceived notions about pack life when he could hardly remember the reason he'd avoided it before. While his past wasn't as sharp in his mind as it used to be, his future couldn't have been any clearer.

The pack finally dispersed, leaving him alone with his new family. Emma put his sax in the case and carried it onto the stage.

She hugged her mom. "You said if I practiced hard and stuck with it, I could get my own saxophone."

"I sure did, didn't I?"

Shane knelt beside Emma and put his hand on the case. The worn leather was smooth against his skin, and the memories attached to the instrument—happy memories he could still recall—would live on in his heart. "You know what, Emma? You can have mine."

She looked at him with wide eyes. "But your mom gave it to you."

"And now, I'm giving it to you."

Emma hugged his neck. "Thank you."

He held her in his arms and blinked back the pressure forming in his eyes. "I have a present for your mum too. The one we talked about before. Do you think she's ready for it?"

She giggled and grabbed Bekah's hand tugging her toward him. "I know she is."

With one knee on the ground, Shane pulled a diamond ring from his pocket. “Bekah, I know you wanted to hold off on becoming mates, so Emma could get used to me…but she assures me she’s ready.”

He glanced at Emma, and she giggled again. “She’s been pestering me to do this for months, in fact. So…” He took Bekah’s hand. “Will you be my mate…my wife?”

A single tear spilled from Bekah’s eye as she pulled him to his feet. “You two discussed this without me?”

“Someone had to make you stop dragging your feet, Mom. We’re all ready.” Emma opened the saxophone case and ran her hand over the brass. “Well, go on and say yes.”

Bekah smiled and took his face in her hands. “Yes, Shane. I love you.” Her eyes glistened, and as she smiled, another tear rolled down her cheek.

He kissed it away. “I love you too, Bekah. Thank you for making all my dreams come true.”

Emma tugged on his shirt. “Can I start calling you Dad now, or do I have to wait until after the ceremony?”

He laughed and scooped her up with one arm, holding Bekah tight against his side with the other. “You can call me Dad whenever you want.”

Emma put an arm around his neck, the other around her mom’s. “It’s about time. I told you that you can’t fight fate, remember?”

He kissed them both. “How could I forget?”

SHIFTING FATE

CARRIE PULKINEN

PROLOGUE

France, early 1600s

Alrick's heart raced as he approached the cathedral. His feet ached from the long journey, but it would soon be worth the pain. A full moon illuminated the stone architecture, the gargoyles perched atop the towers casting soft shadows in its light. A massive circular window was situated in the center of the structure, and three pointed archways held entrances to the chapel.

As instructed, Alrick passed by the doorways and made his way down the left side of the church to a small wooden door near the back. He pulled a folded piece of parchment from his pocket and hesitated to perform the secret knock.

Once he passed through this threshold, there would be no turning back.

But he owed it to his country and his people. Vile creatures had been allowed to run rampant in the villages for long enough. Magic was an abomination, and it needed to be wiped from the face of the earth. The forsaken must be destroyed.

With a deep inhale, he rapped the rhythm on the wood. The door swung open to reveal a long, dark corridor. Torchlight flickered some twenty meters ahead, and as he stepped through the entrance, the door slammed shut behind him. The hall made a sharp left turn where the torch burned, and he followed it to a set of stone steps leading down beneath the main floor.

Excitement hummed in his veins as he descended the staircase. The Sect recruited only the most skilled warriors for its new supernatural army, and Alrick was among the first to receive an invitation. He accepted without hesitation, for how could he refuse being part of the dawn of a new age? An age without magic smearing the face of humanity.

Marie's words echoed in his mind as he reached the bottom of the stairs, and he paused again. "You don't have to do this, Alrick," she'd said. "If you love me, you can find it in yourself to love all beings, mundane and magical alike."

He was indeed in love with Marie, but he loved the woman, not the witch. His feelings for her had bloomed before he had learned about her magic, and he had continued to care for her in spite of her abominable powers. If there were a way to strip the magic from her soul, he would have done so. Alas, leaving her was his only option. To do otherwise would be duplicitous.

Pushing thoughts of the witch from his mind, he continued toward a foreboding set of arched double doors. He knocked the secret rhythm on the wood once more, and the sound of a lock disengaging echoed through the corridor. A man in a deep red robe opened one of the doors and motioned for Alrick to enter.

Five men, warriors from neighboring villages, stood in a line in front of a raised dais. Seven Sect leaders, all in red robes, save for the Supreme, who wore black, sat in ornately carved wooden chairs atop the platform. As Alrick joined the men, the Supreme rose and lifted his hands. Alrick and the others dropped to one knee, bowing their heads in reverence.

"It is with great pride that I, the Supreme Leader of the Sect, initiate the first order of the gargoyle warriors. Your sacrifice for the greater good will forever be remembered and honored. Please rise and remove your doublets and jerkins."

Alrick did as requested, stripping until he stood before the Supreme in only his breeches and boots.

"Magic is a plague on this land, and you, my brothers, will end its reign. Behold." The Supreme descended from the dais and strode toward a great red crystal, at least two meters in diameter, sitting on a stone platform.

"This is Thropynite, the stone that will enable a demon to fuse with your soul. Once the fusion takes place, you will be granted shapeshifting abilities and become the greatest warriors known to man. Under the cover of night, you will transform into your demon and raid the villages, killing everyone suspected of practicing magic. Witches, sorcerers, werewolves, and the like will cower at your feet, but you will show them no mercy, for..."

"The Sect is the one true creed, the Supreme our only leader," they all said in unison.

"As you are aware, your sacrifice is great. When the earth has been rid of magic, you, as magical beings, will be destroyed. Is this sacrifice done willingly?"

"Yes, Supreme." Adrenaline coursed through Alrick's veins. The ultimate sacrifice for the ultimate act of faith.

"Proceed." The Supreme nodded to a Sect member who wore thick leather gloves and a mask. The man used a chisel to break off five pieces of the red stone. With each hit of the hammer, a thunderous boom echoed in the chamber and sparks ignited, illuminating the dimly lit room as if lightning had struck.

"Who shall be the first to accept his initiation?"

Without hesitation, Alrick stepped forward. "I will, Supreme."

The Supreme inclined his chin. "Very well."

Two men took Alrick by the arms and escorted him to a circle carved into the stone floor. A five-pointed star occupied the diameter, and they positioned him in the center of the shape before forcing him to his knees. Alrick obeyed willingly, for he was about to become the first gargoyle warrior for the Sect, an honor he not only deserved, but one he would treasure for the rest of his existence.

The Supreme drew his hood onto his head and read from a leather-bound book. He spoke Latin, a language the warriors did not understand, but as the atmosphere in the room thickened, the intent behind his words was clear.

Holding a dagger horizontally in both hands, the Supreme chanted and then kissed the blade. He handed it to a Sect member, who entered the circle and pressed the tip to Alrick's sternum. Alrick clenched his jaw as the blade pierced his skin. A burning sensation spread through his chest, and the Sect member dragged the tip downward, opening his flesh.

Alrick held in his groan. He had sustained far worse injuries on the battlefield, yet the pain from this small incision ricocheted through his body, making him want to scream in agony. He gritted his teeth, for a true warrior never showed weakness.

The Sect member placed the shard of Thropynite into the wound, and the pain intensified threefold. A traitorous moan escaped Alrick's lips, and the Sect member squeezed his shoulder.

"It will be over soon, my friend."

The Supreme resumed his chant, filling the room again with the energy of lightning. Blood dripped down the center of Alrick's chest, the stone sizzling inside the lesion. A low vibration filled the air, increasing in volume until all he heard was the hum throbbing in his ears.

Alrick's heart raced, and as he peered at his torso, the trail of blood reversed direction, flowing upward and returning to his wound. The circle and star ignited, a wall of fire surrounding him, licking upward to the ceiling. His blood ran cold as the heat, hot as the fires of hell itself, consumed him.

He squeezed his eyes shut, willing his body to bear the pain of being burned alive, when a guttural roar filled his ears. He opened his eyes to find a demonic spirit floating in front of him. Black smoke swirled, taking the shape of a gargoyle, its grotesque mouth, much too big for its face, curling upward into a menacing smile.

Alrick's body tensed in fear. He wanted to run, for even a celebrated warrior like himself was no match for a creature without a physical body. But he was frozen to the spot. The demon snarled, and Alrick swallowed the sensation of a lump of burning coal from his throat.

The Supreme's chanting rose above the noise, and the demon shot toward Alrick, the impact knocking him onto his back. He lay prone, unable to move as the fiend invaded his body, battling with his psyche.

Alrick felt hands on his arms, though his vision had tunneled to mere pinpricks of light. The sensation of being dragged registered in his mind. His arm was lifted, his hand placed against a smooth stone. Another flash of agonizing pain. His chest tightened, the wound healing instantly, the shard of stone embedding in his skin.

As the demon fused with his soul, his hatred of the forsaken grew tenfold. Burning anger seethed in his veins, and he rose, bowing his head to the one true leader. "On my life and my honor, I vow not to stop until every last trace of magic has been vanquished from this earth."

The Supreme bowed in return. "Take your place by my side, brother, as we initiate the others. Your faith has earned you the title of general in our army."

The gargoyle warriors began their crusade that very night. Alrick could never have dreamed the satisfaction he'd feel as he tore the forsaken limb from limb. The taste of their blood on his tongue. The sensation of their bones snapping beneath his fingers. The pleasure almost masked the ache in his heart for the one he'd left behind.

CHAPTER ONE

WITH THE MAGIC OF THE FULL MOON HUMMING IN HIS VEINS, Noah L'Eveque paused on the corner of Royal and St. Philip, across the street from O'Malley's Pub. Tilting his head toward the sky, he inhaled deeply, closing his eyes and focusing on the low vibration in his muscles, the faintest hint of the nearly imperceptible shifter magic flowing through his soul.

Sticky summer air clung to his skin, and as a bead of sweat rolled down his forehead, he flicked it away with a finger. He could almost feel the blast of chilly air that would greet him in the doorway of O'Malley's as he stepped inside, and the draw of his pack's headquarters had his legs moving toward the building involuntarily.

He stopped on the edge of the sidewalk and peered through the window at the activity inside. While the shifters of the pack followed the call of their wolves to the forest to hunt, the rest of them—Noah included—felt little more than an extra burst of energy in their magic this time of the month. A dozen people—all second-borns or non-shifting mates—gathered around the bar, talking and imbibing the free drinks offered monthly, every full moon.

Who said shifters had all the fun?

Normally, Noah would have been inside with them, enjoying the comradery of his fellow second-born weres. He hadn't missed a full moon gathering in as long as he could remember, but tonight, he couldn't bring himself to step inside.

And it was no mystery why.

Amber, the alpha's sister, stood behind the bar, laughing with the others, her blue eyes sparkling with her smile. She'd swept her light golden-brown hair into a ponytail, revealing the delicate curve of her neck, and as she glanced at her watch and bit her bottom lip, an ache expanded in Noah's chest.

Her shift would be ending soon, and if he went in now, she'd join him at the bar, stay there with him 'til closing time, long after the others called it a night, and make him feel things he shouldn't for a woman in the alpha line.

His feelings had intensified so much over the past few months, he could hardly look at her without the crushing need to sweep her into his arms and make her his. But Amber deserved better. She'd made that clear. With alpha blood flowing through her veins, she should be with a shifting wolf.

Fuck. His hands curled into fists. Noah should have been a shifting wolf, goddammit, and if fate hadn't played games with his future, Amber would be his mate by now.

Only first-born werewolves gained the ability to shift...around the age of thirteen...except in a case like Noah's. His older sister was his twin, and if they'd been born closer together, they both would have become shifters. But Noah was breech, and the umbilical cord was wrapped around his neck, complicating his birth. He didn't make his appearance into the world until half an hour later...too late for his magic to activate his wolf gene, leaving him no better than any other second-born werewolf.

Gritting his teeth, he strode past the entrance and made a left on Bourbon Street, heading into the heart of the French Quarter. He needed to get the woman off his mind, and with his friends out hunting, the excitement of New Orleans' most famous street was the next best distraction.

He wiped the scowl from his face, straightening his spine as he strolled into the throng of people and pushing the what-ifs from his mind. *It is what it is.* Focusing on what was, rather than wallowing in what should have been, had served him well enough. Being angry at fate didn't do anyone any good. Besides…things might be changing for him soon.

Laughter and chatter drifted on the air, and the brassy sounds of a jazz band blasted from the open door of a club on the corner. He stopped at the to-go window and bought a beer. Chilled air seeped out from the inside, taming the Louisiana heat as the bartender filled a plastic cup with frothy goodness. Noah took a long sip, savoring the cool, bubbly liquid as it slid down his throat, and he continued on his way.

There was no better place than Bourbon Street for people-watching. College-age partiers all the way up through the occasional couple in their seventies came here to forget their worries and indulge in a bit of sin before heading back to the monotony of real life. The energy of the city called to people, enticing them to tear down their walls and let the good times roll.

"*Laissez le bons temps rouler.*" Noah chugged his beer and tossed the cup in a trash can before stepping inside a club. A cover band blasted an early 2000s pop hit from a small stage near the entrance, and three women in their forties laughed as they danced, trying to entice their husbands to join them on the floor.

Noah made his way toward the bar, but he stopped short when a brunette backed against a wall caught his eye. She gripped her beer bottle, her nails digging into the label as her gaze darted about the room, looking at anything but the hulking man who had her cornered. She swallowed hard, and a nervous giggle bubbled from her throat. The asshole took it as an invitation, reaching toward her and running his fingers down her cheek.

Without a second thought, Noah moved toward them. If he were a shifter, his mere presence would be enough to intimidate the man into backing off, but he wasn't. He'd have to get creative.

"Hey, sis, sorry I'm late." He held out his arms in an invitation for a hug.

The woman furrowed her brow at first, but as the asshole crossed his arms and puffed out his chest, she recognized Noah's attempt and stepped into his embrace. "I thought you'd never get here."

She hugged him quickly and stayed by his side, forcing a smile. "What took you so long?"

"Got hung up on the jobsite." He wrapped an arm around her shoulders. "Who's your friend?"

The man grunted, took a swig of his beer, and, as he stomped away, Noah couldn't help himself. He called on his magic, gathering the energy into his hand until he could feel the atoms in the atmosphere. With a flick of his fingers, he nudged the man's foot with his power, causing it to catch on his other ankle and making him stumble.

The man caught himself, inflating his chest and looking around as if to be sure no one was laughing at him. Noah held in a chuckle. Served the bastard right. He should've sent him flat on his face.

All second-born weres possessed a psychic ability. Some were empaths, while others could talk to the dead or get glimpses of the future. Noah's telekinesis was a power many envied, but he would give it up in a heartbeat to awaken his inner wolf. Maybe someday…

As the man disappeared into the crowd, the woman's breath came out in a rush. "Thank you for that."

Noah released her shoulder. "You looked like you needed a little help. Are you here alone?"

"My friend is in the restroom." She held out her hand to shake, and a flirtatious smile curved her lips. "I'm Tiffany."

He accepted. "Noah." Her skin was warm, but no magical energy sparked from it. Like ninety percent of the people in New Orleans, she was pure human. Her wavy hair brushed her shoulders, and as he released her hand, she tucked one side behind her ear.

"Jeez, Tiff. I leave for five minutes, and you've already picked up a guy. I hope he has a friend," a blonde with dark brown eyes said as she approached them.

Tiffany laughed and clinked the neck of her beer bottle against her friend's. "This is Noah. He saved me from a drunk. Noah, this is Caitlyn."

"Hey." She nodded at him and turned to Tiffany. "This place is lame. Let's get out of here."

"Okay." Tiffany tossed her bottle in the trash and tilted her head at Noah. "Do you want to come with us?"

"Do you have a friend?" Caitlyn batted her lashes.

"It's just me tonight, I'm afraid."

Tiffany bit her bottom lip and swept her gaze down his body. This could be just the distraction he needed.

"Hmm…" Caitlyn shrugged. "I suppose we can share. Come on." She linked her arm through his and tugged him toward the door. Tiffany clutched his other bicep and followed.

Noah instinctively glanced over his shoulder and found the drunk from earlier glaring at them as they made their way toward the exit. With a flick of his hand behind his back, Noah knocked the bottom of the guy's glass, spilling his drink down the front of his shirt.

It's not parlor magic. His buddy James's words echoed in his mind. *It's a unique werewolf gift.*

Not the gift Noah was meant to have…

But he made do with the magic he was given.

He chuckled as they exited the club and turned toward the next one, but his chest tightened, giving him pause. He had an attractive woman on each arm, and a few months ago, he would have been *so* down for this. Now, he couldn't stop imagining Amber's disappointed expression as she chewed her lip and glanced at her watch earlier this evening.

He was supposed to be there with her. He was *always* there for her. What the hell was his problem now?

He tugged his arms from the women's grasp. "It was nice meeting you ladies, but I think I'm going to call it a night."

"But it's early…" Tiffany said, disappointment evident in her eyes.

"I have somewhere to be. Y'all stay safe tonight. Stay together." He nodded and strode to the other side of the street before they could argue more.

Tugging his phone from his pocket, he glanced at the time and cursed under his breath. He needed to march his sorry ass back to O'Malley's and spend the evening with Amber like he had every full moon since gods-knew-when. He should wad up his emotions, shove them into the darkest corner of his mind, and be the best friend he was supposed to be. That was all she wanted from him.

He, Amber, and his twin sister, Nylah, had been inseparable since they were kids. Nylah going rogue shouldn't have changed things between Amber and him. He'd always had feelings for her, from the time he was old enough to understand what feelings were.

They weren't reciprocated, and he understood why. A telekinetic second-born had no place in the alpha line. Amber should mate with a dominant shifter, someone who would pass on the genes a true leader needed.

He'd hinted at his feelings for her once, and she'd shut him down quickly. "I'm so glad we're friends," she'd said. "It's nice not having to worry that you're after me for my pack status." That was when things had gotten awkward, and he'd needed to put an end to that. He could never be the werewolf she needed, but he could be her friend.

"Where is she?" A woman's frantic voice drew his attention down the street. "Goddammit, Mitch, where did she go?"

The woman, in her fifties or sixties, with platinum hair and a thick coating of blue eyeshadow, clutched a bouncer's shoulder outside a strip club and gave him a shake. "You're supposed to take care of my girls."

Mitch shrugged off her grasp and stalked to the end of the building, peering at the closed gate blocking the alley before marching back. "A guy dropped his wallet. I stepped inside for half a minute to return it, and when I came out, she was gone." He shook his head. "I'm sorry, Angel. She probably got a good offer from a tourist."

Angel shook her finger in his face. "My girls are *not* prostitutes. They're dancers."

Shoving his hands in his pockets, Noah shuffled toward the gate and nudged it with his shoulder. It swung freely, so he slipped inside the alley, freezing as the coppery scent of fresh blood assaulted his senses. Though his night vision wasn't nearly as sharp as a shifter's, there was no mistaking the heap of flesh lying crumpled at the end of the passageway.

Pulse thrumming, he moved toward it, his gaze darting about the darkened corridor, searching for the culprit. Muffled music from Bourbon Street filtered in through the gate, masking any sounds of retreat, and a trash can overflowing with three-day-old garbage made it impossible for him to catch a scent. He focused his magic into his skin, feeling the hum of the atmosphere around him. No living energy interrupted the flow. Whoever did this was long gone.

He crept toward the body, covering his mouth as he took in the gory scene. The woman lay on her back, her right leg bent at an unnatural angle. Blood soaked her once-blue satin bra, and in her chest, a jagged, gaping hole was all that remained where her heart used to be.

His stomach turned, and his hand trembled as he dialed the alpha's mate and pressed the phone to his ear.

"Detective Mason speaking."

He swallowed the lump from his throat. "Macey, it's Noah. I found a body in the Quarter. It looks supernatural." He described the scene and the events leading up to it.

"Have you contacted Luke?"

"I will. I don't think her boss has even called the police yet. The killer is long gone, so I thought you should know."

"Who's on patrol with you? Cade or James?"

He hesitated to tell her the real reason he hadn't called the alpha first. "I'm…alone."

She missed a beat in her response. "You're patrolling by yourself?" The wariness in her voice was a knife to his heart. Non-shifters weren't allowed to patrol alone. Macey was the only exception, and that was because she'd been a detective for longer than she'd known she was a second-born werewolf.

"I was at a bar across the street, saw the commotion, and came to check it out." The last thing he needed was to get into trouble with the alpha. His position on the hunting team was fragile as it was.

"Okay." Relief was evident in her voice.

"Don't worry. You don't have to report me."

She paused, the sound of a car door slamming through the receiver filling the silence. "It's not a law I agree with, if that makes you feel any better."

"Thanks. What do you want me to do?" He looked around for any signs of the culprit but found nothing. Whatever took this woman's heart had to have massive claws or a wicked weapon.

"Get out of the alley and call Luke. If you can't reach him, follow the chain. I'll take care of the humans."

"Hey!" Angel's voice echoed down the alley. "What are you doing?"

"Shit." He flicked his wrist, swinging the gate toward her and knocking her back into the street. He cringed at the sound of flesh hitting pavement and scrambled to climb the fence.

"Get back here, fucker!" Mitch plowed through the gate as Noah's foot slipped.

He fell to the ground, smacking his head on the cobblestone, and his vision swam. Mitch hauled him up, slamming him against the brick wall.

"What did you do to her, you sick bastard?" Mitch pressed his forearm into Noah's chest, squeezing the breath from his lungs.

Shit. What now? He glanced around the alley, searching for something he could grab with his mind to fight back, but Angel's agonizing wail pulled his attention to the body.

"Bridget!" She dropped to her knees, folding forward at the waist and covering her face. "Oh my God, someone call the police."

Half a dozen dancers hesitated at the alley entrance before creeping forward, their faces pale, expressions distorted in shock as sirens blared in the distance.

Noah was toast. He stopped struggling, and Mitch eased off his chest enough for him to speak. "I didn't touch her. The alley gate was open, so I came in to look for her."

Mitch's eyes narrowed into slits. "Save it for the police."

Another bouncer, even meatier than Mitch, if that were possible, sidestepped around the dancers and grabbed Noah's arm. He could have fought back, but his second-born strength was no match for these beefcakes. Noah would have to use his magic to have any chance of winning, and he couldn't do that in front of all these people.

Instead, he let them drag him to the street and cooperated as the police put him in handcuffs. Tiffany and Caitlyn, the women he'd met at the bar, stood on the sidewalk a few feet away, but he couldn't meet their eyes.

He had royally fucked up. Whatever the human cops had planned for him would pale in comparison to the punishment waiting for him once he returned to the pack. *This* was the reason non-shifters weren't allowed to patrol alone. They lacked the speed and strength to get out of situations like this. A shifter never would have been caught.

As the officer guided him into the back of the squad car, he caught a glimpse of Macey's face before she headed into the alley. The disappointment and pity in her eyes was enough to tear him in two.

A werewolf arrested by the human police. He was a disgrace to his pack.

CHAPTER TWO

Amber Mason strolled next to her mother up St. Philip Street toward O'Malley's Pub. The hot June sun beat down on them, heating the top of her head and making her reconsider the bar's standard black uniform. It was too damn hot for dark colors.

The surprise lunch visit had been pleasant, her mom filling her in on her parents' move to Jackson, Mississippi, and how her dad was settling into his new role in the werewolf national congress. They talked about family and how Amber was handling running the bar on her own, Debbie placing just enough emphasis on the *on her own* part to make it clear this visit wasn't simply social.

But Amber wasn't taking the bait. If her mom had something to say about her current relationship status—or lack thereof—she'd have to work it into the conversation on her own. Amber sure as hell wasn't bringing it up.

"How long are you in town for?" She opened the door and gestured for her mom to go inside.

Debbie paused and looked at her, tilting her head and giving her that *I can't believe you haven't found a man* look. It was unmistakable: the way her brows drew together and lifted at the same time, the twitch as the corners of her mouth tried to pull into a frown but she forced them upward into an awkward smile.

It was the look of pity, and though Amber favored her mom, with the same light-brown hair and blue eyes, she tried her best to avoid the facial expressions that somehow cut deeper than words.

Her mom placed a hand on her shoulder, giving it a gentle squeeze before she stepped through the door. "Just for the afternoon. I'm heading to Lake Charles to visit Vanessa this evening and staying a few nights there."

Chilled air blasted Amber's skin as she crossed the threshold, a welcome relief from the sauna of the Louisiana summer. Shaded lights hung from exposed beams in the ceiling, giving the quiet bar a dark, smoky haze. A couple sat in the corner, sharing an order of loaded fries and a pitcher of beer, and Chase stood behind the bar, chopping a lemon.

He lifted his head and grinned as he caught sight of Debbie. "Afternoon, Mrs. Mason. Where's the old man? You leave him behind this time?" He stood on a plastic crate and leaned over the bar, stretching out his arms in invitation.

Debbie smiled and leaned in to hug him across the bar. "Us girls need to have a little fun without our mates every now and then. How are you and your witch?"

Chase chuckled and rubbed a hand down his dark beard. "We're good. Perfect, in fact."

"I'm so glad you found someone." She gave Amber the side-eye and leaned against a barstool, crossing her arms over her pressed white blouse.

Amber fought her eye roll. "I'd offer you a drink, Mom, but since you're driving, we better not. I'll tell Luke you said hi."

"Actually…"

Oh lord. Here it comes. She'd all but dismissed the woman. Couldn't she go on her way without bringing up the inevitable?

"I was hoping we could talk somewhere privately about a family matter."

Apparently, she couldn't. Amber rolled the stiffness from her neck.

The headache this conversation would bring was already inching its way into the base of her skull.

She gestured to the side door. "We can go in Luke's office. There's more room in there." And it wasn't in the same state of perpetual disarray as her own office. She didn't need to give her mom anything else to chide her for.

Debbie strode toward the door. "Is your brother here? That would be even better."

I wish. Luke would make the perfect buffer for this conversation. He'd been through all this with their parents already. "He's on a jobsite."

"Too bad."

Amber followed her mom through the swinging door, down a short flight of brick steps, and into the back corridor. A storage room filled with cases of beer and restaurant supplies opened up on the right, and she reached across to the left, pulling her office door shut as she passed it.

The alpha's office lay just beyond the storage room, and Debbie didn't stop to knock before she pushed the door open and disappeared inside. Amber stood in the entrance as her mom ran a hand across the back of a green chair, a sad smile playing on her lips as she stepped toward the massive oak desk and picked up a small Eiffel Tower figurine on the corner.

"I remember when this was your father's office."

"Yeah, well, it wasn't that long ago." She dropped into a chair and crossed her legs. "What did you want to talk about?"

That same scrunched-brow look of pity contorted Debbie's features. "You're twenty-nine years old, sweetheart."

She folded her hands in her lap. "Last time I checked."

A small chuckle emanated from her mom's throat. "You get your sarcasm from your father."

"And his alpha blood and all the laws that come with it. Is that what you wanted to talk about?"

Debbie laced her fingers together and leaned against the desk. "You're obligated to take a mate by the time you turn thirty."

"Which is ridiculous."

She held up her hands. "It's not my place to agree or disagree with the law, but it is *the law.* I don't want you to go through what your brother did if you wait until the last minute."

"You mean when he found his fate-bound, but *the law* almost forced him to mate with someone else when they ran into trouble? Don't worry, Mom. That'll never happen." Amber wasn't meant to be anyone's fated mate. If a wolf in the pack was going to claim her, it would have happened by now. "No one wants me."

"That's not true. Any man in the pack…in any pack…would be happy to take you as his mate. You have—"

"Alpha blood. I know." And that was the perfect reason to spend the rest of her life with someone, wasn't it? Not because he loved her, but because she could bring him into the inner circle, give him a child with alpha blood. *No, thank you.*

"It's within your brother's authority to select someone for you."

Amber's mouth dropped open. Was her mother actually suggesting she let Luke *assign* someone the task of mating with her?

Debbie slid into the chair next to her and patted her knee. "He would never choose your mate, dear, but if there's someone you had in mind, he could…" She shrugged.

"Do you hear yourself, Mother? If I were a man, would you suggest I force a woman to become my mate? Take away her choice, her free will?" Her parents were so old school it was a wonder she and Luke turned out the way they did. This wasn't her father's pack anymore, and she would not succumb to these crusty old antiquated laws.

"No, that would be different."

"It's exactly the same."

Her mother pursed her lips and blew out an irritated breath through her nose. "Your brother nearly brought shame upon our family…in front of the congress, no less. If things hadn't worked out for him the way they did, the congress could have brought in new leadership. Our family could have been exiled."

Her heart sank. Luke *had* to have a mate to become alpha. While Amber would never hold any position of authority, it was her obligation to ensure the bloodline continued undiluted.

"Your father could lose his place on the congress if you… Please don't put our family in another situation like that."

"I won't. I've got plenty of time to find someone I can stomach spending the rest of my life with."

Her mom frowned. "You have six months."

Amber's smile faded, and she placed her hand on Debbie's. Where had the time gone? "I won't let you down."

Her mom rested her free hand on top of hers. "You never have. If there aren't any men in the pack who pique your interest, we could plan a soiree. Plenty of men from the neighboring packs would love to meet you."

"No. Absolutely not. This isn't the 1800s." She tugged her hand from her mother's grasp and stood, pacing around the desk. No way in hell would she allow herself to be put on display like that. She was a grown woman, for Christ's sake.

Debbie nodded. "You're right. That would make you look desperate."

"Which I'm not." She'd dated a couple of pack members when she was in her early twenties. It had quickly become obvious they were more interested in her position than her personality when they preferred having dinner with her parents over spending time alone with her.

"No, you're not." That damned look of pity crossed her mother's face again before she smoothed her features and rose to her feet. "I had better hit the road. I've got an early dinner reservation." She glided toward the door, pausing and turning to Amber. "I almost forgot to ask. How's Noah? You didn't mention him at lunch."

A flutter formed in her stomach, but it quickly turned sour. "I haven't heard from him in nearly a month."

"That's odd. He's one of your best friends."

Was one of her best friends. When he skipped the full moon gathering last month, she'd assumed he was on patrol with Cade or James. But when he didn't respond to her texts the next few days, she'd received the message loud and clear.

"I think he must have met someone." Saying it out loud, the words solidified into steel and pierced her heart. Noah was never serious about anything, especially dating. Whoever was occupying his time these days must have had her hooks in him deep.

Her mother's pity face twisted the blade. "I'm sure he would have told you if that were the case. Noah's kindness and concern for others are some of his best qualities. Wonderful qualities for a potential mate." She raised a brow.

If she was trying to plant a seed in Amber's mind, she was wasting her time. The idea that her feelings for Noah ran deeper than friendship had sprouted a while ago, but right before she could express her interest in him, something about their relationship had changed. He'd backed off, acting awkward around her. She didn't dare risk ruining their friendship by trying again. He was the only single man in the pack who didn't look at her as a breeding machine.

Amber crossed her arms. "I'm sure he'll make a great mate for *someone* someday."

Debbie's lips curved into a sly smile. "I'm sure he will. Give your brother a hug for me. I'm sorry I missed him." She blew a kiss to Amber and slipped into the hall.

Gritting her teeth, Amber shuffled to the door, waiting until her mom exited into the bar before making her way to her own office. She dropped into a high-backed leather chair, spinning in a circle as she chewed her bottom lip. As the chair came back around to face the desk, she planted her feet on the floor and let her elbows thunk on the wooden surface.

She inhaled a deep breath and let it out slowly, willing the tension in her shoulders to ease. That conversation could have been worse. At least this time her mother didn't suggest she lay off the fatty bar food if she ever wanted to land a man. Still, the insinuation that Amber's greatest contribution to the pack would be having a baby sat sour in her stomach like expired buttermilk.

Her second-born psychic ability was occasionally useful. So what if she only had gut feelings about the future and could rarely give specifics? She'd given the pack a heads up about danger on several occasions. Who knew what would have happened if she hadn't? And she ran this bar and maintained the offices and innerworkings of the pack headquarters. This place would fall apart without her, dammit. She didn't have time to fuss with a man.

Unless that man was Noah.

Fisting her hands, she pressed her knuckles against her brow, squeezing her eyes shut and willing the thoughts away. But her will didn't work on her feelings for her friend any more than it did on easing the tension creeping toward her temples.

Her mother was right about one thing: Noah did have all the qualities of a good mate. He was kind, honest, funny, smart, and… Lately she'd begun to find him physically attractive as well, which was weird. Growing up, even when the other girls in school were fawning over him, she'd never thought of him in that way.

Something had changed in the past year, though, and now she couldn't look at the man without a smile tugging at her lips and warmth blooming in her belly. He had thick, auburn hair she wanted to run her fingers through and dark brown eyes she could imagine sparkling with mischief in the bedroom. A shiver shimmied up her spine.

Maybe it was hormones…what shifters called their mating instinct. Amber's wolf was dormant, but it was possible she still had the reflexes. She was getting dangerously close to thirty, and while the arbitrary deadline placed on her was fabricated by the ancient geezers in the congress, most werewolves did find their mates around this age.

After watching her brother find so much happiness with his fate-bound, Amber decided she would never mate with a shifter unless his wolf claimed her as his own fate-bound. She couldn't take that opportunity away from any man. It wouldn't be fair.

Noah's wolf was dormant too, so it didn't matter that he hadn't claimed her. He wouldn't be claiming anyone. Not as a fate-bound… but perhaps as a soulmate just the same. Even humans believed in that concept, so why not?

Whatever it was, she couldn't deny she had feelings for her best friend. She also couldn't deny the jealousy burning in her chest at the thought of him spending so much time with another woman. He could've at least had the decency to reply to Amber's text and let her know he'd be indisposed for the rest of his life.

Especially after what happened with Nylah. Amber and Noah had both been crushed when his twin went rogue, abandoning them without so much as a goodbye.

It seemed hasty departures ran in the family.

She snatched the pile of papers strewn across her desk and shuffled them into a neat stack, tapping the edge against the wood to even them out. It was time to get her life in order. She had an obligation to the pack, and pining over a man who was obviously not interested in her would only hold her back.

The office phone rang with an internal call, and she hit the speaker button. "Yes?"

"Shipment just came in," Chase said. "If you'll man the bar, I'll move the cases to storage."

"On my way." She ended the call and rose to her feet, stretching her arms above her head before rolling her neck and straightening her spine. Her mother was gone, so she could forget all about the ordeal… until her next visit.

She strode through the hallway into the bar, where Chase had stacked four cases of Abita onto a dolly, and the front door swung open before Luke stepped through. She took two strides toward her brother, but Noah entered the bar behind him. Her heart slammed against her chest, and she froze. He hadn't spoken to her in nearly a month, and *now* he showed up at her bar? *Oh, hell no.*

"You can stay here, Chase. I'll move this to the back." With her foot on the crossbar, she pulled the dolly toward her, angling it onto its wheels.

"You sure?" Chase asked. "It's heavy."

"I've got it." She glanced at Noah, and his eyes brightened. Before she could get sucked into their depths, she trained her gaze on the floor and hurried through the door to the storage room.

CHAPTER THREE

Noah's chest tightened the moment he looked into Amber's crystal blue eyes, all the feelings he had for her—which he'd tried to wad up and shove deep down inside him over the past month—bubbling to the surface and making his heart ache.

He didn't realize how much he'd missed her until now, and when she turned on her heel, hurrying to the back without even acknowledging him, all the effort he'd made to squelch his emotions dissolved like a sugar cube in a cup of hot coffee. *Ouch.*

"Great to have you back, man." Chase nodded from behind the bar, and Noah glimpsed a new tattoo near his collarbone. The letters R and A in a cursive script disappeared behind his shirt, most likely his mate's name: Rain. What else had Noah missed in his absence?

He followed Luke through a side door and down the brick-lined hallway into the alpha's office. His stomach soured as he sank into the green vinyl chair. The last time he set foot in the pack headquarters, he was put on a three-week-long probation—a light sentence for his transgression. He was essentially under house arrest, not allowed to communicate with anyone in the pack, aside from his immediate family, and only allowed to leave his home for work. Even then, he'd had to stay by Luke's side like a puppy on a leash at the jobsites.

Noah worked for Luke's construction company, so lucky him, he got to be babysat by the alpha himself. To say it was humiliating was an understatement.

The police still hadn't found the killer, not that they would. The murder had supernatural written all over it. It was a good thing both the alpha's mate and her brother-in-law were on the human police force. They were able to pull some strings and get Noah released with no charges filed.

Now, he'd served his punishment for breaking pack law, and he could have his life back. Lesson learned.

Luke sat in a black office chair behind the desk, and it squeaked as it absorbed his weight. He opened his laptop, punching a few keys before peering at Noah over the screen. "Your probation is officially lifted. Thanks for complying. You made my job a little easier."

"Yeah, of course." What else could he do but comply? If he'd gotten a wild hair and tried to leave his house, he'd have been thrown in the pit—the werewolf prison. Stephen, the alpha's cousin, spent three months in the pit before his exile, and he nearly went insane from the isolation. Noah shuddered to think about it. "I swear I won't patrol alone anymore. That was a stupid decision."

The alpha grunted. "I shouldn't let you patrol at all. The congress would have my head if they knew a non-shifter had taken on watch duties."

Noah's heart sank. He'd worked his ass off proving he was worthy of his spot on the demon-hunting team. "I'll be careful. I won't hunt without a shifter, and if I'm out alone and see something, I'll call it in."

Luke pressed his lips into a thin line, narrowing his eyes before he nodded. "Screw the congress. Times are changing, and your ability is like no other. There's been another murder. We need all the help we can get." He closed his laptop. "Welcome back."

A flush of relief loosened the tension in his chest, his shoulders relaxing as the weight of yet another possible humiliation lifted. "Thank you. I won't let you down again."

The alpha stood and gestured to the door, so Noah bowed his head and strode into the hallway. Luke followed him toward the bar, but as they passed the storage room, Noah paused. Amber stood on the third rung of a ladder, sliding a case of beer onto a shelf.

"Hey, Luke," she said. "Mom came by and said to tell you 'hi.'"

He chuckled. "How did that go?"

She gave him the stink eye. "Same as before. It would've been nice if you'd been there to help me out."

"Maybe next time." He winked and strode into the bar, but Noah hesitated in the doorway. Amber stepped off the ladder and picked up another case.

"Let me help you with that." Noah sauntered into the room and gripped the box. As his hand brushed hers, her magic vibrated across his skin, sending a jolt straight to his heart. All supernatural beings had a magical signature, and Amber's felt so warm and inviting, he couldn't help but imagine his hands gliding across her bare skin.

She jerked the case away and climbed the ladder. "I don't need help." She shoved the box onto the shelf and turned to pick up the next one, but Noah already had it in his hands.

"I've got nothing better to do." He smiled, which earned him a scowl. "Is everything okay?" He set the box on the shelf, using his power to slide it into place.

Amber huffed and stepped off the ladder. "Oh, so we're pretending like nothing happened?"

"*Did* something happen?" He'd been on probation for three weeks, so whatever it was, he'd missed it.

"Seriously?" she scoffed. "You stood me up on the last full moon and then ghosted me. You think you can come back nearly a month later and act like it never happened? What? Did your new girlfriend dump you?"

"Whoa. Amber, that's not what happened. I didn't ghost you for a woman." He stepped toward her, gently gripping her arm.

Her breath caught as she cast her gaze to where he touched her, but she didn't pull away. "Where were you then?" Her stiff posture relaxed slightly, and she angled her body to face him.

"I ran into trouble patrolling alone, and I got arrested on my way to the bar that night. I've been on probation ever since." He cocked his head. "Wait. You haven't heard from me in three weeks, and you didn't ask anyone what might have happened?"

Her mouth opened and closed before she swallowed hard. "I didn't want to know."

Wow. Okay. He gave her arm a squeeze and released his grip. "I could have been dead."

"Then we would've had a funeral." She shook her head. "I assumed you met someone and were done with me. After Nylah left without saying a word, and then you… I was hurt." She lowered her gaze.

"Hey." He hooked a finger under her chin, lifting her head. "I would never abandon you. Okay?"

"Okay." She looked into his eyes, and something sparked in her gaze.

He couldn't recall her ever looking at him like this before, and it was all he could do to stop himself from leaning in and taking her mouth with his. Judging from the way her body drifted toward him, she might have let him do it.

He cleared his throat, breaking the trance he'd succumbed to. "You really had no idea what happened to me?"

She blinked, stepping back as if trying to shake off the electricity that had just charged between them. "If it was something bad, I would have known. That's kinda my thing."

"True." Amber's gut feelings weren't always about the future. Sometimes, she just *knew* things.

"And with all the summer festivals going on, there have been too many tourists in the bar for the guys to talk openly. Luke and Chase have been hush-hush about pack dealings lately, so I never heard them mention you."

Yet you still didn't bother to ask… That hurt more than he cared to admit.

"I'm sorry to put you through that. Whenever I do meet someone, you'll be the first to know." He winked, attempting to lighten the mood, but the thought of being with anyone but Amber sat heavy in his stomach like his grandmother's meatloaf.

She flashed a tight-lipped smile. "Good to know. I…" Her gaze blanked, and she swayed slightly for a moment before she cocked her head at him. "Have you heard from Nylah at all?"

"Not since the day before she left." He clamped his mouth shut. That was a lie. His sister did leave without saying goodbye in person, but he'd found a note on his nightstand the morning she went rogue. Nylah had written that she couldn't tell him where she was going or why, but she promised to return with an answer to his prayers.

The only prayer he'd had was to activate his dormant wolf gene… something Nylah was determined to make happen. Since then, he'd received several cryptic texts from untraceable numbers that could only have been his sister. *I think I know how to find it; it won't be long now,* and *got it* were just a few of the messages she'd sent.

"I have a weird feeling about her." Amber pulled the band from her hair, slipping it onto her wrist before scratching her head. "I think she might be in trouble. No…she's about to be in trouble."

His pulse raced. "Details? Is she close?"

"I don't…" She squeezed her eyes shut, her face pinching as if she were trying to force the empathic magic to expand. "Maybe?"

"Both of you. In my office." Luke stood in the doorway and jerked his thumb toward the hall, making Noah tense. The alpha did not sound happy.

Amber followed Noah and Luke into the office and sank into a chair. She felt like an idiot for assuming Noah had met someone and tormenting herself for weeks. If she'd asked her brother about him when he didn't reply to her texts, she could have saved herself a world of hurt. That was what she got for acting fickle, and from this point forward, she would behave like the strong, independent woman she was. And she'd start by telling Noah how she felt.

As soon as she worked up the courage.

"Tell me what you're feeling about Nylah." Luke leaned on the edge of his desk. "Do you have any details at all?"

"Not yet. The feeling is still building." She closed her eyes, focusing on the impending doom wriggling in her mind, but it was no use. Her ability never could be forced, and the more she tried to will the feeling to expand, the more mixed signals she'd receive.

Luke nodded, cutting his gaze between her and Noah. "I'm going to let you two in on a secret, but this information is not to leave this room. Understood?"

"Yeah, of course," Noah said, and Amber nodded.

"Nylah didn't go rogue. She's working for the congress."

Amber blinked, and Noah let out a long, slow breath. "Come again?" she said.

"The congress approached all the alphas, asking each pack to nominate a shifter to go undercover. She's been traveling the globe, gleaning magical information and helping stop mayhem before it begins."

She looked at Noah. "Did you know about this?"

He shook his head. "She never said a word."

"She wasn't allowed to." Luke strode around his desk and sank into his chair. "She was instructed to leave in the middle of the night without telling anyone, making it appear like she went rogue. Until now, I was the only person who knew."

A mix of emotions swirled through her chest, taking her from happy to relieved to anxious, all in a matter of seconds. Her lips tugged upward before pulling down into a frown, and her brow furrowed, lifting and lowering. She didn't know what she felt at the moment, but she was positive her old friend was about to find herself in a heap of trouble.

"Do you know where she is?" she asked. "Someone needs to warn her."

"I don't," Luke said. "She isn't allowed to communicate with anyone from the pack, including me."

When Noah shifted in his seat, Luke squared his gaze on him. "You two were always close. Have you been in contact with her?"

"I'm in just as much shock as Amber. I have no idea where she is."

"I'll put a call in to the congress. Amber, if you get any more details, let me know." He dismissed them, and Amber followed Noah into the hallway.

"Do you really not know anything?" she whispered.

A strange look gathered in his eyes like sadness mixed with uncertainty. "She abandoned us both."

"Apparently, she didn't. I don't know what to feel about this news, but I'm glad to know she left without saying goodbye for a reason."

Noah raked a hand through his hair, his mouth opening and closing as if he wanted to say something.

Before he could utter a word, sharp pain flashed in Amber's chest, the sensation like claws dragging down into her stomach. This was not good. *So* not good. She blinked up at Noah. "Whatever's going on with her, it's about to go downhill fast."

CHAPTER FOUR

ALRICK CROUCHED ON THE SIDEWALK NEXT TO A SHOP entrance and ground his teeth as he observed the people in their strange clothing walking about, drinking colorful liquid from peculiar vessels, shouting, and laughing in a most obscene way. He'd never witnessed such debauchery in his entire existence.

He'd also never witnessed so many magical beings residing in one location. His demon side longed to destroy them all. It was what he was built for, but he was still too weak to perform his duties.

Duties he'd shirked for a traitorous witch…

It had been almost a month since he'd last ventured out. The heart he'd consumed then wasn't nearly enough sustenance, and he'd needed time to mend and adjust to life. Consuming another heart would help replenish his strength, but he required the Thropynite stone to restore all his powers. A piece of it was close. He could feel it in his bones.

He closed his eyes, opening his senses as he rubbed the tiny sliver embedded in his chest. The Thropynite—a magical crystal from his homeland of Europe—was the source of his power, the only thing that kept him from turning to stone, but the shard he was gifted long ago wasn't enough to give him life. Another piece had found its way to this continent…to this very city now…awakening him from his slumber.

He would find it.

As he opened his eyes, he took in blue trousers and strange red shoes. Lifting his gaze, he discovered a man smiling at him.

"Nice gargoyle costume, dude. Can I get a picture?"

Alrick growled, swiping a hand at the insolent male. He didn't venture out of his pocket dimension for revelry. He was here for sustenance and information.

The man lifted his fists, bouncing on his toes as he laughed. "Uh-oh, someone wants to fight."

Alrick's lip curled. He didn't sense magic running through the imbecile's veins, but the man reeked of alcohol and cigarettes. That was reason enough to eliminate his existence.

Alrick's bones creaked as he rose to his full six-and-a-half-foot height. It was time he gained the knowledge of the years he'd lost.

"Wow. That costume really is amazing." The man took a step back, but Alrick clutched his shirt.

"What century is this?" His voice grated against his throat like gravel, coming out as more of a croak than words.

"Dude, what's your problem?" The man grabbed his hand, trying to pry his talon-like fingers apart, but even in his weakened state, Alrick's demon soul gave him the strength of fifty men.

"I asked you a question," he rasped before clutching the man by the shoulders and dragging him into the alley next to the building. As he slammed him against the wall, the man's head knocked on the brick before lolling to the side.

"What century is this?" He gripped the sides of the human's face, straightening him, and his eyes fluttered before opening into slits.

"It's the 2000s, man," he muttered.

Alrick grunted. It had been nearly three hundred years since his duplicitous witch left him, taking the Thropynite with her and forcing Alrick and his brothers into slumber. "You will show me all you know."

He tightened his grip, digging his claws into the man's scalp, puncturing first skin and then bone. As the life force oozed from the man's head, Alrick absorbed his memories.

Four decades of life flashed through his mind, the human's knowledge of history filling in the gaps and bringing Alrick up to speed with the current times. How things had changed during his slumber… It was all he could do to not go berserk on these fools and murder them all. They had no inclination of the devilish magic that moved among them.

Releasing his grip from the man's head, Alrick plunged his claws into his chest, ripping out his barely beating heart. As he consumed the organ, his spine straightened, the cracks in his stone-like skin beginning to mend before splitting again, causing him to hunch over in pain.

It was time he returned to his pocket dimension to process the new information he received and formulate his plan to find the stone that had awakened him upon its arrival to this land.

In a flash of magic, he transported himself to the woods on the outskirts of the city, the place he and his brothers had been banished to long ago for their grotesque appearance. He sighed as he gazed at the shimmering film over the entrance to his home and then let out a dry chuckle. It was more of a prison than a home.

As he lifted his hand to swipe aside the magic, he felt it. His back straightened again, and his frigid blood hummed in his veins. The stone was closer than it had ever been before.

A growl rumbled from behind him, and he spun around to find a copper-colored wolf snarling at him. Her muzzle peeled back, revealing sharp fangs, and her intelligent eyes sparkled with magic. This was no normal wolf.

She lunged, latching on to his shoulder with her maw, her teeth piercing his rigid flesh. Alrick spun, grabbing her at her haunches and yanking her from his shoulder.

Whirling in a circle, he slammed her against a tree, snapping her spine before dropping her in the grass. His demon rose to the surface, and drool dripped from his fangs. His sole purpose for the past four centuries had been to rid the world of magic, and he yearned to tear her limb from limb. But as this she-wolf shifted into her human form, a blood-red stone attached to a chain glinted on her chest.

He had found the Thropynite.

CHAPTER FIVE

Amber looked up from her computer as Luke peeked his head into her office. She knew that look. Closing the laptop, she raised her brows, urging him to spill whatever news he had.

He straightened and strolled into the room, shoving his hands into his pockets. "You look nice today." Did she detect relief in his voice?

Sure, she occasionally worked a closing shift at the bar and blew off showering to open the place at five a.m. the next day, but she used dry shampoo and applied an extra layer of deodorant when she did. Shifters had sensitive noses, and she knew better than to offend the pack…or attract the wrong kind of attention…with her bodily odors. Luke would be leaving soon for work, so what did he care how she looked?

"We've got a visitor in from the Houston pack, and I need you to show him the city today. Play tour guide."

She shook her head. "No time. The AC guy is coming in at noon, and we have another shipment from Abita arriving soon. Ask Macey to do it."

"She's working. I already talked to Chase. He'll handle the shipment and the AC repair."

Her nostrils flared as she blew out a breath. Yes, as a member of the alpha family, part of her job was to help entertain important visitors, especially since Luke's mate was a police detective and rarely had time, but it irked her to no end when he meddled in the bar's affairs. This was *her* domain, and if anyone was going to rearrange the schedules, it was her.

She folded her arms on her desk. "And who will man the bar while he's doing all that?"

"Kaci. I had Chase call her. She'll be here in an hour."

Her nails scraped across the wood as she curled her hands into fists. "I'm perfectly capable of juggling the schedule at *my* bar, Luke. You do realize Dad transferred the title to me, right?"

He flashed a sympathetic look that reminded her far too much of their mother's. "You're right, and I apologize for overstepping. Will you do this for me?"

"And here I thought you were coming in with news about Nylah."

"The congress hasn't returned my call."

"Did you talk to Dad? Maybe he can speed things along." Her feeling about Nylah had lessened since yesterday, the danger no longer seeming imminent. Now it felt downright strange, flitting in and out of her consciousness and making her wonder if the premonition was real or if it was brought on by Noah's strong connection to his twin and Amber's intense feelings for Noah. But she couldn't explain that to her brother.

"I did. You'll be the first to know when I hear something. I remember you were close…to both her and Noah." A funny look crossed his face when he mentioned Noah, which meant their mother had spoken to him about her impending mating deadline. And that must've meant…

"Strange timing that we'd get an *important* visitor when a supernatural murderer is on the loose in the city. Did the congress send him?"

Luke shook his head, trying to look innocent and failing miserably. "He's just in town to see what our lovely city has to offer."

"Mm-hmm." She opened her desk drawer and pulled a tube of red lipstick and a mirror from her purse. "I suppose I should look my best to ensure he's impressed by what *our city* has to offer." She ran the lipstick in a circle around her mouth, letting it bleed well past her natural lip line. "And I'll be sure to smile." She caked on another layer before brushing it across her front teeth. "How's this, Brother?"

"Amber… C'mon, he'll be here in a couple of hours, and you look ridiculous." He pulled a tissue from the box on her desk and offered it to her.

She yanked it from his hand, but she didn't wipe her face. "I'm not an idiot. Mom and Dad sent him, didn't they?"

He sighed heavily. "You've only got six months to find a mate, and they know how picky you are. They're covering their bases."

She scoffed. "I'd have expected more from you, Luke. After everything you went through…" She scrubbed the lipstick from her teeth.

"I don't like it any more than you do, but Dad's on the congress now. What do you want me to do?"

"Next time, tell me about it so I can put a stop to it before the guy drives all this way. I'm not a piece of livestock to be bought or a prize to be won. I'm a werewolf, and I'll choose my own mate."

"As long as it's another werewolf." He winked. Of course he could joke about the antiquated law now; he got to mate with his fate-bound.

She rolled her eyes. "Yes, of course."

"Just take the guy to lunch. If he doesn't interest you, then send him on his way."

"I won't hesitate to." She gazed at the clown-like smile she'd drawn on her face and grimaced. *Way to act your age, Amber.* She'd played into the second-born, alpha's little sister role for far too long. She wasn't a damsel in distress, nor did she desire to be. It was time she started acting like the capable woman she was.

"I'll give him a chance, okay?" She set the mirror and tissue on the desk. "And I'll find a mate by my next birthday."

"That's all I ask." Luke smiled and turned to leave, but he paused and gestured to his face. "You might want to…"

"Yeah. I'll clean myself up."

In the bathroom, Amber redid her makeup and ran a brush through her hair before returning to her office to stew while she waited for her "date." She couldn't stay mad at Luke. Their mother was persistent at best, and whether or not Amber found a mate would affect him as well. She just wished her family trusted her to make the right decisions. She wasn't as helpless as they made her out to be, even if she acted like a child every now and then.

Fifteen minutes before John Wilkinson, a high-ranking shifter from the Houston pack, was due to arrive, she strolled into the bar and took a long drink from the beer Chase poured for her. Lord knew she'd need it to endure this. She could only imagine the type of man her father thought would be a suitable mate.

Twenty minutes later, a tall, beefy guy with a shaved head and hard-set eyes sauntered in. He squinted as his vision adjusted to the dim lighting, and Amber took in all six feet of him.

He wore jeans that stretched tight over his muscular thighs, and his biceps looked like they might bust through his shirt sleeves with the slightest flex. She was about to consider the "everything's bigger in Texas" motto when her gaze landed on a belt buckle the size of a dinner plate. *The bigger the buckle, the smaller the…*

He cleared his throat and addressed Chase, not even giving her a glance. "I'm here to meet the alpha's sister."

Chase fought a smile and looked at her.

"The alpha's sister has a name." She rotated her stool to face him, but she didn't bother standing up. "Do you know it?"

He scrunched his brow, looking annoyed that she'd spoken and also confused like he really couldn't recall it.

"I'm Amber Mason." She rose and offered her hand. "You must be John."

He raked his gaze up and down her body before taking her hand in a grip so light he must've thought she was made from porcelain. "Hmm." He cut his gaze toward the half-empty glass on the bar. "Are you drinking beer?" His tone held accusation, which made Amber bristle. She received enough judgment from her family. She didn't need it from this guy too.

"I am." She picked it up and took a giant gulp, her gaze never straying from his eyes.

The disgusted look on his face made it evident he didn't like women who drank beer, but he managed to pull a neutral expression as he said, "I'll join you," to her and then, "Give me your darkest brew," to Chase.

Amber chugged the rest of her beer and set the glass on the bar. "We should get going. I want to make it to the restaurant before the lunch rush." Because she could not stand to wait an hour for a table with this Neanderthal. Based on the two minutes she'd known him, it was obvious he was a controlling wannabe alpha. *So* not her type. What were her parents thinking?

John glanced between Amber and her empty glass before saying, "Let's go then."

She faked a smile and followed him into the sultry summer heat. The sun beat down on her from a cloudless sky as they made their way to The Court of Two Sisters for brunch.

They were seated near a front window at a table draped in white linen, and Amber pretended to peruse the menu while she waited for the waitress to arrive. She'd dined here so many times, she had it memorized, and her mouth watered at the thought of savoring her favorite dish.

Lifting her gaze, she stole a glance at John, her would-be mate, if her parents had their way. Actually, this setup had her father written all over it. She could see how a man like John would seem a perfect mate to someone as old school as her dad. He was strong and dominant, so he'd make a good protector. But as she tried to imagine some positive qualities in John, her mind drifted to thoughts of Noah.

If she were going to be superficial, Noah was ten times hotter than John. He was also kind, friendly, and smart. This guy hadn't smiled once, and she'd bet his giant belt buckle was compensating for more than the appendage below it.

Stop it, Amber. You promised to give the guy a chance. An ice cube's chance at staying cold in hell. She couldn't get her mind off Noah.

The waitress arrived to take their order, and as Amber opened her mouth to speak, John cut her off. "I'll have the steak and eggs, and the lady will have the yogurt parfait."

Whoa, buddy. Did he actually order for her? And the cheapest entrée available, while he got the most expensive?

"No. No, I won't." Amber handed the waitress her menu. "I'll have the shrimp and grits, please."

John frowned as the waitress walked away. "Do you eat like that all the time?"

"Do you always assume you know what your dates want to eat without asking them?" She arched a brow and sipped her water, staring at him over the rim of her glass.

"You'll need to watch your weight. I won't have my mate letting herself go."

"Letting herself—" She clamped her mouth shut. Her actions on this "date" affected more than herself. She was representing her pack, so she'd best get it together and make it through brunch without offending the man.

Clearing her throat, she straightened her spine and plastered on a fake smile. "How long are you in town for?"

"Just today. I leave first thing in the morning. My job is demanding but flexible. I can work from New Orleans."

"Mm-hmm." She feigned interest. "Where are you staying?"

"Your father put me up in the Hotel Monteleone."

"Nice." Of course he did.

Their food arrived, and John told her about his pack in Texas, his job, and his family, not once asking her a question about herself. "My alpha tendencies have caused some friction with leadership, so it'll be good for me to join a pack where I'll actually have some pull."

"I see." She shoveled a mound of grits into her mouth.

"We'll have two children. I prefer to only have one, but the second will be back-up in case the first doesn't survive. I must have a shifting offspring."

In case the first didn't survive? What did he think this was? District Twelve?

"Your hips are a good size for birthing, so I'm not concerned about that."

Birthing… She couldn't help but laugh. He was so far off from being anyone she would even consider taking as her mate.

He frowned. "Your laugh is too high-pitched. Werewolves have sensitive ears, so you'll have to work on toning it down."

She laughed louder, and his expression turned even more sour.

When they finished their meals, John paid the tab and looked into her eyes. "Do you prefer your house or my hotel room?"

"For what?" She had a feeling she knew exactly what for, but she wanted to hear him say it.

"Your father said you prefer a fate-bound mate. It's obvious that's not going to happen between us, and that's a sacrifice I'm willing to make. After some time with me in the bedroom, you'll be willing as well." He said it with a completely straight face, as if he actually believed he had a magic dick.

This time, she snorted when she laughed.

Noah sauntered alongside Cade down Royal Street, the midday sun nearly unbearable as he chugged the rest of his sweet tea and tossed the paper cup into a trash can. His friend wore shorts and a loose tank, much more suitable clothing for the Louisiana heat than Noah's jeans and heavy work boots. Sweat beaded on his forehead, dripping into his eyes as he stepped around a group of tourists gathering on the sidewalk.

"I'm glad you could get away on your lunch break." Cade swept a lock of blond hair off his forehead. "I haven't seen you in ages."

"Nearly a month." Noah continued his trek toward the building his crew was remodeling.

"I almost asked Luke for a job so I could make sure my buddy was really okay."

Noah laughed. "I bet that would have gone over well with your boss."

Cade shrugged. "He let me take the day off today. I could've finagled a few more 'mental health' days if I needed to. James assured me you were still alive though."

"Thanks for checking up on me." Noah's brow pinched. At least his buddy had inquired about him in his absence. "Amber didn't bother to ask." He clamped his mouth shut. His sulking was better done in privacy.

"You're still hung up on her? Have you seen her since your probation ended?"

He crossed the street to avoid the crowd watching a musician play the saxophone. Elegant music drifted on the air, and the spicy scent of boiling crawfish drifted out from a restaurant. "Yeah. She assumed I was spending all my time with a woman."

Cade clapped him on the shoulder. "Sounds to me like she didn't ask because she was jealous."

"Doubtful."

"Have you told her how you feel?"

"You know what happened when I tried."

"Damn." Cade stopped walking and peered into the window of The Court of Two Sisters. "I was going to suggest you try again, but this might be the reason why she wasn't concerned. Look."

Noah strode toward him, stopping in his tracks when he saw the view. Amber sat across from a barrel-chested male with a shaved head. She laughed so hard, she wiped a tear from her eye, and Noah's heart wrenched in his chest.

He huffed, turning on his heel and stomping away. Why the hell was he doing this to himself? She'd made it clear she wanted nothing more than friendship from him, yet he'd held on to a tiny spark of hope. Gods only knew why. As if he could actually awaken his dormant wolf with some made-up magic he read about online. *Get over it, man.*

"Hey, don't sweat it." Cade jogged to catch up. "If you mated with her, you'd have to deal with all the politics of being in the alpha family. That would be a pain in the ass."

"You're right. She's out of my league."

"That's not what I meant."

"Doesn't matter. I've got to get back to work."

"Let's go out tonight. With James mated and you on probation, I've had to fly solo the past month, and that's not nearly as fun. You wanna play wingman? Get your mind off things?"

Noah started to say "no," but a night out with Cade might be just what he needed. Lord knew he had to get over Amber as quickly as he could. She'd be mated within the next six months, and it wouldn't be to him.

CHAPTER SIX

"WITCHES," ALRICK GROWLED LOW IN HIS THROAT. HE DESPISED witches...detested them. Of all the magical beings he was created to eradicate, he loathed witches the most. Three hundred years in suspended animation could do that to a man.

A trio of the odious creatures strolled down Dauphine Street, laughing and carrying on as if they belonged in this wretched city. As if they deserved to live. He'd made the mistake of allowing one's existence to continue, and he had regretted it ever since. He wouldn't let it happen again. As soon as he regained his strength, he'd banish every last one of them from the face of the earth.

When they reached a pale green two-story with white trim and a wrought-iron balcony, the witches turned down St. Philip and disappeared through an alley entrance. Perfect. They'd secluded themselves so he could do his job in privacy.

"Oh, check out his costume. I want a picture." A human woman stumbled toward him before he could follow the witches, and Alrick curled his lip.

The strangeness of this city allowed him to be seen near the vile street they called Bourbon without causing alarm, but the inebriated lacked the inhibitions to stay away from danger. Their ignorance was maddening.

"Come on, babe. We'll get a picture tomorrow." At least her escort was in his right mind. He guided her away, and Alrick strode across the street to track the witches.

He grasped the handle of the green door that led into the alley, but he found it locked. No sound drifted toward him, which meant the revolting creatures had already ventured inside their dwelling. Good. This would offer him even more privacy to take his time and enjoy their demise.

With a shove, he wrenched the door open and slipped into the alley. A staircase scaled the side of the building, and a potted fern adorned the second-floor landing. He took the steps three at a time, inhaling deeply when he reached the top. The faint scent of witches, warm and herbal, assaulted his nostrils, and a tinge of something… other…lingered in the air. He couldn't place the supernatural aroma, but it didn't matter. He would eradicate New Orleans of *all* magic.

Ramming his shoulder against the door, he busted it open and stormed into a small living room. One woman screamed, and a man scrambled to the opposite end of the sofa, while the second woman lunged for a bottle on a shelf.

She uncorked it and chanted a spell. What magic she believed would stop a gargoyle, he didn't know, and he almost paused to witness her display of power before he killed her. But the other witch's screams had surely alerted the neighbors to his presence, so he grasped her neck, snapping her vertebrae in his grip and crushing her trachea.

The man lunged, but Alrick simply swung his arm, his stone-like fist shattering his skull and sending him careening to the floor. His mouth watered, the demon inside him screaming for sustenance, so he lifted the dying man from the floor and plunged his talons into his chest, ripping out his heart.

"Jasper!" the witch wailed and dropped to her knees.

Alrick snarled and threw the bloodied, limp body across the room. It crashed through the window and tumbled head over feet to the sidewalk below.

"Look what you made me do, enchantress." Alrick's anger seethed, the memory of another witch's betrayal fueling the fire in his blackened soul. He lunged for her, biting into her neck and severing the pulsing artery. Blood sprayed from the wound, and she gurgled, sucking in a dying breath.

As she lay on the floor, bleeding out, Alrick consumed the man's heart. He shivered as the organ slid down his throat, and he closed his eyes, allowing himself a moment to bask in the feel of his body being restored.

But the shouts of panic from outside interrupted his pleasure. Law enforcement would swarm the apartment soon, and he hadn't yet gained the strength to withstand their weapons. He plunged his talons into the women's chests, taking their hearts, and silently slipped out the door before rushing down the stairs and escaping in a flash of magic.

"What about those two?" Cade tipped his beer bottle toward a pair of blondes at the bar, but all Noah saw was an image of Amber's face as she laughed at whatever the shifter she was dating had said. It had been ages since he'd seen her laugh that hard, and the thought of another man bringing her so much joy gnawed in his gut like termites in an abandoned wood shack, eating away at him from the inside out.

A band took the stage and played a smooth jazz tune, and Noah cast his gaze toward the bar. Rows of liquor bottles lined the shelves, and a massive mirror hung above them, reflecting the revelry in the room. People smiled and laughed, but Noah couldn't stop his frown.

He set his half-empty beer on the table. He should've been happy for Amber. He *was* happy for her. Well, at least he would try to be. "Sorry, man. I'm not feeling it tonight."

Cade sighed as two men approached the ladies he'd set his sights on. "Yeah. Neither am I. You wanna jet?"

Noah nodded and headed for the door. When they reached the sidewalk, a hawker holding a sign that read *Big Ass Beer* shouted at them, motioning for them to enter the club across the street. Noah ignored the man and hung a right, but he cut across the street to avoid passing in front of the strip club where his trouble began. Two extra bouncers stood outside with the women, and he recognized the one who'd pinned him to the wall. He wouldn't be going anywhere near that place for a while…if ever again.

Thick clouds blanketed the dark sky, and the sweltering summer air clung to his skin like a wet electric blanket. The crowds of Bourbon Street thinned the deeper into the Quarter they ventured, the clubs and shops giving way to residences with window baskets overflowing with flowers. Here, the night felt peaceful, but as they made their way toward St. Philip Street, a blood-curdling scream pierced the night.

"Holy shit! Call 911." A man pulled the screaming woman to his chest and took his phone from his pocket.

Instinct drew Noah toward the commotion, but he hesitated. His protective nature was what had landed him on probation last month, and he wasn't about to make that mistake again. Cade didn't falter. He picked up the pace, striding toward Dauphine Street as if he were the police himself.

"Oh, hell." Noah jogged to catch up. Instinct was impossible to fight for long. "Need some help, folks?" he asked as he approached the couple, but the last word got stuck in his throat.

A man lay on the sidewalk in front of a pale green two-story, his lifeless eyes frozen wide in shock, a gaping, bloody hole in his chest where his heart should have been. *Not again.*

"Son of a bitch. I know him." Cade fisted his hands and tilted his head up to sift through the scents in the air.

"Who is he?" Noah asked.

"His name's Jasper. He's a second-born from the Biloxi pack, studying at Tulane. I've hung out with him a couple of times."

"This makes four," Noah said under his breath. A crowd began to form around the body, and sirens blared in the distance. "We've got to go."

Cade's jaw ticked as he ground his teeth. "It's personal now."

"Come on." Noah grabbed his arm. The last thing he needed was to be caught by the human police with a victim from the same murderer. "Let's go find the bastard."

Cade nodded, lifting his nose again as they strode away from the fray. "Do you smell that?"

Noah inhaled deeply, and the faintest scent of rotting garbage reached his senses. "Either someone threw out some rancid meat, or we've got a demon on our hands."

"It gets stronger this way." Cade took off down St. Philip, and Noah followed.

They zig-zagged through the streets of the French Quarter, the scent of demon intensifying in some areas and then dissipating as they moved toward it.

"It's like the bastard disappears," Noah said. "He's not leaving a trail."

"Some demons can do that. They teleport." Cade motioned for Noah to follow him down Burgundy. "If this guy has that kind of magic, it means he's a strong one."

Strong enough to rip the hearts from his victims and disappear without a trace. The pack had their work cut out for them this time. They caught another whiff of demon scent, and as they followed it toward St. Louis Cemetery Number One, a sinking sensation formed in the pit of Noah's stomach. It had been weeks since Nylah's last text. What if she had met the same fate as Jasper, but no one had found her body?

No, he refused to entertain the idea. He had to focus on the issue at hand, which was the fact that their noses had led them straight to the city of the dead.

"What is it with monsters always hiding out in the cemetery?" Noah pulled a file from his pocket, which he always kept on hand for situations like this, and picked the lock. He and Cade slipped inside, and he shut the gate behind them, setting the lock so it looked closed to anyone who might walk by.

They paused at the entrance, listening for any signs of movement within the stone walls. Row after row of above-ground graves created a maze inside the single square-block cemetery, with multiple generations of New Orleanians entombed in each one. Some were well taken care of, with pristine white plaster and flowers adorning the façades, while others appeared weathered, the brick and mortar exposed to the elements after years of neglect.

"That's a new one." Cade nodded toward a massive gargoyle sitting a few yards away.

Noah peered at it through the darkness. If he didn't know any better, he'd say it had blood running down its chin. "It's old enough for mildew stains. Look at its face."

"True," Cade said. "Guess I haven't been here in a while. Meet you in ten?"

"Howl if you find anything."

Cade slipped between a row of tombs and shifted into his wolf, while Noah strode in the opposite direction, weaving between the graves. The rancid scent of demon was strong, so the fiend had at least been here recently, if he wasn't still inside. Noah's half of the cemetery turned up no results, but as he made his way toward the entrance, something felt off. He turned in a circle, taking in his surroundings.

The gargoyle was gone.

A grunt sounded behind him, and Noah spun to find what he'd mistaken as a statue rising to its full height and smelling of fiend. Before he could shout for Cade, the demon planted both hands against Noah's chest, shoving him backward into a tomb. His head hit the brick with a smack, and his vision swam.

Cade barreled in with his teeth bared and plowed toward the demon. The fiend grunted again, taking off in the opposite direction, and Noah scrambled to his feet to give chase. He ran after Cade, but the wolf stopped abruptly, jerking his head around with his ears pricked.

Noah froze, listening, but the demon didn't give away his location. He crept down one aisle, while Cade prowled another. He turned, going up another row and down the next. When they met in the center of the cemetery, Cade shifted to human, his wolf's body shimmering with magic as he transformed.

"The bastard disappeared." Cade pulled his phone from his pocket. "I'll call Luke. You let Macey know the cops were called."

"I'm on it." Noah dialed her number and said a silent prayer to whatever gods might be listening that, wherever she was, Nylah wouldn't cross paths with this fiend.

CHAPTER SEVEN

Amber sat in a green vinyl chair next to Noah in Luke's office. It was six a.m., and the citrusy scent of his shampoo still lingered in his hair. She leaned on the arm of the chair, drifting closer to him and breathing in his intoxicating scent.

Her mating instincts must've been kicking in hard. Noah had always smelled good, but damn. She wanted to wrap herself up and get lost in him…unlike the Neanderthal her father had set her up with yesterday.

She'd managed to rein in her laughter and politely inform him that sex would not change her mind about the pairing, but he'd left New Orleans none too pleased. Once word spread of her rejecting such a "viable male," no doubt the race would be on to see who could win her hand. Wouldn't that be fun? *No, not really.*

Noah looked at her, arching a brow in question, and she realized she was leaning way too close to him. She sat up straight, and her head spun like it always did when her empathic premonitions were about to reveal themselves. Clutching the arms of the chairs, she braced herself for the ominous feeling about Nylah to slam into her psyche, but it didn't come.

This premonition was about Noah. *Change.* Something about him was going to change. She dug in deep, settling into the feeling and hoping against hope that her ability would reveal more.

It didn't.

She blew out a hard breath. Leave it to her to have a gut feeling about the one man she could imagine spending her life with, yet all her ability told her was "change."

"Are you okay?" Noah's gaze held concern. "Did you get something more on Nylah?"

"No." She rubbed her chest. "I think it's heartburn." There was no point in sharing what she'd just felt about him. Change could come in so many forms. Maybe it simply meant their relationship would finally turn back to normal. He'd been acting strangely around her well before his probation, and it was time she got to the bottom of it.

"The full moon is tomorrow," she said. "Will you be joining us this time?"

Indecision tightened his eyes as he held her gaze, and the tendons in his neck tensed like he was grinding his teeth.

Why was he acting so weird? "It's a simple yes or no question."

"Yeah. Yeah, of course I'll be there." He straightened. "Why wouldn't I be?"

She narrowed her eyes. "What's going on?"

"What do you mean?"

She gestured from herself to him. "This awkwardness between us. Where is it coming from?"

He let out a nervous laugh. "I've been gone for nearly a month, and you thought I'd abandoned you, so…"

"No, this started before all that. A few months before, actually. If it's because I started flirting with you, I'm sorry."

He blinked, missing a beat in his reply. "When did you start flirting with me?"

"Well, I didn't, but I wanted to until you got all weird. I thought maybe I'd flirted by accident with the way you've been acting."

"Why would…?" He clamped his mouth shut and shook his head. "*I* started to flirt with *you*, and you shot me down, so I backed off."

"When did I shoot you down?"

His brow rose like he couldn't believe what he was hearing.

Honestly, she couldn't believe it herself. "You said you were glad we were friends because you knew I wasn't after you for your pack status. I know when I've been relegated to the friendzone."

"Relegat—" She huffed. "That's not what I meant by that."

"Sure sounded like it." He cast his gaze to the wall in front of him.

Amber chewed the inside of her cheek and stared at his profile. He had a strong jawline, with coarse auburn hair peppering his skin. He closed his eyes for a long blink, and the air conditioner hummed as the fan kicked on, filling the room with cool air.

"Noah…" She clutched his hand. "I meant that as a compliment. I thought we were becoming more than friends, and I meant I was glad I could trust you. That I could date you without having to worry that you only wanted me to give you an alpha child."

His lips twitched like he was having trouble forming the right words.

"Why didn't you say anything?" she asked.

"Probably for the same reason you didn't ask about me when I was gone. Wounded pride." He shook his head and leaned away from her. "It doesn't matter. You seemed happy with the guy you had lunch with yesterday. Is he going to be your mate?"

Jesus, word travels fast. "How did you know about that?"

"I saw you through the window, laughing. He must be a funny guy. I'm happy for you."

"Are you?" She bit her bottom lip. If anything, he seemed jealous. "Noah, I was laughing *at* him, not with him. He was half-cowboy/half-caveman. I sent him packing as soon as I could."

The door swung open, and she jerked her hand back into her lap.

"I'll make this quick," Luke said as he strode into the office and sat behind his desk. "We're behind at the jobsite, and we need to head there immediately."

Noah straightened, lowering his gaze slightly, showing respect for the alpha. Amber leaned forward in her chair.

"The body you and Cade found last night wasn't the only one. There were two more in the apartment above."

"Christ," Noah said. "Any of ours?"

Luke shook his head. "Witches again. Until this is resolved, no non-shifters are allowed on the streets in the Quarter after dark, Noah and Macey excluded." He looked at Amber. "Are we clear?"

She nodded. "What did you learn about Nylah?"

"She missed her last check-in," Luke said. "The congress hasn't heard from her in a week."

Amber's stomach sank. While the feeling of impending doom for Nylah had passed, something still felt off about her. Like she was out of danger for now…or the threat had already come and passed…but she was standing on a slippery slope.

"Do they know where she might be?" Noah asked. "Where was she when she last checked in?"

"She was in Mississippi last month," Luke said. "After they read the report of the murder you discovered, she was ordered to New Orleans. She hasn't made contact since."

Amber looked at Noah. "Have your parents heard from her? Surely she'd at least contact them if she was in town."

Noah started to answer, but Luke cut him off. "They haven't, and that's no surprise. National agents are forbidden from contacting anyone in their pack."

"Why was she sent here?" Amber asked. "We've never needed the congress to get involved with supernatural policing."

Luke shook his head. "No, we haven't, but this is where things get weird. She was sent to investigate the reappearance of the Grunch."

Noah cocked his head. "I thought that was nothing more than an urban legend."

"Me too," Amber added. "It was made up by kids as an excuse to scare their friends. You drive down Grunch Road, and if you see a goat, the cannibal dwarves will come out and eat you."

"I thought it was an urban legend as well, but the congress assures me it's not. After the demon Noah and Cade encountered last night, I believe it." Luke opened his laptop and punched a few keys. "The Grunch are human-demon hybrid abominations created by a European religious sect centuries ago. They fused demon souls with an army of human warriors and used a magical crystal called Thropynite to give them shifting abilities. They transformed into gargoyle-like creatures—like the fiend you and Cade encountered—and swept through towns and villages, murdering magical beings."

"Are you serious?" she asked.

Luke nodded. "A group of them somehow made it to New Orleans, and that's where the Grunch legend began. No one has seen hide nor tail of them in centuries, but it looks like something woke them."

Amber glimpsed Noah from the corner of her eye, and he'd gone pale.

"Thropynite is real…" He stared straight ahead, not seeming to focus on anything for a moment before he blinked and shook his head. "I've heard stories about it, but I thought it was legend too."

"It was destroyed more than one hundred years ago," Luke said, "but someone stole a sizeable shard and has been selling pieces on the black market. If some made it to the US, it could have awakened the creatures who came here centuries ago."

"Holy crap." Amber slumped in her seat.

"Tell me about it," Luke said.

"We need to find the Grunch. They must have my sister." Noah fisted his hands on his lap, and Amber placed her hand on top of his.

"Her trouble might not even be related to that. I haven't had any feelings connecting the two, so she might just be indisposed. Whatever it is, we'll find her; won't we, Luke?" She shot her brother a hard look.

"If we are dealing with the gargoyle shifters, they only operate at night." He looked at Noah. "I want you and Cade to head to the Grunch Road area at sundown to see what you can find."

"I'll go with them. She's my friend too."

"No, you will not." Luke arched a brow at her. "Noah and Macey are the only non-shifters with permission to patrol."

She straightened her spine. "Then don't call it patrolling. Call it looking for my friend."

"As your alpha, I forbid it." His gaze softened. "And as your brother, I'm asking you nicely not to. Please, Amber. They've already killed one second-born. I won't risk it happening to you."

She pursed her lips, glancing at Noah before returning her gaze to

Luke. She'd concede this time. Her second-born ability wasn't intended for fighting, and her presence could put Noah and Cade at risk if they felt like they had to protect her…which they would. They all treated her like she was fragile, and that irked her to no end. "All right. But keep me posted."

"You do the same if you get any more details from your premonitions." He stood and motioned to the door. "Let's get to work."

Amber rose and touched Noah's arm. "I'll see you tomorrow night, right?"

He nodded absently. "Yeah. I'll be here."

Noah parked his Chevy along the side of Grunch Road and killed the engine before sliding out of the truck and closing the door. Cade and James joined him near the ditch, and all three men stared up at the nearly full moon. A wispy patch of clouds stretched across it, the light giving it a silvery glow against the inky sky, and the summer air was warm and muggy against his skin.

James, the senior shifter and lead wolf on the demon-hunting team, jerked his head toward the trees, indicating they should follow him into the woods. Dead leaves and twigs crunched beneath Noah's boots as he paced behind the two shifters. The atmosphere felt thicker in this part of the swamp, almost as if he could slice it open and get lost inside.

"It's quiet," Noah said. "Do y'all ever hunt out here?"

"Never," James said. "This place has bad energy. Even Odette was worried about us coming out here."

"I'm surprised she let you," Cade said with a wink, which earned him an irritated glare.

"My mate communes with the spirit of death. When she has a concern, I listen to her."

Cade chuckled, running a hand through his short blond hair as he turned to Noah. "Have I told you how glad I am to have you back? This old geezer would rather stay home than go out anymore."

"Someday, when you find your fate-bound, you'll understand," James said.

Noah faked a laugh. "At least I'll never have to worry about having a ball and chain that heavy."

Cade clapped him on the shoulder. "Lucky you."

Yeah, right. His friends had no idea how badly he wanted the ability to have a fate-bound. Especially after his last conversation with Amber. Luke had interrupted them before they could finish, but that was probably for the best. Noah could never be the werewolf she needed…that she deserved…but he had to admit learning she might have feelings for him sent a thrill rushing through his veins.

Hell, it was more than a thrill. Amber reached all the way to his soul.

They trudged deeper into the woods, until Cade lifted a hand and stopped. "This is where the Grunch supposedly lived. Are your Wonder Twin powers picking up on anything? Can you sense Nylah?"

Closing his eyes, Noah sucked in a deep breath and opened his senses. The energy around him pricked at his skin, palpable and thick. But aside from the foreboding pressure in the air and the low vibration giving the area its bad vibe, he felt nothing. Nylah wasn't there.

He tugged a flashlight from his pocket and shined the beam into the clearing. "Y'all go do your thing. I'll have a look around here and see what I can find."

"We'll meet back in fifteen," James said before calling on his magic and shifting into his wolf. Dark gray fur rolled down the length of his massive body, and as his front paws hit the ground, he took off running.

"See ya on the flip side." Cade shifted and followed James, bounding deeper into the swamp and leaving Noah alone with the sickening thoughts that had plagued him since Luke mentioned the Thropynite.

From the moment Noah turned thirteen and his wolf gene failed to activate, Nylah had become obsessed with finding a way to unlock it for him. She felt guilty being the only shifting wolf when they should have shared the magic, and she'd gone to great lengths, trying numerous experiments to reverse the outcome of his delayed birth.

When the local witches couldn't cast a spell to help him, she'd scoured the dark web, consulting with black magic practitioners to find a way to change Noah's fate. But when fate dealt your hand, you had no choice but to play the cards you were given.

In her research, she'd come across the legend of the Thropynite. Supposedly, if a non-shifting were held a piece, the stone would activate their dormant gene, awakening the wolf inside them. She and Noah made a pact that they would do everything they could to find it.

In her absence—or maybe before she left—Nylah must have learned of its actual existence. That was what her cryptic texts were about. It was the only explanation.

Noah grunted, switching off his flashlight and returning it to his pocket. If she got her hands on a piece of Thropynite, that would certainly be the answer to his prayers. But there was no telling what kind of trouble she might have gotten herself into trying to obtain it. Black market dealings were shady at best, downright deadly at worst, and if she'd used her status as a spy for the national congress to obtain it, she could be looking at threats from both sides.

He'd never forgive himself if he was the reason Nylah was in danger. And if the Grunch really had awakened because the Thropynite was here, then he and Nylah were to blame for the recent murders. *Holy hell.*

He sent a text to the last number she'd messaged him from, but he got no reply, not that he expected one. Every text she sent had come from a different number. No doubt they were burner phones, which she discarded frequently to avoid being traced.

Footsteps sounded to his left, and Noah dragged out the flashlight again, shining it into the trees where Cade and James approached in human form.

"Nothing out of the ordinary," Cade said. "Did you find anything?"

A crack in a thick trunk drew Noah's attention to the right, and he strode toward the tree. "Check this out."

The ground beneath the branches had been disturbed recently, the grass flattened to indicate something had been dragged a short distance. James ran his hand along the trunk, peeling away a piece of loose bark as he examined the damage.

"Some kind of fight happened here," he said before he straightened and angled his nose upward to catch the breeze. "It could've been anything. Bobcats, boar…hell, even gators venture this far onto dry land sometimes."

"Yeah, and I know Nylah," Cade said. "She'd have put up a helluva fight if she were in trouble, so she either won this scuffle, or it wasn't her."

"You're right." Noah jerked his head toward his truck and trudged back to the road. Nylah was tough; she could take care of herself. He wouldn't have been worried about her at all if not for Amber's initial empathic premonition of trouble.

And a nagging feeling in the back of his mind said he was the reason for all of it.

CHAPTER EIGHT

AMBER GLANCED AT THE CLOCK AND DRUMMED HER FINGERS ON the bar. Where the hell was Noah? She'd convinced Kaci to come in early and cover her shift, and now the man had the nerve to stand her up after their conversation was cut short yesterday morning? *So not cool.*

Her feelings for Noah weren't just bubbling to the surface; they'd reached a full-blown boil, and she'd be damned if she'd let a miscommunication come between them again.

She'd been thinking about it all day, rolling every scenario she could imagine around in her mind, and they all led to one conclusion. She needed to be up front with Noah. Just lay it all out, tell him how she felt, and demand…in a nice way…that he be honest about where they stood. What did she have to lose?

Her best friend, for one thing. But keeping her feelings for him bottled up was eroding her psyche from the inside out. It was best to rip off the duct tape and spill it all. If he didn't feel the same and their friendship didn't survive, then it wasn't as rock-solid as she thought.

"Are you okay?" Her sister-in-law, Macey, rested a hand on top of hers, stilling her incessant drumming. "You're lucky your nails are short, or you'd have dug holes in the bar by now."

Amber bit her lip and fisted her hand. "Why don't men say what's on their minds? Why do they make assumptions and then shut down?"

Macey laughed. "I think they probably ask the same questions about women."

"I guess you're right."

"Noah?"

She looked at the clock again. "He should be here by now. I think I scared him off."

"He doesn't seem like the type to scare easily." Macey swiveled in her seat to face her, resting an elbow on the bar. "What happened?"

"We were talking yesterday morning before our meeting with Luke, and he—" Amber's gaze snapped toward the door as Noah sauntered in. He wore jeans with a tight gray t-shirt, looking sexy as hell.

One corner of his mouth lifted into a crooked smile as he caught her gaze, and she willed her frantically beating heart to slow. All but one lock of his auburn hair fell perfectly into place, the errant strand curving down across his forehead, drawing her attention to his deep brown eyes. *Damn.* The lid was off the pot, and she was boiling over.

"Not scared after all." Macey gave her a conspiratorial wink before sipping her beer.

As Noah made his way toward Amber, she slid off her stool and met him halfway across the floor. She needed to start this conversation as soon as possible, before she chickened out, and here in the bar, with a dozen second-borns and non-were mates as witnesses, was not the place to do it.

"Hey." His smile widened as she approached.

"Let's get out of here." As she clutched his hand, his magical energy joined with hers, shimmying up her arm and hitting her heart with a jolt. She froze, her head spinning as the feeling of change for Noah that she'd felt this morning intensified.

His brow furrowed. "Everything okay?"

Something was about to change as soon as she confessed her feelings. Hopefully it would be for the better. She shook her head to chase away the dizzying sensation the premonition caused. "Yeah. We haven't hung out in forever, so I thought we could grab a six-pack and head to the park."

He hesitated, glancing at the bar before looking into her eyes. "Okay. My truck's two blocks away. I'll drive."

They stopped by a convenience store to pick up some Blue Moon beer before heading toward City Park. She smiled as he stopped in the lot and slid out of the truck. She'd only said, "the park," yet he'd known the exact place she meant. How many times had they come out here as teens, lounging beneath the massive oaks, drinking beer Amber had swiped from the storeroom when her mom and dad ran the bar?

Noah opened the door and grinned. "What?"

"I was thinking about the time Nylah bumped me with her shoulder. She didn't know her own strength yet, and if you hadn't used your power to catch me, I'd have fallen into the lake." She stepped out of the truck and shut the door.

He shook his head. "Yeah, but I couldn't control it, remember? I threw you back into the bramble. By the time we untangled you from the mess, you were seething."

"I wasn't *that* mad."

He laughed. "Yes, you were."

"Okay, I was." But she got over it. She could never stay mad at Noah.

They made their way to an arched stone bridge and stood at the top, overlooking the stream below. Noah opened a beer and handed it to her before getting one for himself and clinking the can against hers.

"We've had some good times out here, haven't we?" he asked.

"We have." She turned around, resting her back against the railing. He stood next to her, still facing the water, close enough that she could smell his woodsy, masculine scent. Her stomach fluttered, and a slight nauseating sensation rolled through her core.

"Noah, I wanted to talk to you…" She looked at him, and he rubbed his chest, his face pinching with pain. "Are you okay?"

He rolled his shoulders, stretching his neck. "I'm fine. What did you want to talk about?"

"Us."

He raised his brow. "What about us?"

"Yesterday, you said I'd relegated you to the friendzone."

"Ah." He turned around, matching her posture. "It's okay. Really."

"It's not though. I don't want you to be in the friendzone." She held her breath, anticipating his response.

"Well." He blew out a hard breath before taking a swig of beer. Then he opened his mouth like he wanted to say something, but he clamped it shut again.

She'd officially ripped off the duct tape. She might as well keep the confession flowing. "My feelings for you have changed, Noah. I can't be near you without my stomach fluttering; I think about you all the time when we're apart. I'm falling for you…for my best friend. Is that crazy?"

He set his beer can on the railing and faced her. "Amber…"

The fluttering in her stomach rose to her chest, coming out as something between a sob and a laugh. She should have kept her mouth shut. It was months ago when he thought she shut him down. He'd probably gotten over it and moved on. It was stupid of her to think, after all these years, their feelings for each other would bloom at the same time.

She nodded and set her can next to his. "It's okay. If you're not falling for me too, just tell me. We'll go back to being friends, and we can pretend like this conversation never happened.

He held her gaze, and a strange look formed in his eyes. "I'm not falling for you."

Her breath caught, and she swallowed the lump that crept into her throat. "Okay." That six-month deadline seemed a lot more ominous all of a sudden.

He tucked her hair behind her ear before resting his hand on her shoulder. "I fell a long time ago, and I never got back up."

Her heart couldn't decide if it wanted to stop or beat right out of her chest. Her best friend had fallen for her, and she for him. Pressure built in the back of her eyes, her throat thickening as another sob-laugh threatened to escape. "Why didn't you say something sooner? You know what? It doesn't matter." She took his face in her hands and kissed him.

He froze for a moment, and she almost pulled away. But before she could chide herself for jumping the gun, he slid his arms around her waist and kissed her back. A low moan escaped his throat as he tugged her tighter against his body, and when he coaxed her lips apart with his tongue, she couldn't help but lean into him and revel in the feel of his embrace.

That wasn't so hard, was it? She glided her hands over his shoulders and down his back, memorizing the way his muscles felt beneath her palms. His body was warm and hard in all the right places, and the coarseness of the scruff on his face contrasted with the softness of his lips.

He slipped his hand beneath the back of her shirt, and though it was rough from work, his touch was a gentle caress. With a deep inhale, he gripped her hips, first pressing his pelvis into hers and then gently pushing her away. "We can't do this."

She touched her fingers to her swollen lips. The taste of him lingered on her tongue, and she wanted more. "Should we head back to the truck?"

"No, I…" He raked a hand through his hair before fisting his hands on the bridge railing and staring up at the full moon. "I mean we can't do *us*."

"Did I move too fast? I figured, since we know each other so well, we didn't need to wait for our second date to kiss." She let out a nervous laugh, trying to lighten the mood.

He gripped the edge of the railing so tight his knuckles turned white. "Don't get me wrong. That kiss was amazing. *You* are amazing, but I can't… You shouldn't waste your time with me."

"Who says I would be wasting my time?"

"I do. Everyone would if we started dating. You were right when you said I wasn't interested in your alpha blood, but your alpha blood is the reason *you* shouldn't be interested in me."

"I don't understand." Well, really, she knew exactly what he was getting at, but she wanted to hear the words from him. Surely he didn't believe what he was hinting.

"You should mate with a shifting wolf."

Damn. He believed it. "Tell me why you think that."

"You know why, Amber."

She shook her head, lifting one shoulder in a dismissive shrug. "No, I don't. Please explain to me why you think you…or anyone else…knows whom I should mate with better than me." The words came out sharper than she'd intended, but she was done hiding her irritation about this subject. Noah, of all people, should have understood that.

"Your firstborn will be a shifting wolf who will hold rank in the pack. He should have at least one shifting parent."

"Oh, so you're saying you're not wolf enough to make up for my inadequacies. Is that it? That I won't be a good mother without a shifter telling me how to raise my kid? Do you hear yourself?"

"That's…" He winced and rubbed his chest. "No, that's not what I'm saying."

"What are you saying then? I'm listening."

"You deserve a fate-bound. That's something I can never be for you. I wish I could. I'd give my soul to be able to shift, but since my wolf is dormant, I… You deserve more."

"The only person who feels this way is you. Even my mother asked about you the other day, dropping a not-so-subtle hint that you would make a good mate. So if there's something else, you should say so because I'm not buying what you're selling."

"Don't you want to experience that kind of unconditional love? Isn't it worth waiting for?"

"I see. Now you're saying you can't love me unconditionally without magic sealing our fates. Plenty of people—werewolves included—find their happily ever afters without a fate-bound."

"I know. You're right…"

"And I'll tell you something else since we're on the subject of fate-bounds. *I* would never take a shifter as my mate unless his wolf claimed me, and guess what? I know every shifter in the pack, and not one of them has had even an inkling of a bond forming with me…not even the caveman my dad set me up with. I refuse to take away a shifter's chance at finding his fate-bound. They're all more interested in my status than my good looks and charming personality anyway."

He grinned. "You're awfully cute when you get on a roll like this. You always have been."

She narrowed her eyes. "No one—not you, not Luke, and especially not my mom or dad—is going to tell me whom I should be with. I will mate with a werewolf before my thirtieth birthday because I have to, but that were does *not* have to be a shifter. It probably won't be, but if you still think I'd be wasting my time by dating you, then say so now."

"You are—" He doubled over, clutching his stomach and groaning.

"Noah?" She gripped his shoulders. "What's wrong?"

"I don't know." As he straightened, he swayed, knocking his hip against the rail and nearly tumbling over into the water below.

Amber grabbed his arm, tugging him back onto the bridge. "Is it your stomach? Your head? Tell me what I can do."

"It's everything. It's…oh god." He doubled over again, this time landing on his hands and knees.

"Noah!" She knelt beside him, resting her hand on his back as he heaved in a breath. "I'm calling an ambulance."

"No." He shook his head. "No ambulance."

"Can you walk to the truck? We need to get you checked out." She tried to help him to his feet, but he waved her away.

"I don't think this is a medical issue." He groaned, digging his nails into the concrete.

"What is it then? A spell? A curse? Talk to me!"

"I don't know!" He coughed hard. "I don't know what's happening."

"I'm calling Alexis." She tugged her phone from her pocket and dialed the pack's healer, her hand trembling as she pressed the device to her ear. "Please pick up. Please pick up."

She answered on the third ring. "Hello?"

"It's Amber. There's something wrong with Noah. Can you come to the stone bridge in City Park?"

"What's going on?"

"I don't know. He's on his hands and knees on the ground, groaning, and he said it doesn't feel like a medical issue. Maybe it's a spell?

Can you bring Rain too?" Chase's mate, Rain, was a witch who'd recently helped undo a spell that had wiped another werewolf's memory. Surely between her and Alexis, they could fix whatever was wrong with Noah.

"Put the phone on speaker so I can talk to him."

She did as Alexis asked and held the phone toward him, her heart wrenching as Noah let out another groan.

"I need you to describe how you're feeling," Alexis said. "What kind of pain is it?"

"It burns," he said through clenched teeth. "It's like acid in my veins."

"Amber, check his eyes. Are they dilated?"

"Noah, can you look at me?" She placed her hand on the side of his neck and lowered her head to meet his gaze. "They're constricted like pinpricks."

"Oh, shit," Alexis said.

"Oh, shit? What's 'oh, shit'? Don't say that." Panic raced ice-cold through her veins. "What's happening to him?"

"Can you get him in the car? You need to take him to the hunting grounds. Now."

"Why?" She tugged Noah up by the arm. "Walk with me. C'mon, you can do this." With his arm slung over her shoulders, she carried most of his weight as they trudged to his truck. He moaned, tripping over his own feet and nearly sending them both face-first into the dirt. She practically dragged him the rest of the way.

"Alexis, what's going on?" Amber helped him into the passenger seat before darting around to the driver's side and climbing in.

"Constricted pupils, doubling over in pain, blood that feels like acid… It sounds exactly like what happened to Bryce before his first shift. Apparently, the pain is normal if the wolf awakens later in life."

She started the engine and stared blankly out the front window. "Noah can't shift."

"It sure as hell sounds like he's about to, and if you don't take him to the alpha, you might end up his first meal."

CHAPTER NINE

Nausea churned in Noah's stomach, an intense burning sensation pulsing through his body with each beat of his heart. He clutched the door handle as Amber sped down the highway, and he squeezed his eyes shut to ease the pounding in his head.

"Are you okay?" Amber reached across the seat to take his hand.

"No," he ground out through teeth clenched so hard he tasted blood.

"Alexis thinks you're getting ready to shift."

"I heard." He moved in the seat to rest his head against the window, hoping the cool glass would tame the fever threatening to burn him from the inside out. "It's impossible."

Amber winced and returned her hand to the steering wheel. "There is a way," she whispered.

Noah groaned. She was right; there was a way, but in his current state of agony, he couldn't add mental anguish to the pain.

"If Nylah…" She swallowed hard.

"I know." If a first-born shifting wolf died prematurely, the second-born's magic would be triggered, enabling them to shift. It was like a supernatural failsafe to ensure the pack had enough shifters.

He clenched his hands in his lap, pressing his feet into the floorboard and lifting his butt from the seat as his muscles contracted. "Can you drive any faster?" Whatever was happening to him, it was about to reach critical mass.

"We're almost there." She turned onto a side road.

His stomach lurched, and he bent over, pressing his head into the dashboard as he groaned. This couldn't be happening. He refused to believe Nylah was gone, yet he couldn't deny the intense pull of the moon. With every breath he took, he felt the magic growing stronger until his entire body began to hum—no…to vibrate.

The truck bounced as Amber pulled off the path and rolled to a stop. "I'm sure Alexis will be here soon." She rubbed his back, trying to console him, but her hand on his body felt like an electric shock, setting his nerves on fire.

"Ah, fuck." The vibration in his muscles intensified, the burning acid in his veins melting his insides. Every nerve in his body screamed with pain as if he were being shredded into ten million pieces. It was happening. "Get out of the car."

"Noah…"

"You heard Alexis. I don't want to hurt you." His body seized, the magic consuming him. "Run."

Amber's breath hitched, and she reached a trembling hand toward the latch before sliding out of the truck. "I'm here for you, Noah. I know you won't hurt me."

"I don't," he forced out a moment before his wolf came to life.

Amber froze, staring in awe at the magnificent creature lying in the seat. Copper fur covered his body, with a sprinkling of black across his shoulders, and Noah's brown eyes gazed back at her. "You're beautiful," she whispered.

Shifters retained their human thoughts and emotions in wolf form. While he couldn't speak, he would understand her. His fur looked so soft, she couldn't help herself. She reached a hand toward him, and his lips peeled back, revealing white teeth with a massive set of canines.

She gasped and jerked her hand away. "Why don't you come out of the truck?"

A growl rumbled in his chest as he rose to his paws. He lowered his head in what looked like a predatory stance, but he was so big he would have hit the ceiling otherwise. He wasn't growling at *her*. He couldn't be.

Still, she took a few steps back, moving out of the way just in case. When his growl turned into a snarl, her heart slammed against her chest.

He leaped from the truck, twigs cracking beneath his massive paws as he hit the ground with a *thud*. He blew a breath through his nose, and she swallowed hard. *Uh oh.* His head was still down, his ears flat.

"Noah, it's me." Her hands trembled, so she clenched them into fists at her sides. "It's Amber."

He took a step toward her, and in his crouched position, he looked fierce. If she weren't alone in the woods with no way of knowing what was going on in his mind, she'd have been in awe. But Alexis's words rang in her mind: *you might end up his first meal.*

Slowly, carefully, she moved away, not daring to turn her back to him. Leaves crunched beneath her shoes, the sound melding with Noah's low growl like a warning. "Luke is on his way," she forced the whisper through her thickening throat.

He prowled toward her as she backed away. *Oh, shit.*

"Your alpha is coming." Gripping the side of the truck, she stepped on the tire and hauled herself into the bed.

Noah's growl intensified. Her pulse raced.

She lifted her hands, palms toward him, as he stalked around to the tailgate. *Come on, Luke. Where are you?* If she were a shifter herself, she could have sent her brother a mental message. Werewolves had a sort of telepathy in their wolf forms. Of course, if she were a shifter herself, she wouldn't be in this situation, about to become her best friend's dinner.

Noah rocked back on his haunches and sprang, landing in the bed of the truck, inches from Amber.

"Noah, no!" she screamed and scrambled onto the top of the cab. "I know you can understand me. Your wolf's instinct is to hunt, but the man should always be in control." How many times had she heard her father say those same words when he was alpha?

Noah knew the laws. He'd gone through training with Nylah when they were kids and everyone thought he'd be a shifter too. "Remember what you learned," she said as she scanned the branches above, calculating which one would hold her weight if she jumped. They were all too high to reach.

On her hands and knees, she inched backward before rolling onto the balls of her feet. As Noah rocked onto his haunches, preparing to lunge, her foot slipped, and she slid down the windshield onto the hood.

A howl echoed in the distance, and as she peered through the glass, she saw Noah's ears prick. He turned his head toward the sound and leaped from the bed of the truck onto the ground.

Amber rolled off the hood as quietly as she could and gently tugged on the door handle. The clicking of the door opening and the light from the cabin drew Noah's attention, and he spun around as she scrambled into the truck and slammed the door, hitting both locks and exhaling a curse.

Something was wrong. It was as if Noah didn't even recognize her. Like the man ceased to exist the moment the beast took over. Even the youngest, most inexperienced shifters had more control of their wolves.

Another howl sounded, unmistakably Luke, followed by several others, creating a symphony piercing enough to make even Amber's blood hum.

Noah turned toward the trees as a line of wolves approached the clearing. Luke stood in the middle, the biggest of the pack, with caramel-colored fur. Chase, his second in command with sleek black fur, flanked him on the right, and James stood to his left. Cade, Bryce, and Alexis made up the rest of the crew.

Luke held his head high and let out a commanding *woof*, followed by a low growl. Amber didn't need their special telepathy to understand the alpha was telling the fledgling to stand down. But Noah didn't follow orders. Instead, he stiffened, the fur on his back standing in a ridge, and he took a tentative step forward.

The alpha growled louder, moving toward him while the others fanned out in a semicircle, trapping Noah between the pack and the truck. Noah snarled and snapped, and the pack tightened the circle.

"What are you doing, Noah? You can't disobey the alpha." Luke would be fully justified in tearing Noah apart if he continued this insolence.

A knock sounded on the glass behind her, and she squealed. She turned around to find Rain, an elemental witch and Chase's fate-bound, tugging on the door handle. Amber reached across the seat and popped the lock, and Rain slid inside.

"Chase asked me to come in case he was under a spell, but I guess he isn't." She tucked her dark, curly hair behind her ear and gave Amber a sympathetic look.

"With the way he's acting, I'm not so sure. He almost attacked me."

Her brow furrowed. "That doesn't sound right."

"I know. I was hoping Luke could calm him down, but he's acting like the man doesn't exist at all anymore." She turned her gaze back to the confrontation outside.

Luke and Noah stood nearly nose to nose, the alpha calm and stoic, while Noah bared his teeth. Luke didn't waver, and she could sense the dominant, patient vibes he exuded as he tried to get the wild wolf under control.

But Noah wasn't having it. He lunged, latching on to Luke's shoulder and trying to drag him to the ground. The other wolves closed in, and Amber held her breath, praying to every god in existence that her best friend would survive.

"He won't kill him, will he?" Rain asked.

"I hope not." Her brother was a kind, just alpha, but he was still alpha. One out-of-control wolf could wreak havoc on the pack structure.

Luke spun, throwing Noah to the ground, but he got back up and snarled some more. He lunged again, but this time, Luke caught him by the neck and sent him careening into a tree trunk. The wood cracked with the impact, and Noah hit the ground with a *thud.*

The wolves circled him again, and again he rose to his feet, letting out an enraged howl. He barreled toward Luke, and they rolled over each other, snapping and snarling like they were fighting to the death.

"Stop it." Amber's breath fogged the glass. "They have to stop." She unlocked the door and threw it open.

"Amber, no." Rain clutched her arm, but she pulled from her grasp, sliding out of the truck and running toward the fray.

"Stop it! Noah, stop. It's Luke. He's your alpha."

Noah jerked his head toward her and whined as Luke clamped onto his throat.

"Luke, it's Noah." She clasped her hands in front of her chest. "Please. Both of you."

Noah whined again, and Luke loosened his grip.

"Stand down," she pleaded. "Please take control. I can't lose you too."

Something sparked in Noah's eyes, and as Luke released his hold, he bowed his head, tucking his tail and letting out a submissive whimper. Luke stood over him, tail high, chest proud, and Noah licked his muzzle, accepting his place in the pack.

Amber's breath came out in a rush as the other wolves relaxed their stances. Noah was safe…for now.

She leaned against the truck, pressing her fingers to her temples. As much as she wanted to be sure he was okay, she didn't dare go to him. He was docile now, lying on his stomach while Luke and Chase stood on either side of him, but Amber's pulse hadn't yet slowed to a normal rate. She had no idea if he was willingly compliant or if he was merely trying to stay alive.

A smaller, sandy-colored wolf approached, and in a mist of shimmering light, Alexis shifted into her human form. She wore beige cargo pants with a black tank top, and her short blonde hair was tucked behind her ears. Rain climbed out of the truck to stand next to Amber.

"Is he okay?" Amber's hands trembled again, so she crossed her arms, tucking them against her sides.

Alexis sighed, shaking her head. "His wolf is wild. I've never seen anything like it, and I was rogue most of my life."

"Is there any way I can help?" Rain asked. "A calming potion, maybe?"

"We're going to take him hunting," Alexis said. "Hopefully once he's fed, we can help him shift and figure out what's going on. His thoughts aren't on the same wavelength as ours. He can't communicate in wolf form."

Amber nodded. "Will you bring him back here when you're done? I'll wait."

"Luke wants you to go home. He'll be by to get your story later."

"Thank you." Amber waved as Alexis returned to wolf form and bounded into the trees after the others.

"I'm sorry about Nylah." Rain rested a hand on her shoulder. "I never met her, but Chase said y'all were close."

"She was my best friend. Both of them were." Amber smiled sadly, and a wave of dizziness washed over her. She clutched the side of Noah's truck to steady herself as a sinking sensation formed in her stomach. Another premonition was coming on.

"Are you okay?" Rain asked.

"I feel like…" She pressed her lips together and shook her head. It was impossible. "I feel like Nylah's still alive."

Rain tilted her head. "I thought the only way for Noah to shift was if his older sibling died prematurely."

"That's the only way I'm aware of, but these feelings are never wrong."

"How…?"

"I have no idea, but I'm going to find out."

CHAPTER TEN

Alrick gazed at the Thropynite lying in his palm. The she-wolf had constructed a wire cage, attaching it to a chain she'd worn carelessly around her neck like an ornament. Had she no idea of this tiny shard's worth? Of its power? At its simplest, it gave magical beings the ability to shapeshift…an ability no one but the gargoyles should have. In the hands of the powerful, it could be used to meld the souls of two beings. No one knew the true origin of the stone, but the Sect believed it had been around as long as the earth itself.

He fastened the clasp behind his neck, letting the stone rest against his chest and relishing the extra magic it fed into his veins.

"It's only a matter of time now, brothers." He lay a hand on each of the three other gargoyles' shoulders in turn, checking their auras for signs of life. But the small piece of stone he'd retrieved from the she-wolf wasn't enough to bring life to them all.

Alrick was one of the originals, the first of his kind to be created. Later, the Sect discovered they had more control over their abominations if they used the Thropynite to create them, but then forbade them from having contact with it until they deemed it necessary.

His brothers in arms came from the second batch of recruits, and he would need a much larger piece of stone to revive them. Like the one his witch destroyed when she left him.

He gazed at the she-wolf, now in human form, lying unconscious on the bed his traitorous witch used to occupy. Her superficial wounds had nearly healed by the time he brought her into his home, but the blow to the head he'd given her when she resisted had knocked her out for two days. Now, she stirred.

Her long auburn hair spilled out in a tangle around her head, and she had a sprinkling of freckles across her nose that reminded him so much of his witch, his heart ached to look at her. Perhaps she was nothing more than a witch herself and the stone had given her the ability to transform into a wolf. He would soon find out.

"What the hell?" She blinked her brown eyes open and pressed a hand to her temple, rising onto an elbow. Turning her head, she took in her surroundings, confusion contorting her delicate features. "Am I dead?"

He could see how she might think so. His pocket dimension rendered the world around them colorless, as if they stood in a bubble in the middle of a fog.

"You're alive…for now." His gravelly voice startled her, and as she took in his form, she scrambled to her feet.

"Grunch." She tilted her head, squinting at him.

He cringed at the derogatory name. "I'm a gargoyle, not a Grunch. That name was given to us by the humans…the very people we were supposed to protect." They considered him and his brothers a family of albino deformities, with their stone-gray skin, hunched postures, and demon-like faces, and they exiled them to the outskirts of town. In their homeland, the gargoyles could transform completely to their human forms, but the piece of Thropynite they'd brought with them to New Orleans didn't have enough power for full transformations, so they were frozen in this abhorrent in-between state.

She scoffed and shook her head. "Protect them from what? You eat their hearts."

They had to keep their demon sides fed to maintain their power, much like a werewolf was compelled to hunt in his wolf form despite what the man had eaten. "We sacrifice a few to shelter the masses."

"From magic." She crossed her arms.

"Magic is an abomination."

"What do you think made you?"

"You know nothing about me," he growled. He was tempted to end this conversation for good and absorb her knowledge the demonic way, but she could be of use to him alive. "I will not tolerate your insolence, witch. Now, tell me how you acquired the Thropynite."

"I'm not a witch." She called on her magic and transformed into a snarling wolf.

Alrick grunted. She was a she-wolf, after all. The magic he used to create this small dimension normally kept both supernaturals and humans away. They couldn't sense the pocket lying parallel with their world, but they'd acquire a feeling of foreboding unease if they ventured anywhere near it. Perhaps the Thropynite had guided her here.

The wolf rocked back, preparing to spring, and Alrick crossed his thick arms. Baring her teeth, she lunged, aiming directly for his neck, but she slammed into the invisible wall of her cell, bouncing off and hitting the floor with a *thunk*. She sprang to her feet and dove to the side, where she encountered yet another wall.

"You won't escape." He sank into a chair he'd brought in from the earthly realm. "Your prison is fortified by magic only I can unravel." His threat wasn't entirely true. His witch had finally broken the spell after decades of imprisonment, but this she-wolf didn't possess the ability to undo demon magic.

She growled before transforming into a woman. "Do you hear yourself? You're using the very thing you're trying to rid the world of. You're the abomination."

"Indeed I am, as are my brothers." He gestured to the other gargoyles frozen in stone. "We cannot fight our demon natures, but it was a sacrifice we willingly made."

"To protect the masses."

"Precisely. And once we purge all the magic from the world, we will end our lives for the greater good." He cradled the Thropynite in his palm. "Where did you get this?"

She crossed her arms and inclined her chin.

"You will tell me." He rose to his feet and loomed toward her, but she simply shook her head, unfazed by his threatening stance. A strange flutter rose from his gut, her lack of fear intriguing him.

"Maybe you're not aware," she said, "but werewolves hunt demons. That makes me the predator and you the prey."

He lowered his brow. "Yet you're the one in a cage."

"For now." She lifted one shoulder dismissively. "But not for long. We hunt in packs."

He was well aware of how werewolves hunted. The mangey mongrels were the reason he and his brothers fled Europe. It was the only way to survive. Werewolves were intelligent and fierce, and this she-wolf was no exception. Hollow threats would get him nowhere with her.

"My name is Alrick," he said.

She let out a cynical laugh. "I'd say it's nice to meet you, but you've locked me in a cage in another dimension, and once I'm free, I'll send you back to hell where you belong."

He grunted. "I'm familiar with your instinct to rid the world of demons. The cage is simply for your safety."

"My safety? I think you mean your own."

"On the contrary. If you attempted to attack me, I would crush your skull, absorb your knowledge, and devour your heart."

"I'd like to see you try."

Another flutter rose from his gut. "It would be the last thing you saw, she-wolf."

"Don't call me she-wolf."

"What would you prefer I call you?"

"I'd prefer you let me out of this cage so I can kill you."

He chuckled. "You're going to be here for a while, *she-wolf.* Unless you want to tell me where you found this shard of Thropynite so I can acquire more, you'd best get comfortable."

"Bite me."

"Don't tempt me." He returned to the chair. "I was engaged to a witch before the Sect recruited me."

"Poor her." She remained standing, her arms crossed, feet wide. He could almost see the gears turning in her mind as she planned her escape.

"I didn't always look like this."

"Your point?" She pressed her fingertips against the invisible wall, giving it a hard shove before returning to her guarded stance.

"You remind me of her. She was beautiful, intelligent, cunning… *insolent* like you."

"Lucky me."

"I don't want to kill you." Not yet anyway. She was far too intriguing. "Tell me your name."

She pursed her lips, her eyes calculating as she drummed her fingers on her biceps. Her jaw clenched, and she rested her hands on her hips. "It's Nylah."

CHAPTER ELEVEN

His wolf had been ravenous. The magic had been dormant inside him for twenty-nine years, and as it rose to the surface, it had one thought on its mind: to feed.

Noah had tried to take control. Seeing the fear in Amber's eyes as he prowled around her—the way she screamed when he lunged—had ripped into his soul like a thousand razorblades.

He almost killed her.

She was his best friend, the one woman he could see himself spending forever with, and his wolf had tried to eat her. *Fuck.*

Now he sat in the passenger seat of Luke's truck, staring out the window into the swamp while his pack stood a few yards away and discussed what to do about his behavior.

His behavior. More like the behavior of a wild animal who had taken over his body. It wasn't supposed to be like this. He remembered Nylah's first shift as if it happened yesterday. They'd gone to the hunting grounds with their father and the alpha on the full moon after their thirteenth birthdays. When Nylah shifted and he didn't, she didn't try to attack. She'd obeyed the alpha like she would have in human form.

Even Bryce, a human who'd become a werewolf after being

attacked and left for dead, had no problem obeying the alpha after his first shift.

So what the hell was Noah's problem?

Luke said something, though their voices were too quiet for him to hear, and Alexis lifted her arms, dropping them at her sides like she couldn't answer his question. Bryce shook his head and fisted his hand over his heart as he spoke. Chase said something, and Luke nodded before heading toward the truck.

Noah stared straight ahead as he climbed in and slammed the door. Thank the gods his wolf had finally submitted to the alpha. Now the best course of action for the man was not to speak until spoken to.

Luke kneaded the steering wheel, the tendons in his neck tight as he clenched his jaw. "First, I'm sorry about Nylah. I know you're grieving."

"Thank you." He lowered his head. He *should* have been grieving, but he and his twin shared a bond, what Cade called his Wonder Twin senses. Somewhere, deep inside his soul, the bond was still there, unbroken.

It didn't make sense. The only way he could have inherited the shifting ability was if Nylah died…yet he couldn't ignore his gut instinct that she was still alive.

"What the hell happened out there?" Luke started the engine and pulled out onto the road.

"I'd say I lost control of my wolf, but I never had it to begin with. The moment I shifted, the animal took over."

Luke glanced at him before focusing on the road. "You could have killed her."

"I know. I'm sorry." Sorry didn't begin to describe his level of regret. "Are you going to see her now?"

"I am."

"Can I come? I want to apologize."

Luke sighed and gave him a curt nod. "You can. Maybe hearing her side of the story will help you gain some control. I've never seen her so terrified."

His throat thickened. Neither had he.

"Until you do gain control, you will not shift without me present. Do you understand?"

"Yes."

"Tomorrow night, and every other night until I deem it unnecessary, you will hunt with me. Clear your calendar."

"Okay." Noah fought the urge to sink in his seat. It was bad enough being babysat while he was on probation, but this was humiliating. Though, after the way his new wolf had behaved, he understood. He deserved worse.

"And no more patrols until you have control of your wolf. I want you indoors by nightfall unless you're with me."

"Understood." He was a grown-ass man being put back on the leash…a disgrace to his pack.

Luke parked behind Amber's Mazda in her driveway and killed the engine. Noah slid out of the truck and followed him to the door. When Amber answered, her eyes tightened as she met his gaze, driving a knife into his heart.

How could he have done that to her? His wolf should have claimed her as his fate-bound the moment he emerged, not tried to make a meal out of her.

She stepped aside and motioned for them to enter, so he followed Luke into the living room. As Amber joined them, Noah took her hand in both of his. "I'm so sorry."

"I know." She gave him a tight-lipped smile and tugged from his grasp, twisting the knife even deeper.

"Can I get you guys a beer?" she asked. "After tonight, we could all use one."

Noah waited for Luke to answer "yes" before nodding and saying, "Thanks."

As Amber disappeared into the kitchen, Noah sank onto the sofa and Luke took the teal accent chair adjacent to it. A fireplace with a white brick mantel occupied the wall across from him, and he caught his reflection in the blank screen of the television mounted above it. His hair was disheveled, so he ran a hand through it and cast his gaze to the potted ivy in the window instead. He couldn't bear to look at himself.

Amber returned with three bottles of Blue Moon and sat on the corner of the couch, as far away from Noah as she could get.

"Walk me through it from the beginning," Luke said.

Noah took a long drink from his beer, focusing on the way the citrusy bubbles cooled his throat as Amber recounted the incident step by step.

"I'm glad you got there when you did," she said. "I don't know what would have happened otherwise."

"You have to know that wasn't me." Noah scooted toward her and pleaded with his eyes. "I was there, like a floating subconscious, but I had zero control over what the wolf did. It didn't know who you are. It didn't know how important you are to me."

She looked into his eyes, her voice thin. "You scared me."

"I'm sorry." He scooted closer until his knee touched hers. "You helped me. When you got out of the truck and yelled at us, that was what brought me to the surface and let me take control. I don't know what would have happened if you weren't there." *She wouldn't have been in danger if she wasn't, dumbass.*

"Somebody had to talk some sense into you." She gave him a small smile. "Don't let it happen again."

"I won't."

"He'll be under close observation," Luke said.

Like a puppy on a leash. Noah set his beer on the coffee table. Amber took another drink from hers, and when she reached toward the table to place hers next to his, it slipped from her grasp.

Noah instinctively stretched his mind, using the energy in the air to grip the bottle before it could spill. With a flick of his wrist, he positioned it upright on the table. Amber didn't flinch at his use of power; he'd been doing things like that around her for as long as he could remember.

Luke cocked his head. "Interesting. Your wolf was out of control, but your second-born gift seems unaffected by the change."

"Why would it be affected?"

"Most lose their gift when their dormant wolf is awakened. It's rare for a shifter to have any other abilities, unless they have witch or Voodoo ancestry."

"Lucky me." He'd gladly give up his telekinesis if it would tame the rabid beast inside him. Even now, sitting in Amber's living room, his wolf was restless. Though he lacked the connection to understand and communicate with it, he could tell it wanted to run…to hunt… and it took every ounce of willpower he could muster to keep the animal subdued.

"Are you okay?" Amber's eyes held concern…and a hint of fear. "You look pale."

He glanced at the alpha. "The moon is calling me, I guess. My wolf wants to hunt again."

"The pull is always strongest on a full moon. Tomorrow it should be easier to control. You'll sleep in our spare bedroom tonight in case anything happens."

Noah held in his groan. He wasn't just being babysat. Now he had to have a slumber party too.

"Do you want to inform your parents about Nylah, or should I?" Luke asked.

He clenched his teeth. He didn't want anyone to tell them anything. Not while he felt his sister could still be out there. "I will."

"No." Amber shook her head. "Nylah isn't dead."

Luke straightened, looking at her quizzically. "Details?"

"You know by now details are scarce. She's out there somewhere, and she needs us to find her."

Luke rubbed his thumb and forefinger on his chin. "Not to discredit your ability, but is it possible your desire for her to be alive is clouding your senses?"

"I don't think so."

"She's right," Noah said. "I can feel it too. If she were dead, I'd know."

Luke stood and paced into the kitchen to toss his bottle in the recycle bin. Noah looked at Amber, and she mouthed the words, "Thank you."

"If she is alive, how do you explain your new ability to shift?" Luke stood behind the chair, resting his hands on the back.

Noah took a deep breath and blew it out hard. He'd have to choose his words carefully, or he could end up incriminating both himself and his sister. "I think it could be the Thropynite. It has the power to grant shapeshifting abilities, and it can be used to fuse two souls into one body."

Amber gasped. "That makes sense."

Luke sank into the chair and rested his elbows on his knees. "How do you know so much about the stone?"

Noah grabbed his beer and took a long drink, hoping to wash down the knot in his throat. It didn't help. "When you mentioned it the other day, I did some research online. A stone that could awaken my wolf sounded too good to be true, so I was curious." That was only a half-lie. Both he and Nylah had researched the Thropynite extensively, long before she left the pack.

Luke arched a brow. "Do you have the stone?"

"No, of course not." He didn't, but Nylah most likely did.

"The Thropynite must be in New Orleans, and it awakened your wolf along with the Grunch." Amber rested her hand on top of his, and his chest tightened.

Luke lowered his brow. "If that were the case, every second-born in the area would be a shifter now."

"But Noah was supposed to be one," Amber said. "He's a twin… the only one in our pack."

Luke studied him, narrowing his eyes as if processing the idea. "I'll put another call in to the congress tomorrow. We don't have enough information on the Thropynite to confirm your theory. I don't trust the internet; people can post anything there." He rose to his feet and looked at his sister. "Are you okay?"

"I'm fine." She released Noah's hand and stood.

"Let's head home." Luke strode toward the door. "We can swing by your place to pick up some clothes."

"Okay." Noah rose and followed him to the door.

"Do you mind if I talk to Noah alone for a minute?" Amber asked.

"I'll be in the truck." Luke gave his sister a quick hug and strode out the door.

Amber chewed her bottom lip as her brother walked away, and she turned to Noah. "We didn't get to finish our conversation, and I know

now isn't the time. Do you want to have dinner tomorrow night? I get off at eight."

"I have to hunt with Luke tomorrow night."

"Oh, okay." Disappointment was evident in her eyes.

He knew where the conversation would lead. He had a wolf now, so he didn't have an excuse for not being with her. Hell, he *wanted* to be with her. "I'm free the next night."

She smiled. "It's a date."

He turned to leave, but she caught him by the hand. "Is there something you're not telling me about Nylah?"

He forced his gaze to her eyes and shook his head. "I'll see you the day after tomorrow." He kissed her cheek and strode out the door.

CHAPTER TWELVE

Amber sat in her office, her desk in perpetual disarray, and went over the bar's inventory orders for the week. They were running dangerously low on hurricane mix, so she'd have to pay extra for rush shipping. The syrupy-sweet rum drinks were a top seller, thanks to the buy-one-get-one-free special they ran for tourists who signed up for the haunted history tours that operated out of a side room in the bar.

Every evening at six and eight, the place would be packed with visitors taking them up on their special drink offer. Half an hour later, things would be quiet again.

She glanced at the clock on her computer. Five-thirty. It was time to help Kaci get ready for the rush.

A few tourists had already wandered into the bar, their blue wristbands indicating they'd leave with the first tour group. Kaci had set up a row of black plastic cups across one side of the bar and was filling them with ice as Amber lifted the hinged section of the counter and joined her. A cylindrical cooler filled with premixed hurricanes sat to her right, and she grabbed a few cups, filling them with the red liquid.

As she set them on the bar, her head spun, and an overwhelming feeling about her employee seeped into her soul. “Kaci, are you mated?”

She laughed. “Not hardly. I’m not even dating anyone.”

Amber nodded. “You’re about to be soon.”

“Really?” Her eyes sparkled. “Is it Cade? God, I hope it’s Cade.”

“I didn’t know you liked him.”

“Who doesn’t? He’s the hottest shifter in the pack.”

Not anymore. In Amber’s eyes, Noah held that title now. “I don’t feel like it’s Cade, but that doesn’t mean it can’t be. Keep your mind open, though.”

Within minutes, people packed the bar, filling every seat and most of the floor as they waited for their tours to begin. She and Kaci served drink after drink, ran credit cards, and made change until the final tourist strolled out the front door.

“Whew!” Kaci wiped the counter with a dishrag. “Those tours are getting more and more popular.”

“They won a few awards this year, so they’re getting a lot of free promotion.” Amber pulled bottles of light and dark rum from a cabinet and began mixing the drinks for the next rush when a man with long brown hair and a stocky build strode through the door.

“Welcome to O’Malley’s.” Kaci beamed a smile as he approached, and his gaze locked on her.

“Amber?” He stopped at the bar and rested his hands on the surface.

“That’s me.” Amber brushed her hair from her face and moved toward him. “How can I help you?”

The guy looked like it pained him to tear his gaze away from Kaci to look at her. “Hi.” He glanced at Kaci again before continuing. “I’m Judd Wilson. Your father contacted me and suggested I stop by to say ‘hello.’”

Not again. She really needed to have a conversation with her dad. Now he was sending them in unannounced. What was next? A guy showing up in a tux with a ring in his hand? “It’s nice to meet you, Judd, but I’m afraid you’ve been sent here under false pretenses. I’m not in the market for a mate.”

“I see.” He couldn’t seem to stop his gaze from flicking to Kaci.

"I hope you didn't drive far." Amber lifted the flap in the counter, ready to escape to the back room. She didn't need any kind of empathic ability to see what was happening between Judd and Kaci. This was a fate-bound bond forming.

"I came in from Lake Charles."

"Well, you're welcome to stay and have a drink or two on the house. Kaci will take care of you." She winked at her bartender and slipped into her office.

Damn. She didn't realize Kaci would find her mate *that* soon. And at only twenty-two years old. She was a lucky girl.

Two hours later, when Amber returned to the bar for the second rush, Judd was still there, making heart eyes at Kaci as she prepared the drinks. The man exuded love. There was no doubt in Amber's mind Kaci was his fate-bound, and seeing the joy it brought him… knowing the happiness he'd feel for the rest of his life…Amber's resolve to not mate with a shifter unless his wolf claimed her solidified.

So what did that mean for her and Noah?

After the rush, Kaci began to wipe down the bar, but Amber took the rag. "Why don't you take off early? I'll close up tonight."

Kaci bit her bottom lip and glanced at Judd. "Are you sure?"

"Absolutely." She leaned toward her and whispered, "I'm happy for you."

When Kaci left, Amber retrieved her laptop from her office and sat at the bar. It was a weeknight, and no festivals were going on, so the rest of the evening would be slow. She occupied herself with work to keep her mind off her current predicament, but she couldn't stop her thoughts from wandering to Noah. Even with closing time approaching, she remained at the bar, pondering what to do.

"Hey, Amber. You're working late tonight." Odette sashayed through the front door, carrying a big cardboard box. Her curly black hair spiraled down to her shoulders, and she wore her signature colors, purple and black, to honor Baron Samedi, the Voodoo spirit who guided her.

Amber closed her laptop and lifted a half-empty mug of beer. "Not really working. I wasn't ready to go home." Truth be told, she was hoping Noah and the hunting party would stop by for a drink when they were done. "What do you have for me? That looks like more than I ordered."

Odette slid the box onto the bar and took the seat next to Amber. "I brought you some swag to give to your customers." She pulled out a stack of coasters and a small cardboard box. Tape sealed the edges, so Amber tugged her trusty Swiss Army knife from her pocket and sliced it open to find shot glasses with the distillery's logo, a skeleton wearing a top hat, painted on them. Odette was James's mate, and she ran the popular rum company, The Baron.

"Thanks. These are great." Amber wiped the condensation off the side of her glass.

"James told me about what happened with Noah. How are you holding up?"

"I'm fine. I just… I didn't expect…" She didn't expect to nearly be eaten by the magical beast who was supposed to make Noah fall instantly in love with her. "When you met James, how long did it take before his wolf claimed you? Was it immediate?"

Odette returned the swag items to the box and pushed it away before swiveling on her stool to face Amber. "That was a special circumstance, what with the reincarnation business and all. It took him a while to sort it all out."

Amber sipped her beer. "Once he did figure it out, when he knew you were his fate-bound, did you feel it too?" She'd never thought to ask a shifter's mate what it felt like to be claimed. Based on the way Luke and the others talked about it, and how giddy Kaci was with Judd, she assumed the feeling worked both ways. But after the way Noah's wolf terrified her, she couldn't imagine feeling any kind of connection to the beast, no matter how desperately she wanted to.

"I knew he was the one before he did, but again, that was due to our circumstances." She smiled knowingly. Through her Voodoo priestess, Odette had done a series of past-life regressions, so she knew she'd been with James in previous lifetimes. "I don't think it feels the same as it does for a shifter. You and I don't have a second soul to guide us like they do, but I do sense a connection like no other. It feels as if a cord runs from my core to his, tethering us. An unbreakable bond. But I'm a Vodouisant, and you're a werewolf. It might be completely different for you."

"Hmm." She drained the rest of her beer. Aside from being terrified of Noah's wolf, her feelings for him hadn't changed since he shifted. The connection she felt to him was simply a woman falling in love with her best friend.

Odette placed her hand on top of Amber's. "Give it time. Your case is unique as well. Most shifters have known their wolves for ten or fifteen years before they claim a mate. Noah only met his yesterday."

"You're right. I shouldn't have expected him to claim me the moment he came into existence. He's not a baby duck. I have to be patient."

"Your ability doesn't give a glimpse into how it might work out?"

She laughed. "Sadly, I've never had a premonition about myself. And Noah…" She shook her head. "I sensed change coming for him, but my emotions get in the way when it comes to him. I should have warned him."

"I'm sure you did what you thought was right." She slipped her purse strap onto her shoulder. "Even if his wolf doesn't claim you, y'all have a lifetime of friendship behind you. That's the best foundation for a relationship I can imagine."

Amber shook her head. "I could never do that to him. If he doesn't claim me, I'll have to end it." And then she might have to take her mother up on her offer of having that party. She shuddered at the thought of being put on display for other packs, but it would be better than the random ambushes her dad was planning.

Odette stood. "If you want to stop by the temple sometime, we can leave an offering for Erzulie, the loa of love. She might help you." Loa were Voodoo spirits. They weren't gods, but they did have the power to help people in situations like this.

"Thanks. I'll think about it." She slid off her stool, preparing to take the box to the storage closet when her head spun for the second time that evening. She pressed the heel of her hand to her temple as the familiar sinking sensation brought on another empathic premonition. "Whoa."

"Are you okay?" Odette placed a hand on her shoulder.

"There's going to be another murder."

Noah ran beside Luke, twigs crunching beneath his paws as his wolf pushed his body to its limits. He'd shifted easily, his beast coming to the surface on command as if he'd been there his entire life. Following commands from the alpha was another story.

Luke stopped abruptly, his ears pricking as he gazed at a pair of gators lying in the mud near the water's edge. Noah started toward them, his wolf eager for a fight, but a growl from the alpha signaled he should wait. They'd already hunted. He'd satiated his hunger, but electricity hummed through his veins, the urge to engage with the potential prey overwhelming him.

Crouching, he began his advance, and Luke's growl turned into a snarl. The alpha had issued an order, and Noah had to obey. He fought for control, wrestling with the wolf in his mind, but the beast refused to listen. He continued his pursuit.

Luke leaped in front of him, blocking his path and snapping at his face. The alpha's teeth grazed his muzzle, and Noah growled against his will. Luke growled in return, exerting his dominance until finally, Noah's wolf surrendered. With a whine, he lay on his belly and watched as the gators disappeared into the murky water. Luke shifted, and Noah tried to follow suit, but his wolf wouldn't release control.

"Return to human form," Luke commanded.

Noah clawed his way to the surface and was finally able to shift. Hanging his head, he stood before his alpha. "I'm sorry. I swear it's not me disobeying you. I don't know why my wolf won't listen."

Luke walked up the path toward his truck, and Noah followed. "You still can't sense my thoughts? No form of telepathy at all?"

"None. I'm going off body language and instinct." He climbed into the passenger seat and slammed the door. What the hell was wrong with him? All he'd wanted his entire life was to be a shifter, and now that he had a wolf, the damn beast was out of control.

"I've never heard of anything like this." Luke started the engine and pulled out onto the road. "But that doesn't mean it's never happened. I'll call the congress to see if a case like this is on record somewhere."

Noah grunted. "Can we wait a week or two and see if it fixes itself? I don't want the entire werewolf population knowing what a screwup I am." It was bad enough when he was a rare twin who couldn't shift. He didn't need the added humiliation.

Luke shook his head. "If this goes downhill, it's my responsibility as alpha. Issues like this are required to be reported. I'll contact my father. He'll be discreet."

"Thanks, man." Noah rubbed his forehead, cursing himself silently. He had to get his wolf under control, not just for himself, but for his pack.

Luke's phone rang from his pocket, and he dug it out before pressing it to his ear. "Yeah." His jaw clenched, his fingers curling around the steering wheel in a death grip. "Where?" He blew out a hard breath. "I'm on my way."

He dropped his phone into the cupholder. "That was Cade. There's been another one. A Vodouisant this time. Heart ripped out like the others. Can I count on you to keep control?"

Could he? Not really. No. "You know I'll do my best."

Luke nodded, but his expression was grim. They parked in front of a bar on the outskirts of the city, and he killed the engine. "We can't chance your wolf going rogue during a fight."

"Understood." Noah climbed out of the truck and followed the alpha into the woods behind the bar.

Cade met them beneath a massive oak tree a few yards away. "It's back here. The beast had the decency to drag his victim away from prying eyes this time, but it won't be long until the smell draws attention."

"He's getting smarter," Luke grumbled as they made their way toward the body.

The previous corpses had been discovered right in the middle of the French Quarter. No one had witnessed the actual crimes, but the gargoyle-like demon Noah and Cade had found in the cemetery had to be responsible.

James and Chase stood over the victim, and Chase gestured to the chest wound as they approached. "Looks like claws, same as the others, but check this out." He moved to stand at what was left of the woman's head.

Noah exhaled sharply as he took in the carnage. The skull had been pierced in multiple places, as if by claws, and the eyes bulged from their sockets. "Are we sure the same creature did this? The woman I found last month didn't have this kind of head wound, nor did the werewolf we found in the street."

"The second victim did," Luke said. "Do you know if the police have been contacted?"

"Not yet. I believe we're the only ones who know," James said. "I called Odette. She's on her way to identify the body."

"What brought you out here?" Luke moved around the body, examining it. "This isn't the normal patrol area."

"Amber called," Cade said. "She sensed something was going down in the area, so we came out to have a look."

"The wounds look fresh," Chase said. "I'd say this happened less than an hour ago."

Noah ground his teeth, a strange sensation of jealousy churning in his gut. It was ridiculous, but he couldn't help wondering why she chose to notify Cade over him. He'd never been jealous before. Could this be his wolf beginning to claim her? He could only hope.

"When she couldn't get ahold of you," Cade said to Luke, "she went down the chain until she reached one of us."

The tightness in Noah's chest eased. As a former non-shifter, he didn't have a place on the call chain. Of course she wouldn't contact him about this. It was pack business, not personal.

"Do you think we're dealing with the Grunch?" James asked.

"I'm not positive," Luke said. "But based on the information we've gathered, I assume so."

Noah gazed at the mangled body lying in the dirt. If Nylah really did find the Thropynite, the creature might have gone after her first. His connection to his sister and Amber's insistence that she was still alive were the only things keeping him from fearing she'd met the same fate.

The sound of a branch breaking drew their attention to the east, and Luke held up a hand indicating they should wait as he crept toward it. Shuffling sounded, and the bushes rustled like something was attempting to escape.

"Shit. Let's go." Luke transformed into his wolf, and the others followed suit, darting into the trees.

Noah stood there squeezing his fists, fighting the urge to shift, Luke's words echoing in his mind: *We can't chance your wolf going rogue during a fight.* He took a deep breath to steady himself and ran into the woods behind them. But as he approached and found his pack encircling the same stone-like creature he'd encountered before, he couldn't simply stand aside and watch. He had to help, so he shifted and joined the other wolves.

The creature smelled like a demon, of rotten garbage and sulfur, but it lacked the signature red eyes that most possessed. Its skin was gray and cracked, and blood stained its crooked mouth. Not mildew like he'd originally thought.

Luke lunged, snapping his jaws at the creature's flesh, but the demon was too fast. It teleported, shooting deeper into the woods.

The alpha grunted, and the others bobbed their heads as if they had received a message. But Noah's wild wolf heard nothing. He'd be of no use to them if he couldn't follow orders, and he didn't know the plan without the telepathic bond he should have shared with his packmates.

The wolves fanned out around the creature, lunging and snapping, but the beast bounced from position to position, always out of their grasp.

Noah reached out with his senses, trying to manipulate the energy around him, but in his wolf form it seemed he couldn't access his telekinetic ability.

Come on, buddy, he said to his wolf in his mind. *Give me back control.*

He struggled, his wolf battling him for dominance. The beast did not want to let go. The fight continued in front of him, but he focused inward, willing his human side to come to the surface. His wolf snarled then let out a pained yelp. Cade swung his head around to look at Noah, and the demon used the distraction to his advantage, swiping his massive claws into Cade's shoulder and knocking him into a tree.

Fuck. He shouldn't have shifted. In this form, he was nothing more than a hindrance. Cade scrambled to his feet and limped away from the fight to heal, while Noah forced his wolf to grit his teeth, biting until he tasted blood. His body hummed, and though his wolf dug in his claws, trying with all his might to hold on, Noah beat him down and shifted to his human form.

Holding out his arms, he gathered the energy around him, sending out an invisible wave of force and freezing the massive demon to its spot. Luke attacked, sinking his teeth into its side, and Noah released the fiend, allowing the alpha to drag it to the ground.

The other wolves sprang, a mass of fur and fangs covering the creature as they snarled and growled, but a menacing laugh reverberated through the forest.

They froze, silent. Chase backed up, and Noah moved to the side to get a view of the demon, but it was gone. Cade, now healed, took off with James to scout the area, but the gargoyle-demon had vanished.

As the men shifted back into their human forms, Luke looked at Noah. "You held him with your ability?"

Noah nodded. "I never should have shifted, but when I saw all of you on the move, I couldn't help myself. I'm sorry." He lowered his head, preparing for his punishment.

"That's understandable," Cade said. "Remember what it was like when we were kids? If we were around our parents when they shifted, we couldn't resist."

Noah inclined his chin toward Cade, silently thanking his friend for sticking up for him.

"You're right," Luke agreed. "I shouldn't expect him to have any more control than a young wolf would."

Noah's ears burned. The alpha may not expect him to have more control, but *he* expected himself to. He'd never be allowed to patrol with the pack if he didn't get his shit together, and he *definitely* couldn't be Amber's potential mate in this condition. They wouldn't allow his defective wolf to taint the alpha line.

CHAPTER THIRTEEN

"Is this your alpha?" Alrick shoved the tuft of fur he'd ripped from the wolf's hide through the magical prison wall.

Nylah's jaw clenched as she leaned toward his hand, and her nostrils flared, her pupils constricting as the scent registered. He sensed the flush of heat running through her veins, and while her skin didn't turn to gooseflesh, the fine hairs on her arms rose on end. Just as he suspected. The local werewolf pack—*her* pack—had noticed his presence. She would pay for their attack.

"What did you do to him?" The she-wolf moved to snatch the token, but he grabbed her wrist with his other hand.

He jerked her forward, slamming her head into the prison wall and bloodying her nose. The vexatious woman minimized her reaction, so he yanked again, releasing her when her nose broke with a satisfying *pop*.

"Son of a bitch!" She backed away, out of his reach, and clutched her face. Deep purple spread outward beneath her eyes, and she winced as she pushed the bone back into place.

Tough girl. Her abominable magic would heal her far too quickly. He dropped the wolf fur into her prison, and she scrambled to grab it. The blood had already ceased its flow from her nostrils. *Infuriating.*

"Did you hurt him?" Her voice held far more accusation than a woman in her position should dare.

"I did nothing to him, but he did this to me." He gestured to his shoulder, where the biggest wolf's teeth had penetrated his skin, cutting all the way to the bone. The extra piece of Thropynite he'd taken from Nylah had made him both stronger and more vulnerable at the same time. His flesh, which formerly had the strength of stone, had softened, turning to the consistency of skin in some places.

"Next time he'll do worse." She set the fur on the small table inside her cell, the same table where his witch would keep the flowers he brought to brighten her mood.

Alrick's chest ached at the unwelcome memory, and he rotated his shoulder to try and ease the pain. His skin was slowly mending itself, but he'd need to feed a few more times to regain his strength.

"Doubtful. There were four wolves, and they couldn't lay a claw on me. If it weren't for the man who accompanied them, with his blasphemous powers, I could have taunted them until they passed out from exhaustion."

"What man?" Her eyes narrowed, her fingers curling at her sides.

Interesting. He tilted his head. "He was some sort of witch with powers I've rarely encountered before. He held me still with his mind, which allowed the wolves to attack."

She rushed toward him, slamming into the invisible cell wall and rubbing her forehead. When she recovered, she pressed her palms against the barrier. "He's no witch. He's my brother, and if you lay a finger on him, I swear to God, I'll tear you into so many pieces, no one will even know you existed."

Alrick was fiercely protective of someone once, and look where that got him. "Perhaps when I tire of our conversations, I'll let you try. If you continue to take the Lord's name in vain, I'll be the one doing the shredding."

She scoffed. "Do you hear yourself? You were made from a fucking demon, yet you claim to be doing the work of God."

His jaw clenched. "Because I sacrificed myself for the greater good."

"Yeah. Keep telling yourself that."

He turned a chair around backward, straddling it and resting his arms on the back. "Tell me about your brother."

"No."

"Tell me where you found the Thropynite."

"Go fuck yourself."

She was feisty, much like his witch. Nylah's resemblance to her may have been the only thing stopping him from digging his claws into her skull and retrieving all the information at once.

"You love him. I can see that." When she didn't respond, he continued, "I once cared for someone enough to risk my life to protect her." A mistake which added fuel to the demonic rage inside him.

"Your fiancée?" She sat in the chair next to the small table, arching a brow in defiance.

"She was one of the forsaken, like yourself. A witch." He chuckled, though he wasn't sure why. Simply talking about the treacherous woman tore his heart to shreds. "I loved her in spite of her ungodly magic."

"How very kind of you."

"When the Sect recruited me, I was forced to cut ties with her, but my love for her never ceased. We were to raid her village, killing all the forsaken in a single night, but I couldn't allow her to be harmed. I warned her. I bought her passage on a ship to New Orleans and begged her to start a new life, out of the Sect's reach."

"Let me guess. You missed her so much, you followed her here to live happily ever after."

"I missed her, yes, but there is no happily ever after in store for me. She followed my instructions and fled to America, while I stayed in Europe and thinned out the supernatural population."

She crossed her arms. "And what brought you to my lovely town? Your Sect trying to expand its reach? Are there others like you here?"

"We are the only ones, to my knowledge." He gestured to his brothers. "As for what brought us here, it was your kind. The werewolves of Paris organized all the neighboring packs into an army. They were the only ones who could sense our true nature in our human forms, so they attacked us when we were at our weakest, murdering us in masses. The Sect disbanded our legion, abandoning us, so I and my brothers fled to save our souls."

"Your true nature is hard to miss. Have you looked in a mirror lately?"

"We brought a piece of the Thropynite with us, for without it, we turn to stone ourselves." He cast his gaze to his brothers. "But it wasn't enough. We lost the ability to shift from human to gargoyle, getting stuck in this halfway rendering of both our forms."

"And I guess your witch took one look at you and told you to fuck off."

A growl rumbled in his chest. "She would not have me, but I could not live without her. I brought her here to the room you now reside in. Time moves at a crawl in this dimension, so she was mine for one hundred years."

"Then you got tired of her and killed her?"

He should have. "She tricked me and escaped. She destroyed the Thropynite, turning us to stone, and we've been frozen ever since… until you brought a piece here. Where did you find it?"

She pursed her lips and narrowed her eyes, refusing to speak.

"I'll need to feed again to heal this wound. Your brother's magic is formidable. I love the taste of a powerful heart."

Her eyes widened. "You wouldn't."

He laughed. "You know what I am and my purpose in life. What reason would make you doubt my word?"

"Kill me. Take my heart."

"Oh, but I enjoy your company far too much. You'll either tell me what I want to know, or your brother will be my next meal."

CHAPTER FOURTEEN

"You didn't have to cook." Noah sat at the table in Amber's kitchen while she finished making dinner. "We could have ordered takeout."

She set a plate of crawfish étouffée in front of him and took the seat beside him. "I don't mind. I actually enjoy cooking, and it's not every day I have someone else to cook for." She gazed into his eyes, staring longer than comfortable, willing the connection between them to form. Surely if his wolf had claimed her, he would have said something. She'd made her interest in him clear, so there was no chance of him scaring her away.

She didn't feel the tether that Odette described magically forming, so she looked away and shrugged. "Besides, with the curfew Luke put on the pack, it's obviously not safe to be out in the Quarter at night. I couldn't endanger the life of a delivery person."

"Good point." He took a bite of his dinner. "This is delicious."

"Thanks. It's my mom's recipe."

They ate in silence for a while because she couldn't make herself bring up the conversation they'd left unfinished a few nights ago. Honestly, she hoped he would bring it up, but he seemed content to eat his meal, smiling at her occasionally as if the kiss they shared never happened.

"Any news on Nylah?" she asked.

He swallowed his food, his eyes growing wide briefly before he spoke, "The pack is searching the area around Grunch Road and where we found the body for any signs that she might…for signs of her. So far, they've found nothing. Any news on your end?"

She shook her head. "I still feel like she's alive, but that's all I'm getting."

"Me too."

Amber chewed the inside of her cheek. She'd known Noah all her life, and the tension in his shoulders combined with the way his gaze darted about the room made it obvious he was holding something back.

"Luke said you helped them with the Grunch last night." Between running the bar and being the alpha's sister, Amber was privy to more information than a normal pack member would be. Plus, she drilled her brother with questions this morning when she found out Noah had been on the scene with him.

"I don't know how much I helped. The bastard still got away."

"Yeah, but they never would have come close to catching him if not for you. I guess you're getting more control over your wolf?"

"I don't know about that either." He shoved another scoop of étouffée into his mouth, avoiding eye contact.

"You'll get there, I'm sure." She reached across the table and placed her hand on top of his.

His breath caught at the contact, and he looked at their joined hands before gazing into her eyes. "I have no control. I shouldn't have shifted last night when the others took off to fight the Grunch. Cade was injured because of me."

"That's normal." She laced her fingers through his. "With the moon nearly full, and your packmates shifting, how could you resist? Even Luke was like that when his wolf first awoke."

Noah shook his head. "I'm not thirteen. It feels like I've got an alien living inside my body, battling me for dominance. I'm out of control."

She traced her thumb over his. "I'm not afraid of you."

"You should be." He slipped from her grasp, resting his hand in his lap.

Amber picked up her fork and pushed the food around on her plate. "Your wolf knows me now. That won't happen again."

"You don't know that."

"Yes, I do. I have powers too, remember?" Honestly, she *didn't* know. She'd had no more premonitions about Noah since she'd sensed his change, but logic told her she was right. His wolf didn't know who she was then; now it did. Problem solved.

She watched him eat for a few more minutes. Ever since she'd mentioned his sister, his demeanor had changed. He seemed nervous now, as if he had a secret. "What are you not telling me about Nylah?"

He froze with the fork halfway to his mouth before looking at her and returning it to his plate. "Nothing."

"You're lying." She leaned her forearms on the table, holding his gaze. "You can trust me."

Sighing, he lowered his head and tugged a slip of paper from his pocket. He held it tightly, the tip of his thumb turning white from the pressure before he handed it to her. She unfolded it and read the words on the page.

I can't tell you where I'm going or why, but I promise to return with an answer to your prayers.

"This is Nylah's handwriting. When did she give you this?"

"She put it on my dresser the night she left."

She turned the page over, looking for more information, but the single sentence was all she'd written. "You knew she didn't go rogue?"

"No, I had no idea she left to work for the congress. This is all she told me."

She read the words again, realization dawning. "'An answer to your prayers.' Do you think Nylah brought the Thropynite here?"

"I know she did. Look." He showed her a series of texts he'd received.

"These are all from different numbers."

"Burner phones. I've tried replying, but the messages don't go through. My prayer was to awaken my wolf, and Nylah answered it."

"And woke the Grunch in the process. Holy crap." She gave the note back to him, and he folded it before returning it to his pocket. "This is bad, Noah. If Luke finds out…" She shook her head. "If the *congress* finds out she was the cause of the very thing she was sent to investigate…"

"I know. We'll both be dogfood. That's why you can't tell anyone about this. How the stone got here doesn't matter. The pack just needs to find Nylah and stop the Grunch."

She nodded. "You're absolutely right. We'll keep it between us. I'm sure she had no idea bringing the Thropynite here would awaken the Grunch." How could she? Information on the stone was so scarce, it was thought to be merely a legend until now.

"Thank you." He took her hand beneath the table, and his magic vibrated across her skin, stronger than it had ever been.

"What are friends for?" She laced her fingers through his, sandwiching his hand between both of hers. "Thank *you* for trusting me."

As she held his gaze, something passed between them, like the shared secret formed a bond, deepening their relationship. He smiled and brushed a strand of hair from her forehead before gliding his fingers down her cheek in a much more intimate way than a friend would touch her.

Rising, she carried their empty plates to the sink, grabbed two more beers from the fridge, and padded toward the living room. Noah followed and sank onto the sofa next to her. He took a drink of the beer she offered before setting the bottle on the coffee table.

She set her bottle next to his and angled her body toward him. "We need to finish the conversation we started before you shifted. You have a wolf now, so you can't use that argument against us dating."

He took her hand and scooted closer. "I don't want to have any argument against us dating." He cupped her cheek in his hand, running his thumb across her skin.

Being near him, her entire body hummed, and his dark brown eyes held so much emotion, she couldn't have looked away if she tried. "So don't argue." She drifted toward him.

"I won't." He pressed his lips to hers. They were warm and soft, contrasting with the coarse scruff on his chin, and as she leaned into him, she slid her arms around his shoulders.

An *mmm* resonated in his throat as he coaxed her lips apart with his tongue, and she opened for him willingly, losing herself to the feel of his strong arms wrapped around her. Everything about being with Noah felt right. His scent, his touch, his taste. She couldn't fathom why it had taken her so long to feel the spark, but now, the flame had turned into an inferno.

Yes, this was technically their first "date," but being friends as long as they had, they'd already gone through the *getting to know you* part of a relationship. The only new territory left for her to discover was his body, and she couldn't wait to explore every inch.

Gripping the back of his neck, she rose onto her knees and straddled him. His deep inhale sent a shiver down her spine, and as he glided his hands up and down her back, she slid in closer until she met the bulge in his jeans.

He groaned, gripping her hips, and she moved against him. The friction, even through their clothes, sent a bolt of electricity shooting straight to her core. Good lord, she needed this man.

She slid her hands beneath his shirt, and as her fingers met skin, he sucked in a sharp breath. He was soft flesh over hard muscle. The perfect combination of strength and comfort. Everything she wanted in a mate.

"Amber," he whispered against her lips. "Amber, wait." He clutched her shoulders, breaking the kiss. "Before this goes any further, we need to talk."

"You said you didn't want to argue." She kissed him again, and he moaned, sliding his fingers into her hair.

With a sharp exhale, he pulled away. "It's not my argument we need to discuss. It's yours."

And there was her answer. She didn't feel the tether Odette mentioned because it didn't exist. She slid off him and folded her hands in her lap. "Your wolf hasn't claimed me."

He shook his head. "The guys have described what it feels like, and I…I don't know if I'm capable of it."

"Of course you are; don't be silly."

"I mean it. This wolf inside me doesn't feel like it's mine. He hasn't claimed *me,* so I don't see how he could claim anyone else. *I* have feelings for you. I always have, but this wolf…" He blew out a hard breath. "I don't think you want it tainting the alpha line. There's something wrong with me."

"I don't give a shit about the alpha line, Noah, and there's nothing wrong with you. I wanted you before you had a wolf, and I want you still. You'll get him under control."

"And if I don't?"

"You will." She refused to entertain any other outcome.

He leaned forward, resting his elbows on his knees. "You said yourself Nylah is still alive, so this wolf in me must have been awakened by the Thropynite. Wherever my sister is, she has the stone."

"So? Once we find her, she'll still have the stone. You'll still have your wolf."

"What if this isn't *my* wolf? What if the Thropynite didn't awaken the one inside me? What if its magic fabricated one?"

"That's not…" She grabbed her beer from the table and took a drink. "I don't think…"

"But you don't *know*, and neither do I."

She tipped back her bottle, draining the contents before returning it to the table. "So where does that leave us? Are you saying you don't want to be with me?"

"No, Amber." He took her hand in both of his. "I'm not saying that at all. I'm saying you shouldn't want to be with me."

Not this again. "You don't get to decide what I want."

"Then tell me. Knowing what you know about this wolf and what it's done to you…what do you want?"

"I want you." She laughed as pressure built in the back of her eyes, and she blinked, trying to hold back the tears. "I…" She clamped her mouth shut.

You know what? Screw it. She was too old to play games. If he couldn't handle a woman crying over him, it was best she found out now. A tear slid down her cheek. "I have six months to find a mate, or I'll risk bringing shame to my family name. My father could lose his seat on the congress, and Luke… My actions could jeopardize the pack, and I won't allow that to happen. I *will* take a mate by my thirtieth birthday."

"See? I knew you cared about the alpha line."

"I do, and I don't think you'll taint it. You are the only person I can imagine spending the rest of my life with. I think about you constantly when we're apart. When we're together, my blood hums, and I feel like I can't get close enough to you." Another tear slid down her cheek.

"I want to be with you," she continued, "but if you don't feel the same about me, say so. I'm not going to chase you. If you don't want to be with me, I'll move on and look for someone else."

He sat silently, gazing into her eyes, his mouth screwing over to one side as if he didn't know how to break the news. Had she misread the signs? Noah didn't have the best reputation when it came to women. She couldn't recall him having a relationship that lasted longer than a month. Was the passion she felt from him when they kissed merely fabricated? Was it nothing more than the sexual urge of a man for a woman?

He lowered his gaze to their entwined hands, took a deep breath, and let it out slowly. Raising his eyes to meet hers once more, he furrowed his brow. "All I want is to make you happy. I do feel the same, and I do want to be with you."

Her throat thickened, and another tear slid down her cheek. Cupping her face in his hand, he wiped it away with his thumb before leaning in and kissing her. Cool relief flooded her body, but as she tried to move closer to him, he pulled away.

"There's still the issue with this wolf. What are we going to do if he doesn't claim you?"

Her heart ached at the thought. Maybe she should take Odette up on her offer of praying to the Voodoo loa of love. Perhaps there was some sort of spell that would convince the wolf she belonged with him.

Who was she kidding? Magic couldn't force a fate-bound bond. The future of her relationship was up to fate itself. "How about we take it one day at a time? I don't see any reason why we can't enjoy each other's company while you're getting your wolf under control." She slid her hand up his thigh.

"If I get him under control, and he still doesn't claim you?" He placed his hand on top of hers.

"We'll cross that bridge when we get to it."

He folded his arms over his chest. "You mean you'll leave me."

She sighed. "I refuse to be the reason you live your life without a fate-bound. If your wolf doesn't claim me, we can't be together, but I don't want to focus on that right now."

"Neither do I, but…" He froze and clutched his stomach. "Oh, shit."

"What's wrong?"

The tendons in his neck protruded like he was straining, and a sinking sensation formed in Amber's core. Sweat beaded on his forehead as he ground his teeth.

"Is it?" She gripped the arm of the sofa.

He nodded. "Run."

She shot to her feet and darted around to the back of the couch.

"I can't stop it," he mumbled a moment before he transformed into a wolf.

The beast locked his gaze on Amber, and her blood fell from her head to her feet. "Not again." She shuffled backward, trying her damnedest not to make any sudden movements. Noah was in there somewhere. He wouldn't try to attack her again.

The wolf growled, baring his massive teeth, and Amber's back met the wall behind her. "Hey, buddy. I'm supposed to be your fate-bound. Don't you recognize me?" She inched toward the bedroom door, her heart frantically pounding against her ribs. "Tell him, Noah."

Narrowing his eyes, the wolf snarled.

"Or not."

The wolf climbed onto the couch, his enormous paws resting on the back pillows as he glared at her. This felt like the exact opposite of being claimed as a mate. He rocked back onto his haunches, and she darted into the bedroom before he could spring, slamming the door so hard, it bounced back open without latching.

If she'd have thought this through, she'd have headed out the front door rather than trapping herself in a room with no exit, but here she was, backed into a corner. A thud sounded from the living room as the wolf's paws hit wood, and her heart lodged in her throat.

He lurked in the doorway, and a low growl reverberated through the room. He prowled toward her, moving slowly. All he'd have to do was lunge and she'd be dead, if not from his teeth, then from the heart attack that was about to take her under.

Her gaze never straying from the wolf, she fumbled with her nightstand, gripping a lamp to defend herself. He growled, crouching low and inching toward her. She tossed the lamp aside, drawing his attention toward the window, and scrambled over the bed, racing out of the room and pulling the door shut behind her.

Now he finally lunged. He hit the door with a *bang* and howled, scratching at the wood when he couldn't bust it open. Amber gripped the knob, pulling with all her weight to keep it closed as she fished her phone from her pocket and dialed her brother. Luke answered on the third ring.

"It happened again," she said through clenched teeth. "Noah shifted. He's locked in my bedroom."

"Are you okay?"

"Yeah, he didn't attack, but he is not a happy wolf."

"I'm on my way."

This was insane. One minute, Noah was talking to Amber about the possibility of building a future together, and the next, this goddamn beast had taken over, scaring the shit out of her again.

The wolf snarled, slamming his shoulder into the door to get to her. The beast wasn't connected to him on a soul level, so Noah couldn't decipher exactly what he was feeling. Based on the howls and growls, his guess was rage.

"Noah, I know you're in there," Amber's voice drifted through the wood. "You need to take back control. You've done it before, so I know you can do it again."

God, how he wanted to. If he could get this fucking wolf under control, he could spend his time convincing Amber she didn't need to be his fate-bound. The man loved her enough to be happy. If only she could be happy with him.

"It's open," she called, and heavy footsteps sounded on the hardwood floor.

The wolf let out a low growl, his ears flattening against his head as he sensed the alpha's presence. Luke pounded on the door. "Noah, get your wolf under control and shift. That's an order."

He fought to gain dominance, but the wolf refused to let go. It tossed its head back, issuing a long, pained howl.

"Right now, Noah," Luke commanded. "If he can't shift, I'll have to go in and subdue him," he said to Amber.

"Noah, please," she pleaded. "You can do this. I know you can."

Her voice seemed to soothe the beast. Maybe it just soothed the man, but either way, the wolf relinquished control, and he shifted to his human form. He raked his hands through his hair, fisting them and pulling at the roots.

The growl this time came from his own throat, and as the door opened, he whirled around, making Amber flinch. "Goddammit! I'm sorry, Amber. I don't know why this keeps happening."

"I guess it's safe to say your wolf won't be claiming me anytime soon." Her lips curved into a sad smile and flattened again as she lowered her gaze.

Luke stood behind her with his arms crossed. "Until it does, you two are not to be alone together."

Amber spun around to face him. "I'll be alone with him if I want to be alone with him. Big Brother doesn't get to run my life."

"But your alpha makes the rules when it comes to the wolves." He softened his gaze. "I'm only thinking about your safety."

"Thanks, but I can take care of myself."

He blew out a frustrated breath. "Okay, then imagine how Noah would feel if his wolf harmed you. Do you want to put that on him?"

"I…" She looked at Noah, and sadness filled her eyes. "No, I don't."

"I'm going to make a phone call. You two wait here." Luke turned on his heel and strode out of the bedroom.

"I'm so sorry." Noah moved toward Amber but hesitated. His wolf must've scared the daylights out of her, so he doubted she'd want to be anywhere near him.

"It's not your fault." She stepped into his embrace, wrapping her arms around his waist and holding him tight. "We're going to figure this out."

Noah closed his eyes, memorizing the way she felt pressed against him. He'd hugged her hundreds of times since they were kids, but now, knowing she cared for him the way he cared for her, holding her made an ache spread through his body that felt so good, it was almost painful…nearly unbearable.

He nuzzled against the side of her head, breathing in her sweet floral scent. "What if it is my fault?"

"What do you mean?"

"If Nylah is alive, the only way I'd gain the ability to shift would be from the Thropynite, and I knew she was trying to find it. I could have done something to stop her from bringing it here."

"No. Shh…" She leaned back, holding his face in her hands. "It is not your fault. If I were in your place, if I were Luke's twin and couldn't shift, I'd do anything it takes to make it right. Fate dealt you a bad hand. You and Nylah did what you had to do to fix it."

"Amber…"

She brushed her lips to his. Her soft, gentle kiss warmed him to his core, and while he had no idea what his wolf felt at the moment, the man felt an overwhelming urge to protect her. Luke was right; they couldn't be together unchaperoned. It wasn't worth the risk.

"Ahem." Luke stood in the doorway, sympathy pinching his brow as he looked at them.

Amber turned to face her brother, keeping one arm wrapped around Noah's waist. As Luke's gaze flicked between them, she rested her hand on Noah's chest, answering the unspoken question hanging in the air.

Noah made eye contact with Luke, his own silent question causing nausea to churn in his gut. With Amber's position in the pack, their feelings for each other wouldn't matter if the alpha didn't approve.

Luke held his gaze for what felt like an eternity before looking at Amber. Her grip tightened around Noah's waist, and Luke returned his gaze to Noah. The alpha inhaled deeply, and Noah held his breath. As he exhaled, Luke nodded once, and cool relief unfurled on Noah's core. One hurdle had been crossed. Now, he just had to convince his unruly wolf to claim her.

"I'm sending you to the congress for an examination," Luke said.

Noah swallowed hard. He was one step closer to his secret being spilled, and who knew what kind of punishment the congress would deal? "They believe Nylah is dead?"

"They do."

Amber sensed his unease and patted his chest. "When do we leave?"

"You're not going," Luke said.

"The hell I'm not." She released her hold on Noah and moved toward her brother. "I'm not leaving his side. Besides, I can make myself useful. I'll scour the archives for information about the Grunch and the stone. They may believe Nylah is dead, but Noah and I know she's not. We're going to find her."

"I don't want you near him without an alpha present."

"Then come with us."

"I won't leave the pack while a murderer is on the loose. Whether it's a Grunch or not, it's obviously supernatural. Dad's driving out tomorrow to pick him up."

Amber sighed, irritated. "Dad is an alpha. Every member of the congress is a retired alpha. You'll have to come up with a better argument than that to keep me here."

Luke's jaw tightened. "All right, but you're both staying at Mom and Dad's."

She placed a hand on Luke's shoulder and kissed his cheek. "I'll start packing."

Noah fought his smile. Amber's strength and determination were two of the things he loved about her.

"Say your goodbyes. I'm going home, and so is Noah." Luke returned to the living room.

"I'll see you tomorrow." Amber hugged him and gave him a quick kiss on the lips.

He was tempted to lean in for more. Now that he had her, he couldn't get enough of her, but it was best not to keep the alpha waiting. Luke had approved both their relationship and their going to the congress together. He didn't need to press his luck.

"Until then." He tucked her hair behind her ear, pressing his lips to her forehead before heading out the door.

Cicadas chirped in the trees above, their shrill song greeting him as he stepped into the warm night air. A couple lounged on the porch of the neighboring house, and a dog barked from across the street.

Pausing in the driveway, Noah turned to Luke. "Can I ask you a personal question?"

He arched a brow. "You can ask. I might not answer."

"Fair enough." He glanced toward the house where Amber waved from the window. He returned the wave, and she disappeared behind the curtain. "What does it feel like when you find your fate-bound? How do you know?"

Luke pressed his lips into a hard line and glanced at the house. "If she was yours, you wouldn't have to ask."

CHAPTER FIFTEEN

"Come in, come in. It's so good to see you." Amber's mom passed her up, pulling Noah into a tight hug instead. "I'm so sorry about Nylah." She wrapped her arm around his shoulders, guiding him into the living room.

"It's good to see you too, Mom," Amber said under her breath, and she turned to her father. She'd held her tongue on the drive over, not wanting to bring up her failed "dates" in front of Noah. Now, she had to put her foot down. Otherwise, her parents would probably send fertility spells disguised as sweet tea as soon as she mated. "I don't appreciate you meddling in my affairs. Sending those men to meet me was out of line."

He shook his head and patted her back as if she were a little girl. "It's the security of the pack I was concerned about, sweetheart."

"Of course," she muttered. "My happiness doesn't matter as long as I continue the alpha line." Amber moved toward the living room, while her dad disappeared into his study. She took a deep breath, bracing herself for her mother's form of meddling—which didn't seem so bad compared to her dad's—and strode toward an accent chair.

Her mom caught her hand, and, making a *tsk* sound, she ushered her toward the couch next to Noah.

I'm going to strangle you for this, Luke. Her brother was such a tattletale.

"How are you two holding up?" Debbie asked. "How are your parents, Noah?"

He glanced at Amber. "They're holding onto hope."

"Nylah isn't dead, Mom."

"How do you know? Your father said—"

"I just do. Trust me on this. I can feel it, okay?" She gave her mom a pointed look.

"Oh, that's good news, isn't it?" She looked toward the study, but Amber's dad had closed the door. "You'll share details when you can?"

Amber nodded, thankful her mom so easily dropped the subject, while simultaneously bracing herself for the next inevitable line of questioning.

"So, then, tell me what's new with you, Noah." Debbie leaned forward in her seat and patted him on the knee.

Noah chuckled. "You mean besides suddenly inheriting the ability to shift?"

"Yes, besides that." Her mom waved off his comment, grinning from ear to ear and cutting her gaze between them. "Oh, I can't stand it. I wanted you to say it first, but…congratulations, you two. Luke told me."

Noah's eyes widened, and his hands curled into fists in his lap.

Amber closed her eyes for a long blink, letting out a slow exhale. "What exactly did he tell you?"

"Well, that you're together. I can't wait to start planning the wedding."

"We, umm…" Noah gave Amber a desperate look. Poor guy. *Way to scare him off, Mom.*

Her mother's smile faded. "Did he…? Is it not true?"

"We're dating." Amber placed her hand on top of Noah's fist, and he relaxed with her touch. "That's all for now, Mom." She flashed another pointed look at her, hoping she'd take the hint.

In typical Debbie style, she did not. "Nonsense. You've been best friends since you were knee high to a cicada. If romance is sparking after all this time, you'll be mates before you know it."

Amber's dad strode into the room and cleared his throat. "The congress is ready for you, Noah. Amber, would you like to tag along?"

"Absolutely." She started to argue that she wouldn't be *tagging* anywhere—that she had work to do—but she was thankful for the distraction from her mother's prying, so she kept her mouth shut.

"I'll have dinner ready for you when you get home," her mother said. "I'm making my famous meatloaf for Noah."

"Mmm…" Noah said as he rose to his feet. "Thank you, Mrs. Mason. It's been a minute since I've had your meatloaf. I'm looking forward to it."

Outside, Amber climbed into the back seat of her dad's jet-black Silverado, and they headed toward the werewolf national congress headquarters. Luckily, her dad didn't ask any questions about her relationship with Noah. She didn't want to think about what would happen if his wolf didn't claim her.

Instead, they rode in silence. Her dad's gaze remained glued to the road, while Noah stole glances at her through the side mirror. Amber leaned her head against the cool glass, offering him the best smile she could fake while her mind whirred with what-ifs. Until last night, she'd been confident Noah could get his wolf under control, but what if he couldn't?

What if Luke's nod of approval had merely been his way of warding off another forced shift? Both times Noah's wolf had taken control, they had been discussing their relationship, and both times, the beast had stalked her. What if that was the animal's way of telling them they weren't meant to be? Or what if the congress had other plans for Noah and tried to remove him from the pack? They'd have to go rogue to be together if that were the case, and going rogue was something Amber could never do.

Or could she?

Her vision blurred as she gazed out the window at the trees whizzing past, and nausea churned in her gut. There was no need to get worked up about this now. She had no control over what the congress would decide about him, and her energy was best focused on things she *could* do.

Gravel crunched beneath the tires as they pulled off the main road onto a narrow path only wide enough for a single vehicle. A car approaching from the opposite direction had to pull over halfway into the ditch, while her dad did the same as they passed. Oak trees lined both sides of the road, creating a tunnel effect, their branches reaching out to tangle with their neighbors'.

Amber swallowed the bile from the back of her throat. She had the foreboding sense that she was being led to her doom, which was absolutely ridiculous. It didn't feel like a premonition, and her father wouldn't bring her here if she'd be in any sort of danger. She'd simply watched too many horror movies for her own good. From now on, movie night would consist of romantic comedies only.

An eight-foot stone wall surrounded the property as they approached, and an iron gate blocked the entrance. Damn, this wasn't how she imagined the congress at all. She'd pictured a cabin in the woods with maybe a subterranean tunnel system where they housed the archives.

The gate rolled open, and her father pulled into the driveway of a massive nineteenth-century colonial mansion, complete with columns and a long gallery on the second floor. He stopped the truck at the top of the U-shaped drive, and a valet scurried out to open his door.

Amber stifled a laugh. Her father was *so* not the being-waited-on type. Noah opened her door, and she slid out, gripping his hand like this was the last time she'd get to touch him.

"Everything you are about to see is to remain in strictest confidence," her dad said as if reciting a speech written by someone else. "Amber, what you find in the archives must be discussed with Luke before the information is disseminated to the pack, and Noah…" He glanced at her before looking into Noah's eyes. "What happens in the congress's chambers stays in the chambers."

Thanks, Dad. Not helping with the overbearing sense of impending doom. "Can I talk to you in private for a second?" She squeezed Noah's hand and released it before lacing her arm around her dad's elbow and walking him out of earshot. "Is Noah in danger being here? They won't…do anything to him, will they?"

Her dad missed a beat in his reply, and something strange flashed in his eyes before he composed his answer. "They're just going to examine him right now." He patted her hand and gestured toward the entrance.

Yeah… Not helping at all.

Inside, a crystal chandelier hung in the foyer, and hardwood floors stretched down a long hallway. A man around Amber's age sat at a desk in a small room to the left, and when he saw her father, he shot to his feet.

"The witch is getting set up, Mr. Mason," he said. "It'll be a few more minutes."

"Witch?" Amber clutched her father's arm and lowered her voice to a whisper. "You said they were only examining him."

He glanced at her hand on his arm before giving her a sharp look, reminding her that, while he may be her father, in here, he was a congresswolf and should be treated as such. "Let's get you to the archives, and then I'll take Noah to the examination room."

Amber released her hold, taking Noah's hand instead, and followed her father down the hall and up a staircase to the second floor. A line of windows revealed the back courtyard, where stone benches surrounded a fountain and topiaries trimmed into the shapes of wolves dotted the grounds.

The wood floor creaked with their footsteps, and as her dad opened a set of double doors, Amber's breath caught at the sight of the archives. Row after row of floor-to-ceiling bookcases lined the dimly lit space, their shelves filled with antique volumes and boxes of who knew what.

"This is my daughter," he said to the woman behind a raised counter. "She has permission to use the archives." He turned to Amber. "Cynthia will help you get started."

Amber pulled Noah into a hug. He was tense, but as she nuzzled into his neck, brushing her lips over his skin, he relaxed a little. "I'll be here when you're done."

He pulled back, running his thumb over her cheek before pressing a piece of paper into her hand. "I'll see you soon."

"Noah." Her dad stood halfway down the hall, so Noah gave her a half-smile, turned, and walked away.

Amber stepped into the archives and unfolded the paper to find the note Nylah left him when she started working for the congress. She quickly folded it and shoved it into her pocket. "Hi, Cynthia, I'm Amber."

"Hi." She scurried from around the counter, the heels of her patent leather pumps clicking on the floor. A black pencil skirt brushed the tops of her knees, and a light blue silk blouse perfectly matched her eyes. "I'm second-born as well. What's your ability?"

"Empathic premonitions. You?"

"Finding lost things…and people."

Amber's pulse thrummed. "You can find missing people?"

"Usually." She gestured to a table in the center of the room and moved toward it. "You're looking for Nylah L'Eveque, right? She was from your pack."

"Yes. Can you find her?"

Cynthia shook her head, and her blonde curls swished around her face. "I've tried."

"Will you try again?"

"I need an item that belonged to the missing person. Clothing, jewelry, a journal. Anything that had meaning to them. I sat in Nylah's room, surrounded by her possessions, and I couldn't locate her, so I doubt—"

"Will you try one more time? I have a letter she wrote." She pulled the note from her pocket, offering it to Cynthia.

"One more time." Cynthia took the note and flashed a sympathetic smile as she began to unfold the paper.

Amber put her hand on the letter. "It's private." Noah had given it to her so the congress wouldn't find it. She had no idea if she could trust Cynthia to keep his secret.

"Of course." She refolded the letter, clutching it in both hands as she closed her eyes and inhaled deeply.

Amber stared at her, willing an image of Nylah's location to come to her mind. The seconds stretched into excruciatingly long minutes before Cynthia finally opened her eyes.

"Nothing." She handed the letter back to Amber. "It's as if she no longer exists."

"What does that mean? She didn't just vanish into thin air."

Cynthia pursed her lips. "Usually when this happens, it's because…" She cringed before finishing, "It's because the body has been decimated. Turned to ash and spread in the wind."

Amber's stomach sank, and she touched a hand to a bookshelf to steady herself. "No. She can't be dead. I can feel that she's alive, and so can Noah."

"And I can't feel her at all." Cynthia drew her shoulders toward her ears. "But that's why you're here, right? To see what you can find out about the Grunch she was investigating. Come on; I've already pulled some volumes."

Amber followed Cynthia to the table where a stack of books lay on the corner. "Do you have any information about the Thropynite?"

"I'll see what I can find." Cynthia scurried away, and Amber dove into the books.

She started with a thick, leather-bound volume filled with handwritten pages dated 1729. The paper smelled old and musty, and as she flipped the delicate pages, she found an entry documenting the Grunch. She scoured the book before moving on to the next. After two hours of reading, she hadn't gleaned any more information about the gargoyle creatures than what she already knew.

And the Thropynite… Two different entries about the stone stated the person had to have physical contact with it for the magic to activate. If that were the case, it simply being in New Orleans couldn't possibly be the reason Noah could shift. And if the Thropynite had nothing to do with his newfound ability, that could only mean Nylah was dead.

So what was this nagging feeling both she and Noah had that she was still alive? Could they both be imagining it? She was about to give in to defeat when Cynthia brought one more book.

"I found this one. It's an account written by a witch who was supposedly held captive by the Grunch, so I don't know how much merit it has. The creatures killed magical beings. I doubt they would have kept her alive, but here it is." She set the thin book on the table in front of Amber and took the seat next to her. "Have you found anything useful?"

"Not yet." Amber opened the book and read the witch's account.

Her eyes widened as she took in the story, her pulse thrumming in her ears. Her knee bounced beneath the table, and when she finished the short report, she gently closed the book. "While I'm here, would you mind finding the records of how the Crescent City Wolf Pack was formed? I'd like to read our history."

"Absolutely." Cynthia stood and disappeared behind a shelf.

Amber waited a beat or two until her new friend was far enough away before pulling out her phone and snapping pictures of the pages in the witch's book. It was all here, in vivid detail, right down to the leader of the Grunch's name. If the account were true, she knew where Nylah was *and* why Noah inherited the ability to shift.

Noah's stomach soured as he followed his former alpha into the exam room. He'd expected to meet in the congress's chambers to be questioned by the lot of them. Instead, Mr. Mason gestured for him to enter a small room near the kitchen on the first floor. The scents of bleach and patchouli mingled in the air, creating a sickening smell that coated the inside of his nose and reached all the way down to his throat. He swallowed the rancid taste from his mouth and stepped inside.

A hospital bed stood in the center of the room. Leather shackles for his arms and legs lay open on the surface, and a woman in her mid-fifties with long black hair and bright green eyes stood in the corner.

Instinct forced Noah to retreat, and he backed into Mr. Mason's chest. He clutched Noah's arms. "This is Helga. She'll be conducting the exam." He pointed to a large rectangular mirror on the wall. "I'll be watching from the next room. Try to relax."

Yeah, right. Even the toughest alpha couldn't relax if he were chained to a bed, and he had a hunch those leather straps were reinforced with magic. Regular hospital restraints would be no match for the strength of a shifter.

"Do I have to be tied down?" He sat on the edge of the bed.

Mr. Mason gestured for him to lie on his back. "It's for Helga's safety. She's going to ask you to shift, and these restraints have been bespelled to remain intact and hold your wolf."

Noah ground his teeth as he lay back and let them strap him to the bed. Magic tingled on his wrists and ankles, and he rested his head on a thin pillow. The shackles gave him enough room to sit up, but he could only lift his arms halfway to his shoulders.

"I'll be in at the first sign of trouble." Mr. Mason nodded and left the room, closing the door behind him, the lock sliding into place sounding like a nail in a coffin. What had he gotten himself into?

Helga drifted to the end of the bed and hovered her hands above Noah's head. "Lie still."

He lifted his chained wrists. "I don't have much of a choice."

She shook her head, chiding him. "Can you sense your wolf? Describe what you feel."

"I can feel it's there, but that's about it. I don't have a clue about its emotions or what thoughts are running through its mind. I can call it to the surface to shift, but it's hard to regain control to shift back. It feels like it's not mine."

She clutched the sides of his head and hummed low in her throat. Her magic pricked at his skin like static, and her nails digging into his scalp reminded him of the carnage the Grunch had committed. He inhaled deeply, trying to calm his racing heart.

"It's strong, and it's yours. You have a block, though." She released her grip and drifted toward a table filled with glass bottles, dried herbs, and copper containers. She crushed some herbs with a mortar and pestle and mixed them with a yellow liquid in a bowl before bringing it to his bedside.

"Drink this." She offered it to him.

He hesitated, eyeing the bowl and arching a brow. "What is it?"

"A potion to open your mind." She grabbed his hand and shoved the bowl into his grasp. "Drink it."

He gazed at the steaming concoction and curled his lip. No way in hell was he consuming this without knowing what it was. "You want me to take drugs. What's in it? Is it LSD? Mushrooms?"

"It's magic." The witch huffed and glared at the two-way mirror.

"Drink the potion, Noah," Mr. Mason's voice boomed over the intercom.

Noah knew better than to disobey an alpha—especially one with a seat on the congress—so he pressed the bowl to his lips and swallowed the syrupy liquid. There was definitely some kind of root in there, as he could taste the earth and the sharp, bitter flavor of mold. He fought the urge to gag and handed the bowl to the witch before lying back and closing his eyes.

His head spun, the magic instantly taking hold and making him dizzy as all get-out. His stomach lurched, and he coughed, rolling to his side in case his lunch decided to make a reappearance.

Helga began chanting, either in a language he didn't understand, or the drugs were making her speech sound foreign. He couldn't tell which. The air in the room thickened, buzzing with electricity as the witch's magic built. She clutched his head again, rolling him onto his back and sending a jolt of energy straight through his skull and into his brain.

He was falling. Darkness consumed him for a moment before stars glittered all around. Then he splashed down into a sea of inky blue, the water flowing over his head until it was impossible to breathe. He struggled in his mind, swimming toward a light above the surface, but the harder he kicked, the farther away the light seemed.

As he hung weightlessly in the empty abyss, an image formed in his mind. Amber's sweet smile danced behind his eyes, and he rose, breaking the surface and gasping for breath.

"Now shift," the witch's voice grated in his ears.

He shook his head, squeezing his eyes shut and willing Amber's face to stay in his view. If the potion made him see her, there had to be a reason.

"Shift, Noah. That's an order." Mr. Mason's voice filled the room, and he was compelled to obey.

He called on the beast, *his* wolf, according to the witch, and he transformed. The wolf snarled, standing on the bed, the shackles magically tightening around his legs. He locked his gaze on the witch, and though Noah struggled to gain control, he was nothing more than a subconscious energy going along for the ride. The wolf rocked back before springing toward her.

The restraints held, and the bed toppled over, sending the wolf crashing to the floor. He scrambled to his paws and lunged again, dragging the bed as he prowled toward her. Noah tried to take over. He willed his body to shift, but the potion had rendered him powerless against the beast.

The door swung open a moment before Mr. Mason shifted and barreled toward him. The alpha growled, a deep vibration resonating from his chest, and placed himself between the witch and Noah's wolf, baring his teeth and looming toward him.

Thank the heavens Luke had trained the wolf to submit. He lay on his belly, resting his head on his paws and letting out a low whine. As the wolf relinquished control to the alpha, Noah grabbed on and forced the beast to release his hold.

Returning to his human form, Noah sat on the floor, unable to stand due to the restraints. "I'm sorry," he said to both Helga and the alpha.

Mr. Mason shifted and knelt beside him. "Are you in control now?"

"Yes, sir." He lowered his head.

They removed the restraints, and Noah helped Mr. Mason right the fallen bed before he led them into an office next door. Noah sank into a wooden chair while Helga and Mr. Mason conversed.

"What's the verdict?" the alpha asked.

Helga frowned at Noah. "The wolf belongs to him, as I said. However, it has not joined with his soul. This is why he lacks control."

"Any idea how this happened?"

"The wolf should not have been awakened. I sense magic was involved, which made the transformation go awry."

Mr. Mason's brows slammed down over his eyes. "Do you know anything about this?"

Noah's heart sank into his stomach. How much longer could he keep his secret? "Both Amber and I feel like Nylah is alive somewhere. That's all I know." He lowered his gaze to his lap, afraid the alpha could sense his lie.

"Do you know of a way to fuse the wolf to his soul?"

"You must find the magic that awakened it. It can either solve the problem or put the wolf to rest for good."

"In this condition, can the wolf claim a mate?" Mr. Mason asked.

"He wouldn't know it if it did." She clasped her hands in front of her. "He'll be a danger to any mate he might choose."

"Thank you, Helga. Please submit your report to the archives."

The witch nodded and left the room. Noah gripped his thighs, digging his fingertips into his muscles. He couldn't make himself breathe, so he sat there holding the end of his exhale, unable to move. Amber would never be safe around him. Not only had his selfish desire to awaken his wolf brought a reign of terror on New Orleans, but now he'd destroyed any chance he had at a life with the one person who mattered most.

Mr. Mason stood in front of him with his arms crossed. "Whatever relationship you have with my daughter ends now. I won't have you endangering her life."

Noah agreed.

CHAPTER SIXTEEN

Amber slipped her phone into her pocket as Cynthia returned with the books she'd requested. She smiled and thanked her before flipping one open and staring at the page, but her eyes didn't register the words. Instead, her thoughts raced in a thousand different directions as she chewed her bottom lip.

It all made sense now: Noah gaining the ability to shift, his wolf not wanting to obey him, why she was certain Nylah was alive. It was all she could do to keep from bursting out of the archives and intruding on the council's examination of Noah. She didn't need a witch to tell her what was going on with him; it was all recorded right here in this journal.

Her knee bounced incessantly beneath the table, and as the heavy door swung open and her father entered the room, she shot to her feet and started toward him. But she froze midstride when Noah didn't follow him in. "Where is he?" Her voice held accusation, and her father stiffened.

"He's waiting in the truck. Let's go home." He turned and strode out the door, leaving Amber standing there with her mouth open.

"What happened in the examination? Is he okay?" She jogged to catch up with her dad.

"The congress will be meeting tomorrow afternoon to discuss his affliction, so I'll be taking you both home first thing in the morning. That's all I can say."

"What do you mean that's all you can say?" She followed him down the stairs and out the front door, her heart running at a thousand miles a minute. "Dad, what are you not telling me? I'm part of the alpha line; I have a right to know. Or is that fact only convenient when you want it to be?"

He stopped, taking her biceps in his hands. "Your relationship with Noah ends today. He is not a welcome addition to our family."

She scoffed, opening and closing her mouth as she tried to find the words. "Are you serious? Mom has been on me nonstop to hook up with him, and now you're forbidding me from dating him?"

"That was before his affliction." His gaze softened, and he squeezed her arms before letting her go. "He's been deemed an unfit mate."

"Unfit? Why? Because his wolf is wild?" This couldn't be happening. They didn't come all this way with the intent to help Noah, only to have the national congress of werewolves say he was unfit to be her mate. No way. She refused to accept it. "I found something in the archives that expl—"

"Drop it, Amber. My decision is final." He gave her a pointed look, the same look he gave her when she was a kid and had been pressing her luck. The look that meant the conversation was over, end of story.

But this story was just beginning. "Don't you want to hear what I found in the archives?"

He sighed heavily. "Report your findings to Luke when you get home tomorrow. I don't *meddle* in your pack's affairs."

"No, you just want to control your children. First Luke's life, and now mine. Things are changing, Dad. You have to accept that—"

"Your mother has dinner waiting for us." He cut her off as if she were nothing more than a belligerent teenager and gestured to the truck where Noah sat in the passenger seat, staring out the front window.

"Noah." She ran to the truck and pulled on the handle, but his door was locked. She knocked on the window, and he looked at her with sad eyes, shaking his head.

With a groan, she climbed into the back seat, but before she could speak to him, her father joined them, silencing their would-be conversation. Amber buckled her seatbelt and clenched her teeth. Noah would talk to her; she just had to get him alone.

Country music playing quietly through the speakers softened the heavy silence hanging in the Chevy on the fifteen-minute drive to her parents' home. Neither her father nor Noah said a word, and Amber chewed the inside of her cheek, her dad's verdict playing on a loop in her mind. *Noah has been deemed an unfit mate.* That was total bullshit, and if her stubborn old man would allow her to explain what she'd found, he would feel otherwise.

She seethed with anger. She—and only she—would decide who was fit to be her mate. Noah was a better fit than any man she'd ever met.

Her mom was putting dinner on the table as they walked through the front door, and she smiled, oblivious to the news Amber had just received. She set it up so Amber would sit next to Noah, and her dad inhaled, opening his mouth as if to protest the arrangement. When her mom cocked her head, he sighed and took his seat. Amber sank into her chair and gave Noah a small smile, which he didn't return.

"How did the examination go?" her mom asked. "I hope all is well."

Noah cleared his throat and looked at her dad.

"Yes, Father." Amber folded her hands on the table. "What happened in the examination?"

He narrowed his eyes at her before addressing her mom. "We'll discuss it later." He shoved a piece of meatloaf into his mouth.

They ate in silence, the tension in the room so thick it rivaled the mashed potatoes. Amber slid her leg toward Noah, leaning it outward so her knee touched his. He swallowed hard and then shifted in his seat, moving his leg away from hers.

Amber's heart ached. No doubt her father had put the fear of God in him. The man was old-fashioned at best. He bought into the old ways, where the men's—especially the elders'—word was law no matter how irrational it may be.

Under Luke's command, the Crescent City Wolf Pack was finally seeing the light of the twenty-first century. No one—not her dad, not a bunch of old fogies in the congress—was going to send them back to the Dark Ages.

As they finished dinner, Noah stood and picked up his empty plate.

"Leave it," her mom said. "I'll take care of the dishes."

Noah returned his plate to the table, glancing at Amber before looking at her mom. "Thank you for dinner, Mrs. Mason. It was delicious."

She smiled warmly. "Any time, dear."

"I'm going to turn in early if that's all right."

"You two can take the big bedroom at the end of the hall upstairs." She gave Amber a conspiratorial wink.

"They'll be taking separate rooms," her dad said.

Her mom gave her a quizzical look. "Okay… Amber, you can have the second room on the right, then."

"Thank you." Noah pushed in his chair and strode out of the dining room without a second glance.

"I'll be in my study." Her dad stood there for a moment, but if he was expecting a goodnight from her, he would be sorely disappointed. She couldn't even look at the man.

As her father left, Amber picked up the plates and followed her mom into the kitchen. She waited until she heard the study door click shut, and they both turned to each other, speaking at once. Amber closed her mouth, letting her mom go first.

"What the devil is going on? It would have taken a butcher knife to chop through the tension in there."

Amber set the plates in the sink and turned on the water, just in case her old man was listening. "He has decided Noah is unfit to be my mate."

"What?" Her mom's mouth fell open. "That's the most ridiculous thing I've ever heard. You two are perfect for each other. What happened during the examination?"

"I have no idea. He won't tell me anything, except that my relationship with Noah is over. Will you talk to him?"

"Of course I will, but I don't know that it will do much good. You know how stubborn your father can be. Have you talked to Noah about this? What does he think?"

"I haven't been alone with him to ask. He barely looks at me." A sob bubbled up from her chest, but she caught it in her throat and blinked back the tears that threatened to spill.

"Oh, honey." Her mom pulled her into a hug. "I'm on your side. I'll get your father to come to bed early so you can talk to Noah."

"Thanks, Mom. You're the best."

Noah lay in the center of the queen-sized bed, staring at the ceiling fan whirring above. He'd felt his fair share of humiliation lately, but being called an unfit mate took the cake. He could hardly look Amber in the eye, much less have a conversation with her about it.

Anger fumed in his soul. She should have listened to him in the beginning when he told her she deserved better. His wolf awakening had given him the false hope that he might be able to be the mate she needed, and he'd let his guard down, allowing himself to fall completely head over tail for her.

And look where that landed him. Forbidden from taking a mate. Forbidden from love.

He growled and rolled onto his side, cursing his goddamn wolf for emerging when it did, cursing Nylah for finding the Thropynite, cursing himself for not stopping her. He could have accepted his fate and given up on the dream of becoming a shifter, but no. He'd been selfish. He'd put his sister's life in danger, and he'd almost killed Amber twice.

No, he did not deserve Amber or anyone, for that matter. He didn't deserve the air he breathed.

A light knock sounded on the door a moment before Amber stepped through. She wore a pale pink satin nightgown, and the moonlight streaming in through the window gave her fair skin an ethereal glow.

His entire body ached at the sight of her, his throat thickening as she glided across the room and sank onto the edge of the bed. He pushed to a sitting position, leaning his back against the headboard and forcing himself to look into her eyes.

"We need to talk." She folded one leg beneath her, angling her body to face him, her phone clutched in her hand.

"I know." He inhaled deeply before blowing out a hard breath. "I told you from the beginning I couldn't be the wolf you need."

"Stop it, okay? None of you know what I need better than me, so I don't want to hear any more of that. Tell me what happened during the examination."

"It was just me and a witch alone in a room with your dad watching through a window. She made me drink this potion that let her look into my psyche, and then I had to shift." His jaw clenched at the memory.

When he didn't elaborate, Amber rested her hand on his leg. "What happened then?"

He let out a sardonic laugh. "If I hadn't been chained to the bed with magical shackles… My wolf tried to attack, so your dad busted in and forced me to shift back to human. When it was over, the witch told your dad that being with me would put you in danger."

He shrugged and toyed with a loose thread in the sheet. "So here we are. I could be thrown in the pit just for being alone with you right now." Not that he cared. It was worth the risk to tell her a proper goodbye.

"First of all, we're not alone. My parents are asleep downstairs. Second, are you saying my dad is the only congresswolf who knows about the examination? No one else was there?"

"It was just the witch and your dad."

"So the congress hasn't deemed you an unfit mate. That's all my dad's doing." She laughed cynically. "Typical. It's just like my father to make a life-altering decision and expect everyone else to follow along."

"Once he meets with them tomorrow, I'm sure they'll agree. I'm a danger to everyone, and it's only a matter of time before they connect the dots and figure out I'm shifting because of the Thropynite and Nylah is the one who brought it here. She's better off never being found if they discover our secret."

"You're not shifting because of the stone. You'd have to make physical contact with it for its magic to affect you. Look at this." She offered him her phone, and he gazed at the image of an elegant script on a withered page.

"What is this?" He flipped through the photos, taking in page after page that she'd photographed.

"It's a witch's explanation of what happened to the Grunch. She claims the Grunch live in a pocket dimension, just outside our plane. Alrick, their leader, held her captive for a century, the magic of the dimension slowing time so she hardly aged. She managed to escape, and she stole the piece of Thropynite they'd brought here. She created a potion to destroy the stone, which froze them all in their dimension."

He furrowed his brow as he read the account. "If this is true, it's proof that Nylah *did* find the Thropynite. How will this help?"

"I think the Grunch have Nylah. If she's trapped in their pocket dimension, she has ceased to exist on this plane. Since she no longer exists here, your wolf was awakened, but because she hasn't actually passed on, your wolf can't fuse with your soul."

He stared into her bright blue eyes as he processed her words. So much hope filled them, he couldn't help but believe it was true. "That would explain why we both feel like she's alive, despite the evidence that she isn't."

She beamed a smile. "It makes perfect sense."

"When she retrieved the stone from overseas, it awakened the Grunch, and they took her while she was investigating their reappearance."

"She probably had no idea the Thropynite would awaken the monsters; no one even knew they were here. If we can find Nylah…"

"We'll find the stone."

"And the stone can fuse your wolf with your soul." She took his hand. "Then no one can say you're an unfit mate."

"And you found all this out while a witch was poking around in my mind." He laughed. "You're amazing."

"No one has to know what we're doing. I know a witch who will help us with the spell to disintegrate the stone. Remember Snow?"

He nodded.

"Whether Nylah is the one who brought it here or not, it won't matter once it's destroyed."

He tapped his thumb on his knee, his mind reeling with possibilities. "Does the witch's journal say how to activate the Thropynite's magic?"

Amber flipped through the images, scanning the pages. "It only lists a spell to destroy it, but I'm sure Snow can help us with that too."

"How will we find their dimension?"

"We know the general area to look in, and now that we know *what* we're looking for, you can use your gift. I'd bet the bar you'll be able to feel a disturbance in the atmosphere where the entrance is."

He did sense a heaviness in the air when he was there with Cade and James, but he'd chalked it up to creep factor. Maybe he was sensing the entrance to the Grunch's dimension. "It's worth a shot."

"We can fix this." She scooted closer until her leg rested against his. "And we can be together."

He traced his fingers up her cheek, sliding them into her silky hair. There was still the issue that his wolf might not claim her, even if it fused with his soul, but he didn't mention it. For the first time since this ordeal began, he felt hope. No need to kill the mood.

"You're the only person I can imagine spending the rest of my life with," she said, "and I know… I know everything is going to work out. It has to. I love you, Noah."

His heart felt like it burst into a million pieces, swirled around in his chest, and stitched itself back together again. "I love you too."

She climbed into his lap, straddling his groin, and ran her hands up his bare chest to hook them behind his neck. Her fingers felt like silk against his skin. Leaning down, she brushed a tentative kiss to his lips.

"Should we be doing this in your parents' house?" he whispered.

Her only answer was to crush her mouth to his.

He held in his moan, the thought of what her father might do if he found them together making him conscious of every sound they made. He almost stopped her, but as her lips glided down his neck, and she nipped his shoulder with her teeth, he said *screw it*. They were both consenting adults, for fuck's sake. They could do what they wanted.

He ran his hands up her sides to cup her breasts, and her nipples hardened beneath the satin as he teased them with his thumbs. Her lips parted on a deep inhale, her warm breath tickling his neck before she found his mouth once more. She tasted of mint, and as she slipped her tongue into his mouth to tangle with his, all the blood that was left in his head rushed to his groin.

He lifted her nightgown, tugging it upward until she raised her arms, allowing him to remove it and toss it aside. He slid his gaze down her form, taking in her delicate curves and smooth, lightly freckled skin before looking into her eyes. His mouth watered to taste her, and when she smiled, something snapped inside his chest like a glowstick coming to life. He still had no idea what his wolf was thinking, but the man needed her more than he needed air to breathe. He would die before he'd spend his life without her.

He stifled the growl rumbling in his chest and leaned forward, taking a nipple into his mouth while teasing the other with his thumb. She let out a breathy *ahh*, the seductive sound raising goosebumps on his skin.

Gliding his tongue upward between her breasts, he circled it around the dip in her collarbone before continuing his ascent to take her mouth in another kiss. How many times he had imagined this moment, he couldn't recall. But having her here, nearly naked in his arms, he felt complete.

Her hands roamed down his stomach, his muscles tightening as they found their way beneath the covers to grip his dick through his underwear. He shuddered, and she smiled, palming him, sliding her hand upward and back down beneath the fabric to grip his flesh.

An *mmm* resonated in his throat, and she rose to her knees, her gaze never leaving his as she pushed the sheets downward, exposing the rest of his body. Drawing her bottom lip between her teeth, she arched a brow and tugged off his boxer-briefs. She licked her lips as she gazed at his dick, and she took it in her hand once more, stroking it from base to tip, circling her finger around the sensitive head before stroking it again.

"Fuck, Amber. You're so goddamn sexy."

With a wicked grin, she lowered her head, taking him into her mouth. He moaned, closing his eyes and tipping his head back, reveling in the feel of the warm wetness enveloping him. She circled her tongue as she sucked him, and when she grazed her teeth over his tip, he nearly lost it.

"Come here." With his hand on the back of her head, he gently guided her toward his mouth. He kissed her, drinking her in and wrapping his arms around her.

"I need you, Noah." Her voice was a whisper against his lips.

"Then you'll have me." In one swift motion, he flipped her onto her back, and she gasped.

With his hips between her legs, he rubbed his cock against her, the thin strip of satin that separated them growing wet as he moved.

"Please, Noah." She nipped at his earlobe, sending shivers down his spine.

He kissed her neck, breathing in the intoxicating sweet scent of her skin as he rocked his hips. God, he needed her. It took all his willpower to keep from ripping off her panties and taking her right that moment.

But he wanted to savor her. With the uncertainty of his condition, this could be the only moment he got to spend alone with her, and he intended to take his time and relish her body.

He worked his way downward, licking and kissing, caressing every inch of her delicate skin. She ran her hands over his back, gripping his shoulders and gasping as he grazed her nipple with his teeth. He took the other between his thumb and forefinger, and the soft moan emanating from her throat had to be the most beautiful sound he'd ever heard.

Amber was a goddess. Her scent, her sounds, her soul…everything about her called to him, enraptured him. He would do everything in his power to make her his mate, whether the pack approved of their union or not.

Resuming his descent, he glided his tongue down her stomach and pressed a kiss to her navel. Her hips moved beneath his chest, a silent plea for him to continue downward. He paused, resting his chin on her pelvis and gazing up at her. She was the most beautiful woman he'd ever seen.

"Please, Noah," she whispered, and he shuddered at her request. He wouldn't make her ask again.

Rising onto his knees, he slipped off her panties and settled his shoulders between her legs before gliding his tongue from slit to clit. She gasped, her entire body tensing, her hands fisting the sheets. The sweet taste of her made his head spin. He teased her sensitive nub with his tongue before gently sucking it between his lips.

He continued the rhythm, sucking and licking while she writhed beneath him. When he slipped a finger inside, her breath came out in a rush. He could have stayed there all night. The knowledge that he could make her feel this much pleasure exhilarated him to no end, but as she whimpered, another whispered *please* escaped her lips. It was time to make her come.

Slipping a second finger inside her, he rotated his hand until he reached her sweet spot. As he bathed her clit in wet heat, he stroked her until her hips bucked and she gasped, biting her lip to keep from crying out.

He slowed his rhythm, bringing her down gently, and the tension in her body eased. Rising onto his elbows, he gazed at her, and she looked back at him with passion-drunk eyes.

"I need you inside me," she nearly growled. "Right now."

"Yes, ma'am." He crawled on top of her, filling her completely with one swift thrust.

She dropped her head back on the pillow and let out an erotic *mmm.*

Heaven help him, he could have come right then, but he wasn't ready for it to end. He pulled out, taking his dick in his hand and rubbing the head over her swollen clit. Teasing her, he slid halfway in, pulling out again and rubbing himself over her.

"You're driving me crazy," she whispered.

"That's the idea."

As he slid halfway in again, she grabbed his ass, pulling him toward her and lifting her hips until she took in his entire length. He couldn't hold back anymore. Slipping his arms beneath her shoulders, he held her tightly and pumped his hips.

She clung to him, wrapping her legs around his waist to take him deeper and biting his shoulder as another orgasm made her entire body shudder. His own coiled in his core before rushing out in a release so intense it rocked him to his soul.

Collapsing on top of her, he hugged her tighter, nuzzling into her neck and making a silent vow that he would never let her go. As her breathing slowed, she relaxed her hold and turned her face toward him to kiss his forehead.

"I meant it when I said I love you." She kissed him again.

"So did I." He rolled onto his back and tugged her to his side.

She came to him, draping her leg across his hips and laying her head on his shoulder. As she traced her fingers across his chest, his eyes drifted shut, and he basked in the elated emotions swirling in his soul.

But a few minutes later, she sat up, breaking the trance he'd succumbed to. "We finally made it all the way without your wolf trying to eat me."

"Hmm." He laced his fingers behind his head. "I didn't feel him at all like I did before. I wonder why that is."

"I should go back to my room. We need to keep up the charade that we're not together." She rose from the bed and dressed.

Noah sat up and took her hand, bringing it to his lips. He was loath to let her go, but she was right. If this plan was going to work, they had to keep it all a secret. Even if it didn't work, he knew without a doubt he wanted to spend the rest of his life with her. He'd go rogue if that was what it took. "Listen, Amber. If, after we do this, my wolf doesn't claim you, I still…"

She slipped from his grasp and lowered her gaze.

Then he felt it. The wolf inside him rose to the surface, threatening to break free. He clenched his fists, willing the beast into submission. "We'll talk about it later. You should go."

Amber nodded and slipped out the door, taking his heart with her. As the latch clicked shut, his wolf relinquished, and Noah lay back, staring at the ceiling.

CHAPTER SEVENTEEN

Amber tried to look sullen on the drive to New Orleans, putting on a show to convince her father she and Noah were over, but every time she caught Noah's gaze in the side mirror, her lips curved into a smile. Luckily, she was in the back seat, and her dad was focused on the road.

Making love to Noah had been better than she could have ever imagined. If she closed her eyes, she could still feel the contrast of his soft skin and hard muscles beneath her fingers, could still smell his woodsy scent and taste the salt of his skin.

Being with him had felt better than right. It had felt like fate. Now, if she could only convince his wolf to agree. Her heart began to sink at the thought, but she yanked it out of the depths before it could slip into despair. She had to focus on one thing at a time, lest she get caught in the vicious circle of *he loves me; his wolf loves me not.*

Noah loved her, and that was all that mattered for now. Maybe it was all that mattered period.

When they reached New Orleans, her dad dropped Noah at his house first. Keeping up the act, he didn't look at her as he thanked her dad for the ride and climbed out of the truck. Amber crossed her arms, staring out the side window as her father turned toward her.

"Do you want to get in the front?" he asked.

"I'm fine here." At the moment, she fit the role of the teenager he treated her like, but she didn't dare chance blowing their cover. She could hardly contain her excitement as it was.

He sighed. "Suit yourself. I'll drop you by the bar so you can report what you learned in the archives to Luke." He backed out of the driveway and headed toward the French Quarter.

"There's no need. I doubt it's anything he doesn't already know," she lied. "I'll send him a text when I get home."

They rode in silence the rest of the way, and when her dad parked in her driveway, he turned around in his seat. "Amber, honey, you know I love you."

"I know. Thanks for the lift." She slid out of the truck and strode to her front porch. He was a fool to think he had a say in whom she chose as a mate. This wasn't the 1900s.

Inside, she closed her eyes and leaned her head against the door. The wood felt cool against her skin. "This is going to work," she whispered. If only she could make herself believe it.

She waited an hour to be certain her father was well on his way back to Jackson before heading out the door. Humid summer heat engulfed her as she strode onto the sidewalk and hung a right, heading toward Royal Street. Two- and three-story buildings dating back to the 1800s lined the streets. Shops and art galleries occupied the bottom floors, while wrought-iron balconies adorned with ferns and colorful potted flowers covered the second- and third-floor residential areas.

A saxophone player stood on the street corner playing a sad, slow tune, and Amber paused to listen. The music drifting on the air made her chest ache. New Orleans was her home, the Crescent City Wolf Pack her family, but Noah was her soulmate. She'd fought tooth and claw to insist no one but her could decide whom she took as a mate, but she would be taking that same choice away from Noah if she left him. If their plan worked and his wolf fused with his soul but didn't claim her, whether he waited for a fate-bound or not wasn't her decision. If he was willing to give up the chance to be with her, who was she to tell him no?

Her phone chimed with a text, and she stepped into the shade of a slate blue building to read the message. Her stomach fluttered when she saw it was from Noah: *I'm going to enlist help from Cade. He can keep a secret.*

She replied: *If you trust him, so do I. On my way to see Snow now.*

They were taking a risk involving other people, but based on what she'd read about the Grunch, they needed the help. She shuddered at the thought of her heart ending up on the gargoyle's dinner plate.

Her phone chimed again with another text from Noah: *Stay safe. I love you.*

She smiled as she keyed in her reply: *I love you too.* Damn, it felt good to type that.

Yes, they were risking their lives and their positions in the pack by attempting this without the alpha's permission. Hell, once her dad talked to his peers about Noah, they'd be going against the congress's ruling just by being in each other's presence. But seeing Noah's *I love you* put a spring in her step anyway.

She paused outside Spellbound Sweets, a witchy bakery, and peered through the window. Snow Connolly stood behind the counter, her platinum blonde hair glinting in the sunlight streaming through the glass. Her sister, Rain, owned the bakery, and she and Chase lived in the apartment upstairs. Amber took a deep breath, pushed open the door, and stepped inside.

The sweet scents of cinnamon and vanilla drifted on the air, and Snow slid a tray of frosted sugar cookies into a display case before looking up and beaming a smile. "Hey, Amber! What brings you in?"

She paced to the counter and drummed her fingers on the surface. "I need a favor. Is Rain around?"

"She's out running errands. She should be back in a few hours if you want to check in later."

Amber peered at the magical cookies beneath the glass. The witches sold them as "spells" with a wink and a nod for the humans. The "love spell" was heart-shaped and frosted red, while the "money spell" was a dollar sign frosted green. In reality, they all contained the same magic: a clarity spell to help the consumer focus on their true goals.

Amber didn't need a spell to know her true goals. She had to save

Nylah and make Noah her mate…no matter the cost. "Actually, I'm here to see you. I need a potion."

Snow wiped her hands on a dishtowel and closed the display case. "Well, you've come to the right place. What can I whip up for you?"

Amber glanced behind her to be sure no one had entered the shop. "This is a covert operation. If anyone in the pack finds out what I'm doing, I'll be in shit so deep, I'll never dig my way out. Can you keep a secret?"

Snow arched a brow. "Are you kidding? I'm the queen of keeping secrets. Just ask Rain."

"This is what I need." She opened the photo of the spell she'd found in the witch's journal and offered Snow her phone.

Her eyes widened as she scanned the page, and she let out a low whistle. "That's some potent stuff. What are you going to do with it?"

"Noah and I are going to rescue Nylah and put an end to the Grunch."

Snow motioned for Amber to follow her into the kitchen. "Why can't the pack know? Sounds like it should be an *all hands on deck* mission."

Amber stepped around the counter and strode into the kitchen. "Because Noah is the reason the Grunch were awakened in the first place." She explained the situation as Snow pulled various herbs and liquids from the shelves and set them on the counter next to a copper bowl.

"Nylah brought the Thropynite here to force Noah's wolf to awaken," Snow mused, "but instead, she woke up the Grunch?"

"Exactly."

"Damn, girl. That is some deep shit."

"Tell me about it." She leaned against the counter, crossing her legs at the ankles. "But if we can pull this off, no one will ever have to know."

"Let me see the spell again. I think it continues on the next page." Snow held out her hand, and Amber gave her the phone. Pinching the screen, she zoomed in on the ingredients list and nodded. "Elderflower. Got it. Eye of newt. Got it. Did you know that's just mustard seed?"

"I had no idea." Amber peered over her shoulder at the phone.

Snow flipped to the next image. "Oh, wait." She zoomed the screen. "Damn. This isn't just potent magic; it's deadly."

"What is it?" Amber took the phone when Snow handed it to her.

"It calls for wolfsbane-infused DUME oil."

Amber's stomach sank. Wolfsbane was a highly toxic herb that could kill a shifter in under an hour. Supposedly death by wolfsbane was an excruciating way to go, and it was used as a supernatural lethal injection for more than a century. The congress finally ruled it a cruel and unusual punishment, making it illegal for any werewolf, shifter or not, to possess it.

"I'm familiar with wolfsbane, but what is DUME oil?"

"It stands for 'Death Unto My Enemies.' It's Hoodoo black magic."

"Oh, hell." Amber shoved her phone into her pocket. "I don't suppose you know how to get ahold of some, do you?"

Snow took a deep breath and slowly shook her head. "A Vodouisant would be more familiar with Hoodoo than a witch. Why don't you ask Odette?"

"For the same reason I don't want Rain to know what I'm doing. She'd feel obligated to tell her mate, and we can't let anyone find out how the Thropynite got here."

"Gotcha. Your secret is safe with me, but I—" The door chimed, signaling someone had entered the bakery.

"I'm back, Snow. You can take a break now," Rain's voice drifted on the air.

"Crap. She's early." Snow ushered Amber to the back door. "If you can get your hands on the DUME oil, I'm happy to whip up the potion for you. I normally don't mess with black magic, but if I can think of someone who might know where to find some, I'll let you know."

"Thank you." Amber slipped out the back door and made her way up the alley to the street, hanging a right and striding away from the shop before dialing Noah's number. He didn't answer, so she hung up without leaving a message. He wouldn't know where to get wolfsbane-infused DUME oil any more than she would.

"Think, Amber. Think." Her determined strides carried her through the French Quarter like a woman on a mission, though where she was headed, she had no clue. She paced up one street and down another, racking her brain for a solution to this problem. Not only did she need to find and bargain with a black magic practitioner, but she had to get a tincture containing wolfsbane. How many supernatural laws could she break in a single act of defiance?

While the pack had been on good terms with the Voodoo folks for decades, they didn't get involved with Hoodoo practitioners. Those guys were always up to no good, using and abusing the magic for their own self-gain. Hoodoo was like Voodoo, but without the religious or moral compass for guidance.

After half an hour of wandering, Amber found herself on Dumaine, across the street from Odette's House of Voodoo, and she paused on the sidewalk, staring at the dark green wooden door. If anyone would know a Hoodoo practitioner who might help her, it would be Odette.

But she couldn't ask her. She might as well go straight to Luke and tell him everything if she was going to get a shifter's mate involved. She could always slip in and ask one of the other Vodouisants inside for help. But if word got back to Odette, their plan would fall apart faster than a strand of cheap Mardi Gras beads smacking the pavement. She needed to find someone familiar with Hoodoo whom Odette never spoke to.

Of course! She mentally smacked herself upside the head for not thinking of him sooner. Odette's cousin Emile was a *traiteur*—a Voodoo faith healer—who lived out in the swamps. They had a sordid history and never spoke to each other, which made him the perfect person to ask for help locating a Hoodoo practitioner.

A quick internet search provided Emile's number, and she sat on a bench in the shade of a tree in Jackson Square to make the call. While the existence of werewolves was kept a secret from the humans, talk of Hoodoo, Voodoo, and witchcraft was so common in New Orleans, no one would bat an eye at the conversation she was about to have.

A warm breeze caressed her sweat-slicked skin, providing a welcome relief from the sauna of the French Quarter, and she gazed up at the massive statue of Andrew Jackson sitting atop a horse in the center of the Square.

A little girl squealed with delight as she ran by, her brother hot on her heels with a bubble gun, and Amber's chest gave a squeeze. If they could make this plan work, she and Noah might bring their own children to the park one day. Wouldn't it be something if they had twins?

She shook her head, chasing away the daydream, and dialed Emile's number. When he answered, she inhaled deeply before speaking. "Hi, Emile. My name is Amber Mason, and I'm with the Crescent City Wolf Pack. I'm looking for a Hoodoo practitioner who might sell me some DUME oil, and I wondered if you might know of someone who could help."

Silence hung heavy on the other end of the line, and it lasted so long she nearly thought the call had dropped.

"Did Odette tell you to call? What is she getting on about?" Irritation laced his voice.

Amber clutched the phone tighter. "No. No, she doesn't know anything about this."

"Well, I'm sure she can help you with whatever you need."

"Wait! Please don't hang up." She paused, hoping against hope he was still on the line. When she heard a heavy sigh, she continued, "I'm in trouble, and no one in my pack can find out about it. Please, I just need the name of a Hoodoo practitioner, and then I'll leave you alone."

"DUME oil isn't to be played with."

"Believe me, if it wasn't a life-or-death situation, I wouldn't mess with it. I'll be careful." Her knee bounced, shaking the bench, so she rested her hand on her thigh to still her fidgeting. What would her packmates say if they knew what she was up to? Most likely that she'd gone insane. The shifters would want to attack the Grunch, using brute force to vanquish them, despite the fact they'd tried and failed already.

Yes, Amber's plan was dangerous, but far less so than anything the "men in charge" would come up with. A full-frontal attack against who-knew-how-many Grunch would result in too many casualties.

Destroying the Thropynite was the best course of action, even if she had to break a few laws to accomplish it.

"You didn't get this information from me." Emile gave her a name and address, which she scribbled onto the back of a business card.

"Thank you. If you happen to speak to Odette..."

"I won't. Good day." The line went dead.

"Well, okay then." She rose to her feet and typed the address into her phone. "Jeez, that's in Algiers. He didn't know a Hoodoo man in the Quarter?" At least she didn't have to trek into the swamp to find him.

She headed to her house and climbed into her Mazda, turning the AC on full blast before pulling onto the road. Traffic was light over the Crescent City Connection Bridge, the muddy Mississippi stretching out beneath her, and her pulse thrummed as she exited onto General De Gaulle Drive. Her hands went slick with sweat, and she wiped her palms on her jeans at a traffic light.

Was she insane for doing this? Her entire life, she'd stood in the shadow of her brother. A second-born in the alpha line didn't get much attention when her power was passive. Any time she ran into trouble, Luke took care of it. He was a good brother and a good alpha, but damn it, it was her turn to shine. Noah and Nylah were *her* best friends, and she should be the one to save them.

She had a duty to the pack, and Noah was the only man who could help her fulfill it. She had to make him her mate. Besides, it wasn't like Luke or the others never broke any laws for their mates. Amber would do what had to be done. End of story.

"This can't be right." She stopped in the parking lot of a convenience store and checked the address Emile gave her. "The Hoodoo man sells his spells out of a Stop-N-Save?" She killed the engine and climbed out of the car, clutching her purse strap on her shoulder as she entered the store.

Three rows of shelves stood in the center of the space, and refrigerated cases lined two of the walls. A cashier stood behind a plexiglass-encased checkout counter, and as Amber cast her gaze in his direction, he didn't look up from his phone. To the eye, the shop looked like any other convenience store.

Her nose told a different story. While her olfactory senses weren't nearly as powerful as a shifter's, she did have a good sense of smell. The sharp scent of ginger mingled with the sweet aroma of calamus root…not your typical Stop-N-Save bouquet.

She spotted a set of black beaded curtains hanging in a doorway at the back of the shop. The cashier still hadn't acknowledged her presence, so she moseyed back, pretending to look at the candies on the shelf as she moved.

After wiping her clammy hands on her pants once more, she pulled the curtain aside and stepped through the doorway. A shelf with jars of herbs and bottles of who-knew-what stood to her right, and a mobile made of animal bones hung in the center of the room.

"Hello?" Her voice sounded tiny, so she cleared her throat and tried again. "Hello? I'm looking for Papa Fortune." Now she sounded like the confident woman she was.

She reached a hand toward a jar containing a clear liquid and what looked like a body part—was that a human ear?—but she stopped before she could touch it. The last thing she needed was to accidentally curse herself.

"Is anyone here?" She walked deeper into the room.

A set of dried animal hides hung from a line attached to the back wall. She recognized the furs of raccoon, nutria, rabbit, and opossum, but there were a few she couldn't place. Beneath the hides, the poor creatures' severed feet dangled like ornaments.

"What do you need, child?" An old man with weathered skin and milky eyes shuffled through another door. He stopped in front of her and held out his hands, palms up, before making a come-here gesture with his fingers.

Amber placed her hands on top of his, and he clutched them, his grip incredibly strong for someone his age. She tried to pull away, but he held on tighter, closing his eyes and nodding. His magic vibrated on her skin, sharp and strong. When he finally released her, she fought the urge to wipe her hands on her pants.

"I don't get many werewolf visitors." He hobbled behind a wooden counter and slid onto a stool. "What can I do for you?"

She swallowed the lump that had formed in her throat, glancing at the dead animals. Thankfully, he hadn't displayed any wolf hides. "I need a tincture of wolfsbane-infused DUME oil."

His eyes widened briefly. "What do you need it for?"

"I'd rather not say."

"No, I guess you wouldn't." He crossed his arms. "DUME oil ain't cheap, child. Powerful magic always has a high price."

"How much?" She had a healthy savings account she could dip into. She'd spend it all if she had to. Anything to help her friends.

His laugh turned into a wet cough, and she curled her lip, leaning away as he hacked. "Money can't buy DUME oil." He coughed again like he was hacking up something nasty.

She stepped back and gave him the side-eye. It figured he'd require something other than cash. "What do you want then?"

"Nothing you have, but you know someone who has it."

Amber tensed, and her nails cut into her palms as she clenched her fists. They were running out of time. This guy needed to stop the cryptic bullshit and tell her what he wanted.

"Name your price," she hissed through clenched teeth.

Evil sparked in his cloudy brown eyes, his smile looking more like a grimace. "Shifter blood." He raised his brows and leaned back against the wall, watching her as he awaited her reaction.

All the blood drained from Amber's head and pooled in her stomach, churning in a nauseating swirl of defeat. Not only was it against pack law for shifters to give their blood to anyone, but it was a crime punishable by death. "You know that's impossible."

"Do I? If you need the DUME oil that bad, you'll pay the price." He slid off his stool and shuffled toward his shelves, all but dismissing her.

Shifter blood was powerful, and it had the potential to be used in all sorts of black magic spells. Spells that should never be cast. There was no way in hell any of the shifters in her pack would willingly donate their blood because the consequences would be worse than losing Nylah to the Grunch. A practitioner could rain death and destruction on the entire city with a few drops.

Papa Fortune didn't seem like a man who would be easy to fool, but she had to try something. “If I bring you the blood, you’ll give me the oil?”

He laughed and then cleared his throat. “Oh no. You bring the shifter to me. One shifter. Don’t bring no more. Once I see him shift, we’ll do a bloodletting, and then you can have the oil.”

“Is there any other way?” she asked.

“That’s my price. Take it or leave it, but I doubt you’ll find anybody else willing to give a werewolf DUME oil.”

Amber turned on her heel and stalked out of the store. They were out of options. The only way to defeat the Grunch would be to bring in the entire pack, and if they did that, she’d never see Noah or Nylah again.

She climbed into her car and clutched the steering wheel in a death grip, squeezing until her knuckles turned white. Even if she could find a shifter willing to give her blood, she could never let a Hoodoo man get his hands on it.

They were screwed.

CHAPTER EIGHTEEN

ALRICK GLARED AT THE SHE-WOLF AS SHE SLEPT IN HER PRISON, and he contemplated his next move. His loneliness had allowed her to live for this long, but his agitation with her insubordination was beginning to outweigh his need for company.

As he watched her eyes move back and forth beneath her lids, he realized somewhere deep inside him, a tiny bud of hope had bloomed. She knew what he was. She could look at his disfigured form and not laugh…not cower in fear.

Against his will, his humanity had leaked toward the surface, his human heart somehow making room for this magical being, this insult to nature.

A growl rumbled in his chest, his anger seething like poison, seeping into the cracks and dissolving the unwelcome emotion that had tried to blossom. He was a fool to allow such unfounded hope to invade his psyche, like he'd been a fool to believe his witch could love such an abomination as himself.

He was designed to kill. When the Sect recruited him, he'd vowed to give up all relationships with anyone but his kind. These damned emotions were nothing more than a burden. A weakness he'd given in to twice. What would his brothers think if they awoke now? They'd probably tear him limb from limb for bringing another female into their realm, and he would deserve it.

He narrowed his eyes as she rolled onto her side. How dare she entrance him? He had the power to glean all the information he'd tried to coax from her lips with a simple piercing of her skull, yet she'd convinced him to let her live, in spite of her defiance.

With a grunt, he passed through the prison wall and wrapped his talons around her throat. Her lids flew open when he squeezed, and as he lifted her from the bed, she scratched at his hands, her feet flailing in the air.

"Please." Her voice was a wisp of air from her lips, but he was finished showing the she-wolf mercy.

He swung his arm, releasing his grip and hurling her against the wall. Her head hit the invisible surface with a satisfying *thwack*, and she slid to the floor, landing in a heap. She groaned, and he kicked her. The sound of her ribs snapping didn't give him nearly enough pleasure.

It was time for the she-wolf to die, but first, he'd make her suffer. He would kill every member of her pack one by one, and he would start with her brother. Forget the cover of darkness. The entire city would soon cower at the sight of him.

Noah bit into an alligator sausage hot dog and gazed out over Frenchman Street as a five-piece band played a jazzy tune for the tourists milling about in the summer heat. Cade sat across from him at their wooden table on the second-floor gallery, silently sipping his soda as he mulled over what Noah had said.

A dollop of the crawfish étouffée topping plopped onto Noah's plate as he finished the last bite, and he scooped it up with his finger, savoring the last bit of what could be his final meal.

"Damn, man. That's heavy," Cade finally said. "I'm down for a clandestine operation, but are you sure you don't want to get the pack involved? These guys have ripped out the hearts of seven people now, and we don't know how many we'll be up against."

"Rescuing Nylah will be for nothing if she's thrown in the pit for the rest of her life."

Cade took a bite of his Polish sausage and chewed slowly, swallowing before he spoke, "We'll both be joining her if this goes south."

A woman screamed, drawing their attention to the street below, where a bachelorette party was getting an early start. One of the women had tripped over the curb, breaking her stiletto and landing flat on her ass. Her friends hauled her up, and she pulled a pair of flip-flops from her purse before slipping them on and continuing down the sidewalk.

"Six months ago, our only worry would have been which woman in that group we'd be taking home," Cade said. "Now we could be facing jail time, or worse."

"We'll have to make sure we don't screw it up. I can hold the bastard. I've done it before."

"True, but he still got away."

"Because I let go. I thought y'all had it under control, but I'll hold on to the end this time. You and Nylah can take them out while I hold them still."

Cade blew out a slow breath and lowered his gaze.

"She's alive. I can feel she is, and Amber can too." His chest warmed at the mention of her name. "We can do this."

His friend nodded. "I'm in."

After clearing their table, they made their way downstairs and out onto Frenchman Street. Jazz music drifted out from the clubs as they strolled to the intersection and hung a right, away from the busy area.

"When is this going down?" Cade asked.

Noah followed him across the street, into the shade of the massive oak trees lining the neutral ground dividing the road. "As soon as possible. Amber's getting the potion to destroy the Thropynite, so as soon as I hear from her, we'll head out to Grunch Road."

"Are you sure that's where the pocket dimension is?"

"The energy felt different when we scouted the area before. It was heavy, like something was disturbing the natural flow. I didn't know what I was looking for at the time, but now that I do, it makes sense."

"Sounds like a plan." A mischievous grin lighted on Cade's lips. "Do you want to go for an afternoon hunt while you wait for your woman?"

Noah huffed. "I'm not allowed to shift without an alpha present."

He raised his brows. "You're also not allowed to hunt demons or see Amber, both of which you're about to do."

Noah stopped walking and squinted, looking more inward than at anything in front of him. "True."

"It'll be good to get some practice in…just in case you can't hold them with your magic. If the Grunch are as badass as the legends say, we'll need all the wolfpower we can get."

He shouldn't. He was already skating on thin ice with both the pack and the national congress. One slip-up, and he could face life in the pit…or worse. He gazed up at the cloudless sky, letting the sun warm his face. *Screw it.* That was exactly where he'd be headed if their plan didn't work. Why be cautious now? "I'll drive."

They rode in silence on the ten-mile drive to the hunting grounds, which was fine with Noah. Cade was right; he did need to practice shifting without an alpha around before they took on the Grunch. That didn't mean he wasn't scared shitless, though. Who knew what his wolf would do with no form of authority to guide him. He was about to find out.

He parked behind a tree alongside the road, and they trekked deep into the swampy area before shifting. His wolf came to the surface without hesitation, as usual. Turning from man to beast never was his problem. He expected his wolf to challenge Cade like he had the alpha, but instead, he hunted alongside his friend like their wolves were old pals.

For a moment, he let go of all his worries, and just let his wolf run. He didn't try to exert dominance over the beast, didn't concern himself with whether or not he'd be able to return to his human form. He simply enjoyed the ride, and damn, was it exhilarating.

Until the faintest hint of sulfur and rotting garbage reached his senses. Cade skidded to a stop, his nose in the air, and Noah hoped to

Hades his wolf's inborn instinct to hunt demons would kick in. Lucky for him, his beast stopped too, a ridge of fur standing on end down the middle of his back. A fiend was near.

A branch broke to their right, and Noah's wolf swung his head in the direction of the disturbance. Cade growled, flattening his ears against his head, the sound making Noah's skin prick. They stood side by side, crouching low as the demon emerged from the trees.

Noah's growl intensified. This was no ordinary demon; it was the same gargoyle-like fiend the pack had attacked before.

"Where is the she-wolf's brother?" He lifted his head and sniffed the air. "I can smell his presence."

The fiend *did* have Nylah. Noah reached out to his wolf, trying to regain control so he could face the Grunch, but the animal refused to relent.

Cade cut his eyes toward Noah, appearing to speak with his thoughts, but Noah's lack of connection to his beast made it impossible for the man to understand. Whatever Cade was planning, his wolf didn't care.

He lunged, snapping his jaws at the creature and sinking his teeth into a patch of soft flesh on its side. The demon roared and grabbed Noah by the scruff of his neck before hurling him into the bayou.

Muddy water engulfed him. He tried again to shift to his human form, but the shock made his wolf hold on tighter. He paddled, breaking the surface and then swimming toward the bank.

"Stand down, and I'll let you live," the demon growled. "Tell the she-wolf's brother Alrick is coming for him. His heart will be my next meal."

If Noah were in control, he'd have growled. This was the same demon who held the witch captive a century ago.

Cade inched toward Alrick, and the demon backed up until he stood on the water's edge. Noah's wolf locked his gaze on the fleshy area of his ankle. With his paws digging into the muddy bank, he hauled himself up and latched on to Alrick's leg before yanking with all his might.

The demon slipped in the mud and tumbled backward. His size

and the weight of his stone-like flesh caused him to sink, and Noah's wolf scrambled onto the bank before shaking out his fur.

Alrick bobbed to the surface, his arms flailing. "Help! I can't swim." His voice had changed, sounding more like a man than a fiend. The wolves stood there watching him struggle. Noah would have preferred to drag him from the water and tear him to pieces, but for once, his wolf made the right decision and let the bayou be his end.

There were only two ways to kill a pure demon: pierce the heart or cut off its head. Even then, the fiend wouldn't die. It would simply be banished back to the hell from where it came.

Alrick was half-demon. Not even that. The fiend in him had been magically fused with his soul, and it seemed his human side could succumb to drowning. *Good riddance.*

After sinking again, he struggled to the surface and gasped before he spoke, "You're next." Then, in a flash of magic, he disappeared.

Noah's wolf shook out his fur again, sending muddy water in every direction before releasing his hold. He shifted to human and ran a hand through his sopping wet hair.

Cade shifted and clapped a hand on his shoulder. "That was amazing, man. Much better than my plan. Next time, clue me in, though."

"I would if I could." He shook his head. "He's got Nylah. We need to find him *now*."

"Slow down. Your battleplan was pretty detailed, and it didn't involve busting in with our teeth bared. Without the potion that destroys the Thropynite, our friend Alrick seems indestructible."

Noah ground his teeth. "We can't even drown the bastard with the way he teleports. That's one strong-ass demon inside him."

"Tell me about it. He's even out in the daylight. I've never seen a fiend escape a battle with four werewolves. We can't beat him with three unless we can get our hands on that stone."

"You're right. Let's swing by my place for some dry clothes, and…" He tugged his phone from his pocket. Thankfully, it had been absorbed by the magic when he was in wolf form and was still in working order. "Amber called three times. She left a voicemail."

He hit the speaker button and played the message: *We've got a big problem. Meet me at Spellbound Sweets as soon as you can.*

"Uh oh." Cade jerked his head toward the truck. "What do you think the problem is?"

Noah paced by his side and climbed into the driver's seat. "She was working on the potion with Snow. We better get there fast."

They swung by Noah's place so he could rinse off the swamp muck and change his clothes, and then they headed straight to the witches' bakery. A bell chimed when he opened the door, and a dozen different sugary scents blasted his nostrils.

Snow appeared in the doorway leading to the kitchen, and she gestured to the entrance. "Lock it, will you? And come on back."

Noah twisted the deadbolt before he and Cade stepped around the counter and followed her into the kitchen area. Amber ran to him, throwing her arms around him and squeezing tightly.

"What's going on?" Noah kissed the top of her head before leaning back to look at her. "You said we have a problem?"

"We do." She stepped out of his embrace. "But I think I have a plan. Oh, Snow, this is Cade. Have y'all met?"

Snow grinned and offered him her hand. "No, we have not. It's a pleasure."

A faint shade of pink tinted Cade's cheeks. "The pleasure is mine."

Amber pressed her lips together and gave Noah a funny look. Yep, his friend was smitten.

"Snow can't make the potion without DUME oil," Amber said, "and we can only get that from a Hoodoo practitioner."

"Do you need us to help you locate one?" Cade asked Snow.

"I found one," Amber said. "I also paid him a visit, and that's where the problem lies."

Snow winked at Cade before turning around and taking a copper bowl from a shelf. Noah elbowed his friend in the ribs, trying to get him to focus on the problem at hand.

Amber ran her hands down her face, pressing them against her lips before lifting them and dropping them at her sides. "He wants shifter blood, and he won't accept any other payment."

Noah's stomach sank. "That's..." He was about to say "impossible," but at this point, was it really? He chewed the inside of his cheek, pondering whether he was willing to commit a crime punishable by death.

"That's what he wants from you," Cade said. "But what if someone who wasn't a werewolf tried to get some? Surely he'd ask for a different form of payment."

"We tried." Amber leaned her hip against a counter. "Snow went, and he wanted her to sacrifice her first-born child."

"That bastard." Cade's brow slammed down over his eyes.

"Black magic isn't cheap," Snow said.

Noah rubbed his forehead. "You said you had a plan. I've heard rumors about the things that can be done with shifter blood, and I don't want to be the cause of more death." He'd already caused enough.

"Hear me out," Amber said. "I believe, since your wolf hasn't fused with your soul, that your blood won't have the shifter magical qualities if it's taken while you're in human form."

"I don't…" He pressed his lips together, his mind reeling at the idea. It was possible. Much like he was a detached soul along for the ride when his wolf had control, the beast felt like a foreign body inside him when the man was in control. Her plan could work, but… "There's no way to know that for sure."

"I can test it." Snow held a small copper bowl in one hand, a scalpel in the other.

His nostrils flared as he blew out a long, slow breath. If he agreed to this, he'd be committing the crime twice, giving his blood to both a witch and a Hoodoo man. Even if Luke wanted to go easy on him, the alpha would have no choice but to enact the swiftest punishment.

"I know it's a big ask." Amber rested her hand on his arm. "So if you don't want to, we'll figure out another way."

He shook his head. His sister's life was on the line. "There is no other way." He gave Cade a hard look.

"I'm in this, man," his friend said. "Whatever it takes."

Noah nodded and clapped him on the shoulder before looking at Snow.

"Your secret is safe with me." Snow drew an X over her heart.

"Let's do this." He took the scalpel from Snow's hand. "How much do you need?"

"One drop will do it. This is a potion witches use to test the potency of an ingredient before using it in a spell. I enchanted it to look for shifter magic, so if your human blood has the wolf gene in it, black speckles will form on the surface like someone sprinkled it with pepper."

Noah eyed the potion. At least he didn't have to drink it this time. "That's all it will do? It can't be used for anything else?"

Snow shook her head and gestured to a bottle of pink liquid. "It won't, but I'll pour a neutralizer into it and dump it down the sink as soon as we're done."

"You can trust her." Amber squeezed his arm.

Sucking in a deep breath, he jabbed the scalpel into the tip of his finger. Blood pooled on his skin, and he turned his hand over, allowing it to drip into the bowl. He pressed his thumb against the wound to stop the bleeding as Snow swirled the contents of the bowl.

She set it on the counter, and they all gathered around, watching the lemon-yellow liquid as it bubbled and hissed. Amber slid her arm around his waist, reminding him to breathe. The concoction settled, and Snow swiped a spoon through it.

"Nothing." She stirred it in a circle. "The potion is clear."

Noah stepped toward the bowl and stared at it intently, looking for any speck of black that the witch might have missed. He found nothing. A sense of relief mixed with the anxiety churning in his core. They were one step closer to rescuing Nylah. "What do we do if he uses this test?"

"We'll have to make sure the transaction is complete before he does," Amber said.

Snow held up a small burlap bag. "This is binding powder. It solidifies any contract made. Be sure to seal the deal before you give him the blood. Amber knows how to use it."

"Y'all have thought of everything, haven't you?"

"We talked through all the scenarios and the possible outcomes," she said. "And we found solutions for everything that could go wrong."

Noah kissed Amber on the cheek. Her sharp mind was one of the things he loved about her. "How much does the Hoodoo man want? More than a drop, I'm sure." He looked at Snow. "Do you have a bottle?"

Amber cleared her throat. "He didn't say. I'm supposed to bring you, and only you, to his shop. He wants to see you shift and witness the blood draw."

His heart sank. That was a whole other problem he *knew* she didn't have a solution for.

CHAPTER NINETEEN

Amber squeezed Noah's hand across the console in the Hoodoo shop's parking lot. His posture was relaxed, his expression stoic, making him seem much calmer than she felt. "It's very brave of you to do this."

He laughed cynically. "Maybe. Or maybe it's downright stupid. Should we count how many laws we're breaking?"

"I'd rather not."

He turned in the passenger seat to face her. "You're the one who's brave. You found this guy and came here all on your own, having no idea what you'd encounter inside."

She lifted one shoulder. "I'll do anything for you and Nylah."

"I love you, Amber. You have no idea how much I respect and admire you."

Her heart warmed at his words. She did have an idea. He was willing to give up his chance at finding a fate-bound to be with her, and that told her all she needed to know. "I love you too."

"I don't want you anywhere near me when I shift in there. I don't know how my wolf will react to Papa Fortune, but I do know how he reacts to you."

She rested her hand against his cheek. "I'll be careful."

Her pulse thrummed as they entered the convenience store that fronted for the Hoodoo shop. This time, the cashier looked up from his post at the register, his eyes widening as his gaze locked on Noah.

Amber ignored the man and took Noah's hand, leading him through the beaded curtain. He cringed as they stepped inside, his nose wrinkling, no doubt in response to the pungent odors of the Hoodoo man's concoctions.

"Papa Fortune?" she called, her voice sounding much more confident than she actually was. "I brought the payment you asked for."

The old man shuffled in from a back room, his gaze skeptical as he glared at them. "You found a shifter willing to give his blood awful quick. Ain't it a crime in your pack? One punishable by death?"

She stiffened at the delight behind his words. "I can be very persuasive."

"I bet you can. Come." He held his hands toward Noah. "Let me read you to be certain you're a shifter."

Icy dread flushed through Amber's veins. She had no idea the kind of magic Papa Fortune possessed. What if he could tell Noah's wolf wasn't fused? If he figured out their trick, he could curse them both.

She stepped in front of Noah. "You said you wanted to see him shift. Isn't that proof enough?"

He narrowed his eyes at her. "Yes, I suppose it is. Follow me."

The old man led them through a doorway into a small room with dirty beige walls and scuffed linoleum. It smelled of mold and death, and her body shuddered as she entered the space. A large window with thick glass occupied most of the far wall, and a narrow doorway with six deadbolts stood to its right.

"What is this?" Amber padded to the window and peered into the next room. A heavy wooden table about seven feet long stood in the center of the room. A counter lined the left wall, and next to the array of herbs and potions sat a…was that a shriveled-up rat? She shuddered again.

"I'm not asking you any questions, child." Papa Fortune unlocked the deadbolts and opened the door. "I expect the same respect."

Noah stood next to her, and nervous energy rolled off him in waves. "I assume you want me to go in there to shift?"

"Can't have you attacking me now, can I?" Papa Fortune gestured for Noah to enter the room.

"I'll be right out here." Amber filled her voice with as much reassurance as she could muster…which wasn't much. She didn't want to be left out here with Papa Fortune any more than she wanted Noah to be trapped in there with the dead rat.

Noah stepped through the door, and the Hoodoo man locked all six deadbolts. Amber watched Noah through the glass, giving him a nod of encouragement and trying her best not to look worried. She crossed her fingers and said a silent prayer to whatever gods might be listening for him to have control of his wolf.

His body shimmered, and he transformed quickly. As his gaze locked on Papa Fortune, he bared his teeth, letting out a rumbling growl. Amber stepped out of the wolf's view so she wouldn't aggravate the situation more. She could only imagine the beast was having flashbacks to the examination room at the congress's headquarters.

Papa Fortune drummed his fingers together and laughed. "This is the first time a werewolf has graced me with a request. I thank you, child."

Amber slid her hand into her pocket and gripped the bag of binding dust. "There's your proof. Let him return to human so we can seal this deal."

"Not so fast." He turned to a shelving unit and picked up a small knife before shoving the handle toward her. She took it out of instinct, and then he offered her a glass bottle.

"What…?" She didn't need to finish her question. He wanted *her* to perform the bloodletting, and as he unlocked the deadbolts, she realized he wanted her to do it while Noah was in wolf form. *Oh, shit.*

"Fill the bottle, and the DUME oil is yours."

"Are you crazy? You want me to try to cut a werewolf?" Panic laced her voice, and it was no mystery why. Not only would Noah's wolf most likely maim her if she went anywhere near him, but they had only tested his blood while in human form. Drawing the blood from his wolf would give the Hoodoo man access to magic no one should have.

"I ain't about to put myself in danger. You want the oil, you'll get in there and get the blood." He swung open the door, grabbed Amber by the arm, and shoved her inside.

Her heart lodged in her throat, and she spun toward the door, gripping the knob with one hand and slamming her shoulder against the thick wood. At the sound of the locks sliding into place, ice flushed through her veins.

Clutching both the bottle and the knife in her left hand, she slowly turned around to face the wolf, and he crouched, his lips peeling back to reveal his massive canines. He growled, and she pressed her back against the door.

"I love you." Her voice was barely a whisper, so she cleared her throat and tried again. "I love you."

His posture began to relax, his growl softening.

"I love both of you—the man and the wolf—no matter how you feel about me."

The growl turned into a whimper, and the wolf lay on his belly. Amber's breath came out in a rush. It seemed Noah had control… for now.

Think, Amber. Think. She looked at the small blade in her hand and then at the wolf lying on the concrete floor. An idea formed in her mind, and she pushed from the door, taking a tentative step toward him.

"I need you to lie still, okay? Noah, can you give me a sign that you're in control?" She took another step. The wolf studied her curiously.

"I'm going to assume that you are." She looked through the window, where Papa Fortune watched her with anticipation in his eyes. Positioning herself between the wolf and the window, she dropped to her knees and lowered her voice. "Don't move."

Her hand trembled as she scooted closer. The wolf narrowed his eyes. "I love you. I'm not going to hurt you."

She glanced over her shoulder before jabbing the tip of the knife into the concrete next to Noah's leg. The wolf flinched, jerking away from the blade, and she made a *shushing* sound, reaching toward him to calm the beast. "It's okay," she whispered. "I love you, remember? One more time."

Raising the knife above her head, she slammed it down again, grazing the fur on his shoulder as she jabbed it into the floor. The tip snapped off, lodging in the concrete, and the wolf yelped and jumped to his feet.

"It won't work." She rose, turning to the window. "His hide is too tough in this form. We'll have to do it while he's human."

Amber moved toward the door, and the wolf growled. "Let me out, please." She banged on the wood.

The wolf flattened his ears against his head and bared his teeth. Amber sucked in a shaky breath, her pulse humming in her ears as she knocked again. "You need to let me out so he can shift."

She turned to the wolf and straightened her spine. The beast had been fine in her presence a moment ago. Why was he growling now? All she wanted to do was leave the damn room. "You are supposed to be my mate. You can't be treating me this way."

He pricked one ear, and then the other. Amber gripped the doorknob, counting the locks as they unlatched. *One…two…* Her words had subdued the wolf, but she had no idea how long it would last. *Three… four… five… Come on, old man.* As the sixth lock disengaged, she threw open the door, rushing out of the room and slamming it behind her. "What took you so long?"

The Hoodoo man cut his gaze between her and the wolf in the next room. "I thought werewolves could shift on command. Why hasn't he turned human yet?"

Amber gazed through the window. The animal's expression was strained; he was fighting the shift. "His wolf is very powerful. Once it comes to the surface, it takes time for the man to regain control."

Papa Fortune took the knife from her hand and gazed at the broken tip. "That's one hell of a hide."

She pressed her hand against the glass. "Noah, it's time to come back to me. We've got things to do, remember?"

It took a few minutes, but Noah finally returned to his human form, and Amber opened the door. He looked at her in awe. "How did you…?"

"We'll talk about it later," she whispered. Honestly, she had no idea how she got so close to his wolf without being mauled, other than he had finally figured out she was a friend.

Papa Fortune's shoes scuffled on the floor as he entered the room and handed Noah a new blade. "Fill the bottle."

Amber retrieved it from the floor and set it on the table. Noah sliced the side of his palm, letting blood drip into the open container. When it reached the top, Amber corked it and swept it from the surface before the Hoodoo man could grab it.

"I'll handle the rest." She clutched the bottle of Noah's blood tightly, while he pressed a rag to his hand. Hopefully Papa Fortune wouldn't notice Noah didn't heal as quickly as a shifter should. Any suspicion from him could negate this deal.

When Noah furrowed his brow, she cut her gaze to his injured hand before narrowing her eyes. He nodded. "I'll wait for you outside."

As Noah strode out the door, she turned to Papa Fortune. "Where is the DUME oil?"

"It's here." He locked his gaze on the bottle of blood and smacked his lips like he was hungry for it. "Let's make the trade."

"Hold on." Amber pulled the bag of binding dust from her pocket and dumped it on the table before drawing a line through it like Snow told her to do. "This contract has been fulfilled. We take no responsibility for what you do with the blood nor how it works in your spells. Are we in agreement?"

"Yes, yes. Now hand it over." Papa Fortune drew a line crossing Amber's, sealing the deal, and held out his hand.

"With the scattering of this dust, my obligation has been fulfilled. I owe you no debt, nor do you owe me. By order of the goddess, no retaliation is permitted from either side." She swiped her hand through the dust, pushing it onto the floor.

Papa Fortune held the DUME oil toward her, and she clutched it in her hand before releasing Noah's blood. He let out a maniacal laugh, and Amber booked it out the door. While the binding dust spell would prevent him from coming after them, she didn't want to be there when he found out the shifter blood he'd bargained for was useless.

They left through the convenience store and climbed into her Mazda. As she closed the door, her breath came out in a rush of relief. She held the brown glass bottle up in the light, chewing her lip as she gazed at the skull and crossbones on the label.

Noah reached for it, but she jerked it away. "It has wolfsbane in it. You're susceptible to it now."

He fisted his hand and dropped it in his lap. "Maybe not in human form."

"Do you want to take that chance?" She opened the console and set the bottle inside.

"I guess not. Amber, you tamed my wolf in there. I was so afraid he was going to attack you, but you calmed him."

She put the car in drive and headed back toward the French Quarter. "I think you calmed him. Maybe hearing me say 'I love you' helped you take back control."

"I didn't feel like I was in control."

"Whatever it was, it worked. Hopefully we won't have to find out if it'll happen again."

Traffic slowed to a crawl over the Crescent City Connection Bridge, and Amber peered out over the Mississippi. A steamboat loaded with tourists chugged along the surface, making her smile despite their situation. She could almost hear the jazz music a band was surely belting out on the bottom deck. From the opposite direction, a barge carrying a dozen shipping crates plowed through the water.

"Have you ever thought of living anywhere but New Orleans?" Noah's voice pulled her from her thoughts.

"No, I love it here. Have you?"

"Not until recently." He rubbed his palms on his jeans. "If this plan goes south, I might have to go rogue to avoid the pit, and..."

She took his hand across the console. "It's going to work. We will be together." And she would keep telling herself that until the very end. What choice did she have? If she focused on the what-ifs, she'd lose sight of their mission.

He nodded. "You're right. We should take it one step at a time."

After making it across the bridge, Amber drove home and parked in her driveway. "I'll take the oil to Snow and get the potion. Meet me at the park with Cade in an hour?"

"I'll be there." He leaned toward her and brushed his lips to hers before sliding out of the car.

On her walk to the bakery, her phone chimed with a message from Snow: *Rain went out to dinner with Chase, but I don't know when they'll be back. Better hurry.*

She replied, *On my way,* and shoved her phone into her pocket.

The front door was locked, so she went around back and entered through the kitchen. As she stepped through the door, Snow shoved half of a red-frosted clarity cookie into her mouth. "That was fast," she said around the food.

Amber grinned. "Did you just eat a love spell cookie?"

Snow swallowed. "You know it's the same clarity spell in all of them. Only the consumer's intent matters."

"And your intent is love?" She arched a brow.

Snow shrugged. "Everything went well at the Hoodoo shop?"

"I don't know about well, but I got the DUME oil." She offered her the bottle.

Snow picked up a dishtowel and wrapped it around the glass.

"Should I not have touched the surface?" Amber asked.

"It was dry, right? Nothing wet or greasy on the outside?"

"It was dry…"

"You're fine then. It's best not to take chances with black magic though."

"I'll remember that next time." Of course, it would have been nice if her friend had warned her. Then again, if Amber had used common sense, she'd have wrapped it in a towel too. *Death Unto My Enemies* shouldn't be taken lightly.

Snow gathered the rest of the ingredients and ground the herbs with a mortar and pestle before sprinkling them into the bowl. As she poured the DUME oil into the concoction, it sparked, and smoke rose from the surface.

"You won't want to get this anywhere near your skin. It'll melt it right off the bone." She transferred the mixture into a glass bottle and closed it with a cork. "It'll disintegrate pretty much everything it touches, so be careful."

"What keeps it from eating through the bottle?"

"Magic." Snow grinned. "When you get the Thropynite, lay it on the ground and pour this over it. As long as that's the only piece of the stone on this continent, the Grunch should return to their suspended animation states."

"What about the fumes? Wolfsbane is toxic to shifters."

"Get at least ten feet away from any shifter before you do it. Once it finishes sizzling, the fumes will dissipate quickly."

"Thanks, Snow. You're the best."

"Let me know how it goes."

"I will." *If we survive.*

CHAPTER TWENTY

"YOU'RE NOT GOING, AMBER." NOAH HELD OUT HIS HAND, asking for the potion bottle, but she clenched it in her fist.

"The hell I'm not. I've got just as much at stake in this as you do." She crossed her arms and looked at Cade, who averted his gaze and walked to the other side of the bridge.

They'd met at their favorite spot in City Park, the same place where Noah's wolf had awakened the first time. He didn't feel it now, but that didn't mean it wasn't lurking right below the surface. Arguing with Amber wasn't wise. "It's not safe for you," he said in a softer voice.

"It's not safe for you either. For anyone." She shoved the bottle into her pocket. "I've spent my entire life being protected. My dad was alpha. Now my brother is. I get this shit enough from my family; I don't need it from you too."

"I don't want to lose you." He was well aware of how her family treated her, but he couldn't live with himself if any harm came to her.

"And I don't want to lose you," she said. "I also don't want to sit at home wondering if you're alive or dead. Y'all need all the help you can get."

"She has a point," Cade said from his perch on the opposite side of the bridge. "If Nylah…if she's indisposed, that leaves you and me against who knows how many Grunch."

"Don't forget there's wolfsbane in the potion. If it spills on me, it'll melt my skin from the bone, but I'll survive. You can't even breathe in the fumes."

Noah closed his eyes and blew out a long breath. *Damn it.* She was right. His instinct said to protect her at all costs, and while he wanted to haul her home and lock her inside, he wouldn't dare. He'd been friends with Amber long enough to know she wanted a mate who would be her partner, not an overbearing bully.

"What if my wolf tries to attack you?"

"It…whoa." She clutched her head and swayed before gripping the bridge railing.

"What is it?" He took her shoulders in his hands and steadied her. He recognized that look, and it wasn't good. "What do you feel?"

"Your wolf is… There's two, and then there's one." She rested her hand on his chest. "Change. I feel like your wolf is in danger. I feel like…"

Cade approached them, his brow furrowed, and Amber glanced at him before looking into Noah's eyes. "I think… I feel like your wolf will die."

His heart sank into his stomach. Amber's empathic premonitions were often vague, but they were never wrong. "What if I don't shift? I need to use my telekinetic power to hold the Grunch still, anyway. I don't need my wolf for this fight."

She shook her head. "I don't know."

"Hold up," Cade said. "The theory is that your wolf was awakened because Nylah is in another dimension, right?"

"Yes." Amber slipped her hand into Noah's. "As long as she's trapped in the Grunch's domain, she doesn't exist on this plane."

Cade nodded. "Whether you're able to rip open their dimension and get inside, or we have to draw them out to destroy them, eventually you and Nylah will be on the same plane again."

"That's the plan," Noah said.

"What if, when you and Nylah are together again, your wolf goes dormant? If it's only awake because she's not here, once she returns…"

"That could be it," Amber said. "Maybe my premonition wasn't that your wolf would die, but that it would go dormant again. What then?"

Noah leaned against the railing and held Amber's hand between both of his. That theory made more sense than he cared to admit. It wasn't just possible…it was probable. The moment they rescued Nylah, he would probably go back to being a regular second-born with only his telekinesis. He might never shift again.

"I don't care." He held her hand against his heart. "If I lose my wolf, so be it. I love you enough to make you happy for the rest of your life, if you'll still want me."

She traced her fingers across his forehead, brushing the hair from his face. "Of course I'll still want you. I wanted you before your wolf awakened, and I want you now, whether you keep him or not."

Her words seeped into his soul, wrapping around his heart and squeezing it tightly. He loved her fiercely; he always had, and he was an idiot for ever thinking she should be with anyone other than him. That was toxic masculinity at its worst. Noah wasn't less-than because his wolf didn't awaken when it was supposed to. In fact, the wolves could never defeat Alrick without his second-born power. He was enough, and he was the only mate for Amber.

"I love you." He tucked her hair behind her ear.

"I love you too." She kissed him on the cheek.

Cade laughed. "Alrick is going to be disappointed you gave Amber your heart when he was planning on eating it."

"Good. Let the bastard starve."

Amber stepped back and cocked her head. "What are y'all talking about?"

"We went to the hunting grounds so I could practice shifting without an alpha present. Alrick found us and asked for me. I guess he couldn't tell who I was in wolf form."

"Why would you do that?" She parked her hands on her hips. "You could have been killed."

"Nah." Cade grinned. "You should've seen him. He fought like he'd had a wolf all his life."

She blinked, her brow rising. "You fought Alrick?"

"For a minute." Noah shrugged. "He disappeared when my wolf pulled him into the bayou."

She pressed her lips together hard, shaking her head. "Tell you what… I won't scold you for being reckless, and you won't patronize me by saying I can't help rescue Nylah."

"Amber…"

"I want to be there. You need a non-shifter to destroy the Thropynite, and it might as well be me."

A crow cawed from a nearby tree before taking to the air and swooping over them. Noah ground his teeth, casting his gaze upward. The sun had begun its descent behind the horizon, painting the evening sky in shades of purple and orange, and a light breeze provided relief from the sticky summer heat.

This city was Amber's home too, and Nylah was her friend. She did have as much at stake as Noah, so how could he deny her? "Okay, but if my wolf forces me to shift around you, I want you to run and not look back. Deal?"

She smiled. "Let's go get your sister."

They piled into Noah's truck and headed toward the east end of the city to the wooded area around the old Grunch Road. He parked alongside the ditch and grabbed a crowbar from his tool kit before climbing out of the truck.

"The Grunch's skin is mostly stone, but he has a few soft spots." He gestured to his side and the spot where his neck met his shoulder. "If he comes after you, hit him with everything you've got."

Amber took the makeshift weapon and held it in both hands, giving it a couple of practice swings. "It's not Excalibur, but it should do the trick." She smiled as if trying to lighten the mood, but it didn't work.

Their apprehension thickened as they ventured into the forest. Once again, the area was eerily quiet. No birds chirped in the trees above, and no animals, not even a field mouse, scampered by on the forest floor. The air felt thick and heavy, and Noah wrapped an arm around Amber's shoulders, tugging her to his side. The energy around them grew denser the deeper into the trees they trekked.

"This must be the place." Noah stopped, still holding Amber against his body.

"Listen," she said.

"To what?" Cade asked.

"Exactly." Noah released his hold of Amber and nodded to Cade, a silent request for him to keep an eye on her.

Cade moved to stand next to her, and thankfully, she didn't protest.

With a deep inhale, he reached out with his mind, sifting imaginary fingers through the atmosphere. He detected a low vibration running through the normal energy, and it seemed to exist above, below, in, and all around them. It was like a layer of foreboding magic folded into their realm.

"Can you sense anything?" Amber rubbed her arm as if she had chills.

"I can feel it." He pushed with his mind, and the thick veil dipped inward, thinning slightly where he pressed. "It's like a layer of gelatin. I think I can puncture it."

"Hold on," Amber said. "Let's take a few deep breaths and center ourselves."

Though he was tempted to tear the dimension open and barrel in with his teeth and claws bared, Amber was right. This was the toughest demon Noah had ever fought. They needed to go in with level heads.

He gazed up, but he couldn't see the moon through the thick canopy above. The silvery light filtering through the leaves barely illuminated the area, but his vision had sharpened with the awakening of his wolf. He could see just fine. The sultry air hung stagnantly, pressing in around him like a sauna, and a bead of sweat rolled down the center of his back.

"Ready?" He looked at his friends.

Amber nodded, and Cade shifted into his wolf form. Noah focused all his magic into the veil, pressing until it thinned to almost nothing. But a piercing scream broke his concentration. He turned in time to see Alrick grab Amber by the waist.

The gargoyle pressed his nose into the side of her head before licking her ear. "She'll make a sweet appetizer. Your sister will be dessert." With a wave of his hand, the veil around them opened, and Alrick disappeared inside, taking Amber with him.

"Son of a bitch!" Noah reached his arms out, making a clawing motion with his hands and ripping open the veil with his magic. Cade bounded inside, and Noah followed, letting the portal he'd torn open slam shut behind him.

He nearly tripped over the crowbar lying on the floor, and he froze for a moment, his brain not accepting the reality of this pocket dimension. There were no visible walls, and they appeared to be in the same part of the woods. But everything inside looked like a washed-out grayscale version of the forest. He took in the scene, and as his gaze locked on Amber, his stomach sank.

Alrick held her by the neck, his long talons stretching across her trachea as he rested his other set of claws against her chest…over her heart. Cade stood facing them, his hackles raised as Nylah watched, her hands pressed against an invisible wall.

Cade rocked back, preparing to lunge, and Alrick jerked Amber aside, the tip of his claw piercing her skin.

"Wait." Pulse pounding, Noah threw up his hands and gathered the energy around him. If Cade attacked now, Amber would be as good as dead.

Alrick's eyes widened as Noah grabbed hold of him with his mind, but the bastard was strong. He fought back, slipping from his grip and tightening his hold around Amber's neck.

She gasped, attempting to drag in a breath. Blood oozed down her throat.

Focusing his energy on the gargoyle's talons, he wrapped the fingers of his mind around them, prying them off her neck one by one…first the forefinger, then the middle, then the next. Amber sucked in a breath and leaned her head aside, but the fiend twisted his other fist in her shirt.

Noah reached out another tendril of energy, and with a firm push, he unraveled the fiend's claws from her clothes. Amber darted toward Nylah, slamming into an invisible wall and sliding to the floor.

"Amber!" Noah's hold slipped. Alrick lunged. Cade barreled into him, knocking him down and rolling over the fiend until they skidded to a stop at the feet of another gargoyle.

Sweat beaded on Noah's forehead, fatigue making his muscles ache. He could barely hang on to Alrick. How the hell was he going to hold them all? But the second demon didn't move. Neither did the two next to him.

Noah's chest ached. Sharp pain sliced through his core, and an anguished howl sounded in his mind.

He was losing his wolf.

"I'm okay." Amber scrambled to her feet, clutching her head.

Alrick roared, throwing Cade off him and slamming him into another invisible wall. Rising to his full, menacing height, the demon stormed toward Amber once more.

"This ends now, Grunch." Noah gathered every ounce of his strength and hurled it toward the fiend, latching on with all his might. Sweat poured down his face, stinging his eyes as he held Alrick in a mental vise grip. "Where's the stone, Nylah?" he ground out.

"He's wearing it."

"On it." Amber darted toward him, and Alrick pushed back against Noah's magic.

The fiend's arm began to move, forcing its way through Noah's hold. He tightened his grip, grinding his teeth and straining against the force as Amber yanked the chain from around his neck.

"Got it!" Amber backed as far away from them as the pocket dimension would allow, but before she could grab the potion from her pocket, Nylah shouted.

"Wait! He has a piece embedded in his chest."

"I can't hold him much longer." Noah's legs trembled, exhaustion threatening to crumple him.

Cade rose to his paws, shaking off the attack, and closed in on Alrick.

"Hold this." Amber pressed the Thropynite into Noah's palm, lacing the chain between his fingers before pulling her Swiss army knife from her pocket. She ran to Alrick, and as Cade latched on to his arm, she pried the stone from his chest.

Noah's palm heated where the Thropynite touched his skin, and he barely heard Alrick's agonizing wail over the sound of his own pulse pounding in his ears. He fell to his knees. His blood hummed in his veins, his vision swimming as something in his core snapped.

"Noah, I need you to hold on a little longer." Amber's voice drew him back to the surface. "He's weakened, but Cade can't hold him on his own." She dug in her pocket and retrieved the bottle before taking the Thropynite from his hand.

His friend's snarling and the sound of the struggle finally reached his ears, and he blinked his gaze into focus to find Cade on top of Alrick, biting and tearing at his flesh.

Amber laid the two stones on the ground. "Y'all hold your breath for a minute."

Noah forced another pulse of magic toward Alrick, tightening his hold as Amber uncorked the bottle and poured the potion over stones.

They sizzled and popped, melting as the magic neutralized them. Smoke rose from the molten liquid, and the ground around it crumbled until everything the potion touched turned to ash. In a flash of light, the smoke dissipated, but Noah held his breath until instinct forced him to drag in air.

"Damn," Amber said. "Snow wasn't kidding."

The struggle stopped, and Cade backed away from Alrick, who was frozen in stone. He shifted and beat on the walls of Nylah's cell. "Can you open this?" He ran his hands along the invisible barrier. "It's sealed with magic."

"Noah?" Amber placed a hand on his shoulder. "Can you let Nylah out?"

He sucked in a sharp breath and rubbed his chest, his thoughts scrambling to catch up with everything that happened. "So this is what it feels like."

"Noah?" She tugged his arm, pulling him to his feet. "We're not out of the woods yet."

She was right about that. He'd have time to contemplate what happened to him when this was all over. Holding Amber's hand, he sauntered toward Nylah. "Hey, Sis. It's been a minute."

Reaching out with his mind, he felt along the wall of energy. It was the same magic the Grunch had used to seal the entrance to their dimension. As he gave a mental push, he stepped through the force-field and clutched Nylah's arm before dragging her through.

"It's about damn time." She pulled him into a bear hug, squeezing until he could hardly breathe. "I'd had about all I could take from the abusive bastard."

Cade gave the immobile gargoyle a kick. "He's down now, but if another piece of Thropynite makes it to New Orleans…"

Amber picked up the crowbar. "I know your usual method is piercing the heart or beheading. Is smashing them to bits overkill?"

"There's no such thing when it comes to demons," Noah said, and Amber tossed him the hunk of steel. They took turns bashing the gargoyles, saving their leader for last, and Noah thanked his lucky stars the other three never woke up. He stood over Alrick, ready to send the fiend to hell where he belonged, when Nylah put a hand on his shoulder.

"Can I have the honors?"

"Be my guest." He handed the crowbar to his sister.

Nylah knelt beside Alrick and shook her head. "You poor, misguided soul. May you finally find peace." She rose to her feet and bashed in his skull.

As the stone crumbled, the veil separating the pocket dimension from the real world dissolved away, and they found themselves in the forest on their own plane.

CHAPTER TWENTY-ONE

Amber clutched Noah's arm to stop her hands from trembling. The adrenaline coursing through her veins made her feel like she was either going to explode or pass out at any second. Her stomach churned, her lunch threatening to make a reappearance.

Nylah threw her arms around them both, sandwiching Amber between them. "Y'all were amazing. The perfect team. I'm sorry you had to destroy the Thropynite. If I'd known it would wake up that asshole, I would've had you meet me in Europe where it came from."

Amber tugged from her embrace. "The pack doesn't know you brought it here, and it's best if they never find out."

"Good call." Nylah looked around. "Where is the rest of the pack? Don't tell me y'all performed this mission on your own."

Noah chuckled. "Rescuing you wouldn't have done much good if we both ended up in the pit for the rest of our lives. Between you waking up the Grunch and me knowing what was going on and lying about it...we didn't stand a chance if anyone found out."

Amber sucked in a sharp breath. She'd succumbed to her adrenaline, completely ignoring the way Noah had acted in the Grunch's dimension. "My premonition. Your wolf. Is it...?"

"It's fused." He pressed a hand to his chest. "I can feel him. Feel his thoughts and emotions."

"'There were two, and now there's one.'" She shook her head. "I didn't feel that you'd lose your wolf. I felt him fuse, two souls joining into one."

"Wait… You can shift?" Nylah's mouth fell open. "Since when?"

"Since the last full moon." Noah wrapped his arm around Amber's waist. "When Alrick took you into his pocket dimension, you ceased to exist on this plane."

"Holy shit." Nylah shook her head. "We didn't need the Thropynite after all."

"Yes, we did," Noah said. "My wolf didn't fuse with my soul until Amber put the stone in my hand."

"Wow." Nylah's eyes were wide, making her look as dumbfounded as Amber felt. "I guess we better report to HQ and fill Luke in on every…on almost everything."

Their crazy plan had worked. Amber clung to Noah, trying to wrap her mind around it all. His dream had come true.

"I'm not doubting you," Cade said, "but don't you think you ought to make *sure* your wolf is fused before we spin this story for the alpha?"

"Good idea." Noah kissed Amber on the cheek and stepped away. "You two watch her, just in case."

Cade stood between Amber and Noah, and Nylah moved in behind her. "I take it his wolf threatened you before?"

A nervous laugh escaped Amber's throat. "I'll tell you all about it later."

Noah summoned his magic, his body shimmering as he transformed into his wolf. Amber tensed again, her previous experiences with the animal ingrained in her muscles, but now something was different. The look in his eyes, his posture, the way his copper fur lay flat against his back… The man was in control.

"Noah." She slipped from her packmates' protective circle and padded toward him.

"Amber." Cade's voice held warning, but she ignored him.

Reaching toward Noah's head, she brushed her fingers along his muzzle. When he didn't snap, she moved closer and ran her hand down his side. He let out a light *woof* and licked her, his slobbery tongue running from her cheek to her ear.

She laughed. "Okay, mister. That's enough of that."

He shook out his coat, and in a cloud of shimmering magic, he returned to his human form. She threw her arms around him, sagging against him as the last of the fight-or-flight energy drained from her body.

"Hold up a minute." Nylah cut her gaze between them. "Are you two…together?"

Amber smiled, resting her head on his shoulder. "We are."

Nylah nodded. "It's about damn time."

"Amber…" Noah gently lifted her chin with his fingers. "I'm whole because of you, and my wolf—"

"Aw shit." Cade held up his phone. "Text from Luke. I didn't report for patrol duty, and he wants to know where I am."

Noah inhaled deeply. "I guess we better get our story straight."

Cade's phone rang. "We'll discuss it on the way." He pressed the device to his ear. "Yeah, man. I'm sorry. I'm on my way to the bar now."

They squeezed into Noah's truck, and he drove to the French Quarter. He held Amber's hand in a tight grip the entire way, and while they hashed out what details they could share and what they would take to their graves, he seemed distracted. His lips twitched like he wanted to say something, and he glanced at her repeatedly until they arrived on St. Philip Street.

It was most likely nerves. They'd ignored several direct orders from their pack alpha, but Luke wasn't only their leader. He was also her brother, and if he decided to be an asshole, she would have to knock some sense into him.

They made their way to the entrance, and the familiar blast of cold air greeted them, raising goosebumps on her arms as they stepped inside. Rain and Snow sat at the bar with their backs to the entrance, while Chase and Kaci washed beer mugs behind the counter.

Chase looked up, and his mouth fell slack, the rag slipping from his hand as his eyes widened. "Nylah?"

Snow turned around, her smile beaming, and she gave Amber a conspiratorial wink. Nylah stopped in the center of the floor and spun in a circle. “Man, it’s good to be home. How’s it going, Chase? Hi, I’m Nylah.”

She offered her hand to Snow and then Rain. “Witches?”

“Rain is my mate. Snow’s her sister.”

Nylah laughed. “Y’all are going to have to fill me in on everything I’ve missed.”

Luke’s boots thudded on the concrete behind the door, and as he flung it open, he scowled. “What in hell’s name?” His eyes widened as his gaze landed on Nylah. “All four of you, in my office now. Chase, you too.” He turned on his heel and stormed away, and Cade let out a low whistle.

“It’ll be fine,” Amber reassured her friends and slipped her hand into Noah’s. “We’ve got this.”

Nylah tapped the sign on the door as they walked through. Made of cardboard and written in black marker, it read *Employees and Werewolves Only*. “At least some things haven’t changed.”

They filed into Luke’s office, where Chase brought in a stack of folding chairs and positioned them in a semicircle facing the desk. Cade took a seat on the end, and Amber sat between Noah and Nylah, unable to fight her smile.

They’d done it. Two second-borns had concocted a plan to rescue a packmate and vanquish the strongest demon they’d ever fought… and they’d succeeded. If this wasn’t proof she was worth more to the pack than her uterus, she didn’t know what was. Not that she ever intended to assist with a fight again. Simply knowing she was tough enough was all she needed.

Luke opened his mouth to speak, but Amber cut him off. “It’s done. The Grunch are vanquished; Nylah is safe, and Noah’s wolf has fused with his soul.”

Luke narrowed his eyes. “Tell me what happened.”

“I had a premonition. I thought I knew where Nylah was, so the three of us drove out to Grunch Road to see if we could find the entrance to their lair.” She held up a finger before her brother could admonish her. “Let us finish the story.”

Luke tilted his head slightly, a silent reminder that he was alpha, and she needed to tread lightly where the pack was involved. "Continue."

"I found the entrance," Noah said, "but as we were discussing what to do, Alrick dragged Amber into his dimension. I acted on instinct, tore open the veil, and Cade and I went after her."

Luke rose and walked around his desk to stand next to Chase. "How did you defeat the Grunch? Even with Noah's power, four wolves couldn't take him out. How did you manage?"

"We got a witch to make a potion that destroyed the Thropynite. I found the spell in the archives while Noah was being examined."

"What witch?" He closed his eyes for a long blink. "Never mind. It's best if I don't know the details. You're certain they've all been vanquished?"

"The moment we destroyed the stone, the only one awake went dormant," Amber said.

"How did you get the Thropynite from the gargoyle?"

Cade leaned forward in his chair. "Noah held him still; I latched on to a soft spot, and Amber pried it off him with her knife."

"You should have seen your sister," Nylah said. "She was fierce."

A giggle rose from Amber's throat. The shock was wearing off, and everything they'd been through was finally catching up to her. "We smashed them all to bits with a crowbar."

"And then the dimension dissolved," Nylah said. "I got a lot of information out of Alrick while I was in there. He and his three brothers were the only ones who made it out of Europe. They're gone, and I'm alive, thanks to these three." She smiled at her friends.

"We did it, Luke," Amber said.

"Not without law breaking." Her brother crossed his arms, eyeing all four of them like he couldn't decide if he should punish or praise them.

"That's not true," she said. "Cade was with us the whole time. We were never alone, and Noah didn't shift until…" She clamped her mouth shut. Technically they had been alone when they visited the Hoodoo man—and Noah shifted in her presence then—but Luke said he didn't want details on that aspect of their adventure. A good alpha knew when to look the other way, and her brother was the best.

"Until?" Luke arched a brow.

"Until he was certain his wolf had fused with his soul."

"I'm sure it's fused," Noah said. "When I touched the Thropynite, I felt it happen. I can feel him now." He gave Amber a strange look, and her stomach fluttered.

"It's over." Amber squeezed her brother's hand. "And maybe now you won't consider me so helpless."

Luke relaxed his stance. "I'm sorry I underestimated you, but, Amber, if you ever pull a stunt like this again…"

Another laugh bubbled from her throat, whether from nerves or relief, she couldn't tell. "Don't worry about me. That's the last battle I ever plan to take part in. My abilities are best suited for giving the wolves a heads-up, and I'm cool with that. Just don't forget what I'm capable of."

"I won't." He narrowed his gaze at Noah, silently considering him before saying, "Thanks for keeping her safe."

Noah dipped his head and took Amber's hand. "I'm sorry we went in without permission, but I had to save her."

"You did the right thing. Both of you." He nodded at Cade.

"I'll expect a full report tomorrow morning before you head to the congress." He cut his gaze to Noah before looking at Amber and then Nylah again. "As full as the report needs to be."

Amber swallowed down another nervous laugh, clearing her throat. Luke understood some rules had to be broken for the good of the pack. He'd broken a few himself, even defying the congress for his mate. Hopefully he'd understand her relationship with Noah too. "I don't know what Dad has told you, but Noah and I…"

Luke cleared his throat. "There's still the matter of the congress's ruling. They met a few hours ago."

"But their ruling no longer applies. Noah's condition has changed." She laced her fingers through his. "We just vanquished a centuries-old gargoyle. Cut us some slack."

Luke chuckled. "Yes, you did, and while I agree with you, the congress will require some convincing." He rose to his feet and motioned toward the door. “Come in the conference room and prove to me that your wolf is fused, and then I think we can all relax tonight. Nylah, I’ll take you to your parents’ place. They’ll be happy to see you.”

“Do you have room for one more?” Cade gave Amber a wink. “I’m on the way to Nylah’s.”

Noah rose to his feet, and Luke shook his hand. “The Grunch may be vanquished, but I want security detail on my sister tonight to be safe. Can you handle the job?” the alpha asked.

“I won’t let her out of my sight.”

After shifting and returning to human for Luke, Noah drove Amber home, and when he parked in the driveway, he killed the engine and turned to her. “We need to talk.”

Her stomach sank, her throat thickening as the question she’d been ignoring since they left the swamp presented itself front and center. Had his wolf claimed her? Based on his words, she’d wager that was a no. “Come inside.”

She led him up the front steps and into her home. As she closed the door, she leaned her head against the jamb. Maybe he’d changed his mind about wanting to be with her regardless. It would be selfish of her to continue their relationship if his wolf wasn’t on board, but dammit, she didn’t care.

Sucking in a deep breath, she spun around. “Noah, I…” She froze.

He stood motionless, the rise and fall of his chest the only indicator he hadn’t turned to stone. The primal look in his eyes gave her chills. Her mind flashed back to the way his wolf had looked at her when he was last here, but her soul told her she was safe. More than that…

As she stood there locked in his gaze, her core tightened, and an invisible tether formed between them. Her lips parted on a quick breath, and as he moved toward her, heat unfurled in her belly, spreading through her body like wildfire.

“My wolf never wanted to hurt you.” Noah’s gaze dropped to her mouth as he placed his hands against the wall, pinning her in.

“No?” She licked her lips. His deep, woodsy scent wrapped around her, making her head spin.

"No." He moved in, but instead of taking her mouth, he glided his nose along her neck, inhaling deeply before pressing his lips to the dip below her earlobe. "He was trying to tell you that you are mine."

Her skin turned to gooseflesh at his words, and she knew, in that moment, that he would move heaven and earth for her. He would be her partner, her protector…everything she would ever need for the rest of her life.

She slid her hands beneath his shirt, and his muscles contracted with her touch. A growl rumbled in his chest as he leaned into her, pressing her against the wall, and his breath warmed her skin.

Leaning back slightly, he gazed into her eyes. "I love you, Amber. Will you be my mate?"

She arched a brow. "Seeing as how your wolf has claimed me, I don't have a choice."

"You always have a choice."

"I choose you, Noah. I love you."

He crushed his mouth to hers, taking her face in his hands, cradling her like she was precious, yet kissing her with an urgency that said he would die without her. Never in her life had she felt so much emotion in a single kiss.

The man and the beast coming together to claim her was like nothing she could have imagined. Her body trembled, her knees threatening to buckle. If not for the weight of Noah's body pressed against her, she would have crumpled to the floor beneath the intensity of the passion. She belonged to him, and she couldn't wait to spend forever with him.

With his pelvis pressed against her, he leaned back and peeled his shirt over his head. Moonlight streaming in through the window illuminated his muscular frame, and she traced her fingers along the cuts and dips of his abs. He was the perfect combination of soft skin and hard sinew.

He tugged her shirt off and ran his fingertips along the edge of her bra before reaching behind and unhooking it with a flick of his wrist. She let the garment fall to the floor as he stepped back and raked his heated gaze over her form.

Slipping a finger into the waistband of her pants, he tugged her toward him. She came to him willingly, and as she popped the button on his jeans and jerked the zipper down, another growl rumbled in his chest. The sound sent a shiver cascading down her spine.

She worked the denim down his legs and gripped his dick, reveling in the groan emanating from his throat and the way his hands tightened on her hips with each stroke. He bent down, taking her nipple between his lips, grazing it with his teeth as he unbuttoned her pants and slid them down. Rising, he toed off his shoes before stepping out of his clothes and standing before her in all his glorious nakedness. He was built for strength and stamina. If things went well tonight, she'd get to test both.

Kneeling, he removed her shoes and the rest of her clothes. He glided his hands up her legs as he rose, and he took her mouth in a passionate kiss as he teased her folds. She moaned when he slipped a finger inside her, the response making goosebumps rise on his skin.

He kissed her neck, working his way down to her shoulder and across her collarbone, nipping and licking along the way. Stroking his fingers in and out, he clutched the back of her neck with his other hand and brought her mouth to his once more. She clung to him, her legs trembling as he brought her closer and closer to the edge. With his thumb on her clit, he worked her in circles until she panted.

The orgasm coiled tightly in her core, and as it released, she screamed his name. Electricity shot through her body, igniting every nerve and setting her world ablaze. Before she came down, he hiked her leg over his hip and plunged inside her, sending another lightning bolt ricocheting through her core.

With one hand bracing her ass, he grabbed her other leg, lifting her from the floor and pressing her back into the wall. She clutched his shoulders as he pumped his hips, each thrust setting off a chemical reaction in her body that felt like pure ecstasy.

His rhythm increased, his thrusts growing harder until he groaned and pushed himself deeper inside, his body shuddering with his release. They stood there motionless, their breaths coming in short pants before slowing with their heartrates. Gradually, gently, he let her feet slide to the floor, and he leaned back to look into her eyes.

One corner of his mouth tugged upward in a tentative grin. “I lost myself there for a minute.”

She smiled and brushed the hair from his forehead. “I found you. I always will.”

He laughed and swept her into his arms before carrying her to the bedroom. They snuggled in the bed, Noah on his back and Amber curled against his side, and she rested her head on his shoulder, gliding her fingers over his stomach before laying her hand on his heart.

Noah let out a contented sigh, and she smiled. She’d found her fate-bound, and he was her best friend. What more could a girl ask for? After a while, her eyes began to drift shut.

But Noah stirred. “The congress has deemed me an unfit mate.”

She lifted her head and kissed his cheek. “Then we’ll prove to them just how fit you are.”

CHAPTER TWENTY-TWO

Noah sat next to Amber in the back seat of Luke's truck, his leg pressed against hers, their fingers entwined. Ever since his wolf fused with his soul and he realized the beast had claimed her from the beginning, he felt like he couldn't get close enough to her. It had pained him to sit in the alpha's office and hash out the details of what they'd done, when all he'd wanted to do was get her home and make her his.

And now that he had her, the fate of their relationship lay in the hands of, as Amber called them, the old fogies of congress.

He squeezed her hand, and she leaned her shoulder against his. Last night with Amber had been nothing short of magical. He finally understood the way his mated friends changed once they found their fate-bounds. He loved Amber with every fiber of his being before, but now he felt it with twice the intensity because his wolf loved her too.

He would do whatever it took to be with her. He'd challenge every wolf on the congress if he had to. If they refused to reverse their decision, he would convince Amber to leave the pack and go rogue with him. He simply could not live without her.

"What are you grinning at?" Amber looked at her brother in the rearview mirror. Macey sat in the front seat next to him, and Nylah sat on the other side of Amber.

Luke's smile widened. "Can't I be happy my baby sister found her fate-bound?"

Macey turned around, her smile as big as Luke's. "We're all thrilled for you. You're a perfect match."

"Mom's going to be over the moon," Luke said.

Amber rested her hand on Noah's arm. "And dad?" Cynicism laced her words.

"He'll come around." Macey rubbed Luke's arm. "Won't he, hun?"

"I'm sure he will." Luke didn't sound convinced.

Neither was Noah. Not only had they defied congress by deciding to become mates, but Noah had made love with an old-fashioned man's daughter after he'd forbidden it. No doubt Marcus would see it as "defiling his daughter," despite the fact Amber was a grown woman who made her own decisions. Her palm slicked with sweat, and he wrapped his arm around her shoulders.

"Probably best if y'all don't walk into the congress's chambers wrapped in each other's arms," Nylah said.

"Why not?" Amber stiffened. "We're going to be mates regardless of their decision. I don't give a shit what they say."

"Neither do I," Noah said. "She's my fate-bound, and I'll fight to the death for her if I have to."

"I'm sure it won't come to that." Macey gave him a sympathetic look before turning to Luke. "It won't be the first time someone from our pack has defied their orders."

"And anyway," Amber said, "it's not like they don't know why we're here."

Luke cleared his throat. "I requested an emergency meeting regarding urgent pack business. They didn't ask for details, so I didn't offer them."

"This will be interesting." Noah kissed Amber's cheek.

"No kidding," she said.

They pulled into the U-shaped drive, and an attendant directed them to park alongside the building. Noah gazed up at the mansion with its white columns and massive façade. It looked as foreboding as the first time he came, but he was a different man now. It was time he proved it.

He slid out of the truck and offered Amber his hand. She smiled and accepted, climbing out and then walking by his side to the front door. Luke entered first, followed by Macey and then the rest of the group.

Noah didn't release Amber's hand as they followed the attendant down the hall, passing the exam room and heading directly for the congress's chambers. They paused outside the door, and Luke glanced at their entwined hands before giving Noah a nod. He nodded in return and straightened his spine as the thick double doors swung open and the attendant gestured for them to step inside.

Once the estate's ballroom, the congress's chambers had polished wood floors and soaring ceilings complete with nineteenth-century crystal chandeliers. Tall vertical windows lined the wall behind a raised dais, giving them a view of the pristine gardens outside. Fifteen members of the werewolf national congress, including Amber's dad, sat behind a long, curved desk. They wore black robes, and as Noah and his pack entered the room, their gazes bore into him.

Noah tightened his grip on Amber's hand, refusing to be intimidated.

"The Crescent City Wolf Pack is here for their emergency appointment." The attendant bowed his head and strode out the doors, closing them behind him.

Marcus shot to his feet and glared at them, gesturing to Noah and Amber before looking at Luke. "What is the meaning of this?"

Noah understood his anger. As much as Marcus claimed the good of the pack was his top priority, his daughter's safety came first. Now if the man would only listen to their story, he might feel differently about their relationship.

Amber opened her mouth to answer him, but her brother stepped forward and spoke, "We are here to request a reversal of the congress's ruling on Noah L'Eveque in light of recent events."

Noah could almost feel Amber seething next to him, but she held her tongue. She was wise enough to understand when to push her boundaries, and this wasn't one of those times.

"The most recent event was our ruling, yet you bring them here and present them as a couple?" one of the congresswolves asked.

"Quite a bit has happened since." Luke strode toward them and rested a hand on Noah's shoulder. "It's because of these two that my pack vanquished the Grunch and rescued your agent."

The congresswolves murmured amongst themselves, while Marcus ground his teeth and stared at the back wall. After a few minutes, the man in the center rapped a gavel on the desk, silencing the congress. "Please, Luke, apprise us of these events," he said.

"I think it's best if you hear it from them. Noah, Amber, the floor is yours."

"Finally," Amber said under her breath, and Noah laughed.

Together, they recited the story as they had told it to Luke. When they got to the part where Alrick captured Amber, and Noah tore open the veil to save her, Marcus sucked in a breath, his hard expression softening as he cut his gaze between them.

"She's my fate-bound," Noah said. "I would do anything to protect her."

When they finished the story, Nylah filled in the congress on all the information she'd gathered from Alrick while he held her prisoner. "And if it weren't for Noah and Amber's quick thinking, I wouldn't be standing here, and the Grunch would still be a threat."

"But how did the Thropynite find its way to this continent?" the congresswolf in the middle asked.

Nylah glanced at Noah before squaring her shoulders toward the congress. "That was the one piece of information he didn't reveal."

Noah held his breath, praying they would buy it, and Amber's grip on his hand tightened.

"That's a shame," the congresswolf said before turning to Noah. "You are certain the stone fused your wolf to your soul?"

"One hundred percent," he replied.

"He shifted in my presence before we came here," Luke said. "I can vouch that he has full control."

The lead congresswolf inhaled deeply and glanced at Marcus, who nodded. "Your pack is dismissed. We will run another examination on

Mr. L'Eveque and make our own determination. You may wait in the lobby until we're ready for you."

"Thank you." Luke bowed his head. "I appreciate you seeing us on such short notice."

As they turned to leave, the attendant met them at the door. "The lobby is that way." He pointed to the left. "Noah, if you'll follow me to the exam room."

"Right." He leaned toward her. "I'll be back before you know it," he whispered, and he kissed her on the cheek.

Amber trailed behind Luke, Macey, and Nylah on their way to the lobby and glanced over her shoulder as Noah disappeared around the corner. Her clammy hands trembled, so she wiped them on her pants and shoved them into her pockets.

Noah would be fine. He'd been through this before, and now he had control of his wolf. But heaven help her, if they found some other reason to uphold their decision that he was an unfit mate, they could kiss her precious uterus goodbye. Luke and Macey better have tons of kids because Amber would cut herself right out of the alpha line if the congress tried to pull any shit. She sat on a bench and fisted her hands in her lap, pressing on her thighs to keep her knees from bouncing.

"What kind of exam are they doing on him?" Nylah wrung her hands. "They're not going to hurt him, are they?"

"If it's anything like last time, he'll have to drink a potion and let a witch poke around in his psyche. He didn't say if it was painful." And Amber hadn't thought to ask. She took a deep breath. This would all be over soon.

"You did great in there." Luke offered her a smile.

"I agree," Macey said. "You were both very impressive in your delivery. Not bad for a couple of second-borns." She playfully elbowed Luke in the ribs.

"Not bad at all," he said. "Next time there's a supernatural threat in New Orleans, you'll have to help us with our plan of attack."

She smiled. Finally, she was getting the respect she deserved...

from her brother at least. Her father's look of disdain as she'd spoken meant he still required convincing.

The half hour Noah spent in the exam room felt like an eternity. Nylah's knuckles turned white from her hand-wringing, and Amber gave in to the nervous bouncing her knee insisted on doing. She stared at the floor, creating imaginary images in the wood pattern until footsteps drew her gaze toward the hall.

Noah sauntered toward them with a confident gait, and she shot to her feet, her heart leaping into her throat as she stood. She raced to him, meeting him halfway down the hall and throwing her arms around him. He hugged her tightly, lifting her from the ground and spinning in a circle.

"I take it the exam went well?"

He cupped her face in his hands and kissed her. She expected a quick brush of the lips, but he went all in, crushing his mouth to hers and putting so much passion into the kiss, she nearly melted. Butterflies flitted in her stomach, the beating of their wings sending a tingling sensation throughout her body. As the kiss slowed, her cheeks warmed, and she pulled back to look at him.

"The witch confirmed it. My wolf is fused, and I'm no longer a threat."

She grinned. "I always knew you were fit to be my mate."

"She's delivering her findings to the congress now." He slid his arm around her back, and they returned to the lobby to wait with the pack.

It took another excruciatingly long half hour before the attendant told them they'd been summoned to the chambers. Amber held her breath as they entered, avoiding her father's gaze and instead focusing on the lead congresswolf who rose to his feet. Her hand was clammy clutched in Noah's dry palm, and he gave her a squeeze before moving his to rest on her lower back.

The congresswolf cleared his throat and touched his fingertips to the desk. "In light of recent events and a re-examination of Mr. L'Eveque, the congress has reversed its decision regarding his viability as a mate."

Her breath came out in a rush of relief, and she leaned into Noah's side.

"Furthermore," he continued, "at the request of Congresswolf Mason, the congress approves the mating union of Noah L'Eveque and Amber Mason, and plans may be made for a ceremony to occur before her thirtieth birthday."

A sob bubbled from Amber's chest, and she finally looked at her father. A sad smile curved his lips as he nodded once at her and then at Noah.

"This emergency meeting of the national congress is adjourned. The Crescent City Wolf Pack is dismissed." He rapped his gavel on the desk, and the rest of the congresswolves rose and exited the chamber.

In a daze, Amber let Noah lead her into the hall where her father stood waiting for them. A dozen different emotions swirled through her psyche—relief, elation, love, forgiveness—making her head spin. Noah took her hand, and they turned to face her dad.

"Welcome to the family, son." He clapped Noah on the shoulder. "I know I didn't show it, but I'm glad it all worked out."

Noah looked at her with so much love in his eyes, her heart swelled with joy. "So am I."

"I'm proud of you, Amber," her dad said. "And I want to apologize for ever making you feel otherwise. You'll always be my little girl, but I know you are a strong, capable woman. I promise never to forget that."

"Thanks, Dad. I love you." She hugged him.

"I love you too, sweetheart." He pulled from her embrace and turned to Nylah. "Because your cover has been blown, the congress is relieving you of your duties. You may return to the pack."

Nylah smiled. "Gladly. Turns out, the solitary life is not for me."

"Debbie and I would like to have you all over for dinner if you don't have to rush back."

Amber looked at Luke, who nodded.

"That sounds fantastic," she said.

"Shall we?" Her dad led the way out of the congress house, but Amber and Noah lingered.

"It's official." He tucked her hair behind her ear. "We're going to be mates."

"Fate sure took a roundabout route to bring us together, didn't it?" She rested her hands on his chest.

"It did." He pressed a tender kiss to her lips. "But I'll never question it again."

ALSO BY CARRIE PULKINEN

Fire Witches of Salem Series

Chaos and Ash

Commanding Chaos

Claiming Chaos

New Orleans Nocturnes Series

License to Bite

Shift Happens

Life's a Witch

Santa Got Run Over by a Vampire

Finders Reapers

Swipe Right to Bite

Batshift Crazy

Collection One: Books 1-3

Collection Two: Books 4 - 7

Crescent City Wolf Pack Series

Werewolves Only

Beneath a Blue Moon

Bound by Blood

A Deal with Death

A Song to Remember

Shifting Fate

Collection One: Books 1-3

Collection Two: Books 4-6

Haunted Ever After Series

Love at First Haunt

Second Chance Spirit

Third Time's a Ghost

Love and Ghosts

Love and Omens

Love and Curses

Collection One: Books 1 - 3

Collection Two: Books 4 - 6

Stand Alone Books

Flipping the Bird

Sign Steal Deliver

Azrael

Lilith

The Rest of Forever

Soul Catchers

Bewitching the Vampire

ABOUT THE AUTHOR

Carrie Pulkinen is a paranormal romance author who has always been fascinated with things that go bump in the night. Of course, when you grow up next door to a cemetery, the dead (and the undead) are hard to ignore. Pair that with her passion for writing and her love of a good happily-ever-after, and becoming a paranormal romance author seems like the only logical career choice.

Before she decided to turn her love of the written word into a career, Carrie spent the first part of her professional life as a high school journalism and yearbook teacher. She loves good chocolate and bad puns, and in her free time, she likes to read, drink wine, and travel with her family.

Connect with Carrie online:
www.CarriePulkinen.com

www.ingramcontent.com/pod-product-compliance
Lightning Source LLC
Chambersburg PA
CBHW020602310726
48979CB00008B/1316/J

9781957253077